THREATENED BY LOVE

After a pause, Andre said so softly she almost didn't hear, "You could get over that—hating me."

"Never."

He leaned over her, very close. His body carried the sweet breath of pond water, along with his own complex masculine scent that was becoming familiar to her. "Are you sure?" His dark eyes swam and beckoned, capturing hers in a locked gaze. His voice grew softly mocking. "Never is such a long, long time."

Andre's arms, though steely, were gentle as he pulled her onto her side, closer to him. His left forearm hooked beneath her neck. His right hand slid down her back, down her buttocks, and grazed the backs of her bare thighs.

Laura's blood rushed in a torrent from one end of her body to the other, and for once, she was relieved he was stronger than she. Now she didn't have to fight him—and show him she didn't really want to . . . .

ZEBRA'S GOT THE ROMANCE
TO SET YOUR HEART AFIRE!

Captive Melody

Nadine Grenshaw

ZEBRA BOOKS
KENSINGTON PUBLISHING CORP.

*For Evelyn Carpenter, my mother, my friend,
and one of life's true heroines.*

The Prelude . . .

It was July, 1876, though time seemed to drowse and nap for long golden hours over the Sierra Nevada foothills. The sky sagged overhead, so heavy with blue it seemed about to bow inward. Birds sang liquid secrets in the still trees and the air was sweet and musky with summer flowers wherever there was water, as in the crease of one ravine, where a stream seeped along, eventually to fill a pond. A cabin perched above, and a horse shed leaned nearby.

At the pond's edge a young Chinese woman crouched, scrubbing a man's shirts. Her black hair glimmered in a coil at the nape of her neck. Ling was her name. She was newly married and her whole life had suddenly become dreamlike, full of romance and nights of love.

Her marriage hadn't been lightly received. Her father, Kee Soo, had cried to his ancestors. He'd raged that he'd already chosen a husband for Ling, "good Chinese man"—a man so ordinary Ling had hardly noticed him before.

Her new husband's father had reacted similarly, casting his son out until such time as the young man should come back to his senses. For Kee Ling and Andre Sheridan had done the forbidden: They had refused to deny a love that went beyond all boundaries of culture and nationality and race.

They had come to live in this secret place in the Mother Lode, hoping that by bothering no one, no one would bother them.

The Gold Rush was more or less a thing of the distant past here, yet the peace was still rudely broken at times. Men—the kind of men who ignored pleas for privacy—occasionally thrust themselves into tranquil out-of-the-way places like this. Yet it was such an unusual occurrence that when Ling first heard the faint sound of horses today, her mind barely took notice. As the sounds came closer, however, and as she began to hear voices, though they were yet thin and small, she prudently began to gather her laundry into her wicker basket.

Three horsemen galloped over the ridge above the pond just as she finished bunching her laundry away, piling wet atop dry, soaped atop rinsed. "Hey, would ya' lookee there!" called a voice suddenly grown substantial and decidedly masculine. Ling grabbed her basket. The cabin was only a hundred yards up the slope and the door was strong. Andre had left her his shotgun—not that she could really dare use it against a white man, but it might serve to scare them off.

"Looks like a little Chinee gal," the masculine voice went on. "How about a pigtail chase, boys?"

She broke into a run up the steep slope. Behind her the horses splashed and splattered around the shallow end of the pool. She looked back only once, to see one man galloping forward with a rifle in his hand, upheld like a banner. He fired it, sending echoes against the ridges. A voice lifted in a wild "Halloa!" and started more echoes.

Just as she heaved over the lip of the slope onto the shelf of land where the cabin stood, the first horse ran close by her from behind, knocking her basket from her grasp: Andre's shirts went flying. Horses circled her now, cantering round and round until they made her dizzy. One rider bent to pull at her hair, loosening its coil so that it fell down over the side of her face and flopped there like a spaniel's ear. Another charged his mount at her playfully, and they all laughed at her attempt to dodge away.

She would not give them reason to laugh! She stopped running and, though she was quivering and breathless and hot, stood straight and proud. She gathered herself in, as if for some great test of endurance. For even then she knew

8

there was no escape for her.

The three men were young, all wearing cowboys' chaps and curling grins and that sharp glitter of self-assurance. She knew their type. California was full of them, each charging full speed through every second of every hour, looking neither right nor left but bursting like bullets from guns, their eyes settled on prospects no one else could ever see. Each of their saddles carried a bedroll and a rifle. A spiked buck hung lifeless over the rump of a pack horse.

For a moment no one spoke, then the tallest, who seemed to be their leader, swung out of his saddle. She dared not look at him for fear her eyes would collide with something ugly.

"Ah, leave her alone, Laird," said one of the men. The other, stiffly encased in disapproval, added, "What do you want to fool with a chink for? We had our fun; let's go."

"I ain't had my fun," said the one called Laird, smiling at Ling evilly. His eyes, which she had tried to avoid, were copper-colored; they seemed to burn with hellfire. He wasn't handsome, not to her, yet he had a face as striking as a face on a coin. He slowly advanced on her, his spurs spinning through the feathery foothill grass. She made no futile move to save herself, not even when he reached for her jacket and ripped it open so that the fine, clear afternoon light poured over her small breasts.

One

*"Heard melodies are sweet,
but those unheard are sweeter . . ."*
—John Keats

August, 1881. The rooms of Richard Laird's ranch house were decorated with flowers brought all the way out from Sacramento, flowers that greeted with their delicate, fruity scent even before the entering guests saw them.

At eight o'clock sharp, a cheerful, rosy-faced clergyman took his place in the fern-filled wedding alcove—really the transformed bay window of the parlor. Agitated whispering whirred around the room as people made ready for the wedding procession.

Richard entered, accompanied by a vision in white lace. His bride had piled the mass of her dark hair high on her head, and braided it with white velvet ribbons before pinning a coronet of orange blossoms and trailing gossamer veils over it all. Her name was Laura Upton and, like all brides, she was all romantic, languorous whole notes, a love song come true.

The layers of her veiling created a misty barrier to her vision as she dared a glance at the man escorting her. He wasn't exactly handsome, but he was a striking man, arresting in a sharp-featured, reckless, the-devil-take-you way. He had a thin smile and dancing, copper-colored, devil's eyes. Gold lights attractively shot through his

11

nondescript brown hair after the long, hot, Sacramento Valley summer.

She brought her eyes back to his arm that was supporting her hand, back to the white cuff showing beneath his coal-black jacket. But his image remained in her eyes, like the cool afterglow one sees after looking at something very bright.

They reached the fern bower. The violinist seemed reluctant to let his "Wedding March" die, and went on for a moment longer before giving in to the unspoken impatience in the room. When he lowered his bow at last, the candle flames on either side of the bay window stretched and wavered in the sudden silence.

The clergyman said, "Dearly beloved, we are gathered . . ."

The ceremony passed Laura in a blur. When asked if she would take Richard to be her husband, she blinked and hesitated before answering. Later she would remember only three things clearly: his copper eyes and sharp features, his need to force his gleaming gold wedding band onto her shaking finger, and his kiss. Especially his kiss. He lifted her veils away, exposing her face and gazing at her a moment with narrowed eyes—as if she were something made not of flesh and blood, but perhaps of porcelain, something beautiful but really terribly expensive—and then his mouth came down on hers. It was a kiss full of possession, a claim of ownership.

There was tittering before he released her at last, then embarrassed applause as she rose with him and passed into the throng to have their health toasted.

Richard's ranch foreman, Page Varien, had evidently been delegated to offer the best man's toast. The baby-faced, middle-aged man stood in that shambly wishbone style of a cowboy, his legs and feet spraddled farther apart than they seemed to be meant to go, and he began, "Well now, I've known Mr. Laird here a while, and I have to say," he looked about him with a self-conscious grin, "much as I like my paycheck, I have to say it, folks—I never thought he'd do this well by himself." Here he glanced shyly at Laura.

That glance seemed to be all he could handle. The whole responsibility of the toast had been something he'd probably worried about for days, and now he ended quickly with a few more muttered words, some of which sounded like "health and happiness." When he raised his glass to his mouth—the signal that he was finished—everyone drank with him, and grinned until their faces almost broke.

By way of thanks, Laura gave him one of her rare smiles. She liked Page, liked him beyond the fact that Richard said he didn't know how he would run Laird Ranch without him.

The ranch cook, known only as Harriet, a woman of strong hands and ample girth, rolled open the doors to the adjoining dining room. "Set your mouth for supper! Mrs. Laird? You and the Mister coming, or do the chickens get an extra share tonight?"

Mrs. Laird!

The buffet got under way, and Laura carried her plate back into the parlor. Married now, she was readily accepted into one of those rambling, womanly discussions of housekeeping. Harriet was asking a neighbor how she got her lime water to "come off so clear."

The neighbor's wan eyes brightened, and she smoothed the front of her decidedly orange dress. "Well, now," she said, "I set a stone of fresh, unslaked lime, about the size of a half peck measure, into a big crock—"

"I use an unpainted pail," Harriet said.

"Well, now, that might be your trouble," the neighbor said. "I use a crock, and I pour in—slowly, now—four gallons of hot water. I stir it up good, leave it to settle, then stir it two or three times more during the day. And when I bottle it the next day, I only pour off as much of it as pours perfectly clear."

Laura said, "And what do you use it for?"

Both women looked at her as if she were simpleminded. Finally Harriet answered, "It's a good cure for the men's summer complaints, particularly for . . ." She leaned and whispered in Laura's ear.

"Oh."

"That's right," said the neighbor woman, "and one teaspoon added to a cup of milk is wonderful for the kids."

Laura wrinkled her nose.

13

"Well, I sooner think it improves the flavor of milk, don't you, Harriet?"

"It does, and keeps it from curdling."

"I see." Laura felt embarrassed. She could tell these women thought she should know about things like lime water and men's summer complaints if she was going to be a rancher's wife. When they went on, now talking about chicken lice, she excused herself.

She self-consciously joined another group, but couldn't concentrate on the topic. Plate in hand, she glanced around, feeling guilty and vaguely upset that she wasn't as happy as she'd expected to be at her wedding.

Richard and his friends, it seemed, had momentarily budged from talking cattle, and were discussing the latest news about President Garfield. The papers were saying that the end was near, after all these weary weeks since July 2nd when the man had been shot down by an assassin named Guiteau. Garfield was still alive, though almost two months of heat and somnolence had passed, but nobody believed he had the slightest hope of recovering.

Richard for one was getting tired of going out to the corral every blessed day to be greeted right off by one or another of his men asking, "Is he still alive, I wonder?" Even Laura seemed to feel it—as if it were some heavy personal calamity. He hadn't understood her unsettling bewilderment: "Why . . . how could it have happened?" She'd even wanted to postpone their wedding, and he'd had a hell of a time convincing her that if they kept it quiet, it wouldn't be improper.

Hell, the man was taking too long to die!

One of his companions was saying now, "Wouldn't it be a good idea if that Washington jailor allowed Guiteau to escape? There's men who swear they'd kill him the minute he left jail, regardless of the consequences."

Another man added, "That's a good idea! Turn him loose and give the boys a chance!"

Richard's attention faltered. His gaze slid to Laura. He looked her over rather as he was used to examining a promising heifer. She was beautiful! It wasn't just that fancy dress filled to the throat with pristine lace and pulled so tight across her belly and poufed out over her behind. And it wasn't just her slight build, dark hair, white skin and those clear gray eyes; it was the way she carried her head, the way she moved. There was a chaste look about her, an impression of unawakened sensuality, of a beauty unmarked by any man's touch.

What a sheltered life she'd led! What easy pickings she'd been! What fun he was going to have with that innocence of hers!

Truth was, though he'd found the innocence amusing enough during the first months, when he'd been staking her out for himself, once he'd asked her to marry him, you would have thought she'd unbend just a little. Well, tonight he was going to get his. And she was going to get hers.

He moved across the room unnoticed by her, and bent near enough to detect the faint scent of rose water about her.

Laura looked up to find his copper eyes squinting down at her just the way they had before he'd kissed her earlier. She resisted the urge to step away. *I made a mistake, it was all a mistake!*

You made your bed!

That was her stepmother's, Alarice Upton's, voice, which Laura hadn't forgotten, though she'd come three thousand miles to escape it.

Automatically she began her interior arguments: I don't begin and end at my fingertips anymore, Mama! And I don't need to listen to you—I've found someone else to take care of me!

This thought was immediately followed by dismay. How much of marrying Richard was affection, and how much a shabby relief at having her care taken over by someone else again? Too late, too late to wonder now! Only a few hours more and she would, literally, lie in this bed she'd made for herself.

What would that be like? She knew so little of the male sex. Bessie, the woman Laura had been boarding with in

15

Sacramento, had kindly, if somewhat obscurely, explained what would be expected of her: "Since your mother isn't here, I feel it's my duty to tell you . . ." Then she'd started talking about rabbits. Eventually she'd returned to men and women, but only to say: "You might be a little frightened the first time—every woman is, it's only natural—but soon you'll feel right at home with Richard's, er . . . requests." Here came a hand pat. "He won't expect you to know everything. Just try to please him and you'll find it not so terrible. Do you understand what I'm trying to say?"

Laura had understood, in a hazy sort of way. She wasn't stupid, even if she'd been brought up so sheltered. She knew there was more than kissing and fondling involved when it came to being a man's wife. She knew there were *intimacies*. Looking up at Richard right now, she forced down a feeling of panic. His half-closed eyes were on her silken white bodice, and she thought she knew what he was thinking, so she was surprised when he said lightly, "Having second thoughts, honey?"

"No, of course not." She shouldn't be having second thoughts, she really shouldn't! She set her plate aside and impulsively stretched onto her toes to kiss him with an innocent flourish, something she'd rarely done before— partly because she knew she was far less accomplished at kissing than at playing the piano.

"You're getting plenty forward," he murmured, catching her to him with an arm around her waist.

"Mind if I kiss the bride, too?" came an unpleasantly familiar voice. But for once she was glad to see Richard's frequent companion, Ives Zacariah, though she didn't really care for the man. He was a seedy-looking, short, heavyset man whose bulbous nose was invariably red from too much drink. She tried not to pay too much attention to the greasy, curly hair that half-covered his ears, yet to her eyes Mr. Zacariah never looked washed. He took her face roughly between his work-broadened hands and kissed her cheek nosily, leaving a wetness that she wiped away as soon as she could do so unobtrusively.

16

"Well, Laird, my boy! So your little piano-plunker was too smart for you! You had to marry her to get at her blouseful!"

"Not so loud, Zac," Richard said.

"You must be something, ma'am," Zac said with a leer in his eyes.

She couldn't think of a thing to say in answer, and looked to Richard for help.

"Yeah, she is something. What've you been up to, Zac?"

"Well, after you left Aida's last night—" He paused to glance at Laura—long enough for her to remember that she'd heard of Aida's before. It was a saloon, she believed, or something of that sort. She'd seen it on her way to Hammer's Music Store once.

Mr. Zacariah looked back at Richard. "Anyway, I was talking to someone who said he'd come all the way from Texas for your wedding. Fellow named Sheridan." He paused, looking at Richard intently. "Andre Sheridan."

Richard said carefully, "I don't think I know anyone by that name." He added, "You say he's been in Texas?"

"That's right, been out of state for quite a while, 'bout five years. Says he found out you were getting hitched and come back special for it—though I ain't see him around anywheres tonight."

"Did you look?"

"Oh, I been keeping my eyes open."

"Did he say what he wanted?"

"He asked a lot of questions about your bride here." He smiled his wet smile in Laura's direction. "I told him she was a real smart little piece."

"What else did he say, Zac?"

"Nothing much, but that he'd been waiting all these years to hear you was getting married."

Laura sensed there was more going on here than she understood. She could tell Richard wasn't happy about any of it, though he answered casually enough: "Are you sure his name was Sheridan?"

"Yep. Big brawny guy. Bit taller than you. Getting close to thirty now, I'd say. Dark hair, dark eyes—funny eyes," he added, "look right through you."

Richard was clearly bothered. He seemed to recognize the description, though he denied knowing the man. Turning and drawing Laura away with him, he said, "We'll talk about this again, Zac. Keep your eyes open and let me know if you see anything more of him."

Laura was curious. "Richard, don't you have any idea who it could be? I mean, it seems odd that if he traveled all the way from Texas just for your wedding—"

"Oh, if I know Zacariah, it was two in the morning and he was in the process of sliding under his chair with an empty bottle of Beargrass Rye. He probably imagined the whole thing." The shadow on his voice didn't match the sureness of his words.

She noticed that he had led her into the hall. She stopped short. "We can't leave our guests yet."

His arm tightened around her waist. "Sure we can."

"It's rude."

He inhaled deeply, evidently seeking some last scrap of patience. "All right, a little while longer—but I need some fortification if I'm going to last." He pulled her into his arms, heedless of her delicate veil and gown.

She didn't argue further. Lately he could get suddenly furious for reasons she little fathomed. She only knew that it had to do with his hungers. She'd seen him become as enraged as a two-year-old, wanting the impossible—for he must know that she couldn't grant him too many favors before they were married. The more carefully and precisely she behaved at such times, the more inflamed became his impatience.

She could hear the voices of his friends and neighbors only a few steps away, and tried to deflect his kiss to her cheek, but he threaded his fingers through her hair and tilted her mouth to his without a word.

He separated her lips with a hard thrust of his tongue. One hand slid down her back—until it was stopped by her bustle—to press her body closer. After a long moment his mouth slid to her jaw where it met her neck, and he made low sounds, whispered warnings she couldn't make sense of. So often in his arms she experienced this bittersweet mix of distaste and enjoyment. It made her feel just that much more nervous of his desire.

He captured her mouth against his again, forcing her head back, back . . . Then, as suddenly as he'd taken her into his arms, he released her. For a moment she stood quivering in a kind of dazed aftershock, then she backed away quickly and smoothed her rumpled dress and loosened coiffure. Her coronet of orange blossoms felt awry.

His face took on that familiar expression of amusement. "You enjoyed that," he said, daring her to deny it. "You'd like me to believe you're made of ice, but I know better. And so will you, very soon now, honey."

The meaning of his words passed over her head. She was trying to straighten her coronet, but without a looking glass it was impossible. Her nostrils flared faintly. "Sometimes you make me so angry, Richard!"

He took her elbows and looked into her face. "I know. I'm a real son of a bitch, ain't I?" He was always quite willing to use his twisted, mocking wit upon himself. In truth, he didn't seem to care in the least what she thought of him. Sometimes she had the feeling he'd ceased to mind what anyone thought of him.

She said with defensive dignity, "Since you've insisted on behaving in a way no gentleman should permit himself, I'm going to have to repair the damage. Excuse me."

As she walked down the hall with as much grace as she could muster, she heard him chuckle. Oh! Was their relationship always going to be based on this *rubato* rhythm—the lengthening of his notes at the expense of hers?

She entered the bedroom in which she'd dressed before the wedding. It had been Richard's parents' room during their lifetimes, and tonight she would begin to share it with him. A single lamp beside the tall-posted walnut bedstead threw out a dim pool of yellow light, leaving the corners of the spacious room shadowy. Someone, Bessie or Harriet, had been in to turn down the white German-crocheted counterpane and the crisp white sheets. Laura's lacy new nightdress was lying there on the pillow.

Everything was as it should be, yet, dramatically stirred up as she was, she suddenly had a spooky feeling. She moved with slow majesty across the Brussels carpet, pulling off her gloves and gathering her lace train over one forearm. Her gown rustled in the silence.

She felt a sensation . . . as if she sensed a gaze on her.

It was just her apprehension. She went to the cheval glass. Her coronet wasn't as crooked as she'd thought, but her cheeks seemed much too white. As she lifted her hands to pinch some color into them, she saw that her fingers were shaking: Not all of Richard's words had passed over her; some of their portent had sifted down into her awareness, like dust.

She tried to make the reflection in the looking glass regain its poise. She spread her skirts with conscious grace. The corset she was wearing was long and stiff, stoutly whale-boned. This armature had made her stand up terribly straight all evening, and she was beginning to look forward to taking it off, so she could draw a full breath.

Looking at herself, she decided no one could tell that she was not as happy as a bride was supposed to be. She turned her attention to re-securing several slippery locks of hair back into their proper places—until a slight noise behind her stayed her hands.

Two

Had Richard followed her? Laura wondered. She wouldn't put it past him. He was in that mood in which he enjoyed everything and respected nothing. She listened, alert. She heard nothing more, yet that sensation of a gaze, a presence, remained stronger than ever. It touched the back of her neck with a shiver. She peered into the looking glass—and as she did, her eyes went wide.

She whirled to face a large shadowy form moving from where it had been hiding behind the door all along. Revealing its shape an edge at a time, it became a man. A tall man, with wide shoulders and a lean frame, taut and muscled. A man wearing denim trousers, a blue chambray shirt, cowboy boots, and a hat. A man who was also wearing a thick leather belt, pulled down over one hip by the weight of a holster holding a big lethal-looking revolver.

Oddly enough, her first reaction was not fear. There were certain notes and blendings of notes that, having little to do with intellect or rationality or ideas, inevitably caused a chill across her nape and gave her a well-nigh literal feeling of being taken up out of her self. This man gave her that same feeling right now. He was so handsome—it was an awesome, almost overwhelming experience to find him there, unexpectedly shouldering onto the horizon of her life.

Her second reaction, however, was fear, for he was also fearful-looking. Her heart leapt up like a fierce quartet of chords, precisely marked.

"W-who—?" With that first sign of impending speech he started forward so quickly she couldn't finish. A warning choir of brass gongs inside her told her to run. Yet his presence had flabbergasted her; her normal reactions seemed slowed. When she did make a belated move he was already between her and the door to the hallway; she had no choice but to turn for the French doors leading to the veranda.

He was on her in an instant—so sudden and so muscular! Before she could make three steps, his arm circled her from behind, his forearm caught her beneath the lift of her breasts, and brought her right up off her feet against him. She had never felt so light and small and weak. She tried to scream, but he clamped a hand over her mouth. It was a big hand; it covered her nose as well as her jaw. So tightly were her lips and nostrils pinched, she was sure he meant to suffocate her. He clamped her head back against his chest as her long musician's fingers pulled at his thick hard ones. Her face was tilted up; his eyes looked powerfully down into hers.

Funny eyes, look right through you . . . name of Sheridan . . . a man named Andre Sheridan . . .

She felt swallowed by those eyes, so dark, so deep. She was falling into them, into a dark deep pool . . . .

Laura woke to find herself lying on her stomach with her head hanging over the edge of the bed. Her cheek nuzzled the cool sheeting. It slowly penetrated her mind that what she was looking at, the heap of material on the floor, was her wedding dress . . . and her bustle and petticoats and corset cover . . . and there were her white silk stockings. Meanwhile it felt—it sounded as though—as though someone were cutting the strings of her corset.

He was! That man, that Andre Sheridan who had arrived in her life like a cuff in the mouth! She must have fainted. And obviously he'd tossed her onto the bed and started undressing her. Oh! She rolled over so suddenly that if he hadn't lifted his knife just as quickly he would have slashed her arm. There were those eyes again, eyes that seemed to be the keepers of a hundred inscrutable secrets. His voice was

22

only a rustle of breath. "Don't make a sound, Mrs. Laird."

His knife blade seemed to be looking at her, as she was looking at it. Undeniably frightened, she let him pull her corset off. He dropped it among the pile of clothes on the floor. She had nothing on now but her linen chemise, laced up the front with a glossy ribbon. And her underdrawers, of course. And the long lengths of veil pulling her head back uncomfortably because she was lying on them.

Careful of his knife, she crossed her wrists over her chest and tried to conceal her bare shoulders and the curves of the tops of her breasts from his cold stare. He seemed about to say something, but then turned his head slightly. She heard it too: the first guests were departing. How long had she been unconscious? Five minutes? Not more than ten surely. But Richard must be starting to wonder what was keeping her.

She took advantage of the man's inattention to open her mouth to scream—but shrank down into the mattress when his attention jerked back to her. The lamplight glanced off the blade of his knife and lit his face briefly. "Don't do that. Then I would have to get mean, wouldn't I?"

She had no doubt he could, too.

"Come on, we don't have all night." He kicked at the ruined dress that lay puffed on the floor, and moved to pull her veil out from beneath her, relieving the pressure on her neck, at last. He took her wrists and yanked her into a sitting position. With a length of cord drawn from a back belt loop of his trousers, he tied her hands before her.

He was fast; he used the same technique she'd seen Richard's cowboys use when roping a calf. The muscles in his powerful forearms flexed as he whipped the cord around and around and tied it into a hard and intricate knot. In seconds she was helplessly bound.

He put his knife away then. Noticing her wedding band, he squinted at it, as if considering, then tugged it from her finger and placed it carefully on the new nightdress lying on the pillow behind her.

Why are you doing this? she cried mutely.

Now he pulled at the orange blossoms and veiling still fastened in her hair. Tears started in her eyes at his first heartless tugs; she'd pinned it too securely for him to merely

23

rip them out—unless he intended to rip half her hair out as well.

He made an impatient noise, swore, and turned her so he could start pulling out big pins and little pins and combs, using both hands at once, until not only did the veil come away, but also her carefully arranged coiffure. Her dark hair fell around her shoulders and tumbled down her back. She felt immediately shy, and realized it was because no man had ever seen her with her hair loose before.

What nonsense! The man has you down to your underwear and you're shy about your hair?

She saw that not even her chemise was going to be left to her, not intact anyway. With his knife, he jabbed a hole in the material just beneath her waist. He pushed her onto her back again. "Lift up," he commanded, and when she did, he wrenched the skirt portion of the garment away from the bodice and skinned it down her legs.

He pulled several handkerchiefs from his pocket. He seemed to pause, to really look at her for once. He said softly, "What's your name, anyway?"

"Lau—"

It was a trick, for as soon as she opened her mouth, he stuffed two of the handkerchiefs right between her teeth, and quickly gagged her with a third. This was the worst so far; she was dreadfully afraid she was going to suffocate. Her eyes pleaded, and she made a whimpering sound, but all he said was, "It won't be for long."

He stood, wiped his forehead with his wrist, then scooped her into his arms. As soon as she felt the contact of his body against hers, without the usual intervening layers of female clothing, a great shock went through her. She punched at his hard shoulder with the heels of her bound hands as he toted her through the French doors and into the falling coolness of the August night.

Why . . . ? Where is he taking me?

Back inside the ranch house, the violinist had started again. The music sounded far away, gossamer and eerie out here in the dark. Laura kicked and squirmed in her captor's arms—though there really was little chance of her escaping, for he was unbelievably strong. "Keep still, Lorelei," he said softly. But she kicked harder, and even tried to scream behind her gags.

It didn't stop him from covering the distance between the back of the single-story ranch house and the Consumnes River with long strides. A horse was hidden in the junglelike waterside growth. He hoisted her onto its huge back and paused to look up at her. She fell quiet: Would he stab her now?

He didn't get his knife out, but swung himself up to ride pillion behind her. His arms surrounded her as he found the reins and urged the horse toward the river. The animal's strong supple back moved beneath the saddle. Laura leaned back into the man, automatically seeking balance. She hadn't realized how high above the ground a saddle was until now. A sound in her throat was muffled by the handkerchiefs stuffed in her mouth. She clutched the man's rolled-up sleeve with her fingertips. But he needed that arm to brush away some hanging vines. "Hold onto the saddlehorn," he told her.

She did, though the solid leather was only minimally reassuring. Then they were through the vines, and there was the shallow water. It danced with moonlight that broke under the horse's hooves.

Laura's mind searched for the sense of all this. Maybe it was only a misguided prank. Everyone knew people played pranks on wedding nights.

But he's taken my clothes off!

An hour passed. They'd left the ranch. No sound or odor of shifting cattle was anywhere. Her captor stopped the horse and turned to look back, to listen. Laura listened, too, though there was nothing to hear. She craned to see around his shoulder. There was nothing to see, either. She knew Richard at a distance by the head-up way he sat his cow pony, as if he were always trying to look over a ridge, but she saw no sign of him now.

Her captor sat forward again. She cringed as he glanced at her. His hand came up to her chin; he turned her head forward and untied her gag. He pushed the damp wad into his saddlebag, saying softly in her ear, "Make a sound and back in they go—understand?"

25

She sat rigid, unanswering. He brought out a canteen, uncapped it, put it to her lips, and started to tilt it. She had no choice but to tip her face up and try to catch the water with her mouth. He lowered it fractionally, allowing her to swallow just before she choked. With her head still tipped back, her eyes met his again.

"More?"

She shook her head.

He put the canteen away and they rode on in silence.

They traveled in a southeasterly direction, into the foothills of the Sierra Nevadas. He stopped often to listen, but if they were being followed, her rescuers were traveling on tiptoe.

Laura's feet, dangling loose, gradually went icy cold, and then numb. She steeled herself once, despite his threat about the gag, to say in a rush, "Where are you taking me? Why—"

He lowered a sudden glare on her, sustaining it so that she didn't dare finish her questions. When she was totally quelled, he reached for her wrists. She tried to pull away from that reach, which meant she leaned back deeper into his arms and actually made it easier for him. The hand holding the reins braced her hard against him, while his free hand pulled her wrists out from under her chin where she'd tucked them. He did nothing more than feel her fingers, though, as if to see if they were cold from lack of circulation. Roughly, he put a thumb beneath the cords, testing the tightness. He seemed satisfied that she wasn't suffering, and released his hold.

She took the opportunity to wriggle a bit. She'd had no idea that riding a horse could be so uncomfortable. Her thighs felt strung out, and she was getting sore there.

"Not used to riding, huh?"

She glanced back over her shoulder at him, found his eyes reflecting the moon-bright and silver night. She faced forward again quickly, her face hot. She bit her lower lip as his breath brushed the top of her head. "Throw your leg over the horn and sit sideways." When she didn't move, he leaned his head over her left shoulder; the corners of his mouth bracketed the slightest of sardonic smiles. "Throw your leg over."

She slowly brought her wrists up beneath her chin again and grew high-shouldered in a shrinking endeavor to fend him off.

His face changed. "Do it!"

She tried to obey, but clutched his arm and said, "I'll fall!"

"No, you won't. I've got you. Lean into me." He put his arms around her and pulled her into him, then spurred the horse into motion again.

She felt his breathing more intimately now, not only on the top of her head, but the movements of his chest all down her side. The sensation touched her clear to the marrow. She struggled to maintain an inch of space between them.

The moon went down, and though the sky pulsed with starlight, the way was so dark she didn't know how he could possibly know where he was going. She smelled the pungent, spicy odor of sagebrush. The dew, her fright, and her state of undress all combined to make her shudder. She cowered down for warmth. He opened his big hand that was lying around her waist and pressed her even closer against him. She strained against this, but he said, "Here!" and forced her. She gave in and stayed where he wanted her, stiff-spined at first, then, as she tired, leaning more and more into him.

On and on in the blackness, for hours, deeper into the foothills, climbing one hill after another, each hill getting higher and harder to climb, on and on. Her head lolled against his collarbone, so that now his chin and jaw, and sometimes even his cheek, brushed her hair.

When would Richard come? *Richard, please!* Oh, why had she ever come to this uncivilized place?

Adventure, experience, something new . . .

The very first time she'd seen Richard Laird she was being jostled off the high plank sidewalk outside Sacramento's Central Pacific Train Station. The place was a madhouse. A flood of newcomers descended constantly on the state, and Sacramento was a transfer point for all passengers. Hackmen, hotel runners, and loungers added to the crowds and confusion. Passengers ate from vending stands while standing up or walking, some even while running. The engine of the transcontinental train she'd just left was still puffing under the vaulted roof of the arcade, and men were

27

shouting into the cavernous space, "Want a carriage?" "Railroad Hotel!" "Pacific Hotel Coach!" Baggage carts clattered and screamed, bells rang, whistles blew, train masters wearing railroad caps announced trains heading in several different directions. Meanwhile, no gates or guard rails protected passengers from the tracks running through the mobbed depot. Laura got caught in a clutch of people headed out through the ticket office. She needed to retrieve her trunk, but the flow of people moved her farther and farther from the baggage office, until she found herself out on the boardwalk. Here a smell of stock pens floated and mingled with the scent of dust. She heard a station boy say, "Get your baggage for you, miss?" and turned with hope, only to be bumped by another traveler hurrying full-tilt to get out of the mayhem. She swayed dangerously at the edge of the three-foot-high plank walk—and that was when Richard, on the street below, reached up for her.

There was nowhere to go but right into his hands. She hung there, half-balanced between him and the walk, looking down into those glowing yellow eyes and that sly smile. He was a man such as she had never known in Abfalter Village, Massachusetts. He was wearing a black cowboy hat and cropped black cowhide vest over a white shirt, open at the throat, the sleeves rolled to his elbows. The moment lasted while she hung poised, held . . .

Finally he lifted her down to the street. She pushed away from his hands around her waist. "Thank you."

He stood back and gave her an absolutely knowing smile. "That was close, wasn't it, honey?"

She swept her pride cloaklike about her and said, "Was it?" knowing very well that it was.

His smile grew cheeky; his gaze dropped to her lips. It wasn't right. He was a stranger; having done her a service, he was supposed to bow and leave. And if he didn't, she most certainly should. But she'd been lost that day, exhausted and confused after traveling for over a week, and anxious about what lay ahead—and already nostalgic for all she'd left behind. Running away from home, she'd discovered, had two phases: first the adventure, then the doubt. Memories had plagued her lengthy trip, forcing her to plumb all the reasons behind her decision to leave the piano in the parlor of the only home she'd ever known.

And yet the world was so full of so many things—so many people were happy! What else could she have done?

On the other hand, now that she was free, which way should she turn? She had no idea really. She felt lost—and knew she looked it—a small black figure shrouded in dust. And Richard, after saving her from that fall, had found it easy to take her in hand. He was at the station with a wagon that day, to receive some freight. Instead, he collected her large iron-bound traveling trunk and delivered it, and her, to Bessie Gladwin's boarding house, saying, "This'll do better for you than a hotel." And she'd let him make that decision! A perfect stranger! Surrounded as she'd always been by rules—dos and don'ts and can'ts—she was nonetheless so unsure and anxious that she was unable to resist his rather arrogant and lordly ways, even though—or maybe because —he frightened her half out of her wits.

He was right about Mrs. Gladwin's place suiting her, though; and on the basis of the success of that first decision, she let him make a second for her, and then a third, until, in a a matter of weeks, he'd become a *person* in her life. A man. The first man to ever take an interest in her.

The weeks at Bessie Gladwin's passed quickly. There was so much to learn and accustom herself to. She was chagrined to learn it wasn't easy to get work in a place where so many newcomers were looking for work. There wasn't much need for what she had to offer: some genteel rudiments of French and a fine italic writing hand. Oh, she could have found laundry work, or chamber work, or table-waiting, but there were limits to what a lady could stoop to and still remain a lady. She'd never meant to touch a piano again, but as it turned out, she was forced to seek pupils and give music lessons in order to keep herself.

And then came Richard's proposal, only two months after their meeting: "I want you to marry me."

Her smile, shy at seeing him again, slid away. She'd come down to Bessie's parlor to meet him in a peach satin dress, which she hoped made her look pretty—but the dress was forgotten. It was an instant or two before she could make her

29

voice work. "Is this your idea of a joke, Mr. Laird?"

"From the day you got into town, from the minute I caught hold of you and you looked down at me with those big, scared, gray eyes, I knew I wanted you. You're a lady, the kind of quality a man marries. And I've been thinking for the last year or so that it's time I got married, had a kid to take over the ranch some day. I want you for my wife—and I'm going to have you."

"Are cattlemen always this ruthless when they want something?"

"When they want it bad enough, yeah."

To hide her alarm she remained at her most formal. "We hardly know each other, sir."

"I want you, Laura."

What about her? What did she want? What did she know about this man who stood waiting for her answer? What did she know about his background, his circumstances, his disposition—except that he had a ruthless streak that aroused feelings in her, feelings of fear and . . . was it awe? Yes, he impressed her terribly with his purposefulness. But how could she marry a man she was afraid of a good portion of the time?

"I'm flattered, of course, but I must think it over. You understand, don't you?"

"Think what over? If you'd been going to say no, you would've by now."

Would she have? Her head was whirling. She'd played alone as a child. Great heroic adventures had been acted out in her chilly bedroom. In her imagination she was held prisoner there, a maiden in distress. A fine knight always came eventually to rescue her. When Richard walked into her life, unforeseen, unannounced, he seemed the living resolution of all those fairy stories.

"Adventure," he said to her, "experience, something new—you came here because you wanted all that, didn't you? Well, you can have it with me."

She *had* wanted that. She didn't want to grow in just one direction anymore. Yet somehow she felt he was using her words against her. From the day she'd met him, she'd been totally confused, totally out of her depth. She'd never seemed to have an instant of clear decision since.

And just look where that yen for adventure had landed her! On this horse, bound helplessly, abducted by a man she'd never seen before!

Richard! Where are you? Help me! Surely he could have caught up with them by now. Any minute, surely, he would appear. And he would be murderously angry. She hardly dared think what he might do to this poor man.

Poor man? This poor man was abducting her, for who knew what reason! Oh, how could this be happening? This was her *wedding* night!

Her captor's hand slid casually from her waist to her hip. The intimacy of it shocked her into sitting ramrod straight with a jerk. The horse skittered. The sound of its dancing hooves seemed loud. "Sit still—or you'll end up walking on a lead rope, Mrs. Laird."

"Where are we going?"

"Now don't make me gag you again."

She slumped back against him, resigned.

Sometime later they came into a rocky area. She could tell because of the sound of the horse's hooves against the stones. She vaguely made out steep, overhanging hillsides and the sound of trickling water. A scent of ferns pervaded the place, and the smell of moist, cool earth. The man stopped to listen yet again, sitting very still and seeing that she did, too. There were no sounds, though. Her heart ached to hear something, but there were no sounds, never any sounds!

Suddenly he dismounted and reached up for her. His thumbs seemed to measure the narrowness of her waist for an instant before he dragged her off the horse. "What are you—?" She fell into him, shivering and sick with terror. Her feet and legs tingled painfully with the long lack of circulation. When he put her on her feet, she would have fallen if he hadn't tightened his hold on her again. "Please—!" she said, not knowing what he meant to do next. But he only put a forearm beneath her knees, lifted her to his chest, and carried her into a place that was even darker than the night without.

Three

It was as if all light had gone out from the world: Laura couldn't see anything. Her captor set her down on the gravelly floor of what she surmised was a cave. At least the place had the sharp and acrid smell of humus and wet moss and secret crevices of rock. And there was a dead, incredible silence that told of solid walls. "Stay here," was all he said, and he left her sitting with her legs curled for warmth on the chill pebbles.

Sound came from one direction only—the entrance; she heard him outside tending his ebony-colored horse. Evidently they were going to stay. For how long? For what reason?

He brushed by her carrying something—probably his saddle by the leathery smell and creak of it. She heard him throw it down, then heard him rummaging in the darkness. There was silence again. "Are you there?" she asked the midnight blackness, but nothing answered. Breath-held seconds passed, until at last a pale light flared as he struck a match, held it to the bottom end of a small candle to soften the wax enough for him to secure it to a rock; then he lit the wick and the cave brightened.

Their eyes met over the tiny blaze. He tilted his head back and squinted at her from under his hat, as if to set a price on her. She was excruciatingly aware of the fact that she was dressed only in her underclothes. She was glad now for her loose hair. At least she was partly veiled by its thickness and

32

length. Yet that was all she could find to be glad for. Her tongue slipped dryly over her lips and she looked about for some place to hide, some hole or burrow she might crawl into and feel safe again.

His face remained expressionless. He was looking at her but not seeing her. It made her feel diminished, as if she weren't quite deserving of human consideration. She got to her knees in the pebbly gravel and shook the slithery screen of her hair back from her face. "Are—" the word came out funny and she cleared her throat and tried again. "Are you after a ransom? Is that it?"

"No," he said slowly, "that's not it."

The brief glimmer of controlled appetite she caught in his look brought a rise of something close to panic. Since male sexuality was still shrouded in mystery for her, she naturally feared the unknown possibilities of this situation. She ran her tongue over her lips again. "I—I don't think you intend to hurt me—"

"You don't know that at all," he said flatly.

She came back quickly: "Mr. Sheridan, I demand that you release me."

That galvanized him. He stood abruptly, tossed his hat aside, and came to hunker down before her. His black hair gleamed in the light of the candle. He didn't touch her, but those eyes bored into her. "How do you know my name?" His voice was quiet yet urgent. She shrank back and began to twist her wrists within the cords that bound them. He reached out negligently to stop her. The clench of his fingers set her to trembling. This was the hand that had stripped her dress off her, cut her corset from her, ripped her chemise, and dragged it down past her knees. The memories were so acute she jerked away.

He rested his forearms on his knees as he balanced on the balls of his feet. "How do you know my name, Mrs. Laird?"

"A-a man you talked to—Mr. Zacariah. He's Richard's f-friend. He said he'd t-talked to you last night."

"Uh-huh." Her answer seemed to please him, though he didn't smile. "But you've never seen me before. How did you know it was me?"

33

"He described you—tall and dark—w-with eyes that look right through you, he said."

His brows raised. "Do my eyes look right through you, Mrs. Laird?"

She didn't answer, but began wrenching at her wrist bindings again. Once more his big hand clenched over her smaller ones. "Don't. You'll only give yourself rope burns. There's no place for you to go anyway, barefoot and half-naked." He said this quite incidentally, as though he had no inkling of what the words meant to her. "What did Laird say when Zacariah told him I was around?"

"He . . . Richard didn't know who you were."

His chiseled mouth broke into a sour smile. "Oh, he knows who I am, you can bet on that."

The seconds ticked away, small eternities. She inhaled deeply, but her voice, when it came out, was only a breath. "Are you going t-to hurt me?"

His mouth twisted. "I don't plan to. But better not take that as a promise." He stood and stepped away from her.

Her senses sharpened to a keen edge now. With him standing there looking as if he could hardly control an urge to do something horrible to someone—and she the only one near—she knew absolutely that she was in terrible danger.

She looked about the cave with more concern. It wasn't a cave at all, she saw, but an abandoned mine shaft, a relic of the gold fever that had spurred the most famous human migration in history. The excavation had been quickly abandoned, evidently, for it was only about ten feet deep and eight wide. Mr. Sheridan, who was six foot three or four, had to stoop in order not to hit his head on the splintery beams bracing the roof. A pile of rocks to one side of the entrance testified to someone having cleared them from the floor recently, leaving it fairly smooth. A roll of gray blankets lay tossed in a far corner. Obviously he'd planned this with care to details.

He pulled his canteen from his saddlebag and gestured with it carelessly in her direction. "Thirsty?"

She stared at it; she wouldn't be able to lift the metal bottle with her hands bound; he would have to help her again. She

34

shook her head.

"Come here then." He beckoned her to the blankets he was now spreading at the back of the mine. She didn't move, except for her eyes, which went from him to the two heavy gray blankets and back to him again. Without realizing, she began to edge backwards toward the mine's entrance.

"If you try to run, I'll have to tie your ankles." It wasn't a threat, but simply an unemotional statement of what he would do. Cause and effect: Run and I'll have to rope and tie you like a calf for branding.

She halted, sank back on her heels, and watched him with her hands joined, as in prayer, beneath her chin.

"Wise as well as steady of nerve." His sarcasm had a weary sound. "Come here, Mrs. Laird."

Still she stayed where she was.

He lunged to his feet and crossed the space separating them. He came down on her, not with anger, but deadly seriousness nonetheless. With a hand on each arm, he pulled her upright and gave her a little shake. "Look—you're going to have to do what you're told, understand?" She pushed her bound fists into his board-hard chest, as if to keep an animal at bay. The strength of his grip was disturbing, as was the impression of violence that emanated from him. He gave her another shake. "I *said,* 'do you understand?'"

She bit her lower lip and nodded vigorously. And when he pushed her toward the blankets, she stepped onto them.

She looked back at him. He stood slightly stooped to avoid bumping his head, waiting. Which made her feel even more self-conscious standing there, her body unclothed and unfettered to the point of abandon. Suddenly she was overcome with shame, and the seeming small thing he required of her—to lay herself down in his bed—was simply too ignominious. She stood there in the puritanical psychic chains of her upbringing.

Amazingly, he seemed to sense her dilemma. He came slowly forward and reached out a hand and pushed her hair back over her shoulder. With the backs of his fingers he traced the curves of her face and the delicate outline of her jaw. He thumbed her pliable earlobe a moment, while she

35

stood still as a statue. Finally he dropped his hand back onto her shoulder. He didn't exactly push her down, but he did exert pressure. It was something she had to give in to, something that made it seem less humiliating to surrender and kneel on that spread blanket.

He still loomed over her, waiting, watching her dispassionately, his gaze lingering on the fall of her hair.

She lowered herself more. Leaning on her elbow, she sat on one hip. Then she lowered her shoulder, and then her cheek, to the rough wool cloth.

She stared hard at his scuffed brown boots—until he sat on the edge of the blanket to remove them. Then she saw his back—his bare back, as he pulled his blue shirt out of his waistband, unbuttoned it, and shrugged it off. He looked shockingly naked, shockingly masculine.

He left his trousers on, but unbuckled his gun belt and placed it inches from where his head would lie. She watched his shoulders move—ball joints curving into biceps—as he reached to pinch out the candle flame.

In the sudden darkness he stretched out beside her. His bare arm brushed her bound hands, his thigh bumped her bent knees. He seemed very still and tense. Stealthily, she inched away, back toward the rear of the mine, until she was half off the blanket.

His sudden voice was quiet. "I was beginning to wonder if Laird would ever take a wife. Now I'm wondering what kind of woman would marry him. You're pretty enough, aren't you? All sweet and gentle allure, with eyes flecked like clouds." His tone of voice curdled the compliment. "And you're respectable, from what I could gather. So what was it? He inherited a fairly good set-up there from his father. He's not rich, but comfortable. Was it for that? Or maybe you're not what you seem. Maybe you have some little secret in your past. They say you're from back East, out here all by yourself, and you don't like to talk about what you left behind. Why? Your family kick you out for some reason?"

She didn't answer, and that was when he turned on her. His arm went over her hips, the other under her neck, and he pulled her back to the center of the blanket. When she struggled, he crushed her to him. She felt the stone wall of his chest, the muscular strength of his big frame, taut with intention. When she tried to hit at him, he squeezed her even tighter, warning her that he could crack her bones if he should have a mind to. He said, "You're cold as the north wind and I've only got these blankets—and me—to warm you up, so you might as well settle down to the idea of sleeping right here."

He rolled her onto her back and threw his leg over her knees to further pin her. "Now talk to me. Tell me why you married him."

She was as near to hysteria as she'd ever been in her life. It cancelled out all her caution. "None of your business! You're despicable! You're disgusting! Let go of me! Do you hear! *Let me go!*"

His free hand gripped her jaw hard. It hurt—and it sobered her. The hand gentled, slid down her throat. *"Talk* to me," he repeated with mock pleading.

The hand twined in her hair. She shivered, but vowed not to give him the satisfaction of seeing her struggle anymore, when it was clear he had ten times her strength. "T-talk until I think of something to say—like a preacher?"

He laughed softly. It was a velvety sound, though she sensed about him and in his heart a deep bitterness. "You've got grit. All right, I don't really care why you married him. What's important is that someone finally did, and that's what I've been waiting for." The touch of his fingers on the side of her neck was not violent. They stroked, caressed, as if to woo her. They descended in a feathery stroke to her shoulder; his calloused palm smoothed and polished her shoulder bone, then slipped warm down her arm.

Her breathing was quick and deep and every muscle was shaking with tension. She clenched her teeth harder, trembled under his dark weight. He's going to take liberties. I won't cry, though! *I will not cry!* Nevertheless, she felt tears come: a sob rose hard from her stomach. She closed her throat to stop it, yet a sound escaped.

His hand stopped abruptly, as if he only then realized what he was doing. He reached for the other blanket to cover them. "Better get some sleep. We've got another hard day of it tomorrow."

He proceeded to make her comfortable to himself, as if she were a pillow to be turned and molded and adjusted for his complete ease. He rolled her so her back was against his chest, her hips in the curve of his groin—and with the intimacy of this handling, she hiccuped with another repressed sob.

"Christ, don't start bawling on me." His tone was laden with rigid patience.

She goaded herself with another stern vow not to cry. After all, it didn't seem as if he was going to do anything more tonight.

Even so, she didn't believe she could ever sleep, not after all he'd said and done to her already. Not when she was still deprived of the use of her hands—while his were free to seize her at any time.

The minutes passed. At first she was supremely aware of his every breath, for she felt every movement of his chest against her back. Then her focus shifted to his heartbeat. It was strong and slow and rhythmic. Gradually her tension eased. His whole warm masculine length was enfolding her—quite comfortably, really—and his heartbeat went on and on, steady, quiet. She began to feel even the warm beating of the blood in his wrist and forearm that lay a bit heavy over her waist. Was there a golden glow in that blood to make it so warm?

The beat began to underlie a dim echo of the "Wedding March," which came to her mind as muted as music heard through water. It was as if this man had become entwined with her, vein and vessel, sinew and tendon. She dreamed she was a drowned woman wrapped around with clinging water ferns. The music came from below her, and she was sinking toward it, bound, held. She knew she should struggle, but she was so tired she couldn't, she just couldn't. And so she sank, sank, into echoing, revolving, radiant depths.

As soon as he was sure the woman was asleep, Andre Sheridan eased away from her. He felt for his gun and his boots and left the mine shaft.

The black texture of the night had thinned fractionally, though he still couldn't see beyond the narrow glen he'd brought them to. He settled himself outside the entrance of the mine to wait.

An hour passed before he heard the slow clop of horses and a quiet exchange of voices. They carried, in this dead hour, from maybe half a mile away. Slowly the searchers passed by to the south, and he knew he wouldn't be found now. Not until he was ready to be found. He stayed where he was an extra half hour, then stretched and went back inside.

He heard the woman's breathing first, then smelled her. Roses. He eased back beneath the blanket, relieved to find her deep in the kittenish slumber of the young and sinless. He smoothed his hand down her arm again. Skin like rose petals, while the curve of her back and hips and thighs felt rich and feminine against him.

What the hell was a woman like this doing marrying Richard Laird? He'd always figured the only kind of wife Laird would ever get would be hard, or ambitious, and at least knowing. This one didn't seem to be any of those. She seemed soft and demure and—an instinct told him— absolutely innocent. And absolutely beautiful. In all his daydreams of killing Laird, he'd never imagined the event would be witnessed by a woman like this. To be truthful, he'd never given much thought to Laird's bride at all. Or, if he had, he'd assumed she would be just as glad to be widowed early on, so she could get what comforts and properties he had to offer without having to put up with the bastard for too long.

So who the hell was this girl? Could she really love the man? Was watching him die going to do something to her?

Andre fiercely put the thought aside. He had to do what he had to do: revenge, some might call it; he knew it to be simple justice. After all, Ling had been young and beautiful and innocent, but that hadn't stopped Laird.

It had been late afternoon, that day five years ago, when he'd come home from his supply trip to Jackson with the usual reaching of his heart for who he thought was awaiting him. He called Ling's name as he entered their one-room

39

cabin. The first little thrill of alarm ran through him when he saw the splintered laundry basket on the center table, full of soiled, wadded, wet clothes. "Ling?" he called.

He heard a slight sound from behind the curtain that separated their bed from the rest of the room. With a feeling of foreboding, he flicked it aside.

She was there, curled beneath the bedclothes, and he stood looking at her in disbelief. There was a livid bruise on her cheek, and her lips were mashed. "God, what happened?"

She wouldn't answer, wouldn't even meet his eyes. His heart banging with terror, he pulled the bedclothes away to look at her. She had on nothing but her jacket, clutched it over her breasts, though it was filthy and torn. Her whole body was trembling violently. He saw the fingermarks on her white thighs . . . and the horrible withering knowledge seeped in. His breath came out in a short *huff*. He slumped to his knees, too awed by her suffering to dare touch her. "Who did this? Oh God, Ling, who did this?"

Now he tried to remember her smile. He had loved her so, and yet he could never quite remember just how her mouth had bowed into a smile. If only he had that much of her, just that one memory . . .

His arm tightened around the woman—Laird's woman. Damn her! She couldn't be what she seemed—all pretty manners and simple decency! His hand slid to her pelvis. Her underdrawers were pulled tight by her position, and his fingers brushed the nicked hint of her female cleft. At the same time his lips closed over her earlobe. Without quite waking, she took a deep, almost sobbing breath—a little heartbreaking noise. He moved his hand immediately.

No, no, don't sound like that. I never want to hear that sound again. No, I won't hurt you, Lorelei, no more than I have to anyway.

Carefully, he pulled her closer. She was so sweetly and elegantly made—so small! At least as small as Ling. He felt the thrum of his heart in strange places through his body. How many years had it been since he'd held a woman who felt so small and smelled so good? How many years since he'd turned his full attention to any woman at all? How many years since he'd lured an innocent to a bed and laid her down and coaxed her to open—

Stop it! She's not for you. She's bait, that's all! Keep your mind on what you're doing, Sheridan, and off this little piece of devil's temptation.

Nonetheless, he woke with a feeling of wanting her, not once or twice during the short hours remaining of that night, but half a dozen times.

Throughout her unhappy childhood, Laura had been plagued by nightmares. She was having another now: *She'd gone into the woods to play—just for a little while. After all, other children did. But when she got home she found the piano ominously closed, the parlor darkened, the whole house silent. She crept upstairs to Alarice's bedroom and, with a mothlike flutter of her heart, knocked timidly. "Mama?"*

The door swung open. There was Alarice on her bed with her hand flung across forehead. "You missed your lesson."

Missed her lesson! "*But I—*"

"Your teacher has come and gone; he couldn't wait."

"I-I'm sorry, Mama."

"Go away. You've made my head ache again. I'll deal with you later."

"I'm really sorry, Mama."

"Go away."

"Please, Mama, I'm sorry! I'll practice extra hard. I'll go practice right now! I-I'm so sorry," she sobbed. But Alarice's approval, always a bit threadbare, had torn again, and Laura felt herself falling through the hole, falling with a thick feeling of dread.

She flung off the blanket that covered her and rolled to her knees. Her mind was disoriented with dreams. Her loose hair tumbled forward over her shoulders to her bare thighs like a cloak, covering both her and the ruins of her childhood. Automatically she resisted the cords at her wrists, sat staring at them dumbly, twisting her hands to get free.

The man beside her on the blanket didn't move, nor did he

41

try to restrain her. He lay still, his hands folded behind his head, watching her through squinted eyes. He looked huge with his broad chest bared, the mat of fine hair that covered it gleaming. It didn't seem she'd awakened him. Rather she had the feeling he'd been awake for some time, perhaps had even been watching the progress of her nightmare on her sleeping face.

Fully awake at last, she recalled everything—where she was, how she had come to be here, and why she ached all over. She stopped twisting her hands and sat still in a return of fear. Why was he doing this? What were his intentions? What kind of a man was he? Oh God, but she wanted to cry!

She felt his broad hand on the small of her back, and quickly scrambled farther away. "Don't touch me!"

"Bad dream?" he said casually. His hair was tousled from sleep and fell rakishly over his forehead. When she didn't answer, he shrugged with indifference. "Well, we've got to get going." But though he sat up, he didn't immediately move away. Instead, he reached to touch her again. He slid his fingers under her hair to put his right hand firmly where her neck met her jaw and her earlobe. She felt in the touch a message: *I'm not happy about having to do this to you.*

Her reaction was violent; she felt a surging desire to do something reckless, something to show him how angry she was, how she hated him for making her feel so afraid.

He said abruptly, "Are you feeling all right?"

Defiantly she nodded her head, denying the aches and pains she felt nearly everywhere.

He frowned, taking his hand away. "Your arms are bruised." She looked quickly, and found two or three fingermarks—the marks of *his* fingers—on her skin. He said grudgingly, "Sorry."

But by the time he finished pulling on his boots he seemed to have crushed this momentary lapse into compassion. He had that expression of grim decision he'd worn last night back on his face. The rash desire to act out surfaced again. "I think I deserve some explanation for all this, don't you?"

He glanced at her over his shoulder; their eyes held as he buttoned his blue shirt. She nerved herself to look straight back at him, to see if he would offer any reason for what he was doing, any information, any edification at all.

His face told her that he wasn't. In fact, he seemed to forget her question altogether as he stood to buckle his gun belt.

"Why are you doing this!"

He lanked casually to his saddlebags, opened one, and pulled out a clean but crumpled shirt, which he tossed down at her knees. Then he reached for her. She shrank away.

"I'm just going to untie your hands, Mrs. Laird," he said, mocking her reaction.

Which made her want to scratch his eyes out.

Though her struggles had tightened his knots, his strong, blunt fingers pulled them apart with very little trouble. He examined the bracelets of red the cord had left around her wrists, but turned away without commenting. She rubbed the tender skin and waited until he stood before she spoke again: "Are you going to let me go now?"

He dropped the candle stub into his saddlebag. Obviously he didn't think this question worthy of an answer either.

"You'll be sorry about all this once my husband catches up to you!"

His glance was noncommittal. He'd taken out a generous chunk of jerked meat and was knifing it into two pieces; he offered her one. "That ought to keep your jaw busy enough to stop wobbling so much."

"My jaw isn't . . ."

She stopped when she saw the ghost of a smile on his mouth. The man was teasing her!

Four

Laura's captor lounged against the side of the cave eating his own share of the jerked meat. A bluejay squealed outside the entrance, and somewhere a cricket made a noise like peeps of light. The smell of wet earth mingled with the scent of ferns. Laura's bare arms were goosebumped. Later, the day would be unbearably hot, but for now it was cool, especially inside this shadowy mine—especially since she had so little on.

She sat eating in a fury, still dueling with that temptation to do something reckless, to make some daring gesture that would demonstrate just how outraged she felt. It cost her terribly to sit quiet and docile, to wait for whatever fate would befall her.

He finished his meal long before she finished hers. The jerky was certainly enough to "keep her jaw busy": it was tough as leather. She could only pull small strings off with her teeth and chew them down a little at a time.

He stretched—seeming to fill the small space with masculine muscle and bone—and folded his hands behind his head and stared at the opposite wall with a faraway look. She took the opportunity to study him, to see what he was like by the light of day.

His cheeks were shaded with the night's growth of whiskers, but beneath them his face was tanned and totally manly. Straight brows over those black eyes. Firm nose. Wide mouth. His build and coloring testified to a daily life of

44

hard work. Looking at him, she felt a growing, mounting tension, reminiscent of how she'd reacted when she first saw him at the ranch house—that stunned feeling. She'd found him immediately attractive before she'd known his intentions.

Though he hadn't appeared to be watching her, or even particularly aware of her, he seemed to know just when she took her last nibble of the jerky, for that was when he uncapped his canteen and leaned to offer it to her. He was close enough, as he sat there, to hurt her easily. One casual flick of his fist and . . . Still, she risked speaking firmly: "They'll put you in jail for this."

All he did was continue to lean toward her. She took the canteen, raised it hesitantly, unwilling to take her eyes off him for a second. He put a finger beneath the bottle and tilted it; the water spilled over her lips and made a runnel of the little cleft of her chin. She quickly put her mouth to the neck and drank. When she handed it back, he nodded toward the shirt he'd tossed onto the blanket earlier. "Better put that on."

She stared down at it, a man's green flannet shirt, *his* shirt, faded from wear, worn where it had been stretched across his back countless times. A flash of stubbornness tempted her to refuse, but common sense intervened: to what end would refusal lead? She was chilled now, and later, if he really was going to drag her around the countryside, the sun was bound to be hot; her bare arms and shoulders would burn. She shook out the shirt and thrust her hands into the voluminous sleeves.

The cuffs fell over her fingertips. She raised her arms to shake them up onto her wrists, but they fell down again as she started on the front buttons. Andre schooled his face to blankness as he watched her deft fingers work at them. She was like a fragile trembling lute; everytime he touched her, or even got too near, she vibrated like a plucked string. She didn't trust him a bit—and he thought that best, all things considered.

She looked near to drowning in his shirt. The sleeves kept falling over her hands as she nervously tried to get the front buttons fastened. The shirt fit him fine—and for the first time it dawned on him that probably his very size was frightening to her.

He heaved himself up, squatted before her, and began to fold one of the sleeves up her arm. She suffered this, but when he made as if to finish the buttoning down her front, she pulled away. "I can do that!"

"Then hurry up." Again he watched her, mesmerized. He knew she'd been earning her living teaching piano to kids. That would account for the length and flex of her fingers.

When Laura looked up, finished, she saw he had the cord to bind her wrists in his hands again. Her expression must have been crestfallen, for he explained himself for once: "I can't trust you not to head off in the brush first chance you get, and I haven't got the time or patience to chase after you."

She gave him her sternest look. "Mr. Sheridan, you are no gentleman."

At first his face was the same. Then—a wonder!—he smiled. He even chuckled. As he caught her wrists and began to tie them, he said, "You've cut me to the quick, ma'am."

His face was only inches from hers—and for one white-knuckled moment, she considered taking him by surprise with a punch. Not a slap, but a real, fisted punch!

Despite his mockery, it wasn't lost on her that the cord was tied looser—not so loose that she could slip out of it, but not so tight as it had been last night.

She got to her feet. The green shirt hung on her. The shoulders fell halfway to her elbows, so that she was sure she looked like a child playing dress up in her father's nightshirt; yet the tails covered her almost to her knees and for that she could only be grateful. Feeling slightly less undressed, she followed him outside. The early morning light quivered in the shady ravine like a just-spun web. Vines hung over the banks and trailed into the shallow stream she'd heard running all through the night. And nearby grazed two horses. Two.

She recognized the great black stallion they had traveled on last night. He stood where the sunlight fell over him. His nostrils flared at the approach of his master. One eye peeked

46

from behind his mane. He nuzzled the man's shoulder, and in return, Mr. Sheridan's strong hand stroked with unbelievable gentleness down the animal's nose.

Meanwhile, a palomino stood plucking at a tuft of grass at the base of a stony upthrust. She was the color of a new gold piece, with flaxen tail and mane. She gazed at Laura with deer eyes, then snuffed the air with her velvet nose and shook her head, seeming to scatter light as she did so.

Laura worked it out quickly: Mr. Sheridan had left the palomino and an extra saddle here while he went down to the valley to steal her away from her wedding. Such elaborate arrangements. Why?

"Mr. Sheridan!"

His buff-colored hat turned in her direction. Several ways to reprimand him competed in her mind, but with those dark eyes looking straight at her, all she'd meant to say dried in her throat. Instead, she muttered irritably, "Never mind."

"You're going to ride by yourself today. The mare's name is Stingy—I don't know why yet," he said dubiously, "but there's undoubtedly a good reason. She belongs to a sea captain friend of mine, and I borrowed her without asking, so try not to cripple her right off."

He hadn't paused in his packing and saddling-up to say this. In fact, right now he was in the middle of strapping the bedroll onto the black. He turned to the palomino next, heaved a saddle onto its back, and Laura realized that if she was going to ask the thing—the very *necessary* thing that she'd put off speaking about since waking—she'd best do so now. But how to phrase it? "Mr. Sheridan, I . . . that is, I have to . . . I need to . . ."

His finger pointed. "You can go behind that bunch of sage—but no farther. The first time you try anything, it'll mean the end of your privacy. Understand?"

She nodded without looking at him—for she knew her cheeks were flushed—and started to pick her way across the rocky clearing on her tender bare feet.

When she stepped out from behind the bushes a few minutes later, he was waiting for her by the mare. She halted well out of his reach. "Mr. Sheridan, you must listen to me—

47

you just can't do this." It came out sounding awfully feeble.

"Can't I?"

She almost wished she hadn't said anything. No, that wasn't true! Who was he to frighten her and bully her and treat her like this? She straightened her shoulders and faced him squarely. "No, you can't. I won't allow it."

His expression grew mocking. "Mrs. Laird, if you aren't afraid of me yet, you better get that way quick, because, truth is, as far as you're concerned, I can do anything I want."

The coldness of those words chilled her bones.

"Come on now, don't make trouble for yourself." He started toward her.

"Stay away!" She stumbled back a few steps.

"Easy," he said. He held his hands up, clear of the blue-black gun he wore on his hip, palms open and apparently without a hint of menace. He propped one boot against a jutting tree root and offered her what seemed a thin, out-of-practice smile. "I just want you to get on the horse."

She still regarded him with the same apprehension—and with good cause, for before she could realize what he was up to, he moved forward and clasped one of her bound arms. Too late she tried to spring away, as if his touch was fire. But he had her. He said coolly, "Now let's go."

Wisely, she didn't resist further when he pulled her toward the horses, didn't resist as his big hands circled her waist and slung her onto Stingy's saddle. Mr. Sheridan handled her bare legs and feet casually as he shortened the stirrups for her. She wanted to kick out at him, but didn't dare. Maybe she couldn't do much in her own behalf for the moment, but Laura vowed to keep her eyes open and to stay ready.

The morning was heating up fast. Mr. Sheridan's blue chambray shirt was already clinging to his back as he mounted his black. He reined the stallion around. The palomino's neck stretched out and the lead rope grew taut before she resigned herself to being led. Laura had nothing to do but hold on.

Richard, Richard! Where are you? Please help me!

Mr. Sheridan kept them to the labyrinthine gullies and

gulches of the convoluted countryside. They seldom climbed openly over the grassy, summer-bronzed balds of the hilltops. This was a country of sage scrub. The only shade was supplied by scant-needled digger pines. There was no breeze, and the sun was like an eye that followed them. Laura's heart muttered resentfully against being transported hither and thither against her will. She longed to unfasten the top buttons of the green shirt—and it was then that an idea came. Stealthily she unfastened the bottom buttons to her waist. It wasn't easy with her wrists bound, but she managed to tear a piece of the material off the frayed edge of her abbreviated chemise, a strip a mere inch wide and about four inches long. With a pounding heart, she dropped it.

The horses clip-clopped around a blue oak. A minute passed. They entered a rocky area occupied by rugged knobcone pines. She had another strip of the material in her fingers and let it drop.

Her captor looked back casually—and his sharp eyes of course caught the flutter of the scrap. The black halted. Mr. Sheridan looked forward again, bowed his head as if to gather patience, then slid from his saddle. He strode past Laura's mare to pick up the bit of cloth lying innocently—blatantly—among the rocks.

Then he was back, holding onto the cheekstrap of Stingy's bridle. "How many have you dropped?" She held her head erect and stared stubbornly forward. With bold hands, he lifted the tails of the green shirt and reached for the edge of her cropped chemise. He studied it, then looked up at her again. His head was thrown back so he could see her from beneath the brim of his hat. His eyes were narrowed to slits against the glare of the day. And his mood was lethal.

Softly, with no amusement now, he said, "I'm no gentleman, Mrs. Laird; you noticed it yourself. It wouldn't bother me at all to strip you naked. Is that what you want?"

She gripped the horn of her saddle. Surely he wouldn't.

He reached up suddenly and tore her from her seat.

"No!" she said.

He paused, holding her with her feet dangling above the ground, his thumbs biting into her waist. "No what?"

49

"No, don't take my clothes off!" How she hated him for making her say that!

"One more chance then." He set her feet on the ground but still held her so close that she could feel his body heat through his soft cotton shirt. "But only one more." Slowly and inexorably he drew her nearer and nearer. "There's a hundred things I could do to you, and every one would make you misserable. Stripping you is only the first thing that came to my mind. Remember that."

His eyes were so uncaring of her that she could imagine at least a thousand punishments he might think up. When he hoisted her back into the saddle, his hand idly stroked her bare knee. His touch was gentle—but his eyes were still severe. "I really don't want to hurt you. Don't make me."

The morning grew dusty and old. Laura slumped on her horse, discouraged. She glared at her captor every time he looked back, yet she left no more strips of white linen to mark their trail.

At noon, when he reined the horses into a little clearing and helped her dismount, she took the food he offered and ate it without speaking. It maddened her that he didn't seem to even notice her mute anger, let alone care. She began to wish she knew what he did care about. Then at least she might find some means of counterattack.

Their resting place was too open for her to consider making a run for it. Chaparral covered the southward-facing hillside like rough homespun; scrub oaks shaded the north-facing slope. Either would have offered concealment, but she was caught between them in a throw net of sunlight and open air. No doubt Mr. Sheridan had chosen the place deliberately for its lack of hiding places.

In contrast, all afternoon their way was narrow again, and thickly overgrown with sagebrush. About four o'clock they came to a creek lined with reeds. The horses plodded in and the stream wetted their bellies before they came out again. Mr. Sheridan stopped them on the grass of the level bank beyond, and stepped down from the saddle. He helped Laura down, and she immediately knelt to scoop up a drink of cool water in the cup of her bound hands. She drank, and patted some onto the burning skin of her nose and cheeks. He looked to the horses, then got himself a drink. He took his hat off to sluice water over his face and head and the back of his neck—more brusque with his toilette than she.

He wandered in his silent way to sit against an oak. She heaved a sigh, remaining in the calm shade of the trees hanging over the water. She dipped a toe into the stream, wiggled it . . . and soon was wading in the shallows.

Slender grasses grew in the pebbly shoals. Her feet looked tiny among them, refracted like the rocks. She supposed it was decidedly unladylike, wading barefoot like this, but she had done so few prohibited things in her life—and considering her circumstances of the moment—she had few qualms about breaking the rules this once. Her exposed legs had been getting sunburned, and since the water felt cool on her ankles, she went farther out, and farther, thigh-deep into the rush, and just stood there.

The dark and soothing current was hypnotizing. Her mind strayed to the stories she'd heard about Indians who had noted stray shiny flakes in creek beds like this—and had rejected them in favor of ornaments such as beads and shells. Well, neither gold nor shells were intrinsically of any worth, she supposed. It was up to individuals to decide which would become the symbols of wealth.

Every time she glanced to where Mr. Sheridan was resting, she found him looking at her. She said, "Must you watch me all the time? You make me self-conscious."

"Do I?" he drawled. She could hear a smile in his voice. "I'm intrigued, Lorelei, that's all."

"My name is not Lorelei; it's just plain Laura."

He wasn't quick to answer, but at least this time he did answer, eventually. "The Lorelei was said to be a siren on a rock in the Rhine River, all satin smiles and silken deceit. She lured German boatsmen to shipwreck with her singing."

"What's that got to do with me?"

Again he didn't answer immediately. She heard the hum of the bees, the soughing of the rushes before he said at last, "Damned if I know."

He lounged there a few minutes longer, sleepy-eyed, then

called her back to the horses.

"Go to the devil, Mr. High-and-Mighty Sheridan," she said softly, speaking to the long limber plants in the stream and not really intending for him to hear.

But he did. "A curse doesn't work unless it comes from the heart."

She looked at him. "That one came straight from my heart, believe me."

His gaze was for the first time totally friendly and pleasant, nonetheless. "Well, if you don't come out of there and get back on this horse I can promise you a pretty intimate look at the devil—and soon." He'd gone to Stingy and seized her bright mane casually, almost affectionately. Laura found herself suddenly thinking how it would be if he handled her as he was now handling the horse. Her quickly drawn breath gave away a mingling of emotions: fear, yes— and some new, beating exhilaration that tightened her breasts and filmed the palms of her hands with perspiration. It was that same feeling she'd had the first time she'd seen him—a stupid and totally inappropriate feeling!

He was waiting for her, and seemed in a perfectly good-natured mood for once, but she was wary of testing him. She'd learned not to count on patience from him, or easiness, or anything but harshness. She waded ashore.

Before he boosted her onto Stingy, he swung his hat off his head and plopped it onto hers. "That should keep your nose from burning anymore."

Of course the hat was miles too big, and nearly covered her eyes and ears both—she knew she must look absolutely ridiculous—but he was right; it would shade her face. And she was not unaware that the gesture was a kindness extended to her of his own volition.

Then he was on his black, and they were in motion again, in that easy way longtime riders and their accustomed mounts have. One instant the pair of them were standing and the next they were on the move, and there had been nothing perceivable in between. They were stopped, and then they were moving, that was all.

But then, he was a horseman. She wasn't. She'd assumed

52

that once she moved to Laird Ranch she would learn to ride, for Richard seemed to spend most of his days on horseback, but as of yet she had very little experience with horses. She was instinctive enough, however, to sense that Stingy was of a more nervous temperament than Mr. Sheridan's black.

This was soon proved out. They weren't far from the creek when a dragonfly dove at the mare's eyes and startled her. She reared. Laura barely had time to get a good hold on the saddlehorn, and even so, she felt herself sliding backwards out of the saddle. The low sage scratched her legs as the mare half-reared again. Laura leaned forward, threaded her fingers into the flying mane, and clung tenaciously.

She saw the black's blaze in the corner of her sight, then Mr. Sheridan was at her side. From his saddle he leaned to grab Stingy. Taking a left-handed death grip on the mare's halter, he addressed a steady flow of obscene threats at her. (What language! It was really dreadful! And he was so fluent in it!) The mare whinnied rebelliously, but eventually settled down.

Laura's skin felt cold. Mr. Sheridan let go of Stingy and took her arm in his hand. His palm was warm and hard as oak. "You all right?" he asked. "Sorry; if I'd known she did things like that, I would've warned you."

"Oh, don't apologize, Mr. Sheridan! Believe me, being thrown and trampled by a raging horse is nothing to me."

His smile was tinged with respect. It told her that he knew she was frightened and that he admired her bravado in the face of it. "It's probably the lead rein. It's made her temperamental. You want to ride with me for a while?"

She stared at the hollow of his throat. "I-I would rather take my chances alone."

His smile stayed the same. "Well, just remember I gave you the option." He reined ahead. "If you get thrown, it's your own fault."

When they finally came up out of the narrow ravine bottoms, she saw peaks standing in the sun to the east. She guessed that they were now deep into the tranquil Mother Lode—the gold country that had drawn an earlier generation as dry grass draws wildfire. The air here was aromatic with manzanita sweetness. From the top of the bluff she saw miles of foothills stretching away on either hand. To the west was the wide flat central valley, veined with threads of light—the creeks and rivers that laced the valley, branching and re-branching into gentle shining streams that seemed to flow nowhere in particular in the peachy glow of the closing day.

The summits of the Sierra Nevada sat on the eastern horizon like stupendous sharp boulders. Though she had crossed them easily enough by train, she couldn't help but sense the bravery and daring which must have been necessary to do so in splintery wooden wagons.

Andre, too, was affected by the panorama. "Nice view, isn't it? My father was one of the crazy ones who came through here by wagon in '49."

He watched her tilt his hat up out of her eyes and shake her hair back with a movement that unconsciously accented her exquisite throat. She said, "I wonder how the lure of gold could have been so strong."

"Do you?" he asked, his eyes still on that undefended column of her throat.

"Did he find any gold—your father?"

"Drew Sheridan always got exactly what he wanted." She mused, "My father didn't."

Common sense told him not to comment, yet he did anyway. "No?"

"No. He told me he'd wanted to come west once, but my mother—my real mother—wasn't strong."

Andre regarded her for a moment longer, remarking her openness, her lack of guile. Any other woman would have rebuffed his comment on the view—as he'd rebuffed her little comments again and again. Yet here she was, trying to make conversation with him. The girl was too difficult to figure; she had patches of almost unnatural innocence, as though she'd been passed over by life. He sensed he could get her to tell him all about herself, but he held back. He knew by now the one thing he really wanted to know, yet he doubted if even she would tell him the answer to that question—or if he would believe her if she did. In the end, he only said, "Let's go."

He pushed ahead for another hour through the dwindling daylight. He rode with the ease of being accustomed to unending days in the saddle, so used to shifting with his horse that he did it unthinkingly, bending his thoughts to other issues. Although Laura admired his stamina she wished he would recognize that she wasn't so enduring. She wanted nothing more than to slide to the ground and lie there. She'd never felt so completely worn.

They were climbing into ever cooler, ever prettier landscapes. At last, under the final low red glare of the sunset, he announced they would make camp beside a streamlet. As he helped her down from Stingy, she saw signs that his energy was not inexhaustible after all. Yet the weariness in his face seemed more than something caused by just a hard day's travel; it seemed to be of much longer standing.

They were in a wooded area, surrounded by steep hillsides. An outcropping of white granite, roughly as large and as high as a one-story house, jutted into the campsite. Laura headed straight for it and sank down, sure that not even the worst threat could make her budge ever again.

Five

Soon the horses were unsaddled and tethered to graze on the slope. The day was closing up like a tulip. Mr. Sheridan built a small smokeless fire in the lee of the thrust of granite. At the side of the flames he patiently warmed a can of stewed meat. When it was steaming, he took two flat-bottomed tin pans and two spoons from his saddlebags. He divided the stew between the pans, opened a second can, this one of muscat grapes, and divided it in the same way. He placed one pan on the ground beside Laura.

When he untied her hands, his face didn't change, but she was glad that he knew now some part of the discomfort he'd caused her today, for her wrists were chafed and had even bled in one place. He was kneeling on a single knee, bracing an elbow on the other. "Why didn't you say something about that?"

"Would it have made any difference?"

He didn't answer, and she took the spoon he gave her and began to eat hungrily.

When her pan was empty, he asked, "That hold you?" She nodded and he went to the streamlet to rinse their utensils. She remained as she was, leaning against the granite boulder; he didn't tie her again when he returned to the little circle of firelight, but sat nearby and set about sharpening his jackknife. For minutes on end he looked only at the knife, gently polishing the razor steel with small strokes of an oiled rag. A pine cone fell in the forest; his hands stopped. There

56

was only silence. He began the polishing motion again.

Meanwhile, with the resinous wood crackling and snapping in the fire, putting warmth and light between them and the darkness, Laura's eyelids began to droop. Mr. Sheridan returned the knife to his pocket, and rested back against his saddle, his hands under his head and his hat—which he'd reclaimed at sundown—tipped forward to cover his forehead. He seemed comfortable, which was more than she was, she was so saddle sore. Her buttocks and thighs were throbbing. Besides, she kept hearing stirrings in the forest which set her nerves on edge.

He sat up just enough to place his boot against a long piece of pine and shove it farther into the flames. A feather of smoke drifted up. He lay back again.

Laura was so tired. She felt her weariness hovering over her, urging sleep, so that when she tipped her head back to study the jeweled velvet sky . . .

She was awakened by a nightmare about playing Tchaikovsky's Piano Concerto No. 1 very badly. Mama had not been pleased. The music had been so vivid, however, she could almost hear the fading hum of the piano's harp in the forest's silence. She barely opened her eyes. Mr. Sheridan seemed to be asleep. At least he'd gone still, lying in that sloped position against his saddle, his feet toward the dying fire. What she could see of his face looked like the face of a man oppressed by loneliness. He had accomplished his abduction of her so easily, yet he didn't seem terribly satisfied. Maybe that was because he hadn't finished whatever it was he meant to accomplish.

Not knowing his purpose troubled her. It didn't seem his goal was particularly to hurt her—yet she knew his name and his face, and would be able to identify him to anyone. So why should she blindly believe he wouldn't sooner or later turn on her? He had nothing to gain by letting her go. And if he couldn't let her go, then . . . She faced the thing at last. The situation and its most probable conclusion. And her heart beat as hard as if she'd just come to the blackest passage of a scarey story.

She looked about furtively. In the deep dark of the forest,

things whispered. The evergreens muttered with wind and with . . . other things. There were cracklings not of the horses' making, movements which might be anything. Nevertheless, she stood, slowly, her eyes on Mr. Sheridan's face. She took a sideways step, then another.

"I wouldn't," he said suddenly, quietly.

She froze. He gave the pine piece another careless push with his boot. He barely moved there in the fireshine, but she saw now that his eyes were open and studying her. She told herself, however, that if he had nothing to lose—neither did she. She spun—and fell headlong into the deep carpet of ancient fallen leaves and pine needles. He'd tripped her, and as she struggled to get to her hands and knees his hand gripped her ankle, stringing her leg out behind her.

She flopped over to look at him. He hadn't moved much from his spot, only rolled onto his left elbow. His right hand held her foot like a trap, and he simply watched her, waiting to see if she was going to carry this little attempt any further—in which case he would get up.

When he did move, it was with lazy ease. He let go of her ankle and sat up, moving his hat back to direct his full attention toward her. His eyes flashed with firelight. "What a pity you can't say 'damn it.'"

She let her breath out with a little puff of her cheeks. "Yes, a pity."

For a moment longer the firelight moved in his eyes. Then he rose, dusting leaves and pine needles off his back. He squatted on the other side of the fire and began to rake together a mattress of sun-steeped pine straw over which he tossed the two blankets of his bedroll. He looked back at her coolly.

She was sitting where she'd fallen, hugging her knees now. She would not give him the satisfaction of letting him scare her meekly into his bed a second time. If he was going to do her harm, well let him go ahead and do it!

Yet it took all her willpower not to cringe when he lunged to his feet and came for her. He was so big, and yet so supple and lazily certain—definitely not a man to provoke needlessly. She didn't know what to expect from him, and so

58

braced herself for anything.

It must have shown, for when he stopped beside her he frowned and said, "What's that look for? Think I might haul off and kick you?"

"I think you could."

He looked down at her, his face solemn and troubled. She got the feeling he was asking himself if maybe it wasn't true. He squatted, and surprised her by saying, "Look, you're not what I expected. I expected someone more, well, more suited to Laird's sleazy character. Another adventurer hoping to strike it rich in California. I don't know why—I've been thinking it over all day, and I guess I should've known he'd pick someone young and easy. A nice, but not very clever little tidbit. Christ, you're so green you probably think I'm going to murder you." She watched his mouth thin as he realized that was exactly what she thought. A moment passed, then he reached out and gave her hair a painless tug. "Stop worrying about that."

Just that simple: Stop worrying about it!

Suddenly he shoved his arms under her knees and back and lifted her before she knew what he was up to; he stood with her held against his chest.

"Put me down!"

"Sure thing." And he did—on the blankets. She started to scramble up, but his hand sent her toppling back. When she tried it again, he gripped her shoulder. "Don't push your luck, Mrs. Laird." He continued to hold her, making sure she stayed where she was. "What's that look for now? Think I'm going to do something else to you? If not murder, maybe rape?"

"You're hurting—" she said in a half-stifled voice.

He let go of her shoulder and fixed his eyes on her face. Her hand rubbed where he'd gripped her. He said softly, with a tinge of genuine regret, "Sorry—but, goddamnit! If you'd just do what you're told! Now I suppose you'll have another bruise come morning!"

She blinked away the lingering pain, and considered him, so contradictory, so set upon his path and yet so obviously disturbed by it.

"Lie down," he said.

She lay back, stiffly. The smell of pine straw ascended around her.

He took off his boots and shirt and gun belt. The last of the firelight made the hard ripples and depressions of his upper body glow. He stretched himself down beside her, and seemed to gird himself before he reached to take her in his arms. She awkwardly defended herself. "Hold still—look, I can either hold you or tie you to a tree. That's the only way I can get any sleep and still know where you are."

"Then tie me up!" Anything was preferable to this physical intimacy.

"You'd change your mind long before morning." He was all this time wrestling her onto her side and backing her up to him and forcing her to bend her knees so that her hips were cupped in the curve of his groin.

"I wouldn't!" She tried to straighten her legs—did straighten the top one, only to have her knee pinned between his hard thighs.

His voice turned heartless. "Go to sleep, Mrs. Laird."

Along with her sore and strained muscles, she felt a painful knot of anger. "I swear you're going to pay dearly for this! You won't like prison!"

"I'm not going to prison, but I am going to get some sleep, even if I have to gag you to do it."

Not the gag. That was one thing she hated. She remembered how suffocated she'd felt. "Why can't you at least tell me what this is all about?"

She assumed he was going to ignore her question again. This time, however, he said, "Your husband committed a crime he's never paid for—till now."

"Richard?" She twisted around in his arms, causing him to sigh as his work was undone. "Richard isn't a crimnal!"

"Maybe not in the eyes of the law, but . . . The number one mistake of Richard Laird is his belief that other people's grass might just as well be his. Now turn over and go to sleep. We've got another day of it tomorrow." His obstinacy was adamant. She found herself being turned again, and gave in to it, knowing it was useless to defy him.

She tried to stay awake, however, thinking there might be a chance for escape if she did. A half hour passed. She was awake and attentive, but lay seemingly settled in the sinking moonlight. Suddenly he leaned up on his elbow and stared down at her. "I really don't want to tie you to a tree, but— that one right there looks like it'd do, if you don't close your eyes right now."

Her gaze darted to the magnificent ponderosa pine close by their pallet. There seemed to be a movement in its lower branches. Her eyes darted back to him. Which posed the greater danger? His face mirrored a disturbing kindness combined with judicial patience. She realized she trusted him more than whatever might be moving out there in the night, so she did as he asked. And at last, in spite of all her fears, her thoughts dimmed. The wind was lulling in the tops of the pines, and the moonlight came dreamily through rifted clouds, even the whisper of his breath on the top of her head seemed to have an effect on her. Sleep, soft-smiling, drew her down.

It was still more dark than light when Andre's spread fingers lifted the back of the woman's head off the blanket and turned her face so his mouth could cover hers. Contradictory feelings welled within him as she let her lips be shaped to his and even accepted his tongue between her teeth. Part of him was disgusted as he pressed his thighs to hers. Part of him wasn't. She was still half-asleep, but she sure knew how to react to what he was doing. It satisfied something malignant inside him to feel her surrender to this raid.

But she surrendered with such sweetness!

His forearm rested between her breasts; his hand was busy slipping the buttons of the shirt he'd lent her. "No," she breathed, her eyes still closed, "Richard . . ." His hand didn't stop, but delved in under the flaps of the shirt to find her breasts—and that was when she opened her eyes, slowly, and with a start saw that it was not her precious Richard kissing her. "Oh!"

She sat up so suddenly that he lost his hold on her. He sat up, too, though not so fast. He studied her. "Did he listen to you when you told him no?"

She was obviously still fuddled by sleep and didn't understand the question. Nevertheless, his gaze burrowed into her pale gray eyes—eyes the color of fog—trying to find the answer. Reaching out unhurriedly, he drew her against him. His arms went around her and clamped hard, flattening the little mounds of her breasts against his chest. He asked roughly, "How far did you let him go?"

She didn't answer; she was scared now. But for some reason he was angry, too angry to care if he was scaring her, angry at the thought of her letting Laird put his hands on her, and probably his mouth, too, and whatever else the bastard liked to do to women.

His own mouth lowered in slow motion, and took hers with moody possession, as with unrelenting pressure he leaned her back onto the blanket. He lay over her, using enough of his weight to bear her down and still her struggles, forcing her to lie beneath him (she felt so good!) as he slid one hand up her hip. He kept his tongue in her mouth to muffle the pleading sounds she was making as he slipped the buttons at the waist of her drawers. Her mouth escaped his as he lifted off her enough to strip the garment down her legs.

"Don't—oh don't, *please!*"

But with sureness and deliberateness, he lowered himself onto her again, and wedged his hand between her legs to cup her intimately with his palm.

She just fits; I can hold her in my hand!

She kept struggling. Maybe she was the kind who liked it, but felt they shouldn't, and needed to be persuaded first. "Let me, Mrs. Laird. You know you want it."

"Oh don't! Please, don't . . . oh God no!" She was trying her best to twist out from under him—kicking the leg he didn't have pinned, and pounding at him with her free hand. She put up a damned good act, he'd give her that. Or was it an act? He remembered her reaction that first day when he'd touched her jaw. She'd acted as if no one had ever touched her with tenderness before. Was it possible she really was as

62

innocent as she seemed, so totally innocent and naive that a man like Laird could find her gullible enough to take him for a husband? Or was she, as he suspected, a slut in an innocent's guise? That was more likely. Laird had probably had her dozens of times in the past six months. Well, that was what Andre was going to find out now. He needed to know—had to know!

She was still fighting him with all her strength. "All right," he said in a terse voice, "I'm not going to hurt you. Just stop a minute—look—look at me! Now, am I hurting you? Am I?"

Gradually, as his hand remained exactly where it was, his fingers neither moving away nor going further into her, her struggles reduced to a hard-breathing acceptance of his palm being where it was. He felt her pulse throbbing. How warm she was there.

Suddenly he moved his hand. One finger dipped, delved. Immediately she arched away from him again, her hand braced against his shoulder. Her head fell back, and her voice made an odd inhaled squeak. Her fingernails dug into the skin of his shoulder.

His finger nudged inside her (she was like velvet—but not excited, not moist) almost to the depth of the first knuckle before it met the encumbrance. *Goddamn!*

In an instant his whole conception of her shifted. Having her beneath him ceased to be a test and became a heady thing. He wanted to linger, wanted badly to kiss her again, and nudge his finger deeper. If he went slow, if he waited just where he was now and let her get used to the idea, the feeling . . . but no, she was beginning to cry. Beginning to cry, but trying to conceal the sound, and it was that attempt at concealment more than the tears themselves that shamed him. The girl was dazed with fatigue and helpless with terror—and though he wanted her (and he did want her!) he was no rapist.

He withdrew his finger. "Don't cry. Shhh, I'm not going to do anything more." He stroked her once, twice, as he would pet the silky fur of a frightened kitten; then he realized he had to let her close her legs again before she'd believe him.

"Shhh, I just had to know," he said in a husky, guilty voice. "Go back to sleep, little Lorelei, shhh, sleep now. I won't do it again."

He enfolded her. All the fight had gone out of her as soon as he'd left off his invasion; she seemed so relieved to have her legs clamped tight once more that she didn't object to him just holding her close. "That's right, hold on to me, and go to sleep now," he went on in the same forced, husky voice. "And no bad dreams."

God, but she felt good, the way she fit right into him, so small and snug against his chest, her arms wrapped around his neck, her forehead tucked beneath his jaw.

A virgin! Did she know what her soft thighs were pressed up against? Did she know anything at all? "Damn!" he said in a quiet voice filled with frustration.

A boot nudged Laura's hip. Drifting halfway over the doorsill of sleep, she rolled onto her back. A dark shape was standing over her in the sunrise. A man. Standing with his thumbs in his pockets. The tops of pine trees rocked in a slight breeze above his head. "Time to get up," he said.

She lay there a minute longer, disoriented, her hair still all adrift on the gray blanket. Then she scrambled to her knees, coming fully awake at last.

The sun had already diffused a pleasant warmth over the copper dawn. She blinked around her at the fragile light, at the glasslike clarity of the new day.

Mr. Sheridan turned to cover the gray heap of last night's fire. She rose and stepped off the blankets—slowly, for she was so incredibly sore she could hardly move. With that first step she realized she had no underdrawers on beneath her long flannel shirt. The shirt itself was unbuttoned to her waist. She spun to face her captor. He had begun to roll the blankets into a neat bundle the moment she stepped off them. And there were her underdrawers, flung over his shoulder casually.

She grabbed them and retreated, backing behind the big ponderosa. She struggled to untangle the garment and get it on while slow helpless tears wended down her cheeks.

She stayed behind the tree for several minutes, and when she emerged she kept her head down, not wanting him to see how her face was stained. Slowly, painfully, she climbed the slope to sit in the warm sun atop the outcropping of granite.

Why had he done that to her? *Why?* Why was he doing any of this? What had she done to deserve it? She really believed she was, if anything, a fairly harmless person—but harmlessness, in this new and violent state, seemed no protection.

Oh, but she wanted to go home! The thought made her tears start again. She wanted to go home! Back to Massachusetts, to Abfalter Village, home to her own little bedroom hidden under the eaves. She wished she'd never left it now. The troubles she'd faced there seemed so innocuous compared to what she'd stumbled into here.

She had to stop crying. The last tears formed and quivered in her eyes, just short of dropping. She'd never been allowed to revel in the luxury of tears. But now—maybe it was because her strength was worn down with anxiety and weariness. And because of what he'd done to her.

She heard him moving about the camp. She really had to control herself. She couldn't let him see her break down and sob openly. That would only give him the chance to make some sarcastic comment. She'd been sitting bent, with her dark hair falling forward to shield her face, but now she straightened, flung it back.

It didn't stay back; it fell over her shoulders and hung to her fingertips in tangled strings. It helped a little to comb it with her fingers, and the pain of yanking at it helped to calm her.

When he came up the slope to offer her some jerked meat for breakfast, she stopped temporarily, and stared away from him, hiding her drenched, miserable eyes. He sat on the rock beside her, broodingly chewing his own meal. She knew he was studying her. Finally he took her arm and pulled her off her perch. The times when she'd been a small helpless child and her stepmother hadn't spared her came back vividly. He said, "Christ, no need to go pale as milk—you want your hair combed, don't you?" He backed her between his legs. His powerful thighs clamped shut around hers, holding her where she was as he began tugging at her hair with a comb out of his shirt pocket.

At first he tugged rather savagely, until she fell back against him once when the comb caught in a knot. Setting her forward on her feet again, he muttered, "Sorry."

He'd said that to her a total of three times now. Three apologies from a man obviously not used to apologizing. But did it mean anything?

He went at it more gently after that, more efficiently. It was several minutes later that he said, "I'm sorry I scared you last night." His tone was abrupt, dismissive.

She felt a frightening rush. She wanted to bolt, but she also wanted to feel his hands draw her nearer and comfort her as he had then. She shivered. She'd never known such confused feelings with a man.

He finished the combing, then started plaiting her hair into a single braid. She knew braiding was a talent cowboys practiced in making their leather and horsehair gear, so she wasn't surprised that he knew how to do it. What surprised her was that he was doing it for her. Every once in a while he had a mysterious habit of doing something kind.

She shuddered and tried to jerk away, however, when he reached under her green shirt, but he only yanked a thread from the torn hem of her chemise to tie off the end of the thick braid.

Then he turned her, his hands on her hipbones now, keeping her within the confines of his legs. He sat looking up at her, still broodingly, his bronze face illuminated by the pure morning light. His eyes flashed as they went over her face and studied the evidence of her humiliation.

She thought she would melt under the waves of masculinity that seemed to radiate out from him. The tension between them was so thick she could almost see it. His stare bored into her—and she saw now why he had done what he had: he wanted her, the same way Richard did, the way men want women. She realized how vulnerable her ignorance of what exactly happened at such times made her—more vulnerable than any woman in her situation had any business being. She realized she was much more ignorant than she had considered herself at her wedding.

She didn't dare put her hands on his lean, hard chest to push herself away. She didn't dare touch him at all. An instinct warned her that any more contact with him at just this moment might be galvanizing.

"Young and easy."

That was what he'd said about her last night. Something about Richard choosing her because she was young and easy.

"You must have come into town like bread offered up for the multitude. Like an angel cake left right out on the windowsill for anyone to cut a slice. So he threw his saddle blanket over you and asked you to marry him fast. But it must have been hell for him to leave you alone for six months. No wonder he was at a whorehouse the night before his wedding."

He suddenly pushed her away and stood. He took his gun from its holster, checked its loading, then slid it back. His manner was totally brusque and businesslike again. "We'd better get going."

She put a hand out to touch the boulder and steady herself, glad she had a moment to recompose her face while he went down to the horses.

Six

Mr. Sheridan saddled the horses in stark silence, his hands skillful and firm as he pulled the cinches tight and checked the bridles. When he was finished, he stood by Stingy and looked up at Laura, clearly waiting for her to come down from the outcropping so he could help her mount. She fixed her eyes hopelessly on the palomino. She simply could not ride again all day. It was too much for him to demand. But when she straightened her spine (even that movement hurt) and stood her ground, he at first frowned, then adjusted his hat and gave her a knowing look.

"If you're aiming to delay us so Laird can catch up, you might as well know he's not even on our trail. We lost him the first night. They passed by us while you were asleep, passed within a mile of the mine shaft and never even knew it. They went on directly east."

"We were going east yesterday!"

"Not until I was sure we were out of their range."

"He'll backtrack. He'll find us."

"Oh, he'll find us. He knows damn well where I'm taking you."

Her heart lifted. Richard knew!

"Come on down here now," he was saying as if she were a tiresome child.

She refused to budge. He looked at the ground and shook his head. The gesture was full of meaning. He started up the slope. As he neared, she backed away. She couldn't see much of his face under the brim of his pulled-down hat, although she was trying hard.

Suddenly, perhaps because he meant to make her ride again when she already hurt so bad that every movement was an agony—and perhaps because she now had new hope of not being murdered—she shouted, "Who do you think you are, you arrogant, spiteful *animal!*"

He raised his hands as if to reach for her, but then let them drop again. "Let's go."

"No." The word was willful, but even as she spoke it she cautiously took another step away from him. For a moment all she could hear was their breathing, hers quick and shallow, his deep and sure.

"Get down there and get on that horse."

"I'm not going any farther! I don't care what you do to me. I don't care—do you hear? I'm not going another mile!"

A moment ticked by. She saw the hardness of his expression. "You care—or if you don't now, you soon will."

Her legs began to tremble. She was afraid she was going to have to sit down. But with a quick movement he caught her arm and pulled her down the slope to where Stingy stood waiting. Even though she stiffly twisted and squirmed and kicked, and even though Stingy whinnied and skittered, he managed to throw her astride the horse.

As soon as he turned away, however, she slid off again, landing bruisingly on her knees.

He swore. Eyeing her, he pulled a length of cord from his saddlebags. She assumed he meant to tie her wrists, but he used his knife to cut the cord into two pieces. She fought almost as hard when he put her on the horse again, but had to stop when he tied her ankles to the stirrups. "I can untie those," she said, blatantly challenging him.

"And I can tie you over the saddle belly-down like a sack of flour."

"You wouldn't!" she said, stunned, unbelieving. Her voice was the voice of a person observing another walking through what she'd thought was an impenetrable wall.

"Wouldn't I?" He swung up onto his black and turned, looking back at her. "Well, go ahead, try me."

What could he believe Richard had done to him? What could have chilled his temper to such an extreme? Her mind turned and turned, yet found nothing to turn on. The few things she knew of this man indicated that he would be slow to forget any wrong—and careful to extract his full revenge for it.

Richard Laird also mounted a horse that morning, and there he sat, not moving, not seeing his friend Zacariah beside him, but staring ahead morosely, seeing only what was in his mind. He knew where Sheridan was taking Laura, and he knew why. And the irritation and stupidity of it made the veins in his neck stand out.

To think any man could hold a grudge that long! And over a Chinese girl! Richard hardly remembered anything about her anymore. She'd been a whim, a little fun to go along with the fun he was having being out with friends, his parents finally both dead and the ranch his to run as he saw fit. It was all part of the celebration of coming into his own: the hunting trip, the whiskey, and then coming across the girl. She'd just seemed part of it, like she'd been put there in that spot for him to have a little sport with. He'd never for a moment thought she might be married to a white man. Who ever heard of a white man marrying a Chinese anyway? He didn't even think it was legal. Whatever, Sheridan had sure considered himself her husband. And he'd come riding onto the ranch about a week later with his holster greased, ready for an old-fashioned, fast-draw duel.

What was Richard to do but deny the whole thing? He was no gunslinger, and he wasn't about to draw against any man that determined to kill him. What did Sheridan think—that Richard would risk everything, risk his life even, all because of fifteen minutes in the dirt with a Chinese girl. No, like any smart man, he called a few of his men over from the corral, and together they'd tried to teach Sheridan a lesson.

They dumped him in his saddle when they were finished, and Richard thought that was the end of that. But somehow, Sheridan had managed not to pass out, and just before

Richard swatted his horse, the man looked right at him and said, "You're a goddamned coward, Laird, but some day you'll have to face me like a man. I've got a long memory. I don't forget. I never forget."

Richard made his eyes focus on his immediate surroundings again. He'd only been to Sheridan's cabin that once, but he figured it was maybe a day's ride from where he and Zac were now. He also figured, now that he was cooled down a little, that he'd been a fool to come this far with just the two of them. Zac wasn't much with a gun.

He examined the facts: Laura had probably been laid by now. He'd been looking forward to saddle-busting her himself, but there was no doubt in his mind that Sheridan had taken her, probably several times. Richard felt a little twist in his gut. He'd wanted her bad.

Did he still want her? Maybe. Maybe not. But more important, he'd gone the whole route with her, waited six months and even married her, and by God he was mad at Sheridan for spoiling things!

But if he faced Sheridan with no one but Zac to back him up, there was a good chance he'd get killed. No woman was worth dying for. Maybe Sheridan thought so; Richard didn't. Especially when there were other ways of getting her back. If she wasn't a virgin, then it didn't really matter how soon he got her back anyhow. A few more days, give or take, wouldn't make any difference.

A plan was forming in his mind. He would go back to the ranch, get some boys together. He had a cowhand or two who weren't as clumsy with their guns as Zac was, who would like nothing better than to take a "hunting" trip up into the hills. They could move in on Sheridan together, and the man would never know what hit him.

Yeah, that was the best way. Now that he'd thought it through, he wondered why he'd ever come all this way with no one but Zac along. He'd been stunned to find Laura gone, he guessed. Stunned and too furious to think straight.

Damn, that woman had got under his skin! Well, he'd have her back in a few days. And then he'd decide if he still wanted to keep her. God knows, he'd had used women

71

before—but not a used wife. What was the point of marrying her if he wasn't going to get to be the first!

His jaw clenched with jealousy. She'd been *his!* He was going to tell his men to aim for Sheridan's arms and legs. He wanted it to take a long time, he wanted to watch the son of a bitch bleed.

He turned to Zac. "We're going back." He reined west, toward the valley, and spurred his cow pony viciously.

Laura and her captor continued traveling upward through the utterly windless day. Her saddle-sore body was in torment, but she kept telling herself that all this would soon come to an end. Richard knew where this terrible man was taking her, and soon it would all be over. Richard would coddle her and care for her and encourage her to put this nightmare behind her. And she would; she would fold it away, as she had folded a few rose petals from her father's funeral wreath between the pages of an old family album.

Meanwhile, the grueling torment continued.

At midday they stopped. When Mr. Sheridan untied her ankles and pulled her down, she sank to the ground in a boneless heap.

"Here, eat something," he said.

"I don't want it," she mumbled to his proffered jerky.

"Eat." He propped her into a sitting position and held her there. "Come on, open your mouth." And he began to feed her himself, forcing small pieces of jerked beef between her lips. "Water?" he asked as he watched her throat work to swallow the dry meat. He held his canteen for her. His strong arm beneath her shoulders lifted her higher. Her head lolled on his upper arm. "Come on, another sip. You've got to drink something, Mrs. . . . Laura." He tilted the bottle at the last so that the water ran over her lips, down the sides of her face, onto her neck. He rubbed a handful of it over her forehead and eyes, too.

But he wouldn't let her lie down. When he gave her a boost into the saddle again, it was his black he put her on. He joined her and turned her so she was sitting sidesaddle as she had two nights ago. "Lean back against me."

She looked up at him. His face was concerned, but that wasn't enough to excuse what he was doing.

It must have been a long while later that she asked, "Why are you doing this?" She was surprised by the smallness of her voice. "I haven't done anything to you." She was dangerously close to self-pitying tears.

He suddenly tilted her head up to peer at her. "Come on, don't cry now. We don't have much farther to go."

"We don't? Wh-where are we going—at least tell me that."

"My father's cabin."

"Is it really close?"

"We'll be there by dark."

She looked up at the sun. It was only the mid-afternoon; dark wouldn't come until eight or nine o'clock this time of year. That meant at least another six or seven hours of this agony.

She was only remotely aware that he was being kind to her, as kind and gentle as he could be and still force her to continue. "Not much farther," he told her several times. And often he asked her solicitous questions: How did she feel now? Did she want some more water? She in turn became slow-spoken, responding ploddingly—and not always rationally, she was afraid.

The Mokelumne River was an ordeal. Though it appeared to be drowsing away the sunlit evening hours, its deep green current was in reality swift and dangerous. And cold, the offspring of the snowfields of the rugged back country. It was headed down out of the mountains in a deceptively calm hurry; only in the shallow places could one see how its green waters broke and splashed and foamed white.

Mr. Sheridan went at it like a roping cowboy, never showing by word or expression the danger. But Laura knew. How stark the chill of that water was! She could feel the sideways suck of its mindless flow.

How Mr. Sheridan managed to get her and the horses across she was never sure. The icy tug came high on her thighs before it receded again. She thought, in retrospect, that it must have been his will and his will alone that had kept them from being swept away and drowned.

Safe in the shallows on the other side, the black horse shuddered and shivered and snorted. Laura suddenly felt like crying again. She tried to hold back, then stopped trying and let the tears fall hard. "Please . . . please . . ." she sobbed, not knowing exactly what it was she wanted from him anymore.

"Come on now, we're almost there."

"Y-you've been saying that all day."

He threaded her hair back from her soused cheeks, but of course that only embarrassed her. "Well, I mean it this time."

Twilight had settled on the hills when they climbed up out of the river's gorge. They started down again, into a valley so narrow it was almost a ravine. Laura saw that they were now following a set of ruts that had once been a wagon road. Brush loomed close on both sides. Grass had grown in the roadway itself, and here and there a redbud had taken hold. Then a building could be seen through the trees ahead, a cabin.

She felt foolishly overjoyed. Mr. Sheridan, however, seemed suddenly cautious. He reined the horses to a stop. Though Laura listened with him, there was only the normal, summery, woven-fabric sound of the forest and its whispering insects. Was Richard here? Was he waiting? Did Mr. Sheridan sense his presence—perhaps in the quiet where birds should be singing, or simply in a strange feeling he couldn't name? He scanned the ground—for tracks, she thought—then his careful eyes picked over the slopes of the hills. He said softly, "Looks like our shortcut through the river got us to the party early."

Laura's heart fell yet again.

Slowly, keeping her pulled close to him, he moved forward once more, through the day's last dim shadows.

She peered ahead along the narrow, overgrown trail. There in the gathering darkness, with the midsummer moon nestled in the trees behind it, sat the promised paradise. Behind it was a pool of glass-like water fed by a spring from somewhere farther up. The cabin was run-down and rough and weather-stained, but it looked wonderful to her. She was beyond any standards of architectural beauty, beyond anything but the thought of rest.

Suddenly Mr. Sheridan was on the ground looking up at her. He was holding his arms out. She didn't remember him dismounting, but evidently he had. She stared down at him for a moment, at his open hands, and then leaned into them willingly, went eagerly into the strong arms that caught her and bore her into the cabin.

She couldn't make out much of the interior. Only the earliest moonshine, thin and silver, slanted through the east windows. He put her down on a bed in a tiny dark room and left her there while he went back into the main part of the cabin. When he lit a lantern, she saw that she was not in a separate room after all, but only a corner set off by curtains. These were not pulled all the way, and she could see him sink into an armchair of sorts, built of a barrel sawn in half, stuffed with straw, and covered with coarse calico.

The cozy glow of the lantern invited rest, but despite his apparent weariness he soon got up again, stretched extravagantly, and went outside. Laura heard him tending the horses.

When he entered once more, she forced her eyes open long enough to see him catch sight of himself in a little mirror hanging near the door. The long journey had told on him, too. He rubbed his hand over his heavy growth of beard, then stared fixedly at his image, as if the person he saw there was someone he should recognize, but didn't.

She tried to keep watching him; but it was impossible. Her eyes felt as if some feral animal had been scratching at them with long, needle-tipped claws, and whenever she blinked, it was a major effort to open them again. Finally she stopped trying.

Laura woke abruptly, aware of three things: First, that it was nearly morning. The window over the bed, though filmed with dust, was awash with the russet glow of sunrise.

Second, she saw that Mr. Sheridan lay with her between the musty sheets of the little bed. He was sleeping on his side,

75

facing her, his hand open on her shoulder.

Which brought her to her third awareness, that they both lay completely naked beneath the blankets, which had fallen away to their waists.

Her heart fluttered up into her throat so loud that she was in terror that its pounding would waken him. He must have finished here what he had begun at the ranch—undressing her with his knife. How could she have slept through it? Her skin crept to think of him appraising her. And she squirmed to think of his hands touching her, putting her under the blankets before he got under them with her. Had he taken her into his arms as he had during the nights on the trail? Had he touched her *there* again?

Would Richard find out? Oh, it wasn't fair! She hadn't asked to be abducted! But would people realized that none of this was her fault?

The bed stood flush against the wall on her side; she couldn't leave it without waking her captor. She could only slip out from beneath his hand and move as far as she could away from him, suppressing a groan for what it cost her in terms of sore muscles.

From her new viewpoint—her back against the wall and the sheet pulled up to her chin—she watched his upper body move gently with his breathing. She couldn't help indulging in a rapt, faintly shocked visual exploration of him. He was like music picked out with a heavy hand. His dark hair was soft and shiny, she noticed. Yesterday it had been dull and covered with the curious red-colored dust of the Mother Lode. But it was clean now, and he smelled of soap and water. He was even shaved. Evidently he'd been busy before he'd joined her in bed.

She watched him for fifteen minutes, for half an hour. He seemed sound asleep, and she was so sleepy herself . . .

The next time she awoke, she was alone. Her eyes went all around the curtained nook and came back again to the empty place where Mr. Sheridan's head had dented the pillow. Her relief to find him gone was inexpressible.

But where was he? She'd come to know his tight face so well. The sadness there. He seemed to be endlessly hunting for some way to soothe a hurt. If only she knew why he was doing this, perhaps she could reason with him.

His hand appeared on the dividing curtain just then, followed by his head. "Finally had enough sleep?" He pushed the curtain aside and stood there wearing denim trousers but no shirt. Seeing her abashed observation of him, he glanced down at himself. With a little smile, he crossed to a scarred chest of drawers and located a clean blue shirt.

Laura saw how his bronzed shoulders gleamed and how the deep cleft of muscle where his spine divided his back became briefly deeper as he shrugged one arm and then the other into the shirt. Why did she notice these details about him, and why did they make her feel so odd? It was her fear, her wanting her husband, that stimulated this shameless pull she felt. She tried to think about Richard—but it didn't work. Not when this man was *here,* big as the side of a house and bristling with masculinity.

After buttoning his shirt and pushing the tails into his waistband, he bent to pick something up off the floor—the shreds of her chemise and underdrawers. Once flake-white, the rags were now grungy with the red dust peculiar to this area. Nothing wearable remained. He held them casually bunched in his hand. "Ready to get up?"

She tugged the blankets tighter beneath her chin. He smiled briefly, as if just then recalling her situation and finding it amusing. That smile infuriated her, and it was on the tip of her tongue to ask him by what right he had undressed her—but she realized in time that he was exercising the obvious right of a captor over his captive, a right she may question until her tongue shriveled, all to no avail.

He reached back into the chest and tossed her a clean, if faded, cotton shirt, one just like his own except that it was gray. Then he seemed to forget her as he stepped close to the window and looked out. When he turned back, his eyes swept over her dismissively before he turned and went through the curtain.

Warily, she slipped into the shirt, not leaving the protection of the bed until the last button was buttoned.

Every movement was a trial, for her body felt as sore as if she'd been beaten. And her stomach felt like a sinkhole. She was sore and hungry and—and she'd slept *naked* with a man who wasn't her husband!

When she stood, she was outwardly as covered as she'd ever been in his presence, yet she felt more vulnerable than before, for she had no extra layers of chemise beneath it—and no underdrawers! This shirt was thinner than the green flannel, and she feared the shapes of her breasts were completely apparent. Already the slight rub of the soft, faded fabric had hardened the tips to tight points that were clearly visible. She folded her arms over them, and with reluctance slipped through the curtains.

The corners of the main room were beveled by cobwebs. Mr. Sheridan was bent over a small iron stove, blowing on the fire just starting. In contrast to his cleanliness, she felt grubby and coarse standing there with her dirty feet and her arms crossed over her blatant breasts. It didn't help when he looked up at her and said, "Mrs. Laird, you need a bath."

She refused to respond. She watched in silence as he reached for a lacquered container of ground coffee on a shelf, took a paper-wrapped loaf of bread out of the deep drawer of the oak table that stood in the center of the room, and found a jar of jam. These fresh provisions were more evidence that he had planned her abduction in advance.

"Do you know how to make coffee?" he asked, and without waiting for her answer, nodded to an enameled pot. "There's water in the bucket by the door."

She'd never made coffee before in her life, but she filled the pot with water from the white enameled pail, and opened the box of aromatic grounds. Casually she said, "Umm, how much do I put in?"

He gave her a funny look, then said, "A couple handfuls should do it."

His handfuls or her handfuls? Surreptitiously she glanced at his hands and decided she'd better put in four of her own. Four big ones. She put the pot atop the stove and retreated to one of the three barrel chairs. She eased onto one tender hip and tucked her bare knees up beneath the long tails of her shirt.

She watched him move around the room and was aware of a tingling that began in her knees and crept upward toward the insides of her thighs. Her heart seemed to ache for . . . for someone's arms around her. It was the oddest thing, a voluptuous sensation that seemed to have something to do with wearing this flimsy shirt and nothing else.

She supposed she wanted Richard. Yes, that was natural. She wanted to be held by Richard, to hold him back, and feel his body against hers. Her breasts tightened further at the idea of being pressed against something hard, something like Richard's chest.

Richard wasn't here, however, and so she sat disgracefully entranced by her captor, this tireless, rugged man who had caused her more intimate distress—and who had also taken more intimate care of her—in these past four days than anyone else since her mother had tended her in her infancy. There was no question about her heart's devotion to Richard, but the rest of her body kept pulling toward the nearest magnet. It was shameful. She had to conquer it. She looked around for something else to think about.

Seven

There were several curiosities to catch Laura's eyes about the room, including the pretty lacquered box that held the coffee. She noticed a bit of outlandish embroidery hung in a frame between two windows, and a dish edged with an oriental design.

Mr. Sheridan was looking out the windows again, one after another. "What time is it?" she suddenly asked, noticing that the sunlight seemed to be coming in on him from the wrong direction for morning.

He turned back into the room. "About two o'clock."

Two o'clock! She'd slept half the day away.

He cut the loaf of bread into thick slices, two of which he began toasting on the stove. He spread one hot golden slice with dark purple jam and handed it to her. The sweet tasted of wild blackberries.

As soon as she finished that piece, he had another ready for her, and he was eating as well. Between the two of them they ate nearly the whole loaf and drained the pot of coffee— in spite of the fact that it was perfectly awful, blacker than burnt sorghum and every bit as unappetizing. She must have done something wrong.

Once she'd eaten, sleepiness descended on her again. She could have easily leaned her head down on the table and been asleep in an instant. As it was, she sat listlessly in her chair, fighting to keep her eyes open.

He cleaned up the remains of their meal in his careful, self-sufficient way. She watched him rinse their cups in water taken from the pail by the door. In her half-conscious reverie, she realized that those casual-looking, powerful hands of his had become familiar to her. They had taken hold of her waist to help her on and off the horses, held her close in the night, moved comfortingly over her face, plaited her hair, even undressed her—twice. Not to mention the time one of them had . . . No, not to mention that. But the truth was, his hands knew her body much better than Richard's did.

And it was wrong. It was wrong of him to have taken such unfair advantage of her. Wrong.

"It's time you got cleaned up," he said, waking her out of her daze. He stood with his hat on—and his gun belt—with a towel and sliver of gray soap in his hand. When she didn't get up immediately, he took hold of her arm.

"Don't! Who gave you permission to handle me anytime you like?"

"Permission?" He wasn't exactly smiling, but there was a light in his eyes. He was reminding her that she was confronting a man who had already stepped across the line of what was permissible. He stepped back from the chair and bowed formally. "Ma'am, would you do me the favor of taking a bath?"

She followed his gaze down to her dirt-stained knees, her filthy, scratched, naked feet. She heard him sniff pointedly. "You're despicable!"

"So you've said before."

He held the door for her. She exited the cabin, but hadn't taken more than a few tender-footed steps before his right hand clamped down on her shoulder. She turned her head to look at him, wondering what she'd done, and found him scanning the hillsides all about the cabin. She did the same, but as far as she could tell, there was no one about but the two of them.

"None of your stubbornness, now." His heavy hand remained on her shoulder and urged her forward again. She picked her way cautiously down the slope. He patiently kept pace just behind her.

81

Was he expecting Richard any minute? Was that what all this new caution was about? Her heart skittered with hope.

Squirrels chattered from the treetops overhead. The pond lay smooth as glass in the afternoon sun, reflecting an oblong cloud alone in the sky. At the water's edge Mr. Sheridan again scanned the hillsides. With only half his attention on her, he said, "Watch the dropoff. How well do you swim?"

"I don't swim at all—nor do I bathe with an audience."

Now he looked at her. "Go on, get in. You'll be fine as long as you don't go out too far."

She stood her ground, saying with outward bravery, "I am definitely not going to bathe with you watching me." Inwardly she didn't feel so sure.

He breathed deeply, as if seeking patience. "All right, I see you need a little help—and I could use the fun. It's been dull today, waiting for you to wake up and start sassing me." He started unbuttoning his shirt.

She quickly waded into the pond, making small splashes that swam into the reeds. The cold bit her ankles; the silt underfoot was soft as down oozing up between her toes. She turned back to glare at him.

He'd already hunkered down in the tall grass, and his eyes again moved over the ridge behind her. She looked, too, but there was nothing to see but trees and bushes. She realized she stood in the open, while he was pretty much hidden in the grass, and she began to feel like . . . like bait!

"This is part of your plan, isn't it? You don't care if I'm clean or filthy! You just want me to stand in this pond like cheese in a mousetrap."

He stuck a green blade of grass between his teeth, and blinked at her disinterestedly. "Take the shirt off; I don't have another clean one to give you."

"I won't!"

"Think how mad it'd make Laird to watch me come in there and pull it off you and scrub you down. He might do something foolish, endanger himself."

She spun and scanned the hills intently. "Is he here?"

"Damned if I know. But it's a possibility. Now take the shirt off and get to it." He added, awfully casually, as if the

82

thought had just strolled out of the trees, "Unless you *want* my help. You don't have to play coy, you know; just say so, I'd be glad to oblige. I don't think I've ever washed a woman. In fact, the more I think of it, the better it sounds."

Oh, he was evil! He was an evil, evil man! She stood glaring at him. He fingered the buttons of his shirt again. "All right!" she said. Placing her back to him quickly, she unbuttoned her own shirt, hesitated only an instant more, then opened it and flung it off in the direction of the bank. At the same moment, she splashed into the pond.

The contact of her bruised hips with the cool water made her quiver. She felt her breasts tug upward, trying to float. She looked down and saw how she was dwindled, her body distorted, with tapered, wavering legs. How much of her could he see? She saw a place where the bottom canted toward a miniature forest of leaning waterweed. She stepped down to test the feathery strands with her feet—and slid deeper than she'd intended, right up to her chin. When she turned to climb back, she couldn't find any traction.

"Christ, you're bright as a double eagle, aren't you? I told you to watch the dropoff! Am I going to have to come in there after all?"

"I'm all right!" She got her footing and looked up to where he stood with his fists clenched around the towel and sliver of gray soap. "I'm all right!" she repeated.

Seeing she'd escaped any immediate danger of drowning, he relaxed and hunkered down again.

A sudden thought made her ask, "Are there fish in here?"

His eyes crinkled. "Afraid of barracuda?"

"What are barracuda?"

"Man-eaters. Here comes the soap." He seemed full of mischief now, and tossed the worn cake so that it splashed water in her face. She barely managed to catch it before it sank out of sight.

She felt relieved to see he didn't intend to watch her continuously. He still seemed intent on the hillsides. His beige hat tipped up as he swung a slow look at the surrounding pines and brush and mountain slope. When his gaze dropped to her again, he stared at her with that same searching look, as if there might be something hidden beneath the surface of her. She lifted her chin and turned her back on him.

"My, you're a shy one," he teased. "As if I haven't seen you dressed to the hilt, stark naked, and everything in between." His voice paused. "You're sure not like most of Laird's women. But it figures, I guess—if he could have had you without the ceremony, I suppose he wouldn't have wanted to marry you."

Had her? She wasn't sure what that meant. "He married me because he loves me."

"Let's hope so."

"What do you mean by that?" She'd been scrubbing herself beneath the surface of the water. (The soap proved to be so crude it nearly grated her skin off.) Now, however, she turned to look at him.

His eyes were swiveling over the horizons. "I mean I hope he loves you. Don't forget to wash your hair."

She unraveled her braid and lathered her head, all the while trying to forget his ominous comments and observing eyes. The water was soothing, an anodyne to her aches and bruises. Her head felt luxuriously weighted as her hair got wet. She dipped all the way beneath the surface to rinse away the accumulation of dirt that was as red as old rust. Her hair spread out around her in the water like dark seaweed. She came up nose first, and smoothed the water off her face only to find him watching her with a look of troubled fascination. He seemed very far away in his thoughts.

Andre was fascinated all right—by the way she rinsed her hair, by how she flowed under the water in a smooth motion, like a pouring of water into water; by how her face bobbed up again, flowerlike, with her dark hair cascading about her and her gaze hurrying to find him again, as if she didn't dare let him out of her sight for a second. She was like a bathing hummingbird, always balanced for flight. He knew she didn't realize that when she raised her arms to sweep her hair back from her face her breasts raised silvery from the water. Briefly he saw her contracted nipples, like rosebuds closed against wet weather.

Such tiny, demure nipples. Such pretty breasts, small, round, with just the tips kissed with that deep pink color. He considered their fragility, their femininity.

Why did she have to have such a good body? Good, slender bones, roundly fleshed? The pores of her skin knit small and close? He even liked the way her brows arched so neatly at him when she spoke.

"May I get out now?" she was asking.

"Better rinse your hair some more."

Her white body sank down into the lily-green water again, into her feathery entanglement with that waterweed garden. Her head sank beneath the dark surface . . . and came up, her hair sheeting away. She sank a third time, and came up with just her eyes showing above the surface, eyes gone wary, as if she'd finally guessed his game. But no, she bobbed higher in the water, he could see her breasts again, until she brought her hands up and cupped herself. "Now can I get out?"

His own hands tingled. "Might as well." He held the towel out toward her.

Without much hope, Laura said, "Turn your back."

He didn't move. His eyes seemed riveted.

"Mr. Sheridan, I—I beg your courtesy—just this once. It's so small a thing." She swallowed. "Please."

She fully expected him to refuse. And when he didn't, she was shocked. He jerked the brim of his hat down over his eyes with a muttered curse—"shyness of a goddamned fawn"—then stood up, saying, "Hurry up, then." And he actually turned his broad back to the pond! In a flash she realized that it wasn't so small a thing; if there were anybody up on one of those slopes he'd been watching so closely, he'd just made himself completely vulnerable. Oddly, that frightened her.

She waded out quickly, not even pausing when she almost stepped on a toad. It hopped into deeper grass, on its leathery long legs. She shuddered and went on up the bank to stand directly behind him. She took the towel from where he'd draped it over his shoulder. Her shirt was over his other shoulder and she shrugged into it while she was still only

85

half-dry. Then she backed off to perch on a fallen log and dry her beaded, goosebumped legs.

Her hair was dripping. She draped the towel over her head and began to fluff it. Out the corner of her eye she saw him fish in his pockets for his comb. Both her hands were occupied with the towel, so he slid it into the pocket of her shirt. His knuckles grazed her breast, still tight beneath the worn, faded material. She lowered her arms with machine-like swiftness, but he was already stepping away from her, as if he hadn't even realized what he'd done.

The pond winked with light as she worked for nearly half an hour at the task of getting the tangles out of her hair. It was a tedious job, for not only was her mane long and fine, it was thick. But at last the comb went through it easily, and by then it was nearly sun-dried as well. She shook her arms to ease the ache in them.

"Ling's hair wasn't much darker than yours," he said softly from where he lay behind her in the grass, his hands folded beneath his head, his hat pushed low on his forehead.

"Ling?"

"My wife."

"You're married?"

"I was. She's dead."

"Oh. I'm sorry." A glance told her that his profile had taken on an angry precision. Her skin crawled with little insects of foreboding. She fiddled with her hair some more. "Ling is an unusual name."

"She was Chinese."

Laura couldn't think of a thing to say to that. She'd often heard people in Sacramento—Richard was one of them—make jokes about "the pigtails" or "the heathens." Personally, she'd never had any experience with people of different races, not even Negroes. Abfalter Village wasn't exactly a crossroads of the world. Consequently, she had few ingrained notions. It seemed odd to her, though, that a white man would want to marry an Oriental woman. Odd and a bit outlandish. But then, Mr. Sheridan had certainly proven himself to be more than a bit odd and outlandish, hadn't he?

She shook her hair back so it lay over her shoulders like a

cloak. "Mr. Sheridan, can't we talk about bringing this episode to a conclusion? You said Richard knows where to find us, but if that's the case, why isn't he here?"

"I figure he'll show up today or tomorrow. I knew a few shortcuts—and then it might take him some time to remember how to get here—he was only here once before." He sat up suddenly and scanned the hills again, as if recalling that he should be on the lookout. "He'll be along."

At that very moment something moved on the opposite ridge. He snapped to his feet with astonishing speed. He moved behind Laura, slinging his left arm around her and whipping out his gun with his right hand.

She had no thought in her head beyond a burning need to see what was coming. Richard? She peered up the mountainside, her heart banging inside her ribs—but saw only a deer bursting from between some bushes, running toward the pond. When it saw them, it glanced aside, its velvety nose a-twitch and its large eyes brimming with the slanted daylight. Then it vanished, flickering back into the shadows and safety with a flash of dappled rump.

Mr. Sheridan holstered his gun. He didn't move from where he was, but took Laura's jaw into his big hands. He forced her head way back to look up into his eyes. Sullen, jealous eyes. "Want to hear a story about your Richard?"

Her refreshing bath faded from her mind; something bad was about to happen, she knew it; his haunted look warned her. She looked up at him anxiously, feeling her hair down her back and against his legs. His face was as hard as she had ever seen it. His grip on her jaw tightened fractionally. She put her hands over his. "Don't hurt me."

He released his grip immediately, coming around to squat before her, holding her bare knees now. She sat absolutely motionless, willing herself not to pull away, staring steadily back at him.

He let go of one knee, swiveled on the balls of his feet to face the pond. "When Ling and I got married, everybody on both sides treated us as if we had leprosy—so we came up here to live, hoping to be left alone. God, life was good! She made everything new and breathtaking." He paused. "Then one day, when we'd been here a month, I had to go for supplies. She said she was going to spend the day doing the laundry at the pond here. She was only seventeen—did I tell you that?"

"No."

"You know, it's amazing, but there are things about you that remind me of her: She was young and small and beautiful—she was like you in a lot of ways. Innocent. She even had the same tip-tilted roundness to her breasts. I haven't seen that in a long time." He glanced at her.

She self-consciously crossed her arms over her breasts, and he tightened his hand on her knee. "She was here, doing some laundry, when a bunch of riders came over that hill over there." He nodded his head to indicate the place opposite the creek that fed the pond. "They were young, too, and hotheaded, and that might have been enough to pardon them for chasing her around with their horses and scaring her half to death. It *was* enough to make two of them feel big and bad, and they would have just rode on, but the third one . . . It wasn't enough for him. He wanted her—so he took her." He grew hoarse. "He threw her on the ground, beat her up a little while he was at it, and raped her."

He paused; his face was terrible to look at. "When I got home, when I found her, she told me his last name, described him, but then she wouldn't talk anymore. She wouldn't let me tend to her, said I shouldn't touch her, said she was . . . she said she was fouled.

"Do you know anything about the Chinese?" He looked up at Laura fiercely. She shook her head. "They have a code of honor." He looked back at the pond. "I found her the next morning, here—in the water." His eyes slowly came back to rest on Laura's face. "She drowned herself."

Laura couldn't look away. "No," she whispered, "oh, no." She reached out and touched his arm in a comforting gesture, but he yanked back.

His voice rose. "Oh, yes. And the man's name was Laird. And he had sandy brown hair and sharp features—and eyes the color of polished copper."

"It's not true! It could have been someone else—it wasn't

88

Richard!" She wanted to burst into vicious tears, fly at him, beat at him with her fists. "What did the sheriff say? Did you go to the sheriff?"

He smiled bitterly. "Chinese people aren't considered quite human in this country. The law's no use to them. Anyone can as good as murder a Chinese and get away with it. It was up to me, you see, so I went to his ranch."

Laura pictured it, the dry land, the small, ugly, dun-colored cattle that were everywhere.

"He denied it—the bastard's such a coward! He wouldn't draw against me when I called him out—set half a dozen of his men on me instead. The times I've considered just walking up and shooting him—but I couldn't. Seems I haven't got what it takes to butcher a man without giving him some warning. So he's gone scot-free all these years.

"I warned him, though; I told him I have a long memory. And right now I hope it's eating him alive, wondering what I'm doing to his innocent bride." He still held her knee in a clenching grip. "I hope he loves you, Mrs. Laird. I hope he really loves you. I hope he remembers how soft your hair is, how your hands move, how your eyes shine like silver in the sun. The more he loves you, the more his gut's twisting inside him right now. That's what I want. That's why you're here. If he loves you, he'll fight me for you—and then I can kill him."

Tears and a kind of exhaustion stung her eyes as she looked away from his intense face to the reflections of the trees shifting and swaying on the water. "You're mad."

His answer came razor-thin: "I might be."

Her chest heaved with the frightened thud of her heart. "I-I don't believe you. Richard denied it because he didn't *do* anything! This is all for nothing, a-and I hate you for it! I hate you!"

She tried to get up, and fell sideways into the grass when his grip on her knee didn't loosen. When he bent over her, she went for him, sitting up in a dark swirl of hair, her hands made into small knuckly fists. "He didn't do anything to her! He *didn't!*"

He sprawled over her and she was flattened between him and the ground. He got a grip on her wrists. She pulled with all her strength to free them, so she could pound him some more, but it did no good. His chest was hard as stone, his fingers around her wrists were like steel manacles. She strained to get out from beneath him. Her sore muscles were forgotten as she forced them to the effort.

He got both her wrists above her head so he could hold them with one huge hand. The other hand gripped her jaw. "Stop it before you get hurt!"

She somehow shook her chin free of that grip and lifted it to clamp her teeth into his shoulder. She bit down grimly. He stiffened, then shoved her with such force that she was too stunned to react for an instant. When she did sit up, her hair was a mess again. She brushed it back from her face and looked up at him standing over her. A tiny mark of blood was soaking through the shoulder of his shirt. Seeing it, and realizing that she'd been driven to bite another human being, hard enough to draw blood . . . she pulled her knees up and hid her face against them and began to weep hopeless, hysterical tears.

He swept her up into his arms. She tried to squirm loose, but of course he was far too strong. When she braced against his chest, she found it like a rock. "Put me down!" she sobbed. Her fists beat at him again; one caught him in the eye.

"Stop it—or else!" He gave her a quick, merciless, painful squeeze that made her bones creak and forced a squeak out of her. That instant's evidence of his tremendous strength sobered her.

She had to hide her face. Her eyes and nose and forehead pressed into the warm, fragrant curve of his neck. She felt the texture of his freshly shaved skin against her cheek. His Adam's apple was only inches away from her lips. Her palm lay open against his chest. She knew the steady thump of his heartbeat, each one like a resounding chord. Thus she let him carry her back to the cabin, into the curtained bedroom, where he dropped her on the mattress.

She got onto her knees slowly. "I'm the bait. You meant all the time to lure him here and murder him."

"Not murder—I could have done that any time. I'm still

90

offering him a fair fight." His face had gone unbearably sad again. "He raped my wife, and as far as he knows, I've raped his. I've wanted to kill him for what he did, now he'll want to kill me. What could be fairer?"

She met his gaze. "He didn't—couldn't—r-rape your wife." The word felt awful, sounded awful, it must mean something awful, but she had to say it aloud for her own ears to hear, because the story he'd told her was treacherously embedded in her mind.

He didn't argue the point with her. All he said was: "You don't know whether he could or not. You don't even know him. According to the *Sacramento Union* you've only been in California for six months. You got engaged to him four months ago. The way I figure it, he had to keep his ranch running during that time. How often could he have seen you? Once or twice a week? So you had a few Sunday buggy rides together, a few evening walks under the gaslights on K Street. You got to know some veneer he put on for you, but any veneer on Richard Laird has got to be thin."

"I knew him well enough to marry him."

He shook his head, perfectly unmoved. "I doubt that." He brought his hands up and sank his fingers into her hair at either side of her head. "I thought so at first, but I know you better now, and a woman like you couldn't really know a man like Laird and love him."

"A woman like me? Are you claiming now that you know what kind of woman I am? I'm just a means to an end so far as you're concerned. An object. 'Mrs. Laird.' A way to get back at Richard for your imagined grievance!"

His faced was constricted and corded. His fingertips pressed her scalp. "If that's true then why haven't I been able to keep my eyes off you, or my mind . . . or my hands?"

She had no answer for that, and after a long moment, he said, "I hope you don't love him, Laura, because I have to kill him. If it's the last thing I ever do, I'm going to kill him."

"And what about me? What if he doesn't know to come here? It's cruel of you, horribly cruel, to use me and torture me all these days with this stupid fancy of yours, with this ugly plan. If you'd thought about what you were doing . . .

91

but you didn't. In your own suffering you lost sight of everybody else's, Mr. Sheridan. You certainly never cared about mine."

He glared at her, then turned, and slammed out. She sank down on the bed, stared at the dim, cobwebby ceiling. She was dry-eyed at first, then the rhapsody of emotions welled up in her like blood and gushed out.

Eight

When Laura heard her captor come back into the cabin, she realized she'd fallen asleep. She sat up on the bed, her heart pounding from too quick an awakening. She wasn't refreshed by her nap, but felt woozy-tired. He looked in through the curtains. "I brought in some fresh water—it's cold. Want some?"

She nodded, pushing her hair behind her shoulders in a useless gesture of neatness. He brought her a cup and she drank it all. He watched her with his lids drooped over his eyes to cover any emotion that might be in them. It was horrible, she thought, living under the caprices of such a man, a man whose impulses seemed to veer from kindness to cruelty with no stopping points between.

He prepared them a light supper, and muttered as they ate, "I'll try to find you some clothes tomorrow."

"How long before you give this up and let me go?"

"Until Laird shows."

Neither of them ate much, and soon he said, "Come on, let's go to bed." His voice sounded huskier than it should, as if a rasp had been drawn across it.

She was ready with her answer: "I won't sleep with you, not again." The words came out flat with nervousness; she felt suddenly cautious; she was even holding onto the arm of her chair as if the room had become a slippery place.

His look was careful as well. "Since we've only got one bed, and since I'm not about to sleep on the floor, I guess you will."

"I'll sleep on the floor."

"I'd have to tie you up, and I don't want to do that."

"It didn't bother you before."

He tilted his chin and motioned toward the bedroom.

She would have shaken her head, but her body seemed unwilling to do what she ordered. She was trembling inside because so far, every time she'd tried to obstruct him, she'd ended up worse for it. Yet she had to keep trying.

He rose and lit the lantern. He concentrated on the job, staring at the low flame as he adjusted it. The expression on his face had veered from careful; now he seemed to have decided something. He didn't look at her, didn't not look at her. When he spoke, his voice was full of fatigue. "Basically, nothing's changed. You will do what I say. I just wish you wouldn't make me prove it each and every goddamned time." He turned and came toward her, came across the room with purposeful, slow bootsteps.

"Don't touch me!" She shrank back in her chair.

His hand shot out, grabbed her chin, lifted her face rudely. For a moment he looked as if he would strike her—but then he released her chin to pick up a strand of her hair, letting it drift from his fingers. "Come to bed."

A suffocating tightness rose to her throat at that simple order. "No."

All in one motion, he took her by the arm, lifted her to her feet, and ducked and placed his shoulder at her waist. When he straightened she was lifted and slung with her head down his back. "Oh you—you!"

He carried her, kicking, through the curtains and dumped her on the bed. He stood beside it, moving as necessary to block her escape while he took his shirt off. At last she sat back on her knees, panting. Her eyes came to rest on the bluish red marks where her teeth had broken his skin. He glanced at it, too, then back at her. "Get under the blankets."

She looked him full in the face, full in those rich dark eyes that sometimes seemed so sad and pensive. And she said, "I won't. I won't sleep with you."

He heaved a great sigh—"Damn woman!"—then tried

another tactic. "Will you please get into bed? I'm asking you. I'm trying to be patient—but in a minute I'm going to lose my temper." When she didn't move, he leaned over her, his hands sinking into the mattress on either side of her. "I'm not an easy-going man by nature." He smiled. There was something disquieting in that smile; barracudas probably smiled like that.

"I-I can hardly get under the blankets with you holding them down, can I?"

Before straightening, he got her by a little lock of hair again, and yanked it gently. Then he went to turn out the lantern. She heard him taking off his boots and trousers before he sank into the bed beside her. For a moment he was quiet, then he asked irritably, "Why in hell did you come to California in the first place?"

It didn't sound like a question that really wanted an answer, so she didn't give one.

"Tell me, Laura."

The name brushed so softly through the darkness that she realized how harsh he always sounded when he called her Mrs. Laird. The very name *Laird* seemed to roughen his voice.

"I . . ." Rebelliously, she decided to tell him the truth. "I simply wanted to get as far away as I could from home."

He laughed softly, without real humor, almost as if he were saying, "I might have known." Then he turned toward her and propped his head on his hand. "In other words, you ran away. Why? Wasn't your life always just quite sweet enough for your taste?"

Her heart fluttered up into her throat. Her eyes had adjusted to the dark now, and she saw his naked shoulders, saw the dark mat of hair that covered part of his broad chest, frosted in the moonlight from the window. Lower, the blankets outlined his lean waist and hips, which she knew were as naked as the rest of him. She was trapped between him and the wall, trapped and vulnerable, with nothing on but his worn cotton shirt. She swallowed. The best protection would be to talk. "I had to get away f-from my mother, my stepmother. From the life she had planned for me."

"Ahh. The wicked stepmother. Well, what was it? Did she have a husband picked out for you, someone too old for your taste, or not rich enough?"

It was her turn to laugh without humor. "No, there were no men in Mama's plans. I was to be a pianist."

"And you didn't want to be a pianist."

He made it sound so frivolous: a girl stamping her foot, whining, "I don't *want* to be a pianist!" How could she explain? No one knew that . . . that *biting* thing, to be pushed by someone, used, without love. She pictured Alarice, her hair a graying flinty color, a busy little bird of a woman. All she could say was, "It wasn't what you think."

"Tell me what it was then."

A memory welled up. She'd never spoken of it before to anyone, but it seemed the only way to explain herself now:

"We didn't have company much, but one time we did. I'd been sick with a fever for a day or two, and I still didn't feel well, but Mama said I had to come downstairs and be polite. We had dinner, and she kept insisting I eat—to be polite, I guess. Then after dinner, she told the people—cousins of hers—that now I would play for them. I could have done better another day. When I was finished, Mama didn't say anything, just took my hand and led me out of the room. I said, 'Mama, I don't feel well at all. I have to lie down.' The dinner was churning in my stomach and I knew I was going to be sick any minute. But all she said was, 'Sometimes we have to do things whether we feel up to it or not.'

"And after the guests left, she got me out of bed and made me come down and practice until I played that piece perfectly."

He didn't say anything at first, then asked, "How old were you?"

"Six or seven."

He still didn't say anything, and now she regretted exposing so much of herself to him. She said, "I didn't tell you that to make you feel sorry for me. I just want you to understand that it wasn't a whim. I had to get away."

"And did you really think Laird was what you wanted?

Or did you just want to get married and have babies?"

"Doesn't every woman want a husband and babies? What's wrong with that? Why shouldn't I have them? Anyway, Richard's been very good to me. When I got here—it was very frightening, not what I'd expected at all, so rough and crude. Richard looked out for me from the start."

"I bet he did. But does he love you? I know he must want you pretty badly, to go so far as to marry you, but does he love you?"

"Of course he does, I mean, well, can a person ever know if someone really loves her?"

"Yes, a person knows."

He sounded so sure. How could he be so sure?

He said abruptly. "I want you to call me Andre."

The silence hung.

"It's too bad you had to get caught up in all this."

It was too bad!

"But," he went on, "you'll be better off without him. You'll find someone else to look out for you—if that's all you want out of life."

"You assume you're going to kill him, you assume he knows he's supposed to come here—what if he doesn't?"

"He's got to if he wants you back."

"But what if he doesn't come?" She was suddenly afraid. Would he send her home in the same condition in which he'd found his Ling? Hurt and raped? She didn't dare ask. And he wasn't offering any answers. "I hate you," she whispered, "I really hate you."

He was quiet for a long time; he lay back on his pillow and stared into the dark, while she struggled with her anger and her tears and her fears. After a while he said, "You could get over that—hating me."

"Never."

He leaned over her, very close. His body carried the sweet breath of pond water, along with his own complex masculine odor that was becoming familiar to her. "Are you sure?" His dark eyes swam and beckoned, capturing hers in a locked gaze. His voice grew softly mocking. "Never is such a long, long time." His arms, though steely, were gentle as he pulled

97

her onto her side, closer to him. His left forearm hooked beneath her neck. His right hand slid down her back, down her buttocks, grazed the backs of her bare thighs. Her blood rushed in a torrent from one end of her body to the other.

"Stop squirming—I'm not going to hurt you."

"Why should I believe that? You have before!"

He continued to hold her. His hand went on resting under the tail of her shirt, along the turn of the back, the back of her upper thighs. "Do you know what your bridegroom was doing the night before your wedding? Where he goes most Saturday nights?"

"He works on Saturdays. He stays home."

"Oh no." Hie eyes had shrunk to black diamonds. "Ever hear of a place called Aida's?"

That was the place Ives Zacariah had mentioned. She recalled how he had looked at her, that wet, insinuating smile. "It's a saloon. Lots of men go to saloons."

The fingers of his left hand were gently untangling the long locks down her back. "It's more than a saloon, sweet. Aida's is what's euphemistically called a Pleasure Emporium. But a rose is a rose—and a whorehouse is a whorehouse, no matter what it's called. I understand Laird's got a couple of favorites. One's a Chinese girl—not surprisingly. The other's—"

"You're a liar!"

"Did you think he was saving himself for marriage? He's a grown man, and grown men have needs. Still, you don't find most men, grown or not, doing business with whores the night before their weddings. I wonder if he planned to keep it up once you were married? I'd hate to think of him giving you the pox, but Aida herself told me he was one of her more reliable customers."

"You're a liar—a filthy liar!"

"Such a delicate phrase. Makes me wonder where you picked it up."

She writhed out of his arms. "You're cruel beyond belief!"

"Unkind," he murmured, "when I'm going to such pains to keep you from a man whose preferences lean toward sluts."

*　　　*　　　*

She was a Lorelei. Andre wondered what the hell he was doing, telling her about Laird's whores and putting his hands all over her like that? Trying to seduce her? Christ! He'd almost stripped that shirt off her and . . . This was getting out of hand. Sure, she was beautiful, sure she was tempting, but she was his prisoner. Was he no better than Laird, ready to take a woman just because he was bigger and stronger and had the opportunity? Just because he wanted her?

He eased out of the bed. He couldn't sleep there with her. He shouldn't have got in with her in the first place.

Well, maybe that had been called for, so she would go to sleep. But he certainly shouldn't have lain this long with her, easing her back into his arms when she drowsed, holding her like he couldn't bear to let her go. Not when Laird might be out there right now, closing in on the cabin while he lay feeling the tender turn of the backs of her thighs, breathing in the scent of her skin like a lovesick teenager with no willpower.

He slid out of the bed and pulled on his pants, buttoning them over the bulge at his groin with a snort of self-loathing. He knew that was the real reason he'd gotten into bed with her, just so he'd have the chance to rub up against her. God, he was disgusting! She didn't even know, didn't realize what kind of danger she was in. It was crime, letting a woman like her loose in the world with no more sophistication than she had. There were things a woman should know, for her own protection.

He had his shirt on by now, and was carrying his boots out with him through the curtain. He grabbed his gun belt and let himself out of the cabin quietly. There was a stump of wood by the door. He settled himself down there, finishing his dressing. Then he sat dead-still for a good half hour, repeatedly dragging his senses away from where they seemed determined to stray, forcing them back to the sounds and sights out there in the night.

Laird might well show up tonight. If he remembered where the cabin was, and took the route he already knew, then today would have been the earliest he could have shown, tonight was even more probable. Tomorrow, if his memory was bad and he'd had to correct a few false turns.

Andre's mind strayed again. He was going to have to stay away from her. He'd find her some clothes, that would help his willpower; but more important, he had to keep actual inches and feet between himself and her. No more sharing the bed with her.

She was so warm and soft and pliable in her sleep, like a tired-out kitten. He nearly moaned aloud at the arousal that caused him, and shifted his position on the hard stump—stretched his legs out to accommodate the discomfort of the reawakening of his body.

Like a kitten. And he knew he could make her purr. That was the thing, the worst thing—that he knew she found him attractive. Oh, she was scared silly of him, but there was enough attraction there—and he was experienced enough—that he knew he could seduce her if he half-tried.

She wouldn't even know she was being seduced. He could do it. He'd be gentle with her, show her by stages what her body could feel, first by kisses, then . . . her breasts . . . God, to take those breasts in his hands, mold them for his mouth. And then he would pet that fine, scarce down at the join of her thighs, and coax her into revealing the pink and oval part of her. When she was ready, he would go in like a thunderbolt, unchecked, unerring, so there would be no time for her to fear being injured, and—at least in his imagination—there would be no hurt, none. Not if he did it like that, surged into her. But then he would hold still, deep within her, because if it had hurt her, he would want to wait till that passed. And he wouldn't want it to be over too quickly, either; he would want to stay in that high latitude as long as he—

Christ almighty, Sheridan! Keep the hell away from her! Remember what she's here for! Remember Ling, how she loved you, how you failed to protect her. Remember Ling, remember Richard Laird, *remember!*

Dawn crept through the chinks and windows of the cabin and lay curled in the dusty corners. Laura stretched languidly, then tugged petulantly against the fact that the blankets were pulled too tight for her to move easily.

She opened her eyes to find her captor, fully dressed, sitting on the side of the bed. She pulled the sheet up to her chin. He was just sitting there, staring at her, then put a hand on her shoulder. She tried to shrug him off, but he put both hands on her shoulders and pressed her flat into the mattress.

"You'd better leave me alone! Richard might come any time, I warn you!"

He smiled grimly. "You'd better hope so."

Little flares of some feverish feeling flickered through her. "Don't," she whispered.

"Don't what?"

"You're going to kiss me. Don't."

Something of the same glitter in his eyes was in his voice. And his hands, that had her bolted into place, hinted of much more strength than he was exerting. "I could do more than that, sweet. I could take you. Don't you understand *anything?*" he asked very quietly.

She made her own voice as cold as she could, saying, "I resent your constant manhandling, Mr. Sheridan."

He raised his head. A sad smile came to his face. "Laird would've had a lot of fun with you."

She gave him a disdainful look.

He glanced down at her hand, pressing against his chest now as he continued to hold her where she was. He said softly, "Do you even know that you're beautiful, Laura?" He seemed to wait for her reaction, and when she gave none he said, "No, I didn't think so. And you probably don't have a notion in the world what you do to a man, especially when he finds you warm and rosy and fresh from sleep on his pillow of a morning."

He may or may not have meant that as a joke. With him she wasn't always sure.

His eyes narrowed. "What in *hell* did a babe in the woods like you think you were going to do—alone—in a place like Sacramento?" Then, more suspiciously, "Does your Mama know about your recent romantic rise in life? Are you old enough to get married without her consent?"

"I'm twenty-one."

"What month's your birthday come in—and, quick, what year were you born?"

"September, eighteen . . . eighteen . . . eighteen-*sixty!*"

"Took you long enough to figure that one out. Not too fast at subtraction are you? Now what year were you born in? The truth this time."

"What difference does it make? All right, sixty-one! I'll be twenty-one in a week or so," she said stubbornly.

He laughed, almost pleasantly. "All right—in a week or so. Twenty, hard on to twenty-one. But Laird didn't want to wait till you were legal, did he? The younger the better with him. And you went along and fibbed a little. I get the idea you went along with him far too much, sweet." He studied her a moment longer, then took his hands off her and stood. "Time for you to get up, I think."

After breakfast, he found an old brown carpetbag beneath the floor of the cabin. It contained clothing he'd worn in his youth. Although everything was musty and stained with mildew, she resurrected a pair of faded homespun trousers, patched in two places. They would have fit her better if she'd been six inches taller and fifty pounds heavier; as it was, she rolled up the extra length and used a length of his infamous cord to lace through the belt loops. Two pairs of his scratchy wool boot socks served in lieu of shoes. The cabin didn't have a looking glass large enough to show her how she looked, but she knew she must cut a ridiculous figure. He didn't laugh, however.

It was past noon when he decided to use her as bait again. He steered her out of the cabin, under the tall pines, his left arm firmly around her shoulders.

"Must you push and pull me around all the time?"

"The closer I stay to you the less chance Laird has to gun me down from some hiding place. That's his style, you know. He won't come out in the open unless I force him to."

He pulled her down with him while he lounged against the trunk of a young ponderosa. For such a big man, he moved with a striking balance of grace and strength. His eyes, as usual, were roaming the horizons. "Tell me some more about yourself. What about your father?" he said idly.

"You're not interested."

He glanced at her. "You said he wanted to come West."

To think he remembered that! But then, obviously, he was a man who never forgot anything. "Papa . . ." she mused. "It wasn't the gold. He just wanted to see it. He talked about it several times—when we were alone. Mama didn't like to hear about California."

"When did your real mother die?"

"When I was two."

"And then he married Mama. What was he like?"

What was he like? She searched through a lifetime of memories, riffled through them as one riffles through a scrap book, until she came to one of the better moments. "I think of him sitting in his chair near the fire, his paper on the table beside him and his pipe in the ashtray. He never really smoked it much. Mama didn't like the smell, and I think he lit it just to irritate her. It was his one little revenge. And he would have a glass of port—too many glasses of port, I'm afraid." She paused. "Anyway, he would sit there after dinner and say, 'Play something for me, Laura.' He was partial to Chopin."

She hesitated before she went on: "He was a good man, but he was tired and unhappy, and didn't like living anymore. He died last year."

Andre sat silent for a moment, his eyebrows frowning. "Did he approve of your Mama's methods with you?"

"We never discussed it."

"He just sat back—with his glass of port—and let her mistreat you?"

"You don't understand." Home had never been a pleasant place, but Grey had made it better simply by being there. She'd never expected him to do more than that, probably because he never had.

"No, I don't understand how a father could let a sick child be forced out of bed to show off for company, and then let her be punished because she didn't shine."

"You're very judgmental, Mr. Sheridan—for a criminal, that is."

"Andre," he reminded her.

"Very well: Andre, you're very judgmental for a criminal."

"And you're very brave—for a captive. A beautiful, tempting . . . I'm hungry," he finished abruptly.

She had in her hands a small package he'd made of one of his clean handkerchiefs, and now she opened it. Inside was their lunch: the last two thick slices of bread, both spread with jam. She offered one to him and took the other herself. They ate without speaking until he said, "This bread's dry enough to strike a match on." A moment later he added, "My father liked molasses on bread. He made me eat it, too, when I was little. He said it was good for me, but I think he really did it just to let me know he could make me eat sh— . . . whatever he felt like making me eat."

"That sounds just like something Mama would do." She smiled at him, then averted her eyes and occupied herself with brushing bread crumbs from her lap.

"I like that." He was peering at her with his crow-black eyes.

Nine

"I like seeing you smile," Andre said to Laura. "You don't do it often. Even when you came in the bedroom the other night, all dressed in virginal white and smelling of French Milk of Roses, you weren't smiling. As a matter of fact, you looked scared silly. Especially when you saw that lacy nightdress laid out and the bed turned down."

"I'm afraid you had me at a disadvantage, since I couldn't have known I was being spied upon. If you were a gentleman, you wouldn't mention it."

"Yes, if I were a gentleman, I wouldn't."

He lifted his hat and smoothed an unruly lock of hair back from his forehead before he put it back on. Why were her eyes so often drawn to his hands? Why did just looking at them remind her so vividly and constantly of the feel of them at her waist, her back, her legs? Between her legs.

Her stomach all but turned over at that thought and she looked wildly about her. "I suppose Richard's got a posse looking for me."

"I doubt it. But if he doesn't show today . . ." Andre's whole aspect went stubborn and dangerous.

"What? If he doesn't come today, what then?"

"He should show today," he said, in a way that told her the topic was closed.

But it wasn't closed. If Richard didn't come today, then Andre was going to have to decide what to do with her. Would he let her go? Somehow she didn't feel she could count on that. Minutes passed. She felt herself become a hard knot of nerves. Finally, slowly, so he wouldn't be alarmed, she got up.

As she stood there an instant longer, hesitating, he said, "Don't do it, Laura." That was all she needed to set her off.

She heard him curse and lunge to his feet in pursuit. The very thought of him catching her, of those hands reaching out for her, of what they had already done and might yet do to her, made her legs move faster.

She came to an incline and swooped down it heedlessly, only to find herself faced with a solid wall of blackberry brambles at the bottom. She slid to a stop in the slick pine straw and threw a look back over her shoulder. He loomed at the lip of the slope. She turned right, left, frantically searching for an avenue of escape. On one side the brambles had thrown out an impossibly tangled arm, and on the other the ground was too steep to climb.

Meanwhile, he was loping down the hillside, not running, but coming at a casual pace—with a disgusted look that didn't bode well for her. He had his gun out, and was scanning the ridges all the while.

There was nothing she could do but wait for him to approach her. When he did, he holstered his gun and his hands went around her waist and jerked her into him, knocking the breath from her. "Ow!"

"It's no more than you deserve."

"You can't expect me not to try to get away from you!"

Their eyes met, and suddenly she saw him go angry. A sleepily lethal look fell over his features, fell like the visor of a medieval knight's helmet. She tried to ease away from him, but he hauled her back. She fell against his chest, which was hard and flat and stiff as an oaken board. His hands slid down and closed around her hips. They held her, grasped her, seized her—and with his eyes he held her firmer still.

One hand came up to the back of her head, forcing her to look at him by allowing her to look nowhere else. His head lowered and he found her mouth. He opened her lips, pried her teeth open with his strong tongue, and then swabbed the interior of her mouth thoroughly. She felt like melting, like yielding. He shouldn't be making her feel this way!

As soon as she should speak, she breathed, "Y-you're arrogant and overbearing and—and—"

"And dangerous," he supplied. "You'd best remember that next time you get the urge to run away from me. I'm a man, and men aren't domesticated the way women are. We're still hunters, like the wolves, and always hungry. And when we see small game on the run, we go for it."

The afternoon and evening passed. Laura refused to speak to Andre except when it was necessary, and then only with cool indifference. He didn't seem to notice. If he looked out the windows once, he did it a dozen times. She might not have been there, except that if she happened to wander anywhere near the door, he stopped watching out the windows to watch her.

It was still early, barely dark, in fact, when he told her to go to bed. She guessed he didn't want to light the lantern. Did he think Richard was coming tonight then?

To her great relief, he didn't join her in the bedroom. Instead, he strapped on his gun belt and went out. Time passed, and she rose and tiptoed to the door and cracked it open. It was fully dark now. Cautiously she stepped down onto the cold flat stone that served as a doorstep.

"Going somewhere?"

The so-quiet voice came from right beside her. She saw the dark shape of him then, sitting on a stump by the door no more than three feet away. He was mottled by the dappled moonlight coming through the pine boughs overhead.

"I-I need to . . ." She gestured in the direction of the little outbuilding that stood behind the cabin.

He didn't answer at once, but then said, "I haven't noticed you being one to get up in the night for that. I think maybe you ought to go back inside. If you're in real bad need, there should be a pot under the bed."

She felt her face fire up as she ducked back inside. Was there anything he hadn't noticed about her?

When she woke the next day, she saw by his undented

pillow that he had never come to bed. He was shaving when she entered the main room. He had a shirt on, but it wasn't buttoned or tucked.

Seated, with a cup of coffee in her hands, she surreptitiously studied him. She'd never seen a man shave before, and wasn't devoid of curiosity. He perceived her attention, and looked at her over his shoulder as if to say, "Well?" She dropped her gaze. But when he got absorbed in his job again, swiveling his head this direction and that before the glass, his jaw jutting forward and the sinews of his neck standing out, she couldn't help but watch him again. The sight of him performing this totally masculine chore set up a funny pulsating beat low in her pelvis.

The modeling of his face—its flat planes and rounded joinings, the brows and cheekbones and lips—was all handsome, she couldn't deny that. He was handsome, and more rampantly masculine than any other man of her acquaintance. And there was about him always that quiet, disturbing assurance that was his and his alone.

Richard. She must think of Richard. But what she thought wasn't heartening. She was beginning to doubt that he was going to find her. So far it was only a little nagging doubt, yet it was enough to make her think maybe she should be seriously plotting her own means of escape.

Andre passed behind her to put his shaving things away. He was beginning to make her feel ever more anxious. It was plain enough he found her attractive—the cursory passion of any man for a woman he happened to find convenient in his bed, she supposed—but it was enough to make her nervous.

He tossed his shaving water out into the shady yard, then stood boldly unarmed in the open doorway as he scanned the ridge tops and wiped his face with a towel. Eventually he shut the door, and hung the towel and basin on their nails. His face was closed with his own thoughts, and it wasn't until he passed behind her chair a second time that he even seemed to notice her again.

He paused and, with one hand, drew her long tresses back behind her ear, fingering the senstive lobe, and running the backs of his fingers down the side of her neck. "I'm beginning

108

to think he isn't coming, sweet."

She felt a shiver all down her spine and crossed her arms protectively. "He just hasn't found this place yet—since he didn't know where you were bringing me."

He bent over her shoulders, leaning his weight on the curved arms of the chair. The sleeves of his shirt were rolled, showing the muscles cording down his forearms. With his shirt falling open behind her head, she couldn't help but breathe in his musky male smell.

"He knew. You were there when Zazariah told him I was around. What did his face look like then? Did he look like a guiltless man?"

She refused to answer, and he went on: "I'll give him the benefit of the doubt—that he and his friends just stumbled onto the cabin when they found Ling, and that it might take him a day or two more to search this general area to find it again. But if he doesn't show by tomorrow, we'll know he went back for more men."

"Why shouldn't he come with all the men he can get? He knows he's dealing with a criminal. I'm sure he's got a whole posse searching for me. And sooner or later they'll find me—and you."

He pulled a chair around at an angle to hers. She found herself staring at the patch of soft, dark hair on his chest.

"He'll come with a gang of gunmen," he said quietly. "They'll try to catch me alone so they can gun me down."

She'd never seen a man shot, and as she stared at his chest, she had a sudden vision of it punctured with bullets. Blood—there would be blood. She felt as if something had just ripped into her own flesh. Her eyes lifted to his face. "When they come, you must give yourself up."

He smiled slightly, and shook his head. "I'd be a fool to give myself up to your husband. If you can wince like that to think of me taking a bullet, I'd hate to think what it would do to you to see Laird and his men butcher me slowly—and that's exactly what they'd do."

She cleared her throat. "Can we agree at least on one point? That your trap hasn't worked?"

He heaved a sigh. "If he doesn't show today, yes, it looks

109

like we can agree on that much."

"Then may I ask what you're going to do with me?" When she got no answer again, she added, "You can't keep me like this forever."

"Oh? Why not?"

"You have to get on with your life—a life that could be better than it has been. I think I know of a way to make it better. I could even help."

His brows slashed upward. "All right, you've piqued my curiosity, sweet. How could it be better—with your help, of course?" There was a light in his eyes.

"I was thinking, Richard might pay to have me back."

Now he smiled again. A slight, slightly disappointed smile. "That's not what I was hoping to hear."

What had he hoped?

"'Fraid it wouldn't work, anyway."

"What have you got to lose by asking, though? And I give you my word that once I'm home I'll say I don't know anything about you—your name or anything. I'll even give a false description."

He rose from his chair, his face alight with humor. "Forgive me if I don't jump at such a generous offer—or that I doubt for a minute that you'd go all out to protect me—but somehow it doesn't appeal."

"Why not?"

"Laura, don't look so scared. I've told you I'm not going to murder you. Or rape you—violating virgins has never appealed to me. What I *am* going to do with you is something I haven't worked out yet. But I will."

He seemed to hypnotize her with his dark, probing eyes and his low, crooning voice, until he started to buckle on his gun belt in preparation to go out again.

"Wait! At least let me write to him. He loves me. He will pay to have me back. You're wrong about him."

One single raw laugh burst free of him. He stopped working at the buckle of the belt, slung the thing onto the table, and came back to reseat himself. She was encouraged enough by his expression to think he was actually considering her idea.

"Listen," he said at last. Patient again, he gave her all his attention, gave her all the narcotic power in his voice and eyes. "He isn't coming with a posse. You've assumed all along that he'd get the law in on this, but a man like Laird doesn't go to the law if his wife's been stolen. You've got to know he thinks I've had you by now, and that's not a thing he would want printed up in the newspapers.

"I acted on the assumption that he loved you—or at least wanted you enough to meet me face-to-face. I stole you right out of his bed, for Christ-sakes! Well, what a mistake on my part that one was. I gave him too much credit."

"He does love me, he wants me! Let me write to him and ask for a ransom. Why won't you?"

"Because it wouldn't do any good! And as for money, remember I told you my father disinherited me when I married Ling? Well, her death put me back in his good graces. He left me enough money to buy and sell Richard Laird. He found gold on this land, Laura. Not a fortune, but enough to invest where he *could* make a fortune. He started with stagecoaches, then ships, then moved on to railroads—and you know what that means. I'm a wealthy man, Laura."

"You told Mr. Zacariah you'd been driving cattle."

"That's right—*my* cattle. I left California shortly after Ling died—when Laird refused to stand up against me. I knew I'd have to wait until I could force his hand, so I got myself a ranch to occupy me. I had to work, and work hard, in order not to go crazy those first years. Meanwhile, I paid someone in Sacramento to keep an eye on Laird for me."

He gave her one of his caustic smiles. "It's bad taste for me to parade it out for you like this, but I've toured a lot of the world. I'm acquainted with quite a few distinguished and wealthy types; and yes, and I've been to college, your own Massachusetts *Haavaad*." He effected the broad Boston "a" like a native son. "I sold my railroad stock to buy the ranch in Texas and two more ships and . . ." he shrugged, "some other things: farmland here and there throughout the state, a salmon fishery up north . . .

"At home—that's San Francisco, for your information—I manage to keep my mother in enough style that she can be a

111

patron of theater and prose and verse and art and learning. She spends her time funding museums and financing opera and symphony houses and . . . oh, hell, the point of this is, I don't need money, even if I could bring myself to sell you back to Laird—and, mean as I am, I'm still not that mean."

She sat staring at him stupidly. He was wealthy. He didn't need money. And he didn't seem to have any firm plans to let her go.

He leaned closer. "I can hear your heart thumping all the way from here. Are you all right?"

In that moment, some portion of her fear of him snapped inside her. She felt as though he had played a monstrous joke on her, and suddenly she was very angry. "Am I all right? You can ask me that? If I were a man, I think I would put on a gun and kill you myself."

His expression hardened. "But you're not a man, you're a woman. And for the time being you're mine to do with as I see fit. And I find I like having you near, Laura."

She stood now, on tenterhooks, ready to defend herself.

He fixed her with a glance. "Don't do anything stupid."

She grappled with the urge to make a dash for the door, and saw the spark in his eyes that told her he knew just what she was thinking. Trembling with rage, she said, "You can't keep me indefinitely."

"Funny, I think I could—if that's what I decided."

"You couldn't watch me so closely forever."

"I could try. And where that failed, I find a little terrorizing works wonders with you."

She regarded him, this man who had already ravaged her life so thoroughly. He did terrorize her. In spite of the fact that she was beginning to enjoy the sight of his body to a point that bordered on sinful. In spite of the fact that she knew that that line of soft dark fuzz on his chest went down his belly to his . . . private parts. In spite of—or because of—the fact that she was getting accustomed to having her body shaped to his in the night and felt she'd missed something when he didn't share her bed. Yes, in spite of all that he did terrorize her. To her he was an overpowering, vengeful figure. She'd learned not to put anything beyond him.

"I don't understand you. I've never met a man so relentless, so callous. How can you hate so hard?"

"Practice."

She turned to see his gun belt, slung so casually onto the table. Impulsively, she plucked the pistol from the holster. It was heavy; it took her left hand as well as her right to point it at him.

"Put it down, Laura," he said, with a quiet and a restraint that was worse than thunderclaps.

"Not on your life!"

He stood, took a step toward her.

"Stay where you are!" The barrel shook. She was afraid her mouth was going to tremble into tears. She was afraid she was a lot more scared than he was, especially when he got that little smile back in the corners of his mouth.

"Think you can shoot me?" He started toward her again—slowly, his boot heels clunking on plank floor. "Look how your hands are shaking. I don't think you could hit me, even point-blank."

"Stay back! I'm warning you!" Both her index fingers were on the trigger. But they seemed to have no strength in them, not with him harping on her nerves with those gentle, deadly unerring comments.

He came on, and on, and finally reached out and took the barrel in his hand. He forced it toward the ceiling. "This is not a toy; let go of it."

"I won't!"

Holding it with one hand, he used the other to pry open her fingers, until the revolver was his. He slid it back into its holster, then turned to her.

"I want you to let me go!" She was shaking now, violently, bewildered by her inability to save herself.

Suddenly his hand shot to the back of her head, pulled her against him, and he bent his face down. He opened his mouth against hers. She kept her lips closed—so he licked them! He used his tongue to outline their curves and corners, then slipped it along the seam. She tried to say "Stop!" and thus he gained the advantage he'd been waiting for. Now his mouth pressed firmly to open hers, more and more, until his

113

tongue plunged between her teeth. She could only moan.

She was pushing against his shoulders—his bare shoulders, for her hands had slipped beneath his open shirt. She was trying to get him to release her, yet her palms were aware of the feel of his hard, hard muscles. He raised one booted foot into the seat of her chair and wedged the small of her back against his bent and braced leg. The hand that wasn't holding the back of her head began to caress her breasts through her shirt. She couldn't make him stop, though she tried.

Shifting, he tugged at the cord she was using for a belt and deftly opened her trousers. His hand skidded inside and down, forcing her legs apart enough to cup her. She stumbled; he tightened his grip to steady her.

And then he bent his whole body into her, and pressed against her, voracious. His fingers began to move between her legs, to part her, and to slip up and down. He found a place, a nub of her flesh, and two of his flat fingers straddled it.

Suddenly it was all a new wonder, enthralling, breathtaking. She seemed to go completely wet and slack there; her vision burst into warm, shooting sparks of light—sunlight, starlight—against her closed lids. She moaned again. His mouth had left hers to move over the curve of her cheek and along her jaw, then down to kiss her throat. He was taking possession of her as if he had a right to do so.

"Liar," she murmured. "You are a liar. You said you wouldn't rape me."

His mouth moved to her ear. "I'm not raping you; I'm showing you something. Now be still and learn."

His fingers slowly continued to caress her, that hard little kernel of tormented flesh, over and over, up and down. She began to tremble. His fingers dipped into her (she seemed to be all dewed and slippery) then slid back, touching and teasing her, on and on.

She made a little mewing, keening sound. She tried to wriggle her hips away, but he had her wedged securely against his raised thigh and in the iron curve of his arm. Her breasts felt warm and swollen pressed against his chest.

"M-Mr. Sheridan—Andre!" she cried desperately.

"I know, sweet, but soon you'll feel better. Wait."

Something focused, gathered, tightened within her—and fell away once, twice.

"Don't be afraid. Let it happen."

Did he know what she was feeling? They were both panting; he was sweating. She begged, "Please."

But then she was past her own will and could only follow where he led. She took short rapid breaths and felt as if she were climbing a glowing volcano. Deep inside she felt a grip, a sensation, an in-gathering that took its own time and its own path, till at last it splintered around her. As if sensing that very instant, he spoke in a voice insistent and certain: "Now!" he commanded.

He moved one of his fingers down into the middle of her spasms, and his mouth came over hers, as if to taste her cry, and her hips felt like fluid mercury and she was gripped, and gripped again, by paroxysms of exquisite pleasure. He stroked her firmly and rhythmically. Thunderbolts and bullets ran up her spine, riveting her at helpless attention. She arched; the charge spread out from her backgone, went every direction.

It receded. He allowed her a few moments to lie still in his hold. Gradually she found herself again. He was still supporting her, literally, for she was shaking, holding onto him, very close to tears. A muscle in his jaw moved as he looked down at her, and she was aware again of his hand, which was still in possession of her.

Slowly he withdrew his fingers, causing her to gasp with that departing slide. His hold on her head loosened. He put both his feet on the floor. She couldn't look at him; she looked at the diagonal shafts of sunlight cutting across the wall behind him. He placed his hands along the sides of her breasts and turned her to face him. She moved as he directed, like a limp rag doll. Holding her at arm's length, he dropped his hands to her waist, and with seeming reluctance, set about tucking in her shirt and buttoning her trousers, and with snaps of his wrists he retied her belt cord.

The light from the windows gilded his face. His hands at

his sides now, he stood for a few seconds longer, at a tender distance. He seemed to will an unseen boundary between them. She was fixed in place. He suddenly turned his back, as though he could not quite contain his emotions.

"Lorelei." With that one word, he grabbed his gun belt and went out.

She swayed there, afraid to move for the echoing pulsations between her thighs. To think her own body could do that and she'd never known! She had her eyes opened at last to the mystery of passion. She finally grasped why women and men got married. And yet she was full of questions about it.

She followed him as far as the door, where she caught sight of her face in the little cracked looking glass. She stared at the broken reflection of herself, at the bright color of her cheeks and the strange, slack, slightly puffy new shape of her lips, still glistening with his saliva.

She touched them tentatively. Suddenly she felt like crying; she felt guilty.

But she hadn't *done* anything!

Had she?

Ten

The afternoon grew chilly and gray. The sky turned the color of smoke, and a rain-scented wind rose in the uppermost boughs of the pines. The first drops hit the cabin roof like pebbles, then dust scents and rain scents rose together and the steady drum of the rain drowned all other sound.

Andre came back in. He stopped at the door to hang up his gun belt—and to look at Laura where she sat in one of the barrel chairs. He busied himself with restarting the fire in the stove. Finally he said, "About this morning . . ."

She nervously twisted her hair into a rope over one shoulder. She sat tense as a spring, coiled as deeply as she could get in her chair. He stood with his back to the stove. He seemed uneasy, as if he had something to say and didn't know how to begin. "I think I'll make some coffee."

She felt less on pins and needles when his attention wasn't on her. Her gaze lingered on his muscular shoulders as they stretched the fabric of his shirt with every move. Soon the scent of brewing coffee filled the room. "Want some?" he asked. She shook her head.

With a steaming cup in his hand, and a look of regret in his eyes, he took the chair nearest hers. He sat with his knees spread, his forearms resting on them, his hands bracketing his cup. "Somebody's got to explain some things to you, Laura. About men and women. And right away."

His meaning slowly sank to the very bottom of her mind.

He gave the coffee in his cup a slight smile. "When I told you Laird raped my wife, you didn't know what that meant, did you? Well . . . rape hurts. Some men like to hurt women, they take pleasure in it. But most men don't. Most like to make love with a woman. They like it a lot. And when there's a woman around who attracts a man, sometimes it's hard for him not to try things with her, to try to get her to let him make love to her.

"We're in kind of an unusual situation here. Ordinarily, I would never have seen you without your clothes on. Or had reason to paw you so much. But since I have, I'm finding it real hard to keep things under control. I'm trying, but you've got to understand you're a temptation."

He reached across the space that separated them to cup her face with one warm hand, his gaze raking her parted lips before they stabbed into her eyes. "You're a temptation right now," he said quietly.

"I don't mean to be—if you'd let me go, I wouldn't be!"

He put the tip of his thumb over her lips to quiet her. She could only face him, look straight into his eyes, not saying anything, though so much ought to be said. She waited for him to go on, watched his mouth—and realized she thought it was attractive.

He trailed that thumb back and forth across her lips. "I know you're a virgin—Christ, I feel a hundred years older than you, but . . . I've got this crazy wish to be your first."

"I'm . . ." *Married.* Why couldn't she say it?

He half-stood and leaned over her and kissed her then, kissed her very gently, until she opened her mouth to him and let his tongue flow lazily around hers.

He pulled away abruptly, and rubbed his hand over his face. When he looked at her again, he said, "Do you know anything about making love, Laura? No—your eyes give you away. And I bet Laird's the only man you've ever had dealings with. Except me. Didn't anyone tell you anything before the wedding?"

"Mrs. Gladwin," she whispered with downcast eyes.

"Mrs. Gladwin at the boarding house? The one who looks

like a ship's prow?" He smiled that sad smile again. "What did she tell you—no, let me guess: something about birds and bees?"

She couldn't help smiling. "Rabbits," she whispered.

"What do rabbits do, Laura?"

She shrugged. "What their husbands tell them to do."

He muttered an obscenity. "That's what I thought. It amazes me the way they raise girls in absolute ignorance and then, come the wedding night, just throw them to the wolves. You shouldn't have to learn all the answers at once."

She rose, flinging her hair back, and walked toward the snug fire in the little stove.

"I could explain it to you, in clear terms and explicitly, all the peculiar uses a man has for the female body—what lies ahead of you as a woman—but I'm afraid the words alone would revolt you."

"Yes, perhaps you'd better not." She flicked her eyes to the windows where the gray storm veiled the mountains. Where was Richard?

Andre got up. She edged further around the stove. He said, "If you're afraid I'm going to demonstrate again, you don't have to worry—for now." He took his gun belt from its peg, and put his hat back on. "Christ! Don't look so intense and desperate, as if your very life were hanging in the balance!"

"Isn't it?"

"I've been talking about making love, Laura, not murder. I've never killed a woman yet."

She gave him a chary look. "There's always a first time."

"Yes, there's always a first time. For everything."

She felt her face heat up.

An early darkness had drawn in. Night was creeping up the valley. He went out, but only for enough armfuls of wood for the evening and morning to come. With that provisioning done, and bucket of drinking water lugged from the seeping spring, he declared himself in for the night.

He lit the lantern and sat opposite the table from her, sat silent while she tended her hair in the yellow glow of the lantern's light. As she raked his pocket comb through her

119

mane, shadows mimicked her, shooting up the wall and across the ceiling. She was supremely aware of his watching, narrowed eyes.

When she was done, he seemed to shake himself and look about for something to do. He settled on cleaning his gun.

"How did you know I wouldn't shoot this afternoon?"

"You didn't even know how to fire it."

"I only had to pull the trigger."

He grinned without looking at her. "Actually, you have to cock it first." Now he looked at her; his eyes peered up from under their brows. "Did you think I was being awfully brave to walk right up and take it away from you?"

She was beginning to hate that little smile at the corners of his mouth. "Well, now I know, should I decide to try it again."

"You won't. You're too softhearted to shoot me, even to save yourself."

"I would do anything to save myself."

"That's an interesting statement." Another grin. "But would you? You're so damn far from what I expected. It's painful to see how I misperceived . . . misinterpreted . . . misapplied . . ." He shrugged. "In your place, I could have gotten away by now, by any of several means."

"You're stronger, you're a man."

"True, and I'm also more ruthless. I would have . . . oh, hit you on the head with a rock when your back was turned—you could have at least tried that. But you don't think that way."

"That's not fair. You're making it sound as if I don't even *want* to get away."

"Oh, you *want* to. You feel honor-bound to want to. But not bad enough to kill me."

"I wouldn't necessarily have to kill you. I could just shoot you enough to wound you."

That smile came back. "And then you would take off? Leave me to lie in my own blood? More likely you'd cry and say you were sorry and stick around to nurse me well again. And then, sweet, you'd be right back where you started, because I'm not a bit softhearted."

120

"I'm not so sure that's true," she said quietly.

He looked up at her, but she kept her eyes on his hands which were cleaning the weapon with a bit of oiled rag. When it was done to his satisfaction he reloaded the magazine—with very quick movements. It astonished and disturbed her to see how adept he was at handling it. At least as adept as she was at *arpeggio* exercises.

"Are you a good shot?" she asked.

"Good enough, I guess."

"Could you really shoot someone?"

"Anybody can kill, Laura—pushed far enough." He gave the gun a final reverent stroke. "Even you. You just haven't been pushed far enough yet."

All through the cool, cloudy night, a sough of wind ran restlessly through the mountains. The rainstorm was swept away, and the sun creaked over the ridge tops in a glorious dawn. Laura awakened to find the bedroom window open. She breathed deeply of the rain-washed air. Andre was humming a bit of a cowboy tune—a not too inspired melody—while he shaved in the main room.

Despite his singing, she soon found he was tight as a knot. The morning passed without incident, however, since she was wise enough to stay out of his way. Nevertheless, she couldn't keep her eyes from straying to him. As she washed their lunch dishes, she tried to tell herself that Richard would find her soon and then she would never have to worry about Andre Sheridan again. Surely Richard would be here soon!

Andre was out tending the horses and chopping wood for the stove. She watched him out the open door, wondering whether he was occupied enough with his work and his thoughts to allow her to make another attempt to escape.

Never far from her mind was what he'd done yesterday. Was that what making love was like? Or something like that? Did it feel as good as his kisses, which seemed to linger on her lips even now?

He'd taken off his shirt while working, and his broad back rippled with muscle as he wielded the ax. His strong legs were spaced and set; the ax lifted over his head, swung down; his back moved like water over submerged rocks. The smooth ax handle slid through his callused hands. She relived the way he'd pushed his hand between her legs so forcefully, then followed with such a delicate manipulation of her. It made her tingle there to think of it.

His ax swung again. This time it stuck fast in the top of the chopping stump and shivered. He shrugged into his shirt, then stacked the chopped wood into his curved arm.

She was still thinking of what he'd done to her—touched her there, made her . . . yes, he'd known and he'd made her cry out with . . . that bliss. This man she hardly knew!

He crossed the yard and arrived at the door with his arms full of yellow pinewood. She stepped back to let him enter. He dumped the wood in the box and turned to her. His look made her want to cover herself; his eyes were ablaze. "You know, if you don't stop looking at me like that . . ."

Breathlessly, she challenged him: "What? You'll kiss me again?"

"By God, I think you want me to."

"No!" But it was too late. Already he was taking her into his strong arms, wrapping them completely about her. He twined one hand in her hair at the nape of her neck and pulled back gently, so her face was turned upward to his. His eyes were narrowed with emotion.

"Woman," he said roughly, "you've been asking for this. Those big calf eyes following me all day—as if I were ginger beer and you were dying of thirst. I warned you. What can you expect when you practically beg for it?"

She detected a will of icicles and iron, a will she couldn't sway, a will in which—no matter how moving she might be—her arguments would count for little just now. Otherwise why should she feel so frightened?

Then his lips were on hers, hard and exacting, demanding that she open to him. His tongue flicked over her teeth and tested the softness of her inner cheeks. She saw the wisdom of merely keeping still. He was very big, very strong; he held her so close her feet barely touched the floor. Her back was arched into him. She opened to him without resistance,

122

convinced that letting him kiss her was the only way to gain her release.

To her horror, however, she felt desire swell. She liked kissing him. She didn't admit this to herself all at once. At first she only felt weak, limp. Then, at some point, the taste of him became good to her. When he loosened his hold and told her to put her arms around his neck, she obediently slid them up from where they had been trapped between his chest and hers. Then he pulled her close again, and she bent her body into him in response. She didn't know how to assess her emotions; she knew she was yielding, yet it all seemed beyond her control.

He started to lift his head; her mouth blindly followed after his. Then she realized that he was trying to break away, and she felt her face go scarlet. She belatedly remembered she should be protesting. But trying to pull away from him felt like pulling away from a chunk of herself. Anyway, he wouldn't allow it. He lowered his head as if he meant to kiss her yet again—but then brusquely released her. She stumbled back, very shaken.

His eyes roved over her. He started to curse, and kept it up for a good fifteen seconds, with fluency.

And then, this menace, this brutal man she hated so, had the audacity to whisper, "You didn't kiss Laird like that, did you?"

Laura was hiding in a dark closet. Andre was looking for her. She saw the closet door move, saw his strong hand on it as it swung open, not quickly, but inexorably. His eyes danced and shone with a gleam of light that struck from across the room. There was music, too, a slow and sensual measure in a minor key. She pressed herself into the farthest corner, but he found her. A smile was on his lips. She tried to speak; her mouth and throat worked, but her voice wouldn't come. A moan remained soundless as glass in her throat as he reached for her. The motion was smooth and controlled, timeless in its seductive power. He took hold of her arms and pulled her to him, and . . .

"Don't" she cried, the word wrenched from her.

"Laura—wake up! You're having a dream."

She opened her eyes. The terror shivered on through her as she found Andre's face bent over her, night shadows in the lean angles of his jaw and temple. She lay tremulous against his bare chest. What had he been about to do to her in the dream? What kind of fear had that been?

"What was it, sweet?"

"You—it was you," she said haltingly.

"What was I doing?"

"I was hiding but you found me and I was afraid."

Taking her even deeper into his strong arms, he whispered, "Don't be afraid. I'll never hurt you again. You're safe with me now."

She hungered for safety, and just now it seemed he really meant to provide it. She'd never known such a sensation. Her arms crept around his neck. His bare legs were hard against hers. She could feel his hands on her in a new way—protective—and she clung to him. Her fright faded, and all consciousness of right or wrong. She understood only that he was with her, holding her, sheltering her in the dark. With her arms about his neck, she fell dreamlessly asleep, safe in his warm, strong embrace.

Though she hadn't waked again, Laura had felt Andre's hands through the rest of the night, along with a new and strange kind of frustration that wouldn't subside. In the morning she opened her eyes to find the room filled with the hazed, honeyed light of early September. He wasn't holding her now, but lay awake on his own side of the bed, and she wondered if perhaps she'd dreamed the whole thing. Yet his eyes lightened as they greeted her. And as she marked the heat behind them, her cheeks burned a little, which seemed to amuse him. "I guess I was a nuisance last night."

He gave her a lazy smile. "You had a bad dream."

"I don't remember it now."

"No? Well, that's the way with dreams." He swung his legs

124

over the side of the bed to pull on his trousers. Her eyes went involuntarily to the hard muscles of his back and lingered there, until he went out to start the fire in the stove. She listened to the noises he made—the clunk of wood against wood, the striking of a match, the clatter of metal—and all the while her eyes rested on the curtains where he'd gone out. Something was changed, she knew it, without having an inkling of what it was.

Her eyes were waiting for him when he returned. Her heart beat hard in her throat. Those dark, dark eyes of his held a bottomless look. Her whole body quivered as he sat on the edge of the bed and leaned toward her.

He kissed her with lips both tender and ravenous. Her own lips clung to his as if afraid to let him go.

"Let me make love to you, Laura." His voice had gone gruff and surprisingly deep, betraying him.

No.

Her mouth formed the word, though her throat refused to voice it.

He touched his lips to her eyelids. "Little virgin, you excite a man beyond bearing, do you realize that? Especially a man filled with years of longing. Will you at least let me look at you?"

No.

He ignored that unvoiced protest, and pushed the blankets down as far as her thighs, then began to slip the buttons of her shirt one by one. Her hands came up to stop him, but then, as if she'd lost all control of them, they only covered his and lay there lightly as he went on with what he was doing.

When the buttons were all unfastened, he slowly took her hands away, placed them on each side of her, and then folded the shirt open, revealing her breasts. "My God," he whispered, "you're so beautiful."

She felt her small nipples hardening, clenching oddly. She made a whimpering sound as he looked down at her silken nest; he was in awe at the sight. She seemed to be seeing herself through his eyes. She nearly reached to cover herself;

125

she was so shamefully aware of that part of her body suddenly. Did she *want* him to touch her like that again?

One of his hands hovered there, but then came up to cover a breast, and he seemed pleased by the ripples of feeling his touch sent speeding through her. He gathered both her breasts with his hands, sending streaks of sensation up her torso, down her legs. She felt stiff and shocked, like a person who has begun to drop from a great height. Her heart almost stopped—and then pounded.

Squeezing her breasts lightly, he said, "I feel your heart beating, like a bird trapped in my hand."

His thumbs and forefingers took the nubs of her nipples and pressed them, and pressed them again, repeatedly, until the sensation became intense and almost unbearable. She couldn't speak, was afraid to arch her back, afraid to tense her stomach muscles, though she wanted to do all that.

He leaned to kiss her eyelids again, and her forehead where her hair began. He kissed her temples, her lips. His hands smoothed up from her breasts to stroke her shoulders delicately. "So fragile," he murmured, his voice deep and slow and voluptuous. With his hands exerting a slight pressure, as if to hold her where she was, his head lowered.

But not to her lips. He took one sensitive nipple into his mouth, wetted it all around, lifted his head to admire its pink, taffeta sheen, then moved to the other. Colors filled her imagination. She felt softly bewildered. She closed her eyes. This was wrong, yet she wanted it to go on.

She should stop him.

She didn't want to.

For another moment she was balanced like a drop of water on a leaf; then the balance shifted, and two tears rolled down her face, two smooth, snail-paced tears.

He said something beneath his breath, then suddenly gathered her up off the pillow and embraced her, holding her tight, as if apologizing. She was trembling with strange music, even with those tears of guilt on her face.

"You're not ready yet," he said, gruff with emotion. "It's all right, I can wait. I want to please you, so you'll never forget, no matter what happens." He burrowed his face under her hair, into her throat, and smoothed his cool hands under her loose shirt up and down her back, up to her nape, down to the curves of her hips. And pulling her closer, he sighed, "I have tremendous patience, sweet. Patience sometimes achieves more than strength."

He felt her back some more—and her breasts once more when he laid her back on the pillows. Tears still stood in her eyes; she gazed up at him imploringly. There was in his face the patience he'd spoken of, which made him seem for the moment more formidable than ever.

Evidently holding to his resolve, he stood, slowly, turned away without another word, and went back out to the main room.

He left her just like that. As easily as a great storm retreats over the mountains, leaving broken trees, limbs strewn, leaves everywhere in its wake. He simply walked away. She wanted to scream. At him, at herself. She put her own hands on her breasts, covering them momentarily against the remembrance of his. Inside her was a clamoring of feelings, all sorts of feelings, too many for her to sift through or make sense of.

Neither of them spoke over their late breakfast. She didn't trust her wits or her voice. Her stomach was in such a twist she hardly knew what she was eating.

When she rose from the table, he didn't stop her. It had become her habit to tidy the bedroom each day, since she was usually the last to leave it. Alone in there now, with the semiprivacy provided by the curtains, she tried to understand what was happening to her.

He was deliberately trying to seduce her. Why? Was this some new way to goad Richard? His plan hadn't worked, and yet he wouldn't let her go. At first he'd treated her as if she were an object, a carved decoy like hunters use, and now he was enticing her with his mouth and his hands and words he couldn't possibly mean. The manner of his war was to muddle her mind and make right and wrong unclear to her. And it was working! She was awash with fear—and with her knowledge of her duty to her husband.

Her *husband!* Richard—try to remember Richard!

She leaned her forehead against the windowsill. She couldn't go on like this. Somehow she had to get away.

After a while, he came through the curtains. She spun and gave him an accusing look. A muscle of his jaw contracted. He turned and soon she heard the door slam.

Eleven

It had to be four in the morning. Andre couldn't sleep. He left the cabin and saddled his black horse. Laura wouldn't even know he was gone. Unless a nightmare woke her. Once asleep, she was pretty much *asleep*. He smiled to realize he knew so many intimate details about her. He knew a lot more about her than Laird ever had.

The stallion's quiet steps took him to a high ridge overlooking the cabin. In daylight, it was a sunny, airy spot. He'd once talked to Ling about building a house here. When she died, this had seemed the natural place to bury her.

Her father, Soo, had been the only other person to attend that burial. Andre had knelt by the mounded grave a long while. To Soo he'd said, "Laird. She told me his name was Laird. I'm going to find him and make him pay for this."

Soo's face held that implacable Oriental expression. "You forget soon."

"Forget! No, I won't forget. I wish to God I could forget. But I never will."

"You kill him—this Laird?"

"Yes."

Soo eyed him. "I never forget, either."

After five years, the little headstone now stood ankle-deep in fallen leaves and pine straw. Andre's stallion moved restlessly as Andre swung off him. The gravestone's granules of mica and quartz sparkled in the moonlight. He went down on one knee, bracing his forearm.

"I haven't forgotten," he whispered.

He hadn't, but there was something new moving in him now. Everything seemed new with Laura. When he'd fallen in love with Ling, he'd learned that certain choices were made with the mind, and that others were made with the heart, and that of the two, it was the latter that endured. He'd vowed to avenge his beloved, yet now there was this wholly overwhelming need he felt for Laura.

He scowled, remembering her this morning, her engaging innocence, her defenseless reaction to him. "What am I going to do about her, Ling?" He had to make a decision—tonight, because by tomorrow Laird would come for sure, with enough guns to blast him to pulp.

He figured he had several choices—some of them choices of the mind, others choices of the heart:

He could use Laura as bait again—tie her out in the yard, place himself in a good position, and ambush the very men coming to ambush him. That would be fair enough—in his mind. But what would it do to Laura, to be used in such an immediate way, to helplessly watch men die? And then there was always the chance she might get hurt by a stray bullet.

Or he could simply leave her. Laird would arrive, find her, and take her home. She was still a virgin; he would soon enough ascertain that. But what about Andre's vow to Ling? And how could he, in all conscience, let Laura go back to that bastard? An innocent like her, bound for life to a man who had no subtlety, no honor, no pity?

It bothered him that he was worried more about what her life with Laird might be like than he was about fulfilling his vow to his own wife.

He sighed, and brushed some of the leaf mold away from the gravestone. "Ling," he murmured.

So that left a third choice. Was it justifiable? Was it a betrayal of what he'd once felt for the woman buried here? Was it even sensible? Or was it sure to end in pain and bitterness?

Kneeling there, he suddenly and vividly tasted again the warm and responsive sweetness of Laura's tongue. He felt her at his fingertips, open to him down to her core. He shuddered with want—and need—for it had been such a very long time since a woman had been more than just an object to relieve him of certain bothersome sensations. He'd been fighting it for days, but every time he closed his eyes, he saw her.

He closed them and saw her now—her coffee cup brought tenderly toward her mouth, her lips opening to cover the rim gently, her eyelids lifting so her eyes met his, just as the fluid met her mouth.

More and more often his visions were becoming fantasies —her easing closer to him in bed, rising to her elbow above him so that the dark curtain of her hair swung around them both. She looked down at him with those big gray eyes. (How had the sea mist gotten into her eyes?) She touched her mouth to his, and whispered, "Let me feel you," as her palm brushed the heated rigidity of him . . . .

Jesus H. Christ! What was he going to do about her? Another man would have taken her this morning. Without her consent he couldn't, though. Anyway, the sensuous novelty of seducing her gradually was sufficient delight for now.

For now—but what was he going to do in the future? Time was passing; he had to decide. He had to decide tonight.

"Ling, what shall I do? She's ripe for love—innocent as a spring flower and hungry for love, ready for any man who treats her well. If she could just obey her body, she'd give herself to me—and I'd be gentle with her. It's very exciting being the first," he said. "I remember how it was with you."

With a rough curse, he got to his feet. What did he think— no! He couldn't possibly . . . could he?

"Damn it to hell! It's in me to do it! It really is!"

Andre was already dressed when he got Laura up. It was terribly early by her standards; the sun hadn't even put in an appearance. "We're moving out," he said, pulling the blankets off her and urging her into her clothes.

Still blurred by sleep, she slumped back down onto the edge of the bed and mumbled, "Moving outside? Why?"

131

He laughed curtly. "You're not much of an early bird, are you?"

She sensed he'd come to some decision; his mood was charged. He'd been wakeful when they went to bed. Several times she'd been startled half-awake by him taking her into his arms, and once he'd slithered his hand under her shirt to hold her breast. She hadn't fought, for there had been a desperation in him.

But now he only seemed cranky. "Come on." He pulled her into the main room and handed her a cup of hot coffee. "Drink that." She did, while he loaded his saddlebags and checked his gun and slid it back into its holster on his hip.

They were on the horses just as the first sunbeams threaded down through the forest. She asked warily, "Are you taking me home?"

He considered for a moment, then said, "Yes."

She felt shocked.

"What's the matter?"

"Nothing, I-I . . ." What could she say? "I just wish we didn't have the journey to get through."

"Don't you like the horseback way of life? Smart girl. At least you'll never end as a gimped-up saddle stiff."

They followed a different route than the one by which he'd brought her. The Mokelumne River had to be crossed again, but this time on a rickety-looking bridge. They moved along roads that were overgrown, old links in the eroding chain of dusty tracks that had once joined the gold camps.

They paused at noon at a place with a panoramic view. Oak woodlands and foothill pines slid together down the long slopes to the savannas of the Great Central Valley. He looped the reins of the horses over a stump and stretched himself beside where she sat in the grass. They ate jerky again, as they had on that first journey, and washed it down with plain water from his canteen. Neither of them spoke. She was still trying to come to grips with her feelings. He was taking her home. She watched a red-capped woodpecker without really seeing it.

As Andre boosted her back onto Stingy, he said, "Those clouds'll bump into the peaks behind us, bounce back a little, and then settle down to drench everything by tonight."

She looked skyward at a cluster of clouds sailing out above the flat land. A breeze had come up. It was pressing down the grass of the slopes and stirring the leaves in the oaks. "Will we have any shelter?" she asked.

"Only if we sift right along the next couple of hours."

She waited for an explanation as they moved out side by side. He finally told her, "We're going to a house. My house, left to me by my father. After he moved Mother and me to San Francisco, we missed this country, so he built a summer house outside Jackson. My mother still spends a few weeks there every year. It's no mansion, but you'll find it more comfortable than the cabin."

He paused, but she could tell there was more he wanted to say.

"It'll be closed," he went on. "There's a servant, but he doesn't know we're coming."

She cast her eyes sidelong at him. "A servant?"

"Soo. He cooks and takes care of the place for me. He's been there for years. He's . . . He was Ling's father."

"Oh."

The wind blew easily at first, then rattled branches and flattened the grasses. Laura said, cautiously, but in a voice loud enough to carry from her horse to his, "Andre, I don't mean to pry, but, well, I can't help but wonder how you came to marry Ling."

She thought he wasn't going to answer, but then he did. "I was only fourteen when I first met her. I happened to be in the kitchen when she and her father knocked on the back door of our place in San Francisco. They were begging for something to eat."

The wind was in Laura's hair, her eyes. She tried to imagine him fourteen. She found it hard to picture him young and boyish—small enough to fit the pants she was wearing.

"They were pretty bad off. Ling was coughing; she had a fever. They were newly arrived from Canton, and had gone to live in a mining camp the month before—French Corral, in Nevada County—but in January all the Chinese were driven out, their cabins destroyed."

A little girl with a fever forced out into the snow. The touch of fellow feeling at Laura's heart was quite deft and sure.

"One of the whites was actually tried for that business, by the way. He got a hundred-dollar fine." He gave her an ironic smile.

The dry storm crackled, whipped the leaves all around them.

"There were close to a hundred and twenty-five thousand Chinese in California then, and a lot of people had strong feelings against them. After all, they were funny-looking, skinny people, with yellow skin and slant eyes." He sighed. "For some reason I pleaded with my mother to hire Soo, and they stayed on."

"And you fell in love with his daughter," Laura said, trying to subdue her blowing hair.

He laughed. "She was only nine. I hadn't yet taken up robbing the cradle in those days." He gave her an odd, meaningful look. "But I did grow up with her. She was one of the people I missed when I went off to Harvard."

He seemed to think for a moment before he took up the strands of his story again. "Harvard, then Europe for two years—the required Grand Tour. And when I came home again, she wasn't nine anymore. It was autumn, the time of the Moon Festival and she was . . ." his voice went inward, "she was beautiful.

"It was a bad time. Another twenty-two thousand Chinese had arrived in the state just that year, most of them coming to San Francisco, and all of them looking for work—with fifteen thousand unemployed Americans already living in the city. The newspapers were full of commotions caused by a bunch of hoodlums who called themselves the Workingmen's Party. 'The Chinese must go!'—that was their slogan. Everybody seemed anxious to take sides. Including my father.

"He fired Soo when he found out how I felt about Ling. But we found someone to marry us . . . and we had two good months." Now his voice turned acrid. "Just two."

After a while, he seemed to make an effort to continue. "After the wedding, my father made it clear that as long as I was living with a Chinese woman, I wasn't to consider myself his son. He changed his will when she died, but we were never reconciled. He died himself two years ago."

"I'm sorry," she murmured. "You must wish . . ."

He looked over at her. "That I'd seen him again? Made it up with him? You didn't know my father. He wasn't sorry— nothing dented Drew Sheridan for long—so why should I have any regrets?"

Somehow she didn't believe a word of that. The wind swept down, soughing in the trees, fluttering the tails of the horses. Laura said, "But he left everything to you."

"He did do that, yes."

"Surely you meant something to him."

He didn't answer, and she wondered what he was thinking. He had an advantage over her in that he often seemed quite adept at reading her thoughts, sometimes even before she herself was aware of them, while she seldom knew what his were.

Her mind wandered to immediate problems: This was all ending now. She was going home. Richard would be so relieved to see her. And she would be so happy.

Wouldn't she?

Would there be questions from the sheriff? Would Andre be caught? If he wasn't, would she ever see him again? And if he was, would she have to damn him with her testimony in a courtroom? She had to convince Richard to simply let it go! She could argue that the scandal of a public trial would follow them all their lives. Somehow she had to keep the events of these past nine days a secret. Somehow she had to forget.

She wondered if Andre's relenting meant he was giving up his notion that Richard was the one who had abused poor Ling. It was such a ridiculous idea; Laura could never have married a man like that. No woman could. And surely she would know, she would sense it. Oh, Richard was rustic, and he could be indelicate, but he wasn't the kind of man who could force himself on a woman. Not hurtfully. He wasn't

135

capable of real violence. He was easily impassioned—yes, that was true. And perhaps a little unrestrained at times. Tough, too, and headstrong and vehement—yes, all that, certainly—but not savage. Not brutal. Surely not.

Surely not.

She shook back her hair yet again. Andre was looking at her, scowling—for no reason that she could think of. Except that his plan hadn't worked and now he had to take her home. He seemed about to say something, but then looked forward once more.

In the slanting afternoon light they crossed yet another oak-wooded knoll and then fell into single file along an eroded trail, steep and uncertain at places, the outer edge of which tended to fall away abruptly. The view of the hills was rough and canyon-cut here.

Andre stopped his horse and waited for Stingy to come abreast. Facing forward, he said, "There's something I have to tell you. I'm not taking you back to Laird. I don't mean for you to ever see Laird Ranch again."

She felt herself blanch, felt her stomach become weightless. "You said you were taking me home."

"I am. My home; it'll be yours, too, from now on."

"You lied to me!"

"Not exactly. I just let you believe what you chose to believe. And it's proved something to me: you've been in a stew all day. I think the best thing is for Laird to get a letter telling him that you realized your mistake and that you're filing for an annulment."

Though she saw his mouth move, she heard none of this. All she heard was her heart pounding and her blood drumming in her ears.

"Are you going to faint on me?"

She impulsively dug her heels into Stingy's sides. Before the horse could bolt, Andre's hand darted to the bridle. He couldn't hold her, however. Stingy neighed and reared, her ears pricked, her nostrils strained. Laura did her best to hold on to the saddlehorn; nevertheless, she felt herself tumbling from the animal's churning back. The deep canyon yawned beneath her. At the last moment she flung herself sideways between the horses. She hit the road and lay flat on her back, while both Stingy's and the black's hooves danced dangerously near her head.

The wind was knocked out of her; the day became dark and dim. An onslaught of enormous black flowers burst into soundless bloom before her open eyes. Her ears filled with a sound like an excitement of wings in the air. Vaguely she heard Stingy quieting down, and the stallion whickering irritably somewhere nearby. "Easy girl!" Andre was saying to the mare. "Easy! *Eee*asy, now. Everything's going to be fine, everything's going to be just Goddamned dandy." Then Laura saw him hunkering down beside her.

She rolled onto her knees. His hands were on her shoulders, but somehow she managed to slip from his grip. She scrambled a few paces on her hands and knees, then was on her feet, running.

Her flight was short-lived. His arms circled her from behind. "Take your hands off me!" She twisted violently to face him, to better fight him.

He put a leg behind her and backed her over it, tripping her and lowering her to the ground. Then he straddled her on all fours like a wrestler. A part of her knew that he was using only as much strength as was necessary to restrain her—she got a sense of being carefully surrounded by a cage of pure muscle, hard and flexed. But he was unwilling to hurt her, and that care angered her even more. Her fingers curled like claws and went for his face, where she had every intention of doing as much damage as she possibly could.

"Damn it!" He caught her wrists and pinned them on either side of her head. She winced, because he wasn't being quite so careful not to hurt her now; yet still she bucked and writhed.

"Settle down!" He was back-lit by the cloud-covered sky. She could barely make out the particulars of his features. Except for his eyes.

"You!" she said. "I know what you're planning now—to ruin my marriage. You couldn't get at Richard one way, so now you want to try another." She strained against his hands.

"If you don't stop this—"

"What—what will you do? What can you do that you haven't done already?"

"Plenty! Come on!" He hauled her to her feet.

As he let go of her right wrist to reach for his horse, she twisted in front of him and gripped the handle of the pistol at his hip. "I *will* shoot you—I'll prove to you I can!"

His hand came over hers the same instant. That was when the smoke of her fury cleared—when his powerful fingers lifted hers away from the handle of the gun, curled her whole hand within his big fist, and squeezed. She whimpered with the expectation of pain. Lush concertos rumbled through her mind, all lost with the loss of her hand.

The pain didn't come, however. "Is that what you want, Laura, for me to hurt you? Would just breaking your hand be enough, or should I work my way on up your arm?"

She knew he could do it. He could mash her fingers, pulverize the bones, crumble them into small pieces, into powder.

"Is that what you want? Would that salve your conscience?"

By degrees, he released the pressure until she could have slid her hand out of his. But she didn't. What did he mean about her conscience?

"You don't want to go back to Laird," he said, cutting the matter entirely open. "Admit it, you never loved him, not the way a woman should love a man she's got to spend the rest of her life with. Christ, in a grotesque way I saved you from him—and you're glad I did, you know you are. I've been watching you all day. You were almost sick thinking I was going to take you back to him."

There should have been a clamor of sound, like a mountain sliding into ruin. But there was only the whisper of grass, the heavy breath of the wind. Beside them the stallion dipped his head and shook his blowing mane disgustedly. "I'm his wife," she said in a small voice. "I have to go back to him."

He glowered at her, and traced a finger over her lips. "You're not going anywhere except with me, and if that

138

means I have to keep treating you like a captive for a while, then I will. It won't be hard—you're about as strong as a twelve-year-old boy. You'll stop fighting me after a while, though. You know you will. Don't you, Lorelei?"

"It sure looks empty as hell to me," Ives Zacariah said, none too quietly. He and Richard were lying on their bellies behind a rotted log atop the ridge behind Andre's cabin. There were four men with them, in basically the same position. They'd been like this for a good twenty minutes, waiting for some sign of life to show itself below. But none had. There weren't even any horses in the shed. "Laird, boy, there ain't nobody there," Zacariah said, even louder now, impatiently.

Richard nodded his head, then stood, slowly. "All right, let's go check it out." He felt less foolish when they found fresh horse dung in the shelter, and a coffee cup still half full on the table inside the cabin. Though the coffee was stone cold, the stove still held a little warmth. Richard went into the bedroom, tore the blankets off the neat bed, and picked a long dark hair off the inside pillow. "They were here."

Zacariah said needlessly, "But they ain't here now. Looks like we just missed 'em. What do we do next?"

Richard let the hair fall. "I don't know."

"Have any idea where else he might take her?"

Richard shook his head.

"Might as well go on home then, that's my advice."

Richard was getting mighty tired of Zacariah's advice. For two cents he'd bust the man's jaw.

No, it was Sheridan he wanted to bust, if it was the last thing he ever did.

Twelve

As the afternoon went darker with the coming storm, Laura fought Andre tooth and nail. He forced her to ride with him, and her elbows poked his ribs and her head knocked against his chin—until in self-defense he squeezed her so she couldn't breathe.

Her retaliation was to call him every name she could think of, trying hard to insult him. She called him a malicious criminal, a thug, a common outlaw, a contemptible, clumsy, sulky clod, a beast—an *unclean* beast!

The weather grew steadily grimmer, and Andre seemed to grow fairly bleak himself. After listening to her for quite a while he said, "If you can't come up with anything more colorful than thug, then it's time you grew out of the bawling years and into the cussing." To help her, he proceeded to unleash a string of obscenities so vile her ears felt raw.

After that she said not a word, nor did she glance ahead farther than the horse's ears. It wasn't until Andre commented, "Looks like we're in for some thunder," that she grew aware of the dour piled clouds in the darkening sky. From afar came a faint boom. The sun slid under the layers of clouds, glared at them for a minute, then set behind the coastal mountains. Laura began to droop. The journey was catching up with her.

It grew ever darker. They rode in silence, the rush of wind whipping about them. Their route was steadily downhill now. Andre carefully skirted the little town of Jackson and kept off the roads. Laura felt a few threatening drops of rain. Thunder rolled and rumbled along the mountainsides, warning of the storm's swift approach.

At last, amidst the woods that drifted across the landscape, they came upon an isolated house. It was an attractive two-story brick, with a wide porch running the length of the front. A leafy vine grew up the north end of the porch, and the south end was sheltered by a large overhanging black oak. The front windows, edged with white shutters, were all dark. The place looked deserted.

Exhausted as Laura felt, when Andre stepped down from the saddle, she didn't follow him. She ignored his waiting hands. He lifted the brim of his hat and glowered at her. In another minute he would drag her down. To foil him, she got off by herself, on the wrong side. He crossed under the horse's neck and took hold of her waist, looking as if he might finally lose his temper. "Laura, if you don't stop this, I swear I'm going to make you regret it."

Obviously his famous patience was at an end. Nonetheless, she wouldn't budge when he urged her toward the house. "I'm not going in there."

Slowly, enunciating each word individually, he said, "Yes—you—are." And he hooked her firmly around the waist and lifted her under his right arm like a sack of potatoes.

She kicked, to no avail except the satisfaction of making him breathe a little harder as he passed the hitching post, went through the gate, and up the narrow brick walk. He set her down on the porch, but kept his arm around her, and banged on the door. "Soo! Open up! It's me!"

A light shone through the frosted glass oval of the door. Then the locks rattled and Laura saw a man not much larger than herself, though older, heavier, and Oriental.

Andre pushed her into the hall. "Soo, this is . . . well, she's Richard Laird's wife, but only for the time being."

He pushed her into the first room on the right. As he lit one lamp after another, the placed showed itself to be a parlor. He ordered her into one of a pair of wing chairs upholstered in cornflower blue silk, which stood before the hearth, "Sit!" She sat slumped while he knelt to start a fire. In her bruised state of mind she all but forgot Soo—until Andre stood and looked over her head and said, "I'm going out to get the horses settled in the barn. Watch her."

He was gone perhaps fifteen minutes. Laura tried to ignore the fact that she was being guarded. The chair was comfortable, the room tasteful—there was even a piano standing in one corner. It drew her eyes like a magnet. A Grand Chickering. Music stood ready on its rack. She told herself it was only curiosity that prompted her to strain to read the name.

So her new place of captivity came equipped with Brahms? Why should she be glad of that? Why should she feel the need to clasp her hands tightly against an itch to get up and try the ivory keys? She leaned back in her chair, bone-weary, and very confused.

Andre returned, paused in the hall to hang his hat and gun belt on a rack that already held a shotgun, then said, "How about a tray, Soo? We're starved." The man shuffled away. Andre dropped into the chair beside hers. She jerked her eyes away from him peevishly, ignoring his raised eyebrows and soft warning: "Behave, now."

Soo returned shortly with a tray of cold meat, which he placed on the little marble-topped table between the two chairs. Andre filled one of the plates with quick efficiency. He placed it, with a white linen napkin, in Laura's lap. "Eat."

She was too hungry to deny herself. As she began, however, Soo said, "You take his woman?"

Andre gave him a certain look. "Yes."

"He fight you for her? You kill him?"

"No."

"Why you bring her here then?"

"Because I want her."

The jellied chicken was probably delicious, but in her mouth it turned to wood pulp.

Soo left without asking any more questions.

"Eat, Laura." Andre's eyes were grim embers, but he ate, too, with absent concentration. Not even a sudden flash of lightning out the windows drew a comment from him.

Another jagged bolt split the sky almost over their heads; hollow thunder clapped so loud Laura jumped.

"It's getting close," she said, in spite of herself.

"We got here in the nick of time—no thanks to you." He set his empty plate aside and stretched his long legs toward the fire. They both fell to staring into the flames. A light drumming sound announced the rain. Lightning crackled, thunder boomed and resonated and lingered. The sense of shelter, the food, the comfort of the chair, the warmth of the fire, all conspired against Laura. She tried to hide her yawn behind her hand. "You put in a hard day," he said sarcastically, and rubbed his ribs where she'd elbowed him. "I'll take you up."

He showed her down the hall to the dining room, where a graceful curving staircase led to the second floor. He gestured her to lead the way. Opening the first door on the right in the upper hall, he ushered her into a spacious room decorated in pale blue and white. Soo had been busy here: a lamp was burning low on the night table. An enormous bed took up a good deal of the floor space. In the looking glass over the low marble-topped bureau she caught the first clear sight of herself she'd had since the night she'd seen Andre advancing on her from out of the shadows in Richard's ranch house. "Oh!" she groaned. She looked ridiculous in his clothes. And her hair was tangled from the day's wind.

Amusement played over his mouth. She saw it and turned, as if to fly at him again. He lifted his hand to caution her. "You come at me one more time . . ." He left the threat dangling. She backed away, not doubting for a minute that he would do something despicable. The angry energy that had carried her through the afternoon was gone. She didn't want to battle with him anymore.

Andre heaved a sigh at the way she backed off from him. He wouldn't really hurt her, didn't she know that? It broke his heart to see her standing there so small and tired and whipped. It made him feel ashamed for some of the things he'd done—using that kind of language to shock her into silence, and carrying her up the walk like a sack of corn. He had twelve inches and eighty pounds on her—surely he didn't need to sling her around like a sack of feed.

His hand fell to the ornate footboard of the bed. "I hope you like this room. I always did."

She wouldn't look at him. Her cheeks were pale, her eyes were swimming. That hurt him, too. "Is there anything you need, anything you want?"

She didn't respond.

"I thought you'd be glad to be back in a regular house."

Her eyes were still shining. "How can I be glad when you're going to . . . Will you give me tonight? I'm so tired— please, I'm begging you, not tonight."

That made him feel about two inches tall. "Laura, what do you think, that I'm going to force you? I wouldn't, not tonight or any other night." He didn't know what else to say. She didn't even know what he wanted from her yet, what making love was. She had to be scared silly. "Go on, get into bed, and we'll talk about it tomorrow."

He folded back the white hobnail bedspread, revealing a white blanket beneath. He knew he should just leave then, but her lips were too soft-looking to resist. He stooped and tasted them. He kept it brief, though he could have lengthened it—she was too tired to resist. His tongue just touched hers before withdrawing. "Get some rest, sweet. I'm going to talk to Soo, then I'll be up again." He paused, then added, "I, uh, I'll be right across the hall tonight. I'll have to lock your door, but if you need anything, just call out."

Her mouth looked too good; he couldn't withstand the temptation. He stooped again, and opened her lips and took another kiss from her. This time he let his hands slide around her back and down, to squeeze her buttocks. She must be saddle sore again. Under different circumstances, he would rub the soreness out for her. But for now, he'd better get out of here while he was still in control.

Laura heard the key turn in the lock after he went out. She stared dumbly at the doorknob. He was going to let her sleep alone then. A taint of disappointment welled up in her. She tamped it down, and turned to bathe her hands and face in the water that was in a pitcher on the bureau. She undressed and poured more water into the bowl and sponged her entire

144

body, relishing the fresh sensation.

She didn't want to put Andre's soiled shirt back on, so rummaged through the bureau, through his collars and cuffs, his linen necessaries and shaker-toed stockings, through several snow-white shirts all pressed and folded exquisitely, until, in the bottom drawer, along with a pair of red wool flannels—which looked as if they'd never been worn—she found a starched nightshirt. She chose that to serve as her nightdress. Then she crawled into the crisp-sheeted bed.

Outside, the wind scoured the trees, swept the grass; lightning flickered, followed by mutterings of thunder, and under it all came the continuous sound of the rain.

The bed seemed too big. She smoothed her hand over the undented mattress beside her. It was strange how easily she'd gotten used to resting in his arms, to easing against his body, basking in its heat. There was a certain danger, of course. He was a light sleeper; just drawing near him was enough to wake him, and then, shifting, he would close her in his arms. He gave his warmth for a price.

The smooth cloth of his nightshirt rubbed sensuously over her skin. She experimentally put her hands to her tingling breasts and felt the tiny hard nipples. She was aware of that same tingling elsewhere, but forbade herself to put her hands there. Andre had put his hands there—was it only yesterday? The very thought made her blood gush through her veins, made her face—and other parts of her—burn wickedly.

As she tossed and turned, the lightning passed over. The night grew darker and darker yet, as if the fire behind it had gone out completely. The rain kept up a slow tapping on the roof. Her thoughts turned inevitably to Richard. Laird Ranch seemed a thousand miles away. Would she ever see it again? Oh God, what was going to happen to her? What did Andre mean when he said he was going to keep her?

She turned over on her stomach and buried her face in the pillow. The tears she'd held in so that he wouldn't see them came now, leading her at length into an exhausted daze. Dimly, she wondered what he was saying to Soo downstairs. The design and fabric of her future, and her freedom to weave it as she pleased, had become nebulous, something to be set aside indefinitely according to the rise and fall of his voice.

The first seeping light of the morning came with the sound of runoffs of rain trickling in the aftermath of the storm. The clink of china from the dining room downstairs reminded Laura that she was not in a miner's cabin anymore. Yesterday came flooding back: He wasn't going to let her go home. He planned to keep her, and continue seducing her—right to the fearful brink.

When she was dressed, she found her door unlocked. Downstairs, though the table was set, the dining room was empty. As she started down the hall she made out Andre's shape through the frosted oval glass in the front door. She sidestepped into the parlor—

—and clasped her hands against the sudden tide of compulsion engendered by the sight of that lovely Chickering occupying the far corner. Before she had time to analyze this nostalgic feeling, Soo's voice from the dining room announced, "Breakfast ready!" Andre came in the door and filled the hall—such a powerful man! She could only stare at him. He came into the parlor and put his hand under her elbow. She stood, looking up into his eyes. What was this funny-hot-breathless sense of anticipation she felt? Why was he smiling so, with that smug gleam in his eyes? He raised her chin and squeezed it gently. The gesture was one of possession, of knowing. He said, "Breakfast?"

They ate oyster sausages and buckwheat cakes and he talked pleasantries and silliness: "Have you ever noticed how you eat? It says so much about you."

"How do I eat?"

He took a sip of coffee and assessed her. "The way I suspect you do everything. Very unpurposefully. You nibble a little of this, a little of that. You never seem to like one thing better than another, you just take whatever you're given. Christ, I've fed you nothing but jerky and water for days at a time and you didn't even grumble. Just took it and ate it, as if you'd never had better in your life."

"Richard has never complained about the way I eat."

"I don't imagine he noticed, he's apt to be such a self-inflated son of a bitch."

Soo came to clear the dishes. His shaped eyes were cold when they looked at her. He cleared the table without delay, and though he didn't seem to look at her after that first cold glance, she felt he was very much aware of her. His presence was like a shadow in the room.

His presence caused a change in Andre, too. First he fell silent, and then said roughly, "'Morning, Soo."

The old Chinaman nodded without looking up.

"How about some fresh air, Laura?"

She murmured an agreement, and the two of them stepped into the lowering autumn. It was cool out, even within the curve of his arm. It wasn't raining just now, though battlefronts of clouds still scutted overhead. The fresh-washed breeze fanned her face and lifted her hair back. The garden was old-fashioned and overgrown. Emerald moss framed each crumbling brick along the path. They were spongy cushions, full of rain water that soon soaked through the two pairs of Andre's boot socks she was still using for shoes.

"You need some clothes," he muttered. "I'd like to see you in skirts again."

She was glad when he dropped the intimate subject of her apparel and chatted of uniportant things—the weather; his business interests, which were being managed by his lawyers just now; the wounded President's chances for recovery. (He'd found a recent newspaper among the mail piled on his desk, and evidently President Garfield was no better.) His eyes fixed overhead in the shaggy crown of a sycamore tree. He pointed out a limb that seemed rotted. "I should get up there and cut that out before it falls on the roof." Thus she got new glimpses of him: the businessman, the citizen, the homeowner.

Yet her mind was only half-engaged by all of this; the other half was gnawed by her predicament and how she might get herself out of it. As she searched for a way to bring

147

it up—he'd said they could talk about it this morning—he led her to the part of the yard that lay beneath her bedroom windows. The house was perched on a hillside, so that the back of it peered down a moderate slope. "Anyone trying to jump from those windows would probably get a broken leg, don't you think? Or a broken neck."

"You're so subtle." Despite her anxiety, his small talk and the fresh air had relaxed her a little. She even offered him a smile, though it fluttered a bit undependably.

She wasn't prepared when he pulled her into his arms, his mouth seeking hers. She protested immediately, arched away from him and whispered, "Don't."

He mocked her objection. "Sorry, but if you don't want to be kissed, then you shouldn't sigh and gaze at me the way you did in the parlor. Or smile at me like you just did." His head lowered again. His tongue nudged her lips, and suddenly her pretense of unwillingness evaporated. She opened to him, opened like a blossom, and for a long moment she forgot altogether that she was supposed to be afraid of him and hate him.

Each time she thought he was through with her, he started up once more. Her arms became water, merely resting against his shoulders. Long moments later, his mouth slid down her throat, and he said, "There, that wasn't so bad now, was it?"

She was too shaken to answer. All about her came the sounds of the wet earth, and the sounds of his heart in his chest against her ear and his breath against her cheek, all joined in a full-toned romantic *legato,* all smooth and flowing and unbroken, music in her mind.

He put his mouth to hers once more, but this time only to softly bite her lower lip. Then he straightened. "Your feet must be ice-cold. Shall we go in?"

Though he'd dropped his hands from around her, she realized she was still leaning into him, with her breasts flush against his chest. Slowly her bones came alive; they moved inside her skin; she took a step away, straightened her clothing and hair. "Y-you shouldn't have done that."

Again he smiled at her, that mocking smile. And his hands

came up and his fingertips ever so nimbly grazed her nipples, which were hard to the touch beneath her shirt. She didn't even try to stop him. Nothing was keeping her there. He wasn't holding her. She was unbound and ungagged. He's winning, she thought. And whatever had possessed her to be unafraid of him melted from her heart and left her petrified.

A gust of reborn wind whipped the grasses. He slung his arm around her and asked, "Are you cold? Is that why you're trembling again, sweet?"

She was shivering, yes, but she wasn't cold.

Laura sat in the rocking chair listening to the great soft pillow of sound the rain made. It had started again almost as soon as Andre had brought her back upstairs. The light coming in from the windows was dim; all the gold of summer was faded out of it.

She didn't look when she heard the key turn in the door. She knew who it was.

"I found some." Andre tossed a pile of clothes onto the bed. He'd told her he was going to see if his mother might have left some things in her closet. "They'll be a little loose on you, but at least they're skirts."

She stood and lifted up a rose-colored, Princess-style dress. "Your mother isn't as tall as you."

He grinned. "She'd look a bit odd, don't you think?"

There was almost everything she needed: a white cambric petticoat, complete with lace and frills; a pair of dainty high-buttoned boots; black and white stockings, underdrawers, even a corset and bustle.

She hesitated, torn between a petulant desire to refuse anything provided by him, and a purely feminine desire to be properly dressed. Making her decision, she said stiffly, "Are you sure Mrs. Sheridan won't be offended?"

"Mother's never been short of clothes. She probably left these here because she didn't fancy them anymore."

"But they're almost new, and so fine." She was stumped for what to say beyond that. Rules of etiquette failed her, under the circumstances.

"I'll be back in fifteen minutes," he said.

The bodice of the dress was loose enough that she could have managed without Mrs. Sheridan's serviceable corset—but it felt good to be decently whaleboned and bustled again. The overskirt of the dress was drawn tight across the stomach and held with ribbon bows at the sides. The long sleeves had deep, turned-back cuffs edged with small frills.

She was before the looking glass, raking at her hair with the small comb she'd found on the bureau yesterday, when Andre returned. He closed the door quietly and stood watching her, then moved forward and reached around her to place a wooden case on the bureau. "That's for you. A birthday gift. They belonged to my grandmother."

Her birthday! She'd forgotten all about it. It had been yesterday. She met his eyes in the looking glass, those odd eyes that imparted such odd sensations.

Inside the case was a fine, hand-carved, wooden-backed, natural bristle hairbrush, a complete set of brass hairpins, and tortoiseshell combs. "If these were your grandmother's . . ."

"They're yours now."

"Thank you," she said simply, reduced to it by emotions she didn't even try to understand.

He filled his hands with her heavy hair. "I want to kiss you again."

An exquisite sensation rushed through her body. She stiffened against it. She needed to tread warily—she felt unusually sensitive and hesitant. "You think you can give me some hand-me-down clothes and a present and—" She was trying her best to sound firm. "Do you think I'm for sale, and so cheaply?"

"Not for sale," he said softly, "but vulnerable. Uncertain. I don't give presents in hopes of return—but on the other hand, I take advantage of my opportunities."

She swallowed, averted her eyes. Her heart, her treacherous heart, wouldn't beat at the right speed. A delicious and betraying sense of anticipation rippled through her. All the principles she was trying so hard to stand on seemed like gossamer, threatening to rip.

He released her hair, letting it fall in a cape down her back again, and turned her. "Look at me."

She remained rigid. She would *not* look at him. She even lowered her head and her lashes.

"Will you ever stop resisting? You know by now, don't you, that I'm very patient—if not very good-hearted. I'll wait you out, Laura, you and your nagging little sense of loyalty to someone who doesn't even deserve you."

She was shaking all over. He was going to kiss her, and she . . . she wanted him to. She would respond to him, and then . . . then what? Biting at her lower lip, she raised her face quickly, as if to get it over with all in an instant.

She found him smiling at her leisurely. He had such a striking attitude of possession! He skimmed his hands around her, under her arms and around her back, and pulled her to him. He was pleased, yet so matter-of-fact, so at ease, that she knew he took it for granted that he would conquer her.

Because you've never proven any ability to resist him!

Her hands seemed ridiculously small against his powerful chest. She stood trembling as he pressed his lips to her forehead. He smelled of bay rum from his morning shave. "Yes," he murmured, "just let me kiss you for once without all that pushing and straining away."

151

Thirteen

When Andre pulled Laura even closer, fitted her against him, she felt signals within her like . . . like the first time she'd ever visited the seashore. Though she'd never seen it before, she'd known it was near—the new taste in the air, that sensation of an opening out ahead, marking the end of the land and the onset of that ancient uproar and endless coming and going, and the sound, the penultimate hush. And this, or something very near it, was what she felt now in Andre's arms.

"I haven't even kissed you yet and you're trembling," he teased. "Anticipating?" His mouth moved to her shaking lips, opened them, his arms wrapped tightly around her, settling her even more firmly in his embrace. With a little sigh, she went limp against him. In truth, she was trembling too violently to stand alone. Her hands were caught between them, against his shirtfront, and she felt his chest muscles flex as he bent into her.

His kisses seemed never to finish. When one was completed, another began. And gradually she became lost in the whirlpool of them, absorbed, swallowed up.

Still, there came a point when she groaned beneath his mouth and strained away. But his hold couldn't be broken so easily. His lips left her to play against the corners of her mouth, against her chin, her temples. "Stop fighting me," he murmured.

"I have to." Her voice was husky with tears.

"No, you don't." His lips traveled down the side of her throat. He seemed reluctant to stop at the jabot of her new dress, yet he did stop, and raised his dark head. One hand came up to smooth a stray tendril off her cheek. "You see how it is with us? How it could be?"

She gave a little muffled wail of shame, and yet the driving want he'd started in her wouldn't go away.

"You don't need to be afraid. I'll take you slowly, Laura. I'll be gentle with you; I can be gentle."

"No."

"Yes!" he insisted. And then added, more murmurously, "You hardly know what I mean or what I intend, but I'm going to be good to you, and soon—soon now." He gave her an affectionate squeeze before he stepped back. His eyes wandered over her face. As hers wandered over his.

Part of her couldn't deal with this, it was too extravagant, it was happening too quickly. Another part of her felt a tug at fibers in her body she hadn't known were there; she was being called in ways she didn't understand; she couldn't even define the sensations she was feeling.

He broke the spell by laughing lazily. "Soo says lunch is about ready. Let's see how fast you can put your hair up."

Of course, with him watching, her fingers were clumsy. She settled for a simple chignon held by her new combs and pins. When done, she turned. Her rose-colored skirts fanned in a short train behind her. She was transformed, a lady once again. He bowed slightly in recognition of it, and opened the door for her.

But then, as she turned for the stairs, he caught her arm and smiled and bent sideways to kiss her mouth lightly again. She was afraid to lift her eyes, afraid he would see the desire still there, and find her lascivious and easy, instead of the restrained lady this gown reminded her she should be. But he ducked his head even further, and caught her downward gaze, deviling her. She couldn't help but smile then, at the mischievous look on his face.

He kissed her again. "A very lovely flower you have here," he said against her lips. He flicked her lower lip with the tip of his tongue and then kissed her yet again. She fell into that

153

third kiss as she would lie down in a warm bath. When at last he lifted his head, she lay in his arms completely defeated. He whispered her name as though in love with the sound of it: "Laura." Then added, not particularly eager, "Lunch first, then maybe—"

"No." She pulled away from him slowly, trying desperately to restart the wheels of her mind. As the gown had reminded her, she was reared to be a lady. She reminded herself that she was married, another man's wife. And the things she'd let Andre do! An edge of repentance ripped through her. Alarice Upton's voice suddenly sounded loud in her head: *You're wicked! A sinful, wicked girl!*

She got down the stairs somehow—like a somambulist. Andre went at his asparagus omelet vigorously, unaware of her inner remorse. He smiled easily, looking up from his plate at her. Just that look—that smile that was like matchlight—re-ignited the inward flames she'd felt so recently in his arms. It was such a strangely pleasant feeling to be set afire like that—it *must* be wicked!

A movement alerted her to Soo's presence in the kitchen doorway. She caught a new gleam of contempt and loathing in his eyes as he came in and busied himself about the table. Andre's smile fell away. Laura realized why: he was thinking of Ling! A crystal chill froze the heat she'd felt only a moment before. Outraged, she pushed her chair away from the table, rose, and for a moment, petite as she was, the man seemed daunted. "You're a dreadful man, Andre Sheridan!" The words came out with such intensity and such groundless courage that even she was impressed. "You can't treat me like this!" She turned for the stairs—at least in the bedroom she would be spared the speculation of that hateful Chinaman's eyes.

As she reached the bottom step, she heard Andre's chair scrape back. "What the hell's the matter? Come back here!"

There was no source of heat in the bedroom. Laura searched through the clothes Andre had brought her and found a shawl. She pulled the rocking chair near the windows and watched the rain dropping like beads onto the garden below. The afternoon seemed endless. As dusk fell, the idea that had formed in her mind during the past hour firmed to purpose. She stripped the bed, got the sheets, ripped them in half lengthwise, then tied the four strips together. One end she attached to the bedpost nearest the window. The wad of material was thick, and she wasn't at all sure of her knots, but even if she fell, the ground must be soft by now, with all this rain. She raised the sash and threw the end of her makeshift rope out into the blustery evening.

That was when she heard Andre's footsteps on the stairs. Panic paralyzed her. There was no way she could hide her attempt. He wouldn't like it; they would quarrel; and he would win again—and then he would feel it necessary to prove to her that he had won.

She stood stiff as a ruler, listening as the footsteps came closer. At last she hoisted up her draped skirts and lifted one leg out the window. His steps were coming along the hall already. She ducked her head under the window—and banged the top of it painfully. She was lifting her other leg out when the doorknob turned . . .

"For Christ-sakes!" Just as she started to push off from the sill, he grabed her under the arms and yanked her back inside. He swung her onto the bare mattress. She bounced, then scrambled across it, and stood facing him on the opposite side. He stared at her for so long she couldn't bear the suspense, and said defensively, "Prisoners are expected to try to escape."

He was wearing a work jacket of brown duck, one she hadn't seen before. He took it off, flung it over the footboard.

"I'll scream if you touch me!"

He came around the bed. She crawled back onto the mattress. He caught her easily, and gripped her arms and shook her a little, saying, "Scream your head off—who's to hear?" A muscle worked in his cheek. "First that silly show of temper—for no reason!—then sulking up here all afternoon. And now this! I can't help but wonder why you waited so long. Surely, if you were really that eager to cut and run, you would've tried it earlier."

"I am eager!"

"For what?"

"To get away from you!"

"Are you?" He leaned over her, and she shrank back into the mattress. His hands smoothed around her corseted ribcage, and came up to capture her breasts beneath the dress. Her nipples at once formed little caps too tight to bear. All day, ever since his morning kisses, she'd been racked by shameful longings. She closed her eyes, fighting the rush of sensation.

For once he misunderstood her expression. "Christ! Little Miss Chastity! I must be crazy. Any other man would have had you days ago and to hell with all this nunnishness! When I think of all the nights you've lain in my arms ripe for the taking—and you are ripe, Laura—but I made myself a promise—I'm not going to give you any reason to say I forced you or coerced you or tricked you in any way. I'm going to make love to you—don't shake your head at me; I am!—but not until you tell me you want me to."

"I never will!"

"We'll see." His lips touched hers with a tenderness that wasn't in his voice. He deepened the kiss gradually, and her mouth opened to him, easily, indecently. A little sob of shame caught in her throat. He pulled away and looked down at her. "I've never met a woman more virginal than you. Maybe I should have left you for Laird to feast on that first night. I guarantee you wouldn't be so damned innocent now if I had. But no, I had to be sure I was taking you while he still wanted you so bad he was hurting for it." He laughed bitterly. "And now I'm hurting for it. If I didn't love you so—"

He stopped in mid-sentence, realizing what he'd said. "Christ!" he said, thoroughly disgusted. "Am I in love with you?" His dark eyes rested on her in disbelief. He groaned. "Jesus—how did you manage that, you teasing little . . . ?"

She hardly realized she was allowing him to kiss her again. He took her into it as if she were the author of all his despair and agony. Then he pushed her away, abruptly, and got off the bed. He laughed uncomfortably. "This isn't turning out the way I expected, either. I'd better get out of here for a while, cool off and think."

He grabbed his jacket and headed for the door. His face gave away nothing as he turned back to reel in the torn sheets still dangling out the open window: "I'll take this with me."

An hour passed. He didn't come back. Laura didn't think the door was locked. She tried the knob; it turned. She stepped out into the hall, tiptoed to the curve of the staircase. The dining room was empty. She descended and walked down the central hall, careful to stay on the silencing carpet. But as she reached for the knob of the front door, she heard a quiet, "Going out?" Andre leaned his hand against the door, cutting off her leave-taking.

"I guess not." She couldn't look at him.

He bent near. She smelled the now-familiar tinge of bay rum on his skin. "I'm surprised you're trying my temper again so soon," he said. "I thought you were smarter."

The wind whistled through the crisp autumn evening outside. He lowered his hand and put it around her waist. She tried to shrink away, only to come up against the door.

"Afraid, Lorelei?" He tilted her face up with a rough finger.

She thought it best to remain silent, since his mood seemed fairly black.

He turned his head. "Soo!"

The old Chinese, his features arranged in a scowl, seemed bent on voicing his feelings for a change. He came through the dining room chanting a string of singsong syllables. Andre cut through his jabber to ask, "How soon's dinner?"

"Five minute you let me cook it!"

"Keep it warm. We're not going to be ready for half an hour or so."

Soo turned his back—leaving a chill behind him.

Andre looked at Laura again. "In the parlor."

She took the chair she'd been assigned last night. He remained standing, studying her. Her heart beat like a drum beneath her bodice. "Must you stare at me?"

"Yes."

157

A mighty sigh of wind pressed against the windows. Her eyes jerked to the panes.

"Say something, Laura."

"What do you want to hear?"

"Where you were going just now, for starters. Or better, explain why you kiss me the way you do, if you really feel such everlasting devotion to Richard Laird."

"You're not being fair."

"Fair? Fair is for games—for baseball and poker and twenty questions. I'm not playing a game here, Laura. It's never been a game."

"Still, you're doing something that is foolish at best, and criminal at worst."

"Maybe. But I've loved and I've hated and love's better. And I'm not going to let Laird take it away from me twice."

Love. He meant it only in the physical sense. He didn't really care a button for her. "Nonsense; you're simply using me."

"I love you. I didn't mean for it to happen—believe me, it was the last thing I expected. But it *has* happened. I love you, and I think I can make you love me."

Her eyes veered away. Her voice was a whisper. "What do you want from me?"

"You know damn well what I want. Well . . . maybe you're a little vague on the specifics, but you know in general. You're an intelligent woman."

She could hardly breathe. "I can't let you."

"I don't think you can stop yourself."

"I'm Richard's wife. You're proposing adultery."

That goaded him. He swung away from her, swearing. "You're not his wife, and you never will be! You made a mistake, but you're going to get an annulment, and then you're going to marry me!" He spun back. "Consider us betrothed as of right now."

Her throat closed around a whimper. After a moment she said what had to be said. "I promised to love, honor, and obey my husband. I gave my solemn word before witnesses."

He knelt at the side of her chair. "We'll get you an annulment," he said, his old patience back. "You weren't of

158

age. It'll be easy."

"I don't know about that—but even if it were possible, I think I would always feel I'd cheated. I promised, I gave my word of honor, Andre. I can't go back on it, I couldn't do that to Richard."

He burst into a bitter laugh. "He did far worse to you: He abandoned you to a man who held a blood grudge against him."

"I don't believe that."

He threaded his fingers through his hair. "Isn't any of this going to be simple? I want to stop treating you like a captive—but you're so full of I-should-do-such-and-so and mistaken honor and noble stupidity. What else can I do, Laura, but keep you locked up? If I give you any leeway you'll be off and running to Laird in a minute, and I can't allow that. You haven't got a notion what he's really like."

"You don't have the right to make that decision for me. I don't belong to you."

His face hardened. "I say you do. And I think tonight's the night to prove it."

She felt her face go white.

"It won't be your fault, Laura. I thought it would be best to wait, and let you come to see it on your own, but now I think I have to play the bad guy. Your conscience can't handle what your heart and your body want to do—so it's up to me. It's not really wrong, either—we'll be married soon enough. Meanwhile, I'll keep you—whatever that takes— because I can't let you go back to the kind of life he'd lead you. It looks like I have to save you from yourself."

"Andre—"

"No, love, don't look like that. You might be afraid now, but after . . . after, you'll wonder what all the fuss was about, I promise you."

"You *can't.*" The words came out sounding very uncertain.

"You know I can."

"Andre, don't."

He only smiled tenderly, then leaned to cup her breast in one hand. A now familiar ache spread through her body at once. That new want was awake in a moment. "Andre," she whispered, "it's wicked."

He laughed again, the sight and sound of which made her ache all the more. "All right, if it makes you feel better to say so. But I intend to do only good to you, sweet. I give you leave to call me anything—and struggle as much as you can. The only thing I won't let you do is stop me."

Laura's appetite was affected at dinner; her mind was a-clamor. She hardly heard Andre when he said, "I have to go out and check that damn horse of the Parrys. She's been off her feed all day. I'll give you your choice: I can lock you upstairs, or you can give me your word that you won't try anything, and I'll let you sit by the fire in the parlor. Laura, did you hear me?"

"Oh, I-I prefer the parlor." She thought it best to avoid the bedroom at all costs.

"Give me your word then."

She stiffened, irritated by his tone. "My word is my obligation, and I don't like to be obligated to you."

"I could make you come out to the barn with me, but I don't want to drag you out in the rain—and I don't want to lock you up if I don't have to. Just tell me you promise not to run off this once."

"I won't promise any such thing!"

"Like hell you won't."

"Like hell I will!"

"Don't use bad language."

"You do!"

"But you shouldn't. Now give me your word."

"Like—"

"If you say that again, I'll cane you. I might anyway; I think it would be good for your contrary soul."

The tenseness of the atmosphere was shattered. She almost smiled. "Oh, Andre, you know you won't do anything of the sort."

There followed a short silence. "You suspect me of kindness?"

"Sometimes," she said cautiously.

Amusement and approval twitched his mouth. "Good. Now give me your word."

"No."

He sighed, then fixed her with a stern look. "You know, if you try to make a run for it, I'll catch you. It's a good five miles to Jackson, which gives me plenty of time to round you up."

It started raining again a few minutes after he went out. She stared into the flames of the parlor fire, trying to concentrate on some plan of action; but all she could think of was that he'd said twice now that he loved her. Even Richard had never said that to her. Could it be true? No! She must hold firm, no matter what methods he used.

When she imagined a noise on the porch a scant five minutes after he'd gone out, she gripped the arms of the blue chair. Was it him? Did he mean to make love to her now? She wasn't ready! Oh, truly, she didn't want him to!

It wasn't him, but she realized she had to get control of herself. She needed something to occupy her mind.

And there sat the piano. An unwanted image sprang into her mind: her hands sweeping the keys, creating melodies.

No, she didn't want to play!

Well, all right, she did. And why shouldn't she, for a few minutes? What could it hurt? After all, no one was making her; she could quit when she liked. She took the lamp from the table and carried it to the instrument.

Without sitting, she ran her fingers up a scale. A bright ripple of hammered strings came forth. She was immediately moved; she'd never expected the sound to hit her like light— soul-sweetening light.

She sat down and automatically began with a warm-up, a little exercise in thirds. Her fingers felt like sausages. *Keep it light, light as a soufflé.* Loosened up, she went into a Bach "Invention." Her fingers drummed out the intricate contrapuntal with quick precision, just as if she'd practiced it for hours, day after day, month after month. Which she had. She played it with her eyes half-closed so her hands only flickered in the borders of her vision.

She followed this with a quieter melody. The piano grew

more personal and intense with the haunting "Nocturne" her papa had loved best. She warmed the notes, overlapped them into a streaming *legatissimo* . . .

When Andre stepped onto the porch, he was satisfied to hear the piano. At least she hadn't taken off. He entered the house quietly, a little curious about this side of her.

What he learned in the next few moments of standing silently in the door of the parlor stunned him. Her hands hovered like butterflies above the keys, summoning from the instrument a flood of harmony. It seemed a kind of miracle. The lamp threw an amber circle over her gleaming forehead, over her pale skin and dancing fingers, over the piano's shining surface that was as serene and deep as a lake among the Alps. It was a moment of bewitchment, revealing a hidden, graceful, wonderful woman beyond the one his eyes knew, a woman who could take him into worlds there were no words to evoke, worlds as insubstantial as clouds, iridescent as dragonflies, and sweet as the heart of a rose.

When she finished the second piece, there was a silence he didn't want to break. He stood absolutely still.

The music died away, and Laura felt herself return to the room. She dissolved the lingering resonance by leafing through the printed music left on the rack by Andre's mother. She felt eyes on her back, and turned to find Andre. An odd expression had captured his face, and he was advancing on her with his hat still on and his gun belt in his hands.

He placed the gun on top of the piano. "I had no idea," he murmured, sweeping his hat off and tossing it into a chair. He was golden-skinned in the blush of the dancing firelight. She inhaled his smell of straw and stables and leather and oil.

It took her another moment to realize he was referring to music. "I told you I play. *Used* to play."

"I expected . . . I don't know, a peacock-pretty sort of talent, not . . . what I just heard."

He was staring at her as though he thought her no more than moonbeams, which amused her in a distracted sort of way—and then irritated her. "The same way you expected Richard's wife to be a hard cold creature without feelings?"

He took one of her hands upon his wide palm and studied the tendony fingers as if he'd never really seen them before.

"Really, Andre, there's no sense making such a bother." She moved her hand out of his, into her own lap.

"You're an artist."

"I'm not. Not anymore."

"A person who plays Bach and Chopin the way you just did is an artist."

He'd correctly named the composers. Would he never stop surprising her? She dismissed his opinion, however, with, "I've been told I play too delicately."

"Well, you'll never make a piano-pounder—or a Beethoven, reaching out at the keys like Atlas—but you make up for that in finesse and agility." He paused, thoughtful. "You have precision; passion begins with precision."

"You seem to know a lot about it."

"My mother was a performer in her youth. She knows her way around stage circles—actors and singers and musicians," he said by way of the briefest of explanations. "So this is the career . . . and you weren't sure you wanted to pursue it? Hmm, play some more for me. The 'Raindrop Prelude.'"

Fourteen

Part of Laura was gratified for Andre to hear her play the piano and think she was good at it. Another part insisted that this was not what she wanted him to respect; it was not a true thing about her, not even a thing she liked for certain. It was merely her training, her everlasting training. Nevertheless, her fingers were shaking. Now why should that be? "I don't want to play anymore. I think I—I'm tired."

"Liar," he said, in so gentlemanly a tone she couldn't think how to answer him back. "But I'll take you upstairs."

"Oh! No, I'm not tired!"

He was looking at her peculiarly, as though he felt some new and infinite tenderness for her. Was it surprise?
. . . Awe?

Ridiculous! Andre Sheridan in awe of her? She folded her hands together, ignoring the fact that they were still light with the remembered feel of ivory beneath them. "Andre . . . ?" She inclined her head to one side, intrigued and bemused by the emotions softening his face. She moved a little on the bench, appealing to him to break the spell he seemed to be under. *"Andre?"*

He asked without ceremony, "Did Laird ever hear you play?"

"Once or twice."

"Did he appreciate it?"

Richard, she realized guiltily, was growing distant and

164

shadowy, a blurred figure, very far away. Andre, on the other hand, was here, vividly present, and she'd won his regard and admiration and . . . yes, that made her feel (it shouldn't!) utterly happy.

"Did he?"

She gave him a little shrug.

He turned away from her with a curse, went to the fire, kicked at it—then crossed back to her swiftly, swift as a wolf, despite his size. He pulled her up into his arms and kissed her deeply—worked her lips apart and roughly probed her mouth. Her breasts were crushed against his chest as his hand pulled open the jabot of her dress. The buttons of her bodice quickly followed.

His mouth trailed downward over her throat. He pushed the bodice back onto her shoulders, managed to do the same with her chemise, and then her breasts were naked. He put his mouth to them, his hands. He murmured, his voice muffled against her skin, "Tell me you want me."

She wanted . . .

She wanted to be held hard and harder still. Her response came as a rude and inconvenient shock, but there was no denying it, there was no denying this rushing pleasure in being crushed to him. She felt as if she were in a dream, a wonderful dream—but it was time to wake up. *Wake up, Laura!*

She brought her hands up to push him away. He captured her arms and forced her to face the really dreadful expression in his eyes. "What frightens you more—that I'm going to make love to you, or that you want me to?"

She blinked at him, pushed against his chest. "I don't, no, I don't, Andre! How dare you even say I do!"

"I've already dared so much, why not that?" His tone was incisive with warning.

He lifted her, and she was held helplessly as he sat on the music bench with her cradled to his chest. She was aware of the hard brawn of his arms, the ridged muscles in the thighs across which she lay. Her hair slipped away from her combs, came down from the knot she'd put it in, fell over his supporting left arm. His right arm now held her waist. She covered her breasts with her hands. "Let me go." Her voice came out too small to sound convincing, even to her.

He stared down at her hands on her breasts, apparently enthralled. "You do want me to make love to you. You're innocent, Laura, and young. I love you for being all that, I guess—but don't try to tell me you don't want me, because I know it just isn't true."

She was mesmerized by the song his words made, recognizing a *libretto* when she heard it. Her mouth went dry just to look at him. She used the only defense she could: "It doesn't matter if I want you or not. I'm married. I know well enough that you're prepared to defy all convention and authority—you scorn things that shouldn't be scorned, Andre! Duty, obligation, honor—those aren't cheap words to just throw away. They mean something, they mean something to me, and make demands on me."

His smile made her shudder. "A most affecting argument; I wonder how I resist it? I'm supposed to care about your wronged husband? I was married once, too—that didn't stop him. And it wouldn't stop him from withering and suffocating you. Now more than ever, I realize I can't let you go back to him. But we're talking about us right now."

He brushed her hands from her breasts, and when his own fingertips touched them that look of awe wreathed his face again. She didn't have the strength or the will to deny him a second time.

His hand, callused, slightly rough at the fingertips, glided over the firm rise of one breast and then the other. She focused on his mouth, suddenly so close above her own. She thought he was going to kiss her, but all at once he rose, with her in his arms. Time seemed to stop as she was held by the dark mystery of his eyes; she hardly realized he was carrying her down the hall, up the stairs. It was as though she were held *senza sordine* all the way, as if each of their heartbeats and breaths were pedaled and held, creating a dreamlike swirl of sounds.

When they reached the upper hall, she stirred in his arms,

yet he didn't put her down. That was when she knew. She started to struggle, but not until they entered the unlit blue bedroom did he finally allow her feet to touch the floor. Even then he didn't speak. He lit the lamp by the bed, then unbuttoned his cuffs. She watched him, knowing she couldn't get by him to the door. Her dress was still pulled open over her shoulders; she was covering her breasts with her hands again. "Damn you, Andre Sheridan."

"Keep on like this, and they'll say *I'm* teaching you all those swear words."

"You . . . you bastard."

"Well, I suppose you could have got that one from me."

Her voice continued soft, deceptively unemotional. "You will have your revenge, won't you?"

"I've wanted you from the first minute I saw you. And you wanted me—that first night in Laird's bedroom, I saw it in your face. You were so naive you didn't even know you should hide it." He moved toward her, emitting a vivid impression of tremendous, controlled energy.

She backed away. "This is only part of your plan. I mean nothing to you."

"You know better than that."

"When Richard didn't show up at the cabin, you decided—"

"I decided to claim you. And I am."

She glanced quickly around the room, looking for an avenue of escape. He extended his hand to catch the edge of her sleeve. She couldn't fight him without exposing her breasts. He used her hesitation to push her bodice and chemise further down her arms. "I can't wait any longer, Laura. I want you, and I'm going to make love to you. Fight me if you can. It won't stop me. And in the end, it won't stop you."

"You're despicable!" Her voice was icy. She stepped beyond his reach, came up against the wall. "You can't carry a woman away from her wedding, keep her prisoner for—how long has it been? Two weeks?"

"Eleven days."

"Eleven days and then expect her to let you . . ."

167

Her challenge lay like a flimsy barrier to be felled with a single blow. "Are you sure?" He moved closer.

She panted with panic as his hands closed on her bare shoulders. He held her there, remaining at a little distance, and despite the considerable gnawing and churning going on inside her head, she knew she didn't really want to withdraw from that hold. She knew how things really stood with her. She had run away to California to get something more out of life than she would ever be allowed at home. She'd felt a need—to taste the wind, to take part in the world, to see things far away. She'd married Richard looking for those things—but she'd never felt with Richard what she felt with Andre.

"I love you," he said softly.

"Oh, no more lies!" she pleaded, turning her face aside. "You've got me so tangled in lies, bigger and bigger ones. They'll break my heart if I believe them."

"You love me, too."

They stood looking at one another. Part of her wanted to fight him; part of her wanted to step forward into his arms, feel his soft cotton shirt against her bare breasts, her mouth against his throat.

The dark windows were rain-washed. The glass panes rattled with the wind. The silent looking glass above the bureau watched their every breath. Andre broke the silence. "Say it, Laura. You love me." His eyes glinted.

She swallowed. She'd made vows, vows of fidelity and faith. But when she looked outward with her heart for Richard now . . . she couldn't find him.

"I . . ." her voice was thin, "I'm attracted to you," she confessed. But added quickly, "This whole business is so senseless and foolish, though."

The room was cool; did that explain the chill that shimmied down her spine? Her teeth wanted to chatter. A shudder took her.

"You're trembling. Are you cold? Afraid? Don't be afraid, sweet."

Her answer was barely audible, even to her. "I'm not."

He held her at arm's length again, his smile full of tenderness. "I'm going to take your clothes off, then you can get into bed." He pulled her hands from her breasts, and bent to kiss the exposed hollow of her throat. She stared up into his black eyes as he slipped the dress off her. One by one, he expertly divested her of her clothes, until she was completely naked. Then he pulled the combs from her already loosened hair.

She stood rigid, ashamed of the intense desire she felt to lean into him, to stretch lengthwise against him, to feel the hard length of his clothed body against her bare skin. At the same time she fought not to cover herself or turn away from his gaze. Never had she felt so vulnerable.

He lifted a hand to pluck at the trembling pink of one breast through the cascade of her hair, then whispered, "Under the covers with you."

She started for the bed. He reached out and got her from behind by both breasts, tugging her back to him. She did stretch against him now, leaned back against his chest and exulted in the feel of his warm callused hands on her. Then he let her go.

She felt warmer in the bed. He finished his own undressing, keeping her eyes locked to his all the while, as if to keep her charmed, as if to hold her pinned to the mattress. His body exuded power. The lamplight carved the muscles of his back when he half-turned to throw his trousers over the rocker where his discarded shirt already lay. He made no attempt to hide himself; he came to her naked and muscled and unashamed.

Then he was uncovering her a little, not taking her into his arms yet, however, but allowing his glance to drift over the slopes of her breasts. She stared up at him, trying to launch herself into this agreed-upon surrender. He pulled her onto her side against him, fully against him, and his hands moved up and down her back. She felt awkward; she didn't know what he expected of her. She lifted her face to touch his lips with her own. When she pulled back, he was looking down at

169

her, his eyes gone very dark. "Touch me," he said.

Her hand lowered, went between them. At first she was startled by his size, but then said wonderingly, "It's soft."

He smiled to himself, his eyes closed. "I hope not."

"It *is*—I mean—"

"I know what you mean, sweet."

He opened his heavy eyelids, and she wrapped her arms around his neck and brought his mouth back to hers. He took control of the kiss and opened her lips. Hot and swift, his tongue plunged in, filling her mouth. Her hands ran over his chest and across his broad shoulders. With a groan he lifted his head an inch. "Are you sure you've never done this before?" There was affection in his eyes.

"Fairly certain."

"Then how did you get so good so quick?"

He pushed her back into the mattress. His hands went to her breasts. At first she held back, but then his dark head dipped. His tongue flicked a nipple; she felt it grow rosy and erect. He enfolded the other breast, rolling it beneath his left palm. Now both felt tight. She didn't try to pull away from what he was doing, and thrilled to know she couldn't have done so anyway, for his right arm was banded around her waist so tightly, she was as good as welded to him.

He pushed the blankets lower, his mouth followed. His lips trailed hot kisses down her abdomen, pausing at her navel. Her breath lifted and fell like a pulse in the hollows along the sides of her belly. When his hands urged her thighs apart, she half-rose, reached out to stop him.

He came up to kiss her lips again. "All right, sweet. But I'd like to look at you sometime, and kiss you there."

Suddenly, with a groan of male satisfaction, he covered her. His powerful thighs straddled hers, making her aware of the urgency of his desire. He crushed her pleasantly beneath him, all tenderness gone from his kiss now. She cradled him in the valley formed by her upper thighs. He seemed awfully big, but she wasn't afraid, especially since she'd handled him and found him so velvety.

His hands explored her, all her rounds and shallows and corners and joints, and though his touch was no longer gentle, neither was it so rough that she didn't like it. Strangely, she gloried in it; she felt she was awakening to the world more and more.

The contours of his rippling muscles fascinated her. She traced them experimentally, then cupped his neck with trembling fingers—for he was approaching her thighs once more, stroking them, and she knew enough of what he was about to cling to him expectantly. He pressed his knee between her legs, opening her, spreading her, running his fingers smoothly up her legs.

The tip of his tongue tasted the concavity at the base of her throat. "I'm just going to touch you now." And he did, reaching into her drenched furrow and coaxing it open with his finger and thumb. She gave a terrible shudder, then relaxed with his light, stroking movements. He worked her until she arched wantonly. Her body seemed a flame of soft silver fire.

She made sounds. Her hips lifted against his hand with the mounting tension within her. He encouraged her to open her thighs wide, and she did, not caring about modesty or prudery or anything except that he must not stop. She thought she would scream; she felt an odd need, a need she could only equate with emptiness. Her legs moved restlessly, her back arched, her body chimed and jangled.

He immersed a finger within her, deep, and she cried out, consumed with want. Her breathing came hard and fast. The pleasure—*the pleasure!*—it ascended to its very peak. She felt herself expand past the limits of her body, an explosion of beautiful force rocked her. There was that thing her body could do, that extraordinary breath-held grip closing inside her. She throbbed rhythmically with its intensity. "Andre," she exhaled. She tingled and pulsed and knew that no matter how often this happened it would always be profound.

He looked down on her as she recovered, and though she felt spent and quivery, she lifted her head to kiss him with an

171

impetuousness born of all her new knowledge. He loosened from her embrace and pushed her legs wide again, placing himself where his fingers had probed.

"Wait!"

"Now don't be scared," he murmured, feeding a little on her trembling lips. "Do you know what I'm going to do?"

"I-I think so—I *am* afraid!"

"Sweet—"

"It's going to hurt! It's too big!"

He kissed her deeply, then whispered against her mouth, "Love, it's what you're made for. And what I'm made for. It might hurt just a little at first, because you're a virgin. But then it won't. You'll like it. Don't you like the other—when I touch you?"

"Yes," she said reluctantly.

"This will be good, too. I promise you."

He showed her how to draw her knees up for him. She lay still, waiting, with her eyes closed. He took her mouth as he eased himself into her. He slid in slowly, barely pushing, until she felt stretched to the tearing point. He pushed a bit further. She pulled her mouth away from his, spurning his kiss with a sharp intake of breath.

He lifted his upper body onto straight arms, pulled out of her, then pushed in again, creeping deeper this time. She tried not to resist, but he felt enormous. Her eyes opened wide in a silent appeal to him for mercy.

"I don't like to hurt you, sweet," he said. "Relax, open yourself to me."

She tried to. It felt indecent, but before she could tighten again, he lunged into her. It happened so quickly. "Oh—*oh!*" She splayed her hands over his flexed chest. Tears started and rolled from the corners of her eyes into her hair. Some obstruction, some opacity within, had been broken. He was in her body. She was widened and opened—and stuffed mercilessly.

She wept another pair of silent tears as he looked down on her with contrite affection, murmuring. "Sweet, my sweet, I'm so sorry." He waited a moment, keeping himself deep

172

inside her while she adjusted to the new sensation of being distended. Then he began to move, carefully at first, gently. "Can you bear that?"

"I-I guess."

He slipped out of her a little ways, then pressed back in. "All right?"

It dawned on her that this was how it was done. And next time, she felt a pang of some sort. "Ooh!"

He stopped.

"Oh, no—do it again!"

His grin was brief. He did as she asked, and went slightly deeper, and she felt a deeper pang, not of pain, but of pleasure. "Like that?"

"Yes, oh yes."

The next one was exquisite. Her arms slid around his neck. It was like a signal to him; he came down upon her.

Yet she sensed he was practicing self-control; he was purposefully inducing a heat within her. She felt the slowly churning muscles of his back. He was taking his time with her, letting her find that if she arched to meet him, her pleasure was doubled. Each time she did, lovely tremors erupted somewhere near the base of her spine; they formed chords.

His thrusts became gradually more vehement. "Laura, I love you," he said in the midst of a plunge.

She didn't answer, but let the sonorous chords flow through her as she urged him on. He grew more demanding, his body lay heavier on her. Her reward for bearing it came rushing at her, taking her outer edges first, radiating in waves toward her center. There was a split second pause of nearly unbearable sensitivity, an undulation passed through her and shook her with a force that drove its way up into her throat; she gasped.

"That's it, that's it, sweet," he said. "I feel you, God, I feel you!" His breathing stopped abruptly, and his arms crushed her to him with strength barely checked. He made one more deep and total lunge into her, making her cry out, and then clamped her to him. She almost felt the upward rush within him. His final turgidity awed her. Then the shaft of him pulsed and pulsed again. She could feel his surge, his bursts—four, five of them . . . and another . . . and then another . . . and then the last.

He was holding her hard, her lips were pressed against his shoulder. She tasted the salty sheen of his skin. After a moment he seemed to realize he was near to crushing her. He let go a little and looked down on her. He still occupied her, was still erect. Her blood still pounded through her veins. "Laura," he said, "you feel so good." He moved within her tenderly, once, twice, forcing out the last spasms of delight. "I'm sorry for hurting you," he whispered.

"It doesn't matter now. And I'm glad it was you."

His eyes crinkled when he smiled. "So am I."

He reluctantly withdrew from her, with a flow of warmth. She felt his hot fluid between her legs for the first time. It was rather startling. "I'm messy."

He rose and washed himself and brought a cloth dampened in water from the pitcher. She reached to take it, but he said, "Let me." As she suffered him to uncover her, he said, "Don't be shy with me anymore." He sat on the side of the bed and kissed her belly. Then he leaned on one hand to examine the cleft between her thighs. She was shocked! She felt swollen and flooded and very very naked. But if this was something he desired . . . she stirred up her courage.

"You bled some." He used the cloth to cleanse her. She was so sensitive, the feel of the nubby material, though he was being gentle, was almost unbearable. He discarded it, and now his lips grazed her, touched her bud. Gently, gently, he caressed the edges of her opening, which still felt engorged. Her breasts shivered lightly, yet she suffered him to explore, to search, to heal any remaining injury. He made a low and throaty sound.

Suddenly he stretched up beside her again, and took her head onto his shoulder. She pressed closer to him, running her fingers through the mat of hair on his chest. (How often she'd wanted to do that!)

"You're mine now."

174

She didn't argue. She closed her eyes and snuggled into his neck to sail and dream and remember, to better savor this new feeling of tingling, of total, satisfied exhaustion. Yes, if he would have her, she would belong to him, to this man, this wonderful man.

This is my life now, she thought. He has claimed me. He's given me a place beside him. She felt a great relief. She had the moon. She had it in the palm of her hand.

Fifteen

Rain from the close and leaden sky pecked at the windows as the first scud of daylight grew. Clouds tumbled over one another, pushing and shoving in their hurry to get out of the way of the wind. A lone blackbird, caught out too far from its nest, tipped a wing, caught the full force of the blast, and was whirled away. It was a dark dawn, the kind to instill dark premonitions, the kind when one could imagine winter coming and enduring.

Laura rolled her head. Andre wasn't there. Perhaps it had only been a dream. No, the tenderness between her thighs, the trickle of remembered passion was no dream.

She stared up at the moving rain shadows on the ceiling. The dreary morning and her conscience combined to make her feel she'd done a terrible thing. She shivered as she washed and dressed. Her clothes felt dank with a cold that seemed to go to her bones.

She stared out the window at the shadowed wilds of the foothills. She put her forehead against the smooth glass and closed her eyes. She could see everything with almost unbearable clarity: Andre had only wanted her because she was Richard's, and now that she had betrayed Richard—why should either of them want her?

She straightened. With her hair in a neat crown of braids, she left the room. She felt like that bird facing into the wind, leaning against the pressure with an almost combative smile.

Andre came into the room when she was halfway down

176

the stairs. She stopped several steps from the bottom. His ear to ear grin daunted her. Was he going to ridicule her?

His sleeves were rolled to his elbows, exposing his arms, his strong, firm, supple arms, the muscles rippling sensually under the thin cotton. His shoulders seemed broader than ever. He seemed tanner. As he moved toward her, she was aware as she hadn't been before of his legs. They were long and muscular like his arms, perfectly formed, and covered, she knew, with dark soft hair.

"Sleep well?" he said mischievously. He blocked the bottom of the stairs. "I didn't have the heart to wake you when I got up. I knew if I did, then I wouldn't have the heart to get up."

When she didn't answer, his expression changed. "Regrets, Laura?" Did it only seem he was less certain of himself suddenly? She searched his face in vain. He was so handsome! A lock of dark hair had fallen onto his forehead. A warmth shot through her stomach at the sight of it.

He climbed toward her until his face was on a level with hers, and took her arms in his hands. They felt huge, those hands; they gave her a little shake. "Talk to me."

She turned her face away. "Do . . . do you . . . ?" She looked back at him, tears standing in her eyes. "Are you finished with me now?"

He leaned nearer. "What's that supposed to mean?"

"I—I gave you what you wanted. Surely your revenge is complete now. May I go?"

He regarded her. "You gave me what I wanted?"

She looked away, trying desperately to blink away the glaze over her vision.

"Are you saying . . . ?" He seemed on the verge of saying something blistering, then seemed to check himself. "No, you think I used you," he said quietly. "If I didn't know how inexperienced you are, I'd be mad as hell. Mad as *heck*—I have to start watching my language. But that you could even *think,* after what happened between us, that I didn't love you—or is it that you never believed I did? You thought it was all a lie, didn't you?" He seemed on the edge of losing his temper again in spite of her inexperience. "How can I convince you? What will it take?"

There was something in his eyes, something she believed, something reassuring. It prompted her to whisper, "Oh, Andre, I'm so ashamed."

"Ashamed! Of what?"

"I shouldn't have let you, I shouldn't have let you."

"Make love to you? Is that what you're talking about? Laura, what we did was good, it was right. You know that, don't you?"

"No." She forced a tight smile. "I don't."

His face was creased with concern. "I told you I was going to take you whether you cooperated or not."

"But I did cooperate, didn't I? Please, you don't have to keep pretending to like me. I know what you must think of me now—"

"Don't talk like that," he commanded.

"—what any man would think of a woman who—"

He leaned his head to brush her lips with his. And when she still tried to speak, his mouth took complete control of hers with a long, liquid kiss that rushed through her veins and melted her vertebrae. She was too dazed to go on when he freed her. Too dazed and . . . she hadn't come up with a word for that sudden moistness down there yet.

He said, "I shouldn't have left you alone, not for a moment. I should have realized how you'd feel. Come down here." He pulled her down the remaining stairs. She tried to resist, but lost her balance, and fell against him. He supported her until her feet were firmly on the dining room floor, then he embraced her. "I'm not very good at lying abed, but now that I've got more reason, it shouldn't be a very hard habit to acquire. If I'd been there with you this morning, believe me, you'd know right now how much I 'like' you." She hid her face under his chin; his voice rumbled against her forehead. "I wouldn't have given you time to feel ashamed of anything."

"But I was so . . . so . . . surely a lady isn't supposed to . . ."

"To enjoy it?" He laughed a little. "You don't know the half of it yet. There are so many ways . . ." He laughed again, so that she raised her eyes. A peculiarly tender and great-hearted smile played about his mouth. "There are so many ways, sweet." He laughed again, teasingly this time. "In fact I'm tempted to give you another lesson right now. How about there."

"On the table?" She tried to push out of his arms, and when they tightened fractionally, she struggled in earnest. "You wouldn't—Andre!"

"Of course I wouldn't," he said agreeably, but with a sly, lid-fallen look. "Mmm, your eyebrows are as soft as moth's wings." Yet even as he spoke so affectionately, with his lips moving against her brows, he began to back her toward the table.

"Andre—get away from me." She knew only too well that she was quite capable of being seduced by him again. Maybe even in a dining room.

He was biting his bottom lip to hold back his grin. "I bet you had no idea men and women did things like that outside their bedrooms. You need to fling off all these tortured, niggardly thoughts about sex, sweet. You know you have a mind to let me, but you're holding back. Not me, I'm ready—and not a bit ashamed of it." He pressed his groin against her, to show her that he was strong and hard, and now flashed a broad grin, so that there was an unmistakable rush of warmth into her cheeks.

As if he'd just noticed, he said, "You know, there's not much of you, is there? Mostly eyes. Eyes big enough to swallow the world. Why, if a man had a mind to throw you on a table—"

"Andre, stop."

A mock-delicate, disgusted grimace came over his face, "'Will he?' she wonders. 'Will he really? On a *table?* In a *dining* room?'" He bent to whisper confidentially, "He might, sweet, and you might like it. Why I bet there are women all over the world being made love to on dining tables this very minute, and all liking it, yielding their honey in dozens of far-flung hives."

She didn't know whether to believe him or not.

"Think about it, me entering you, filling you till you can't

179

hold anymore . . . ah, such large, abject, imploring eyes."

His bawdy talk might very well have exploded the old powers holding her, but just as her hips touched the edge of the table, scuffing footsteps came in from the door to the kitchen. Andre let go immediately. "Soo!" he said with more embarrassment than irritation. "Uh—we'll have breakfast in the parlor this morning, by the fire. Is that all right, Laura?"

She nodded, keeping her face downcast. She could feel Soo looking at her.

"She your woman now?" he asked Andre plainly.

"That's enough, Soo."

The old man's eyes seemed to flicker with a quaint and reckless heat. "You say you kill Mr. Laird, but you only take his woman. Aieee! What about my daughter? What about you kill Mr. Laird?"

"Soo—" Andre's huge hands had knotted into fists, yet his tone of voice remained placating.

The old Chinaman shook his head as he turned and scuffed out again.

Andre looked at Laura. "I apologize for him." After a moment, he took her chin, forcing her to look up at him. She knew her face was stricken; she couldn't help it. "Don't let him upset you. I'll speak to him later."

"And what will you say? 'Don't ask uncomfortable questions around my whore'?"

Suddenly he was angry—at her. "God damn it, I don't want to ever hear you say that word again!"

She learned too late that now his anger had more power to frighten her than ever. Nonetheless, she said, "Well, it's true, isn't it?"

He collected himself. She watched him visibly tamp his rage down; it was a process that took several seconds, and even then was incomplete. With eyes still smoldering, he said, "You're my fiancée."

"I know what I am," she said miserably. And knew, looking at him, what she would remain. "I must get used to it, that's all."

She glanced back at the door to the kitchen as he drew her toward the parlor. Soo. She suspected the old man had reasons for saying what he'd just said, reasons and motives that were hateful.

They ate a quiet breakfast. Soo remained sulky as he took the leavings of their meal away. Finally, Laura said to Andre, "I'm sorry."

He gave her a puzzled look.

"For using that word."

He smiled sadly, then seemed to rally. "You've behaved badly all morning—doubting me, doubting us. I think you're going to have to be punished."

She wondered at the glint of mischief in his eyes, and braced herself when he rose and pulled her up out of her chair. He laughed. "Don't look so worried. I won't punish you much." He nuzzled his shaven chin against her cheek. "They were understandable offenses, after all." He ushered her across the room and seated her at the piano. "Your punishment is that you must play for me." He narrowed his eyes and tried to mask a shy grin.

Her vision blurred. It wouldn't hurt her to play for him—if only her hands would stop shaking! She fingered the rosewood fretwork and the ivory keys, and stammered, "Any requests?"

"How about Brahms' 'Intermezzo'?"

He turned the nearest armchair and took a seat, while she bent her attention to the piano. She waited to hear the music within her before she ever put her fingers to the keys. Her first tentative touches quickly grew courageous as she waked echoes out of the deeps of the piano. Music filled the air, filled her heart. She felt no faltering or tremor in her hands now. The "Intermezzo" came to her with grace and elegance, very light, like fresh water, crescendoed, then was again sweet and delicate.

When she finished, she couldn't bear to look at him. It wasn't the nervous fear of criticism which she'd always felt with her stepmother. It was, for some reason, that she wanted very badly for him to be pleased.

He said quietly, "That was lovely, Laura. You're *good.*"

Stimulated by such praise, she played for an hour. She was bent over the keys, feeling as though the "Moonlight

Sonata" was being squeezed from her soul right then and there, the bass tones necessarily held *tenuto* style—pedaled, sustained, held—when she realized there were tears on her cheeks. How stupid! How could she get so carried away? She stopped mid-phrase and rose from the bench quickly. "How silly," she said, using her wrist to wipe her face, "I don't know what brought this on."

Andre met her and kissed her deeply.

That kiss remained firm and sweet in her mouth during the rest of the morning; it seasoned everything that passed her lips at lunch; never was there such a flavoring for ordinary food.

"You haven't studied in Europe yet?" he asked as they lingered at the dining table.

"Mama had savings for that, but, well, I never really cared about going. I never cared about being a pianist at all. It was her idea. She'd had some talent when she was younger, but not quite enough, so I was the one who was to achieve her dreams. All those years she kept me at it . . . and she would've kept me at it for the rest of my life."

"She worked you pretty hard?" he said casually.

"It wasn't just that, it was . . ." She was embarrassed to admit it. "Before my wedding, I'd never been to a party, or owned a fancy dress. I don't know how to dance." Her voice dropped. "I've never had a friend." She stole a glance at him. "People in Abfalter thought I was odd. And I am. I don't know how to cook or sew . . . or make lime water . . . or what to do with it once it's made. I'm really very ignorant."

"I gather Laird was the first man to ever court you."

She couldn't bear to hear him speak badly of Richard. She felt guilty enough without that. "He was good to me."

"He wanted you."

"What's wrong with that? At least he didn't *steal* me! He didn't choose me because I was someone else's wife. He chose me—me!—and he didn't give a damn if I couldn't cook and clean or—or play the piano!"

"Don't curse," Andre said without thinking. After a moment he added, "Germany. That's the place for you. You can start your studies there right after Christmas. I don't think Wagner's the one to teach you. He's not accepted in America anyway, and Mother says he's a fault-finding old son of a . . ." He cleared his throat. "Mother says he's cross. But I've met Liszt myself, and I think he just might do. He's a handsome old fellow: white hair to his shoulders and fierce eyes that don't miss anything. He's like a walking volcano. I'm sure Mother would write to him, to introduce you."

She blinked in disbelief. "You've met Liszt?"

"I think you'll like him."

"But . . . no, I don't want to go to Germany!" She felt a panicky loss of control. She'd traveled too far and endured too much only to end up back where she'd begun.

He went on as if he hadn't heard her. "I was there for Christmas when I did my tour, and it was . . . well, you'll have to see it. Thousands of twinkling lights and dazzling trees in the cities—huge fir trees. And the toys in the shops! Booths full of handcrafts along the squares. And if you have a sweet tooth, the marzipan—any object you can think of shaped out of marzipan. I remember feeling it was all wasted on a lone man. It's a city for lovers and children."

"It sounds wonderful." She dreamed, despite herself. It was only an instant of a dream, a sliding elsewhere into fantasy, into a brightness much different from her past. But then she awoke. "I would like to visit there sometime," she said flatly, "but not to study music."

"Laura . . . damn! You're like a horse that bucks and bolts without even a thought to where you're going, as long as you get away. Lessons don't have to be torture, you know."

She laughed lightly, without humor. That was one subject she knew much more about than he did.

He frowned thoughtfully. "I think maybe you were right to run away from home. If your mama is responsible for this denial . . . I don't think I like her one bit."

"And I'm sure she wouldn't like you."

"Probably not. Laura, you have to go to Europe. You have a talent that can't be ignored."

"It certainly can. Just watch me."

He looked as if he might like to slap her. "You'll go to Germany—with me—for Christmas." His face softened.

"Just think of it as part of our honeymoon. I'll take you to Vienna and Paris first, just for the opera. You can absorb Grisi and Malibran, and see how it should be—not a punishment, but a joy."

She answered him with stubborn silence.

She refused to play for him anymore that day. He didn't insist. The storm wrapped about the house. Wind-driven rain rattled the windowpanes, underscoring the sense of comfort inside. The scent and light of a glorious wood fire filled the parlor. Leaning back in his chair, he asked, "What are you daydreaming about? Me? You want me to kiss you?" He wore an expression somewhere between a tease and a caress.

She glanced at him from the corners of her eyes. "Actually, I was thinking about clothes."

"Women!"

"Well, if I'm to stay with you," she felt herself blush, "I can't go on wearing the same gown day after day, nice as it is. All my things are at . . . I don't suppose I can expect to have my trunk sent to me."

"You could always slip into one of my shirts. I have one or two you haven't modeled yet." He held out his hand lazily. "Why don't you come over here and sit on my lap and we'll talk about it?"

She smiled, but didn't go to him. She hadn't quite adjusted to their new relationship yet.

He stood, tended the fire, then suddenly scooped her from her chair into his arms and reseated himself. "I hope you learn to do what I tell you one of these days, because if I have to keep lugging you around all the time, I'm going to be bent like an old man before I'm thirty."

"What a pity."

"Ha! You're cool as the underside of a pillow this afternoon."

She squirmed a bit. "What if Soo should come in?"

"He won't."

"You can't be sure." She wished the man wore shoes with heels you could hear coming.

Andre made a disparaging sound. "Even if he does, you're

staying right where you are." He drew her nearer, holding her inescapably. She was exquisitely aware of the strength in his arms. He said, "I can feel you glowing red right through your dress. Don't you like being near me?"

"This is something I'm not accustomed to."

"What, cuddling? Relax; lie against me, yes." He smiled, and gave her comforting strokes along her hip. "You might as well kiss me, too."

She gave him a businesslike kiss. He grunted. "Your lips will wither if you purse them up like that too often. But what about these clothes? What do you need so badly?" Languorously he stroked down her hip, again and again.

"Only a change of outfits. And I could use another corset. This one is a little loose."

"I don't like corsets." He felt the one she was wearing beneath her gown. "They're ridiculous—all that steel and whalebone. Aren't they uncomfortable?"

"Sometimes. But everyone wears them. And some are pretty, ones with lace."

"Lots of lace then, your breasts shored up with Chantilly lace. Mmm, this is an interesting topic after all."

She gave him a sidelong look, a look that was cut short when his hand curved behind her neck and slowly, deliberately drew her face to his. His lips skimmed warm across hers. After a long minute passed, he said, "You were saying?"

"What . . . ?" Her head lay limp on his shoulder; she was studying the hammering, hypnotic pulse at his throat.

"You were telling me you need some lacy underthings." His finger traced a line from her forehead to the barely indented cleft at the tip of her nose. He raised a brow, a knowing smile curving his mouth as she floundered to recall.

"A corset," she said at last. Her voice was dreamlike, a-tremble, very soft. "And a change of dresses."

"Something smooth and heavy, all cascading silk, that I can take by the handful and lift . . ."

A log in the fire broke, powdering into flames that leapt upward while he nuzzled her throat. She caught his face between her hands and brought his mouth back to hers.

Harpsong sounded.

He murmured, "Maybe we should go upstairs to discuss this. What do you say, my bold, my very brave little virgin?"

In the blue-carpeted bedroom he undressed her, whispering things about her skin, her pale and luminous skin, perfect as a perfect ocean pearl; and he loosened the weaving of her hair, pulling it free so that it fell in a waving cloak around her upper body. Then he undressed himself and lay down with her in the big masculine bed.

When her arms went out to him, he smiled, a slow warming of his face, and he allowed her to explore him. He seemed to curb himself while her fingers threaded the silkiness of his dark, thick hair, the strength of his back, the shape of his shoulders, the curvature of his chest. The stormlight from the windows set his strange eyes under eaves of shadow, threw the great brawn of his torso into sharp relief, and highlighted the strong ropes of muscle over his lower ribs. She envied the fact that using his hands on her seemed to come easy for him. From the first his hands had steadied her, guided her, caressed her—or seized and held her—and always with such confidence.

"I'm not sure what to . . . I mean, how to please you."

His voice was soothing and seducing. "Do whatever you like and I'll like it, too."

Her fingers moved gingerly down. She found him large, pulsing. A tremor of amazed pleasure passed through her as she stroked that immoderate flesh so exotically covered with silk plush. The smooth head of him seemed the same texture as her own lips—specially made, sensitive flesh. With light strokes, she caressed, circled. "Do you like this?"

His laugh came deep and low. "I like it fine—but I won't break." He placed his own hand over hers, showing her she could squeeze harder. "Yes, that's good, very good."

A sharp, hot sensation shot up her thighs. She wanted him, wanted to take him in and feel him in her and over her.

He caught her hand and rolled suddenly. "My turn." He kissed her eyes, her cheekbones, her neck, her breasts. He lay half over her, unreleased, still tight and hot, just glancing her thigh, making an instant fire between her legs. She raised her knee to press against him. How solid he was! She watched him draw a circle around her nipple with his tongue and another pang shot through her. Her breasts stood up brazenly. He saw; he lifted his head.

Their mouths met once more. Then he bent again to her breast and drew as much of her as he could into his mouth. She arched to offer him more. His hand reached for her other breast and encompassed it.

But then he pulled away and threw the covers off and sat up, just wanting to look at her, it seemed, to look at her with eyes cachéd with days of anticipation. At first she lay with her arms crossed over her chest and her hips half-turned, one leg drawn up in concealment. Because of the light falling from the windows behind him, his face was in shadow, while she felt exposed, with every nuance revealed. But his hands pulled her arms down from her breasts, rolled her hips, straightened her leg so that the stormlight fell over all of her.

She lay still, still upon the silken sheets that covered the feathered softness of his bed, and she allowed him what he wanted. And oddly, her body seemed to become beautiful, even to her: her lips, her breasts so unremittingly fondled by his hands, and the path between her thighs he had so freely breached. That she felt beautiful and proud was a source of surprise. Proud was indeed the word, however; she felt illumined by it, as though from within.

Sixteen

Andre reached for Laura, seizing her upper arms and dragging her against his warm nakedness. As he moved her beneath him, his eyes shimmered. He held himself poised, then went into her cautiously. She tried to make herself open to him, yet a small cry escaped her at that smooth, sliding entry. He wrapped his arms around her and nuzzled his face in her hair. "All right?" he whispered.

"Yes, oh, yes," she said softly, with her heart. She had never dreamed she was capable of so much abandon, such intense pleasure.

They lay perfectly still for some minutes; then his movements began, tentatively, barely discernible. Her lips parted, her eyes closed. She pressed herself upward, seeking more of that incomparable feeling of him so hard within her.

Encouraged, he gave her a great delving thrust. She cried out, and he withdrew all the way and lunged again, deep, and again she cried out, louder. Her outcries weren't prompted by pain, even with his shattering drives, even with his flesh going into her flesh and his great weight over her and his arms closed around her so tightly that each cry was *forced* out of her as much as it was called out by how he was pleasuring her.

Their bodies moved together with the cadence of passion. She cried out again and again, like a plucked string. She watched the music of it in her head: braiding lines of melody that streamed from thin, intense rays to throbbing blushes that spread and dissolved; chords layered like the petals of flowers; notes descending like feathers. The pleasure and music mounted like wind before thunder, until—

He paused, holding himself on his forearms. He looked down at her, whispering, "My incredibly beautiful, my indescribably lovesome Laura; I want to stay inside you forever."

She was speechless—and burning to keep him stirring in her. Yet he was making himself heavy; he was pressing down on her to keep her still. She knew the sensation of being completely at his mercy.

"Don't move, sweet," he coaxed. "Kiss me." His mouth came hungering down. His wide palms bracketed her breasts while his lips controlled her lips, directing spasms of desire through her.

She wanted to move so badly, wanted to feel him plunge into her again. She wriggled a bit and groaned. Yet his thighs were so tense they were like stones bisecting her. "Not yet," he said.

"Andre, please . . ."

"Look at me."

She opened her eyes as though drugged, pleading silently until his mouth came down to find hers open, waiting, yearning. He lifted his head a bare fraction of an inch, so that when he murmured now, the movement of his lips, the very words he spoke poured over her mouth like liquid silk. "Now you're going to tell me what you feel for me."

All at once her heart was thumping harder, her wits racing one way and another.

"You said you were attracted to me." There was an instant's pause, then he lifted and delved into her, following her as she arched like some soundless symphony. He stroked once more as she moaned and fell back, shuddering. But then he pressed her down again. And he could be very, very heavy. His strong arms wrapped about her. His tongue slid over her mouth, outlined it.

"Andre . . ."

"Tell me." He didn't move a muscle, he didn't smile.

She felt close to tears. *But I'm terrified, Andre, terrified of all of this and what it means.*

"No, don't cry, sweet. Just say, 'I love you, Andre.'"

There was a terrible wrenching in her mind. "You're a monster to do this."

He murmured, "It's no use calling me names, sweet." He dropped a kiss upon her cheek.

"I hate you."

"Do you, Laura? Do you?" Again he moved, and she gasped and drew her knees higher and strained up against him. He seemed to listen, spellbound, as waves of pleasure washed through her. "'I love you, Andre,'" he prompted.

"All right, I—" her voice seemed to come from a great distance, "I love you."

His eyes blazed with a shocking passion. "What a cautious little heart you have! 'All—right—I—love—you!' *Mean* it!" His voice hadn't risen, but there was a hint of steel in the tone. He clenched his arms about her and thrust into her, saying at the same time, "'I *love* you, Andre!'"

Cautious he called her heart. Torn and tenacious it was, and it swung between her unresisting body and her uncompromising mind. Finally she cried out, "I love you!"

She felt the smoothness, the density of his column, heard the smoothness of his voice: "Again."

"I *love* you!" Then and there, she took her destiny in both hands and welcomed it gladly with a heart spilling with hope. "I *love* you, Andre!" She felt a loss of her self, lost track of where her self ended and he started.

"Yes, you do, and I love you. I am you and you are me. You won't run from me now—God, I love you so!"

She felt he had become a great golden spear with a tip of fire. He drove into her and penetrated to her very heart, and when he drew out, it felt as if he were drawing her heart out with him, leaving her utterly drained by her love for him. The pain and the severe pleasure of it made her moan. The sweetness, the intensity was so desperate she couldn't possibly wish it to cease, nor would her soul be content with anything less ever again.

"You're so beautiful, so magnificent, the way you move for me."

190

It was then that that ecstasy, that miracle of her woman's body, began once more. He arched up, tamping even more rapture into her. Another exclamation . . . and that drawing in, that gathering. Her head tilted forward, her forehed touched his working chest. Gold under pressure, blurred, flowing, molten, alight. Rivers of fiery gilt. That incredible gripping inside, harder, stronger than she had yet known it.

Oh, who would run, who would hide from such bright ruin?

She was finally silent; the great wave had let her down, let her down tranquilly and easily into the presence of him and the earth and the stormlit afternoon. He lifted, raised himself on his elbows, put his hands on the sides of her face and locked his gaze with hers. The silver rainlight flickered in his face. She watched him read the emotions she was unable to conceal. Smiling, he leaned down and kissed her, experimentally, slowly. And she, still stunned by the confession he'd forced out of her—yet with a leap in her blood of pure anguished joy—kissed him back.

Smiling, still thrust far into her, gazing down at her, he moved a bit. He was still rigid and ready. He moved slowly, gently, profoundly within her, and then, like a languid re-enactment of that original great drive, he withdrew and pressed inward again, to the bone.

He did it again and again. Each time he penetrated to that depth, and his eyes almost closed, but didn't quite—not enough to cut the cable of joining between them. He murmured betweentimes, "My Laura . . . my love . . ." between short tender kisses, "my treasure . . . my sweet . . ."

He traced the open circle of her lips with his tongue as her hands ran down and up his back. She clasped him close and began to move with him, in that ancient, slow, and vigilant dance, until with deep and quiet joy she received his climax: the series of beats, repeating and repeating like a heart torn from his clenched and gasping body.

The love she felt had been a gnawing pain within her since . . . she hardly knew how long she'd felt it! Perhaps since he'd walked out of the shadows and into the lamplight in that room in Richard's ranchhouse. Her lips moved: "I

191

love you, Andre." And she knew that something was widened in her heart, forever.

The rain finally stopped after dinner, and with it the wind. Andre took Laura upstairs to bed early, not to make love to her again—he feared injuring her—but to have the pleasure of overcoming her objections to undressing herself in front of him.

At first she demurred modestly, when he lounged on the bed and said, "Take off your things."

"Don't watch me."

"I want to watch you."

"I know you do," she answered, more than a little scandalized. But little by little, she did as he wanted, and stood in her chemise.

"Take that off, too, let me see you." But she wouldn't, and so he pulled her toward the bed and got her on it.

"No," she laughed as he teased and tickled her gently, "No, no, Andre." As he pulled her chemise up, down she pushed it. But then—"Oh!"

Finally her breasts were bared, her thighs opened. "Ooh," she sighed again, and yielded then, and lay quietly for him. How exciting it was to overcome that needless modesty!

He had his arm slung over her now. Her backside pressed agaist his stomach and her hair lay loose all over her and him and the bed. She'd been asleep for an hour or more. In the soft dark he studied the cleanly etched profile of her face. He'd been thinking random thoughts, such as how he would hire a carrige and driver from the livery stable in Jackson until they left for Europe. Once there, he would buy a rig— she would need one when she went to her lessons, did her shopping, made her calls.

Laura! How could this have happened? How could he be so lucky a second time? His arm tightened around her, pulled her closer, so that the top of her head was tucked under his mouth and jaw. Did she understand what she was to him now? Not his woman! And never a whore! And not his prisoner anymore, either. At least he hoped she could never leave him willingly. He hoped he held her bound with the cords of his passion, secured, captured as utterly as he was.

But what about Laird? Could she see that she'd never loved the man, and that he'd never loved her?

Oh, Laura, I want you, and you want me, and can't we, just this once, have what we want? Despite my word given over a grave? Despite yours given in a false ceremony?

When he thought about it, what had she given to him if not her word? "I love you!" she'd said. And she'd given him even more, more than she'd ever given to Laird: her *self*. That was an act of allegiance; that was her testament as surely as any vow of marriage. They were in all respects as much man and wife as the present facts would let them be.

Yet he knew, in all honesty, they couldn't cancel out their pre-existent commitments so blithely. In her case, an annulment was required. How ignorant her stepmother had kept her, for her to not know that such a thing was even possible! How hard it must be for her, believing she was irremediably married to one man and knowing she was irredeemably in love with another. He had to ease her mind on that as soon as possible.

Her breath came and went under his chin. Yes, as soon as possible!

She moved in her sleep, turned toward him, her knee nuzzled between his legs; he felt her naked against his nakedness—and felt once more that wondrous, sensuous, amazed desire she had stirred in him from the beginning.

He felt her gradually waken, and he propped himself on one elbow over her. She seemed unsurprised by his wakefulness. Her fingers combed through the hair on his chest, and stroked lower, going between them to touch his belly, and still lower. He gripped her wrist, pulled her fingertips to his lips and kissed them.

"Let me touch you," she breathed, giving him an imploring look. It was his dream, his fantasy come true. He felt heavy with surrender as he fell onto his back.

She explored him. She'd gained years in boldness and womanhood since last night. Intuitively she put her hand on his slack manhood, surrounded it with her fingers, lifted it.

Soon it was hard and lifting itself, and throbbing. When he couldn't bear her touch any longer, when it had engorged him beyond endurance, he pulled her over him. "Laura," he groaned, "better stop."

She hid her head on his chest and murmured something. "Make love to me," he was sure she'd said so bashfully.

He sighed. "I want to—you don't know how much—but you must be feeling tender. I don't want to hurt you." He could feel her retreat, sensed that she thought he was rejecting her. He stopped her from pulling away. "You've never felt yourself inside, sweeting; I have, and believe me, you're delicate as moonlight—and awfully new to all this."

She bent her forehead against his chest again. When she looked up, he saw her lips tremble. He framed her face with his hands. "Laura, tell me you'll stay with me now. No more running away. Promise me."

She said, "I'll stay with you, I promise. I'll never leave you, never. Oh, I love you!"

He wrapped his arms about her and rolled, settling her down in the bed with himself half over her. "You're mine."

"Yes, I'm yours."

Yet the specter of the man to whom she legally belonged seemed to remain between them. Andre was sure he felt it, and he kissed her almost brutally because of it, crushing her mouth with his lips and his teeth and his tongue. She moaned under him, at the mercy of his heartsore frustration. When at last he released her, she breathed brokenly. He felt things— traces of anger and pain and grief and resentment—and they must have been in his face, because when he lowered his head to kiss her again, she turned away. Immediately he braced himself above her. "I'm sorry. Sometimes I can't help myself."

"You're angry."

"No, I'm not, I'm not, believe me."

Evidently she did. As though water were washing through her, he felt a calm descend on her. Was it a sense of release? Had she put thoughts of Laird aside?

He looked down at her. If she could only see herself. She was genteel, refined, stuffed with virtue since birth. He

194

wanted to say things to her, love words freighted with delicious significance. How he looked forward to teaching them to her, to demonstrating in the weeks ahead the forbidden answers to all her questions.

He kissed her again, and yet again, slowly, whispering, "You're mine . . . mine . . ."

And she also whispered and whispered.

"Andre, can't we do it just one more time?"

"Shhh—look at your skin," he said, trying to direct her attention elsewhere. "It's so white compared to mine, and polished as porcelain." He was holding one of her white breasts with his big brown fingers. "Watch." He bent forward to take a nipple into his mouth, not working it, but just holding it with his lips and resting his tongue against it. When he took his mouth away, the hard tip had relaxed and flattened into a puff of pink. "See? They're like rosebuds that open in warm air."

She probably didn't realize that her breathing had slowed. She reached to touch his temples. Thinking that he'd distracted her, he turned his face into her wrist, nibbled at that sensitive inner skin with his teeth.

She whispered, "How long do we have to wait then?"

He moved with silent laughter. "What have I unleashed— the real Lorelei?" Her own shamefaced giggle earned her an embrace of grand keen relaxation. And then they were both laughing, the hushed private laughter of lovers abed.

She seemed interested in getting to know his body, however, whether or not they were going to make love. She lay with her hand on his chest. Her fingers trailed along his ribs, from under his arm, up and over, under the other arm. "You have a big chest," she said.

With a chuckle, he spread a hand over her breasts. "Hmm, you have a nice, soft, bumpy chest."

It set her to laughing again. He put his hand over her mouth, remembering with a pang that Soo was in the house.

Soo! What am I going to do about Soo? He didn't know. He would think of something, but . . . *I don't know!*

"You're a noisy one in bed, you know that?" he said. But now she had the giggles in earnest, and in the end he had to kiss her quiet. When he lifted his mouth, he murmured, "I can't believe how good you are."

She sobered instantly, and turned her backside to him.

"Laura—what's the matter? Oh Christ, are you hurt? Was I too rough earlier?" His hand delved between her thighs to cup her.

She closed her legs, shutting his hand in, and turned on her back once more. "No," she said in a small voice.

His chest came down tenderly on her breast, brushing, his lips barely kissing. She clutched him and buried her face in the hollow of his shoulder. "Oh, Andre, I'm not good, I'm bad."

"The hell you are! You're so damn good you—"

"I'm an adulteress."

"You are not! That marriage wasn't legal. Don't do this to yourself. Don't do it to us. You *are* good! So beautiful and good!" He comforted her against him now, and kissed the top of her head where it rested beneath his chin. "Whatever blame there is is mine. Not yours. No, sweet, don't cry. I'm going to make it right; I'm going to take care of it. We'll be married before Christmas."

"We can't."

"We can. I'm going to see to it, I promise."

He knew she didn't believe him, yet she asked, with a gratitude that made him feel like scum, "You really would marry me?"

"My God, yes! I want to be with you like this every night for the rest of my life."

She was quiet for a moment, then whispered, "Andre? Can I stay with you even if we can't get married?"

He sighed. "Nothing's going to keep us apart."

"Can . . . can we make love every day?"

He hid his smile and said soberly, "Only if you'll take your chemise off for me next time I ask."

"Well . . . you have to promise not to tickle me."

"I promise—but only if you let me make love to you on the dining table."

"Oh, Andre, that's wicked!"

"I know, but you'll let me, won't you?"

"Well . . . maybe once . . . someday."

He wanted to shout with laughter and triumph. Here she lay clasped to him, her eyes still bright with tears, her thighs warm with ready passion, and suddenly he felt lost in this amazement of love and friendship and intimacy he'd found.

She said after a while, "I hear your heart."

He tightened his arm around her more. "Your heart." His voice seemed smoky to his own ears. "I gave it to you when I stole that little cautious one of yours."

In one of the dark, dark hours before dawn, Laura half-heard the palpitant tread of a saddle horse galloping away from the house. The sound was unmistakable, but in her dreams she confused it with the sound of Andre's heart—her heart now—and she wasn't alarmed.

Seventeen

It was just after dawn and the sky was soft as lake water when Laura discovered Andre's absence in the bedroom. She knew it was his habit to rise early, but as the minutes ticked by, the silence of the house seemed to become a strangely living thing. It made her nervous. She decided to dress and go find him. He was probably having an early cup of coffee by the fire in the parlor. She would surprise him, since he thought her such a lazy lay-abed.

She felt disappointed when she saw his gun belt gone from the shotgun rack by the front door, along with his hat. The parlor was empty—and cold, too, which was unusual, for lighting a fire had always seemed his first thought in the morning.

She checked his study, the room opposite the parlor. She'd never been in it before. The view out the windows was latticed with patterns of dark branches from the dark walnut tree, but a rose and beige floral rug and several botanical prints lightened the shadowy feel. Andre wasn't at the big rolltop desk, however.

She heard a sound in the dining room. She went back down the hall, putting on a smile for him. "Oh—Soo. I was looking for Mr. Sheridan."

Soo didn't answer, and the moment began to slide into a curious feeling of timelessness. Something about it frightened her. She looked for the root of that fear: what came to her was the sound of those galloping hooves that seemed to have threaded her pre-dawn dreams.

"He gone."

"Gone?" She shook her head and smiled. "Where? Riding? Hunting?"

Soo didn't answer. Still smiling, she said to that odd look on his face: "No."

Before her own face could crumple with fear, she turned and took the stairs again, so fast she tripped on her hem once. She hauled her skirts up to show rather more of her ankles than was seemly, and kept going. She re-entered the bedroom breathlessly, as if borne on a high wind. She went to the bureau. His shaving equipment—he'd moved it in here with great ceremony yesterday, along with his clothes. She pulled open each drawer, she looked about the room—every article he'd moved in was gone.

Gone!

All this she saw in the space of a minute, then she spun back out into the hall, running to look in each room, chasing echoes of her own making.

Finally she went back to the head of the stairs. Soo was there, in the dining room, waiting. "He gone."

"He's not . . . *Andre!*" Desperate, and feeling the abyss, the unbearable hurt, yawning ahead of her, she started down the stairs. *"Andre, where are you? He wouldn't leave me! He loves me!"*

Soo only stood there.

She stopped dead at the foot of the stairs. Pain stabbed through her. She suffered such a sudden ebbing-out of trust and faith that she cried aloud—and stumbled, blind, all but dead, toward a chair. She felt something beyond mere grief; it was a sense of herself suddenly incomplete, bereft of a vital part; something had been ripped away, leaving a ragged edge, a wound. She knew that life was going to be forever different now . . . . Then, abruptly, all emotion left her, al feeling, all sensation, and she sat staring at the Chinaman blankly.

Soo watched a shiver run through her, and then another. He watched despair, black and ruinous, creep in upon her. He watched it with satisfaction.

He brought her coffee and pressed a cup of it into her hands, peering into her pallid, washed-gray eyes. He brought her food, for it wouldn't do for her to faint. She took a few bites, but then she spoke again, "Did he . . . say anything?"

"He say you better go back to Mr. Laird now."

She seemed dazed, didn't seem to register the words. After a moment she asked, "What?"

He almost grinned. She was weak—a pitiful thing—not like his daughter. This one wouldn't take her life rather than face her husband dishonored. The very thought of Ling brought back to him that green evening of July when he'd watched her burial, and heard *his* promise: "I won't forget; I'll never forget." The words thundered into Soo's mind and left it enraged for several seconds.

He recalled what he was about. "I take you town. He leave money for you buy ticket for stagecoach. You go home Mr. Laird."

"Home? No," she shook her head stupidly, "he loves me."

His gaze measured her lack of assurance. She looked up at him, and he was surprised to see she was hardening her features in an effort to keep from showing what she was feeling. "No, Soo, I don't believe—"

"He say I put you on stage." And the sooner the better, he thought.

She stood—but didn't move any farther. She acted as if she'd already forgotten what he'd said. She stood staring at nothing. "You get things upstairs, we go," he said impatiently. He was glad she wasn't crying, but he wished she would move a little quicker. "You got to go."

"Yes . . . I suppose there's nothing else to do." Her voice was the voice of a dead thing. She pushed off from the table and headed for the stairs.

Later, when he saw her onto the stage in Jackson, he couldn't resist delivering one last blow between those watery eyes. "Missy." She turned to look at him from the door of the stage. "He leave one word for you to tell Mr. Laird: Revenge. You tell."

She winced. "Oh!" she whispered, "oh, God!"

*   *   *

The bone-jarring Concord coach ride out of Jackson was something Laura would never remember clearly. It was all a jangle of harness, a clip-clop of hooves, a grinding roar of wheels—and the pain of unshed tears in her throat. It was as if an unseen line connected her to Andre, a line that was being pulled more taut with each mile that separated her from him, a line that was being tested, that would soon break.

The break came early the second day of her journey, with a raveling, tearing agony. Finally the tears slid down her cheeks, heedless of her fellow passengers.

In the lower foothills, the sunshine dabbled, the terrain became less vehement, more unassuming. Grass-covered slopes followed one after other, gradually leaving the steep V-ed gullies and canyons behind, until the open savannas of the Great Valley, scattered with dark valley oaks, came into view. The stage driver yelled and pulled his rig to a halt at the entrance to Laird Ranch about the time the setting sun was turning the western cloud caps pink. The driver voiced his concern that Laura would have to walk the mile-long road that led to the house, but she ignored him—she acted like she was a bit tetched in the head—and since he was a bit late already, he released the coach's brake and slapped his reins at the rumps of his team.

Laura walked with her only luggage—the wooden case that had once belonged to Andre's grandmother. (If she could believe even that much of all the lies he'd told her.) From far away she saw the rough cluster of barn, bunkhouse, and ranch house. From the pastures behind the fences, cows watched her. One bull, a great, blunt-headed brute, seemed to accuse her angrily.

Everything was quiet. She saw that a new branding corral was being built. The lumber lay in a ranch wagon waiting for the men to drive the rest of the tar-dipped posts tomorrow. It seemed everything was going on in a normal manner. A stranger couldn't have found much indication that the owner's bride had been missing for two weeks, after being abducted on her wedding night.

Finally Laura stood at the front door. She stood there a long while without opening it. She wasn't quite sure what to do, really. Did she have the right to just walk in now? She envisioned finding Richard in his office, so surprised and shocked that his face stared vacantly into hers, as if he'd forgotten who she was.

She fumbled with her hair, and turned to scan the empty bay windows wherein she'd made her vows to him. The glass reflected the billowing pink clouds over the western mountains. An ocean of silence roared in her ears. At last, her hand trembling, she reached for the doorknob.

But then she removed her fingers again, cautiously. She backed away, and surely would have turned back for the road if the door hadn't opened by itself just then.

Richard was there, right there, within the frame of white woodwork. Quick, restless, impatient Richard. Built for walking with his long legs, though he never went anywhere except on a horse. Bravely, she looked up at him. He was squinting slightly in the brightness of the last gleams of the sun. His mouth hung a little open—in just the way she'd feared it might. They stared at one another while seconds ticked and ticked by. Her heart had clenched and was trying to beat again. She felt caught between flight toward him and flight away.

A preoccupied voice came from the hall behind him. "Barbed wire for a mile of fence—even saying we only use three lines—I don't think we can get by with less'n a thousand pounds. Mr. Laird, you going out or what?" Page Varien, the ranch foreman, poked his good honest face around Richard's shoulder and saw Laura. "Well!" he said, with amicable uneasiness.

The spell broke. Page edged past his employer to tap the brim of his hat in the merest of greetings, then he disappeared quickly. Laura couldn't help but notice that his reception, cool as it had been, was still warmer than Richard's. Her husband looked at her as though she were a long way off—or was it that he wished her a long way off?

A cruel suspicion came over her then, a dark idea, an unworthy idea. Others followed it, however, each as black and ugly as the first. She drove them off as Harriet, the housekeeper, appeared. Always conservative about her employer's choice of bride, she eyed Laura with an especially skeptical look now.

Richard's reception continued cold. Coldness was in the set of his mouth. In his silence. In his hard, proud eyes which probed Laura's face and hair, the dress he'd never seen before, even her body, as though he were looking for fingerprints. At last he said, "Looks like you've come back." He moved, allowing her entrance at last. "She's back, Harriet," he said stiffly. "Aren't you, honey?"

"Yes." ·

She couldn't bring herself to say she was glad.

He didn't seem to notice. At least his face didn't change. "Harriet'll take care of you. Harriet, get her whatever she wants." He seemed eager to shuck her off onto someone else. "You want anything?"

She believed she was better off wanting something than nothing. "I—I think I would like a bath."

"A *bahhth*, huh? Yeah, Harriet can get you that."

Laura followed the housekeeper's square, solid back to the master bedroom, where she stood near the edge of the big walnut bedstead in a sort of stupor. She'd escaped for two days now into her mind, where she'd found the illusion of control. The time had come to emerge, to face the world. There were things going on here that she couldn't ignore.

She smoothed the white crocheted spread with her open hand, trying to think. What kind of a welcome was this? They were treating her so strangely: Richard seemed dismayed to see her; Page acted as if she had leprosy; and Harriet . . .

Without speaking, Harriet was going through the process of bringing in a tub and several buckets of hot water. In the meantime, Laura took the tortoiseshell combs from her hair and brushed it out.

"Thank you," she said when the tub was full and steaming. The woman nodded curtly. "Harriet . . ." Laura hesitated. She'd felt before her marriage that the housekeeper nursed misgivings about her, but the few times they'd met, Laura had taken pains to reassure her that the new Mrs. Laird had no great desire to turn the ranch house upside down with new ways, and Harriet had seemed to gradually come to accept her. That was all vanished now. "Harriet, why are you angry with me?"

The woman actually sniffed. "I'd think that was clear."

"I'm sorry, but it isn't." She couldn't know, could she, that Laura was an adultress? It wasn't possible.

"You marry a man and run off the very same night with another one. And then you come back—just show up on the doorstep! What happened? Your fancy feller leave you high and dry?"

"Fancy fel—" She responded with her nerve ends now. "I didn't run off! I was taken, *stolen!*" She swallowed several times. Then, unable to hold back any longer, she cried, "How could you think that?"

Harriet remained admirably cool. "Mr. Laird told us about the letter you left."

"I didn't leave a letter. How could I? The man was there," she pointed behind the door, "and he threw me around until I fainted and cut my dress off and tied me up and carried me out to his horse. There wasn't any letter!"

"Now Mrs. Laird, don't get so riled." She drew herself up. "I only know what the mister said."

Laura sobered. "Richard told you there was a letter and that I ran off with someone."

"That's what he said. Now, I don't think this is none of my business. You and him got to settle your own differences. It's nothing to do with me. I just work here. Your tub's getting cold. Better use it while you can."

Laura didn't linger in the bath. She found fresh clothing in the chifforobe and slipped into a beribboned chemise, then a chamois gown with a ruffled collar. Taking a deep breath, she turned toward the door. She was terrified of what lay before her now: facing Richard again.

The parlor had long ago been divested of its wedding bouquets and banners. It was back to its staid convention, its dark green horsehair furnishings and gold draperies. The view out the jutting bay windows was still peaceful, however. Richard was standing in them, looking out. One window was cracked open a little, letting in the evening air, which had a

204

trace of mugginess to it from the recent rains. Laura came to a stop behind the marble-topped center table.

He turned slowly, and after a moment said, "You don't look too much the worse for wear."

"Why did you lie to Harriet? What's been going on?"

He shrugged. "I needed some explanation for you being gone."

"What was wrong with the truth?"

"That Sheridan took you?" He moved lazily, around the table, reached out a long arm. She moved away a little, but his arm encircled her waist, forcing her near him. Suddenly he squeezed her roughly.

He knew. Richard had known all along who had her. She felt sick. "Take your hands off me," she said in a voice she didn't know she owned, a low, fierce, venomous voice.

He didn't, though. Instead he pulled her to the green horsehair sofa. She braced herself, but it was useless; he pushed her down and sat beside her, lithe as ever. He had on a quizzical, intrigued, partly amused expression of having stumbled onto a novel sort of game. His smile was faintly derisive. He deliberately kissed her full on the lips.

She pushed him away violently. He laughed. For the first time she noticed that when he laughed it was hard sounding. Now that she thought about it, it seemed his laughter had always been at hidden things, things men laugh at with each other. In the last light coming through the windows, his copper eyes flashed. "Where'd he take you?"

"To . . . but you *know,* don't you?"

He laughed again. "But I want you to tell me. Tell me the whole thing, from start to finish. And don't leave out the good parts."

She was frightened suddenly. That smile on his face was really frightening. To avoid it she stared at the collar of his white shirt that lay folded back against his dark skin.

"Come on, honey, let's have it. Start with when he took all your clothes off. That must've been fun for him. I know how much I was looking forward to doing the same thing."

"Richard . . . oh, Richard . . ."

"How far did he take you that night before he had a go

at you?"

That stung her. "It was you he wanted that night!"

He laughed outright. "Who'd he want the next night then?" All her life she'd been told about hell, but never before had she seen it reflected in a pair of eyes. He spoke lazily. "You'll tell me everything sooner or later—and I want to know *everything*, honey. I wouldn't bet so much as a Mexican dollar you weren't saddle-broke five miles up in the hills." He jerked her chin up so she had no place to look except into those devil's eyes of his. "Did you like it?" His lips thinned when she didn't answer. "Did he like it?"

"Go to hell."

He blinked slowly. "Taught you to talk plain, did he?"

She jerked her chin from his grasp and got to her feet. She would have turned with a swirl of skirts and left the room, but he stood just as suddenly and stopped her with a painful yank of her hand. His posture seemed suddenly intimidating; she was reminded that he was a head taller than she. When he ran his hands down her body, she pushed against his chest, which was as unyielding as a barn wall. One hand held her while the other slid onto her buttocks. "Round and firm and warm, ain't you? And you're my wife, remember? I've got rights." His head came down.

She was his wife—oh God, she *was!* After reminding Andre of it for so long, how could she have forgotten with such fatal swiftness? Her mouth trembled under his kiss. All her safety teetered. The kiss seemed to go on forever. When at last he lifted his head, there was a brooding expression in his face. "What else did he teach you besides how to cuss?"

"Richard, don't," she breathed, catching his wrist as his hand moved from her bottom to her stomach. The tendons she felt were tight as steel. Perhaps he wasn't quite as strong as Andre, yet he was strong enough to tear her apart at the seams. "I—I'm feeling a little sick—I haven't had anything to eat since yesterday morning."

He released her slowly. "I'll tell Harriet to fix you something hot and bring it in the bedroom."

She caught up her skirts to flee. "I—I don't think I can wait. I'll just have a cold snack in the kitchen."

206

His smile was shrewd. He gave the impression of being as alive and supple as an animal. "Don't try to play with me, Laura."

How softly he spoke, but she felt the blade below those words. Her mouth went dry. So it was all true, every bit of it. A girl had died, a man had lost his wife, and to the one responsible it was nothing, merely a shadow in his memory. And he was her husband. "Richard?" she whispered, and licked her lips, "why did you marry me?"

"'Cause I wanted you."

"But you never loved me."

Again he smiled—smiled the way a whip cuts, the way a snake bites.

Laura had eaten as much as she could of the unappetizing meal Harriet gave her: a slice of fried ham, a mound of pickled red cabbage, and a slab of homemade bread daubed with rancid yellow butter. Back in her own room, she lit the lamp and saw herself in the cheval looking glass. Her reflection refused to look even remotely happy. Her eyes had less color than smoke on a sunny morning.

She slipped out of her clothes and into a new nightdress trimmed with princess lace. It was the one she'd meant to wear on her wedding night. Fine threads made designs of butterflies edging the neck and sleeves.

She took the tortoiseshell combs from her hair; it fell to her waist. She brushed it carefully; then, as she placed the brush on the dressing table, the door opened and Richard leaned there. His hooded eyes burned her. "Well," he said, with slow caution, "the wedding night was shot to hell, but I guess we can have some fun together anyway."

Some fierce sense of the ludicrous moved her to a fretful laugh.

"Did I tell a joke, honey?"

Her heart was pounding, pounding, pounding. Why was it she hadn't considered the inevitability of this moment during all the hours she'd traveled on that stage?

He pulled his shoulder from the door frame, shut the door

and crossed the room. As he advanced on her, she backed away. "What's this? Shyness? Were you shy with him—in your underdrawers?"

"Richard, I've been through a terrible ordeal."

"Yeah," he said in a cheerful voice as false as mockery, "well, I won't take too long with you tonight, then you can get some rest."

She backed away until she came up against a bedpost. As he clasped her arms, she said, "Are you going to rape me—the way you did his wife?"

She continued to stare at him for the time of a heartbeat, stared at the malicious light in his yellow eyes, the grin that twisted his thin lips. During that length of time something ugly hung between them.

His arms went around her. She didn't struggle. The truth was, she was afraid to. His nostrils flared; his grip on her became hurtful. He pressed a deep kiss to her mouth. It grew intense on his side, but seemed more desperate than passionate. His tongue swirled around and around, then he hungrily sucked her tongue into his own mouth. Somehow she suffered through it. When he lifted his head, he studied her unwaveringly. "Do you know how much I wanted you?"

"Not enough to save me from him."

He bent his head. "Such a soft mouth," and kissed her again, gently this time. She forced herself to stand still for it. He opened her lips—then suddenly bit her bottom lip painfully. She tried to push away. He drew her back possessively. His hand forced her face upward.

"Please, don't," she begged in a jagged whisper.

"Tell me, Laura, how did he do it? Did he tie you up?"

"No."

"Knock you out?"

"No!"

He considered the import of that. "You really should learn to lie now and then, honey," he suggested softly.

Abruptly, he gave her a savage push that sent her stumbling back onto the bed. He didn't fall on her, however, but only stood looking at her carefully held expression and blanked eyes. She knew his hair-trigger temper had been pulled. She had never considered that he could be truly dangerous to her. She'd never considered she could be hurt. Now she did.

"So he took the trouble to sweet-talk you. And you fell for it. How long did it take him? A day? A week?"

The lampglow highlighted only parts of his face. She saw a muscle standing out in his jaw, saw his fingers clenched into fists. What passed for a smile was really only a baring of his teeth.

"I shouldn't have come back here."

"Why did you?"

She flinched at the cold rage behind those words.

"I wanted you . . . bad. But I'm not sure I want you now." He turned from her, striding toward the door without looking back again. She was left sitting at the side of the bed, as dizzy as if she stood at the edge of the universe.

What was going to happen to her? At the very least he would throw her out. At the very worst . . . my God, the things he might do to her!

Oh, Andre, Andre, when did this plan form in your mind? Before or after you made me love you?

And she *had* loved him.

She'd been blind.

She was not now.

Eighteen

"Did you like it?"

"I won't answer questions like that!" Laura whirled despite the elaborate cascading bustle of her bright green daydress, and stood with her back to the parlor hearth. Her hair was parted in the center with the sides swept back into a chignon, loose ringlets hung down her nape.

Richard slouched in a chair, unmoved by her outburst. He'd spoken no threat—but there was his look, and that was enough. Balanced on his knee was a brown bottle, and as she watched, he swigged down a double swallow of whiskey.

"You've been drinking a lot of that."

He wiped his lips with the back of his hand, glancing at the bottle. "Seems like it, doesn't it?"

She'd never seen him drink before. Between the liquor and the situation, he was growing increasingly insulting, increasingly vicious.

"You haven't answered a single one of my questions, honey. What am I supposed to think about that?"

Laura went to the bay window and held the gold draperies aside. The afternoon was full of wind clouds and cross-grained weather. The blue oaks quivered in their stiff way. The yellow pastures looked faded. And the longhorns, those unlovable beasts with horns double the width of their bodies, simply looked mean. Though his men were hard at work bringing cattle down from the summer pastures, Richard had stayed at home today—to drink and to torment her, it seemed. The first of the returned herds was arriving now. Through the closed windows came the rumble and bellow of cattle on the move. But even that didn't seem to interest Richard.

She asked bitterly, "What do you really want to know?"

He slouched on negligently, crossing one booted ankle over the other thigh. "Didn't you even try to get away?"

"Every time I saw an opportunity." She turned to face him. "Now I have a question: Did you look for me at all?"

"Yeah, sure. Me and Zacariah, at first, then we came home and rounded up a couple of boys and went to Sheridan's cabin. Looked like we'd just missed you."

She stared directly into those copper eyes. She was thinking of the hope she'd nourished for so many days, and Andre's smug arguments against it. She turned to look again at the high-spread sky. "He loved his wife."

She heard Richard move from his chair, felt him close behind her. "Did you like it—when he had you?" he said.

A deadly silence filled the room. She felt his intense stare on her back. He gripped her arms, forced her to face him. She was certain her pounding heart would burst right through the bright green material of her dress. "Tell me all about it, honey." Some demon, some crazy phosphorescence, glittered in his eyes. She had seen traces of that look before, and it had always frightened her. It had a quality of wildness that yanked her stomach. "Tell me."

She didn't like this. He was scaring her.

"Tell me, goddamnit!" He suddenly shook her, hard. "I have to know!" He raised his right fist, held it cocked at the level of her chin, like a loaded rifle. Then he seemed to calm himself, though the fingers of his left hand still dug into her arm. "Why can't you just say it out?"

"Say what?" Such a silly prevarication!

"That you liked it."

"Richard—"

"Say it!" He shook her.

She couldn't speak, yet her silence was condemning.

"Bitch!" He gave her a fierce shove. She fell against a sidetable, and then to the floor, knocking over a lamp. It shattered; the smell of oil filled the room. He stood over her, white-lipped, his hands bunched on his thighs.

"How dare you judge me," she said. "How dare you." She got to her feet and stood quaking, but not with fear, not anymore. "Where were you all the days and nights I was telling him you were coming to help me—when I was warning him you would kill him to protect me? He *laughed* at me for believing in you! When he realized that not even stealing your wife could make you face him, he started on me. He took his hate out on me! You're to blame for what happened!"

"You spread your legs for him like a whore," he said, with a grimness about his lips. "You didn't even fight him."

"I fought him harder than you did! If I'm a whore, you're a coward." She laughed a little crazily. "Yes, I slept with him. He told me he loved me! He even made me believe it! The two of you had me so confused, so frightened . . . . What an easy conquest I must be! First you, with your lying love-honor-and-cherish, and then him, with his lying kindness and seductions! Oh, I've been so stupid!"

She turned and ran from the house. She wanted only to get away from him. She ran past the busy corrals and stock pens, dodged between piles of new and not-so-new cow dung, and, sucking in great gulping breaths, stumbled over the rise of a knoll. Her hair was a-tumble, and as she ran down the opposite slope, she reached up to pull out the tortoiseshell combs before they could get lost. They were all she had of Andre now, and, God help her, she still treasured them.

She sank in a heap at the base of the far side of the knoll, a place protected from the wind. "I loved you, I *loved* you, Andre!" she cried hysterically, until she heard the slow steps of a horse approach and stop. A creak of leather indicated a man dismounting. Cold knifed into her.

But it was only Page. "Ma'am, it ain't safe here." His voice came to her muffled. He had a blue bandanna tied over his nose and mouth, to keep out the dust of his work. "We're going to run some cows right through here in a little while." When she didn't heed him, he pulled the bandanna down, so it hung at his throat. The upper half of his face was filthy with dust and sweat; the lower half was relatively clean and boyish. This was the half that smiled; his eyes didn't.

She turned away and struggled to swallow down the sobs that seemed to choke her. He squatted at a little distance, awkwardly, took his dusty hat off and swung it by the brim in one hand. "Guess you're upset about something."

She straightened her clothing and hair a little, wiped at her eyes and nose, and stared off fiercely at the yellow ochre of the distant foothills. The wind had swept the air, and they seemed closer than usual. Near at hand a half dozen cows stood ankle-deep in short dry grass. They didn't move. It was as if they were painted there, against the hot windy beauty of the pastures and the cloud-trailed sky.

"Richard told you I ran away with another man."

A pause, then, "Yes, ma'am, he did."

She looked at him, saw his eyes; they were ice-blue taffeta behind their dusty lids; she looked away again. "It was a lie. I was taken, stolen—and Richard could have saved me, but he didn't." She sat staring at nothing, the tears dammed up in her.

Page didn't seem to know what to believe. He studied the ground between his feet, scratched his cornsilk hair, then settled his hat back down on his head. "The boss, he said he had a letter saying you were running off with a feller you knew before you met him." He plucked a stem of dry grass and studied it.

She folded her arms tighter about herself. "I never saw the man before. He took me because of something Richard did to his wife a long time ago. A-and now I'm not a virgin anymore and Richard . . . Richard doesn't want me."

He was suddenly a bashful shambles. "Oh. Well."

"I don't know what to do. I'm so confused."

Though she could not, try as she might, hold the disappearance of Andre before her eyes for more than a few panic-stricken seconds, she was necessarily recognizing her present condition: what she was chained to, and how tightly. She was locked in marriage to a man who seemed to hate her now. She thought of all that she now knew marriage implied. His rights, her duties. And she knew she couldn't let him touch her. He sickened her; the thought of having to spend a lifetime with him sickened her.

Well, maybe you needn't.

Hope started up in her, a guilty desperate thing. She turned a ghost of a glance on Page. "Have you ever heard of a marriage being annulled?"

"I reckon I've heard it, but I wouldn't know too much about it."

She hung her head. "No, neither do I."

A minute more passed while he seemed to consider his own helplessness. Then he straightened, came closer, and offered her his hand. "Let me take you back to the house, ma'am. Harriet'll give you a cup of coffee. Or tea—I guess that's what ladies drink in the afternoon. You have a cup of tea and things'll look brighter."

"No, Page, they won't." She found herself remembering, all in one trembling moment; she found herself gathering the pieces of everything that was shattered, of everything her life had been for a scant day and night and was not now, and she ached with them, all she wanted them to be again.

"Page," she gripped his hand, "I need a ride to town, tomorrow morning, early."

"Now, ma'am, I don't know. The boss—"

"Please—if you can't drive me, just harness a horse to a wagon for me. I'll never ask anything else of you. Can't you see that it's best if I go? He doesn't want me anymore. And, Page, I-I'm afraid of him."

Harriet had just put the tea kettle on the stove when Richard came into the kitchen. "Well, isn't this cozy?" He fingered the ceramic tea pot waiting on the wooden table for the hot water. "Tea! I'll have some, too. You ladies don't mind me joining you, now do you?"

He had with him his bottle of whiskey. By the look of him, he'd spent the last hour in deep conversation with it. He brought it to his mouth now and took a drink, and Laura saw the strong spirits flash in his eyes.

He sat opposite her at the table, and hooked a third chair

with the toe of his boot. "Sit down here with us, Harriet, right down here. That's right. Laura told you about her little wedding trip? Laura, honey, tell Harriet about you and your . . . now what should we call him?" He drank again, and became that much more ferocious. She saw by the slant of the bottle that there wasn't any great quantity left in it. She sensed he was purposely working himself up.

"Lover! That's the word! Did she tell you about him, Harriet? No, don't go—sit down. Laura here has some real good stories—but she's been keeping 'em to herself." He lifted the bottle again, and swallowed repeatedly, tilting it up little by little until it was drained. "Come on, honey, I need some new conversation for when I go to Aida's. She's heard about everything, but she listens 'cause she gets paid to." He dug in his pocket and tossed a gold coin out on the table. "There, I'll pay you for your services, too."

The coin was still spinning when she was on her feet. Her chair fell with a crash behind her. "You're disgusting!"

"Am I now? 'N what's that make you?"

The tea kettle began to whistle frantically in the background, but no one moved to take it from the stove.

"Come on, Laura, what's that make you? Let's hear some of your fine eastern words now. Or better yet, how about some of those dirty words you learned from him?" He leaned up toward her with a smirk.

"You smell putrid."

"Mrs. Laird," Harriet warned, rising and coming to put her hands on Laura's shoulders, "there's no point in arguing with him, not when he's on the prod like this."

"No, Harriet," Richard motioned her away, "that's all right." He sat back in his chair. "Did you like it, Laura? Did he kiss and cuddle you real nice? He's got money, doesn't he? Was he a real gentleman? I never was quite gentleman enough for you, was I? Tell me, how do gentlemen do it? Did he use his mouth? Did he lick you, Laura?"

"Stop it!" She hid her face in her hands.

"Or maybe he was rough. Admit it now, you like a little roughness, don't you, honey? You never even let me get a good feel unless I got a little rough. When I think how prissy

215

you were—you had me panting, didn't you? But I knew underneath you were hot as hell. Hot as hell. Admit it, there were times you wanted it, didn't you? I should have—"

"I said stop it!" She headed for the door, but he stood abruptly and blocked her way, his fists clenched into bony mallets at his sides. One hand shot out to take her wrist in a grip so pinching her legs buckled. She dropped to her knees at his feet with a gasp of pain.

"Now, that's enough!" Harriet said. "Stop that, Mr. Laird, or I swear I'll get the frying pan and make you stop!"

Only gradually did he release his hold. "You're nothing but a fancy-talking little whore, Laura."

It seemed to Laura that she must have aged another twenty-one years in the last few days. Harriet, who seemed more uncomfortable than ever around her, brought dinner to her room on a tray, but Laura hadn't been able to eat. She sat at her dressing table, her hands gripped in her lap. Every once in a while her stomach seemed to turn over. She knew what she had to do. And she didn't think she could wait till tomorrow morning. She'd already packed her things, and was only waiting until the men were settled in the bunkhouse. The foreman's room had its own entrance. She planned to steal out and persuade Page to harness a horse to a wagon for her tonight. If he wouldn't, well . . . she had to get away from here if it meant walking all the way to Sacramento.

Nine o'clock, and the lights in the bunkhouse were still on. How late could men who worked so hard stay up? She got up to roam the room. Her body was running on nerves. She'd hardly slept for two nights. She looked at the bed, thinking that maybe if she just took off her button boots and stretched out for a few minutes, on her side so she wouldn't have to remove her clothes and bustle, since she had to wait anyway.

The bed felt like heaven. She fell into a fitful dream in which she was pursued by a groping terror that seemed ready to seize her any moment. And she woke—

—to the feeling of someone stroking her bare shoulder.

216

Richard sat on the bed, leaning over her, smirking. Her bodice was all unbuttoned and pulled off her shoulder; her chemise was unlaced. "What do you want?" she asked, sitting up cautiously, pulling her clothes together, trying to keep her voice under control. She sensed he'd drunk himself into a yet more violent mood. Fully alert, she scanned the room. There was a whiskey bottle on the dressing table next to the lamp she'd left burning low.

She eased away from him. Surprisingly, he let her get off the bed. "I'm not sure," he said, getting up himself. "I'm not sure if I want you or not. You're a bit used now, but I've had lots of women who were used, and had 'em good. So I don't see why I couldn't have fun with you. All I have to do is not think of you as my wife." He was leaning against the bedpost, his eyes narrow and glittering. "But I'm finding that kind of hard."

She stared back at him for a moment, considering what he was saying, then in an instant turned for the French doors. He followed swiftly.

"Don't!" she cried as his arms circled her from behind.

But it was too late. Her sudden action had sparked his violence. He slammed her against the nearest wall and proceeded to tear her bodice open again. Her chemise ripped to the top of her corset, exposing the aureolas of her thrust-up breasts. He held her wrists above her head with one hand and looked fixedly at her, tugging her chemise open more, indulging himself. "Little roses—isn't that a laugh? I always imagined these—" he pinched one nipple cruelly, "would be like little roses. Like your lips." He studied her mouth, then, with casual viciousness, backhanded her. Her head was braced by her raised arms; she took the blow full in the mouth, and tasted blood. His hand whipped again. She flinched, turning her face as much as she could and shutting her eyes. His palm caught her cheek and temple in a smarting blow that made her cry out.

He hauled her back to the bed and threw her on it, falling on her, nearly crushing her. Her pelvis was arched to him by her bustle. He rolled to one side, keeping his leg over hers and pinching her wrists in the one hand above her head again. His free hand closed on a breast. "Damn bitch, you with your rosebuds!" His thumb and forefinger nipped at her painfully.

"Let me go!"

"Not yet." He watched her squirm with drunken, bright-eyed malice. Then his mouth attacked hers bruisingly.

She wrenched free. "I hate you!"

His hand came up, warm from her breasts, and hit her again. His open palm smashed her cheek against its bone. Her head was jerked sideways by the force of the blow. Her skin shrieked, then seemed to go numb. A buzzing blackness threatened to suck her under . . .

After a blank, she found herself still lying on the bed, still in the place where she'd lost consciousness. Her eyes were open and fastened on Richard—they had opened on him before her mind saw him. Her legs lay slightly parted, and he was rubbing his hand up and down the front of her skirt, kneading her stomach, pressing between her thighs. "Is this how he did it, honey?" he said in a soft, treacherous voice.

"Don't, don't touch me," she managed to whisper.

"Don't touch you!" he said in pretended shock. He even sat up abruptly. "You're my wife, my beloved wife!"

With a burst of blood pounding through all her veins, she rolled away, off the bed. She made an attempt for the door to the hall, but he caught her by the flounces at the back of her skirt. She felt like a mouse caught by a cat, caught by her tail. He spun her, so that her hair swirled and covered her face, and when he threw her against the wall this time she wasn't prepared. The side of her head slammed into it so hard she thought her skull cracked.

He leaned into her and went on as if there had been no intervening action. "If a man can't touch his faithful wife, who can he touch?" He held her pinned there, and gradually his voice turned to a quiet whine. "How'd he do it, Laura? How did he get you to spread your legs for him? I *married* you. You were supposed to be *mine.*"

She opened her mouth, then closed it again.

The palm of his hand came up, it closed into a fist, and when she saw his eyes, she knew he meant to keep hitting her

218

until she gave him an answer. "He made me fall in love with him," she said breathlessly.

"Fall in *love* with him?" Disbelief registered on his face. Then there came that demon-look, that look of uncontrolled wildness, and she knew her answer had been the wrong one. With his fist poised to strike, she somehow found a way to wrench aside. Before she could get two steps, however, he delivered a blow to her ribs. She felt the air explode from her lungs as she was sent careening.

She came up hard against the dressing table. The lamp tottered, his whiskey bottle fell and rolled against the leg of the stool, where it gurgled out its remaining contents. When she turned, he was right behind her, both fists ready now. She dropped to her knees; her hand found the bottle, gripped it by its long neck as he pulled her up by her hair. She swung the bottle back, then with all her strength brought it forward again. The heavy brown glass met the side of his head with a horrible sound—just as his fist crashed into one of her squeezed-shut eyes.

He dropped to the floor as she fell back onto the stool. Somehow she got to her feet again, and swayed there, bent at the waist, holding her ribs. He lay still. The silence was wild. She put her hand to her face. Her lips were swollen, and her left cheek and eye were numb. And her head felt . . . funny. There was very little pain, and yet somehow she knew there was soon going to be a lot of pain. She had to move while she could.

The room whirled as she took her first sliding steps; she felt sick and faint. She made it to the door, lurched across the hall, through the kitchen, and fell heavily against Harriet's door. She managed to stand back and lift one hand to knock.

Before she could, the door opened. The housekeeper was in her nightdress, her graying hair in a braid over her shoulder. Even in the dark Laura saw she had a grumpy, sleepy look on her face—the look of a woman who holds on grimly to the threads of her well-earned rest. But then her expression to open-mouthed surprise. "Mrs. Laird? What's happened?"

Laura mumbled words, but her lips were getting misshapen; it was hard to form them. Harriet turned to light her lamp. Laura followed her into the room, weaving, and without permission, sank down on the side of the woman's still-warm and rumpled bed. The lamplight flared. She felt her hair being lifted away from her face. Harriet bent closer. "Oh no."

Laura only said, haltingly, "Got to leave." She was beginning to feel some of the pain now; her head especially hurt. Her vision was growing dimmer and she knew she had to speak quickly. "Page . . . a wagon . . ." But that was all she managed before she slipped over the edge of consciousness.

She awoke. The room was dark. Her hands were one over the other on the place where Richard had hit her in the ribs. The pain there was sharp with her slightest movement. Nevertheless, she roused a bit when she saw light coming from the kitchen. It came closer, came around the corner of the door, beamed like a brilliant shatter of sunlight in her fogged eyes. She squinted into it to find it was only Harriet with her lamp. But then a man was bending over her. She held up a defensive hand and whimpered.

"What in Holy H. Heck—?"

"Here! She's not decent." Harriet quickly threw a shawl over her torn bodice.

The man said, "Don't be scared. It's only Page, ma'am."

"Page . . ." Something was wrong with her vision. He had a blurred, moonish face. "Help me."

Page looked at Harriet. The woman said, "Best to take her into town. You need to get a doctor for the mister anyway—though I think he's only got a bump on the head. Well, go on, get a wagon hitched."

Laura was vaguely aware of him being gone for a while, and then he was back. He hesitated by the bed. "Ma'am, I'm gonna have to lift you up."

"Careful, the way she's holding herself, I think he broke her up inside."

"Lordy lordy. I'll try not to hurt you too much." His hands fumbled beneath her, trying to dig beneath her fussy rear-draped skirts; then she was being lifted. She moaned with the

220

singing fire of agony it cost her. And moaned again as her head fell back over his arm.

And for a moment, because only one other man had ever held her like this, she thought he was Andre. She whimpered, "He hurt me."

"I know, ma'am, I know."

Page. This was Page. Andre was gone.

They left the house. Page said, "I can't hardly believe a man would do a thing like this. It makes me feel ashamed. Hitting a woman, and such a *little* woman. It's not right, I don't care what he says she done."

"I'm not so sure anymore he told us the truth. Did you see any letter? And who cut that wedding dress right to pieces like that? She seemed awful proud of that dress, like she'd never had nicer."

Page placed Laura in the back of a buckboard half-loaded with hay. "My trunk," she mumbled.

"What's she saying?" Harriet asked.

"Something about a trunk."

"Well, maybe that's best, too. She put her things in it earlier—I saw when I took her dinner to her. I'll help you carry it out, then you'd better git before he comes to."

Laura heard the scrape of the trunk being slid into the bed of the wagon beside her; then came the snap of reins and the first jolt of the wagon's movement. She bit back a cry and gripped her side. And then darkness kindly effaced the terrible pain.

221

Nineteen

Laura slept with her limbs drawn up like a child's, and like a child, she stirred restlessly. The movement relieved some of her pains and increased others, and still others hurt no matter what.

Sometimes she dreamed—of riding a knight's black stallion, of magical love—sometimes of the taste of blood. Other times she dreamed of waking in an ordinary bed in her old room at Bessie Gladwin's boardinghouse, so that she grew bewildered whether the wedding and the theft of her and her betrayal—and that *other*—had really happened. Now and again she dreamed that Bessie sat beside her, listening while she spoke of things she recalled, making a muddle of them and struggling to put them into sequence— of Andre, of Richard, and what they had done to her.

And then of a sudden her cheek lay against a soft pillowcase, her side pained her sharply, and when she strained to sit up Bessie truly was sitting nearby, saying, "Don't try to lift your head."

She paid no heed, though her head hurt terribly.

"My dear, don't fret; lie back."

She couldn't remember how she'd gotten here. Then, with a slow settling of recollection, she did remember: there had been two sets of voices, Page's and Harriet's, and then only Page's, and a buckboard half-filled with hay.

She felt her face, her swollen cheeks and eyes and lips. And in that moment wariness and toughness replaced some of the youth in her. She had traveled outside the safe world. She had memories, when she closed her sore eyes, of physical pain, and also of a sickening slide between life and death.

Andre.

Yes, she recalled him, most of all.

There were tears on her face. Someone tucked the sheet about her and touched her shoulder. A face lingered in her sight. "Bessie?" she said aloud. Pain—her very tongue was sore. "He never loved me. It was all a lie."

"No more of it," murmured the woman, who seemed to be crying, too. "You've suffered so."

No more of it. Her eyes dimmed. She laid her head back on the pillow. No more of it. She was broken, but mending.

Andre felt a twinge of doubt as he plodded up the front steps. The evening was falling but there were no lights on in the house, except in the kitchen. Would Laura have gone to bed so early? Maybe he would find her just sitting in the dark, missing him. He could hardly wait to see her face, to hold her, to tell her that his lawyers would have her free of Laird within a few weeks. It had been a long trip—three days to San Francisco, two days working frantically there, (lawyers could drive him crazy with their slowness and their caution!) and three days getting back. He felt a bit saddle-weary—but not enough to stop him from loving her tonight. And loving her again, as many times as he could manage and she could bear.

He went inside, looking forward to teasing her, seducing her, relishing his own dangerousness. He hung up his hat and gun belt above the shotgun on the rack. "Anybody here?"

Soo's whispery footsteps came from the kitchen through the dining room. He was carrying a lamp.

"Where is she?"

"Gone."

"What do you mean?"

"Go home to husband."

It took five full seconds for that to sink to the bottom of his mind and mean anything. "She *what?*" he said softly.

"Go home, back to husband. Day you leave, she leave."

Andre's gut clenched; he never got sick, but it felt like he might be sick now.

"She read letter you leave. She say, 'Soo, I go home to husband now. Don't try to stop.' She go through your desk, find money in little drawer—for stage, she say. She leave."

Andre looked at the man, and looked right through him, to a vision of Richard Laird. He saw Richard Laird holding Laura, holding her in bed, thrusting into her; he heard her crying out as she'd cried out for him. And he damned her. In his heart he damned her forever.

"You go get her," Soo was saying. "You kill Mr. Laird and get her back."

Slowly Andre focused his eyes on the old Chinaman again. "I don't think so. If she wants him that bad, I think I'll let him keep her."

"You kill Mr. Laird! You make promise!"

He'd made a promise. Goddamn, she'd made a promise! *I won't leave you now. I love you, Andre!* What was Soo saying? Andre couldn't think right now. He had to think.

Laura, how could you do this?

Bessie Gladwin's boardinghouse was something of a showpiece in its neighborhood. It featured a cupola, a widow's walk, and all the railing around its sunny porches that modern architecture could provide. Built by Sam Gladwin when his dry goods business was booming, the house was one of those marvelous, roomy places with wide halls, high ceilings, hardwood wainscoting, and a plethora of bedrooms. The late Mr. Gladwin couldn't have provided better for his widow than he had done inadvertently by building this house, which was now her livelihood.

Slanting sun streamed through the white muslin curtains of the front upstairs bedroom this afternoon. Laura had been watching it do that for the past five days, since she'd first regained consciousness. She hadn't spoken directly about the great sunset of a bruise that was the left side of her face, or the tight bandages around her ribs that kept her from moving too suddenly or breathing too deeply. And neither had Bessie. And not once had either of them mentioned Richard Laird's name.

The news had come today that President Garfield was dead. The newspaper on her bedside table was banded in black. Around Sacramento, flags flew at half-mast. Businesses were shrouding themselves in mourning. The death had been announced during the festivities at the State Fair, and it was said there was to be an early closure, cancelling the grand fireworks display scheduled for this evening.

This all came to Laura through Mrs. Gladwin, who had read the articles aloud. The news washed over her as she recovered in her bed. She was still able to get up only occasionally. Her concussion had proved her most troublesome injury. But her aches and pains didn't consume all her attention anymore. For a while, she hadn't been able to move, hadn't been able to blink without a fresh stab of misery. Now, however, she mostly felt anger, and resolve.

Mrs. Gladwin, in dark blue skirts, fussed at the bureau with an arrangement of late chrysanthemums. Laura said suddenly, "I'll be leaving Sacramento as soon as I can, Mrs. Gladwin. I have a little money left and—"

"My dear, where will you go?"

"San Francisco. I'll get a job—or I can teach piano if I have to."

The deep red brooch the older woman wore at her throat flashed as she passed through the sunlight on her way across the room. She looked down at Laura with sympathy, her eyes gently probing the violet and green smudges that Laura knew marred her face. When Laura offered her hand, she took it and sat down on the edge of the bed, not looking at her. At last she straightened—with an ominous creaking of whalebone stays. "Perhaps it's not a bad idea. I have a little money, too. I could spare you some."

Laura squeezed her hand. "Thank you," she said, touched to the heart, "but I owe you too much already. There is one thing I would like to ask, though: promise me you won't tell anyone what he . . . what happened to me—or where I've gone."

On Tuesday, September 27, Sacramento's two newspapers both carried identical notices in their personals sections:

Attention. As my wife Laura has deserted my bed and board, this notifies all persons against crediting her in my name. I will pay no bills of her contracting. Richard Laird.

Laura was spared reading this, because early that same morning, wearing a hat with a heavy veil, and with all the money she had at her disposal folded in the black Russia leather purse clasped tightly against her still-tender ribs, she left Gladwin's Boardinghouse. She took a last look at the grand, gingerbread structure, the well-kept garden where a few yellow leaves had flittered down onto the dew-sodden lawn. Autumn sunshine flooded the scene with an amber glow. She said good-bye to it, for she knew she would never return this way.

In the vaulted arcade of the Central Pacific Station, she stood waiting for her train, apparently calm, though her heart was racing. Unreasonably she feared someone might try to stop her from making this escape.

No one did. She traveled to Vallejo uneventfully, and there embarked on the ferry that regularly crossed the San Francisco Bay.

San Francisco was like another country. Where Sacramento lay under the spell of its long, dreaming Indian summer, San Francisco's sky was a watery lead color. So many nationalities mingled on the streets that Laura wasn't at all sure she hadn't left the United States altogether. She knew Andre had a home here somewhere, but in all likelihood their paths would never cross. After all, here was a metropolis: factories and great stores, schools and chapels, newspapers and theaters, benevolent institutions and municipal works, stagecoaches and mails, trains and steamers, a city of bright bustle and magnificent dissipation. The hills, steep as stairs, were mazed with streets that climbed right up to that place where sight stalled out in the mist. A small, lone woman could easily get lost among all these tall, narrow-shouldered buildings.

She hadn't the time to look for lodgings as clean, well-located, and reasonably priced as Mrs. Gladwin's. She asked a cabdriver, and it was already dark when he dropped her and her trunk outside a shabby building on Mission Street. Soiled elbows had left stains up and down the unlit staircases. She took a room under the name Mrs. Laura Upton.

She'd decided to pose as a widow; she believed that would give her more stature, make her seem less vulnerable. It also explained her black veils. She noticed the landlady looking at her hand, and belatedly realized she'd forgotten the detail of a wedding ring. She made a note to get herself one at a pawn shop first thing tomorrow.

Her new "home" had a little window overlooking a sand and weed backyard. A gray woolen blanket covered the bed that stood within a recess. The whole had a slutty, shut-in look, like a box for a human rat. Nevertheless, here she must wait out at least another week—she had to let the last bruises on her face fade completely before she could look for work.

At last, her complexion clear again, she dressed simply in one of the black gowns she'd worn while mourning her father, and went in search of a way to earn her living. She'd felt prepared to be turned down, but she was surprised to be told, "You're too young—and too slight, Mrs. Upton. And frankly, you don't look well." She could have said that she'd looked much worse recently, but of course she didn't. And she didn't admit, either, that she felt a little queasy now and then these days.

There were other interviews that didn't go well for other reasons, mostly her lack of experience. She had to keep trying, however, for she had so little money.

Sometimes she felt a little like the Chinese child Ling, cast out in the cold in the dead of winter. (Would Andre take pity on her if he knew?) These were the times when she said, I can't do this, I don't want to do this, and then she had to

227

answer herself: *Time to grow up, Laura.*

Meanwhile, she had her expenses: her rent, fares for street cars, the meager amount of food she ate.

Eating seemed the least of her problems, since her appetite had dwindled to the point where often she didn't care if she missed a meal or not. In fact, none of what was happening meant much to her. Every incident seemed bland. When she thought about it, she realized she'd felt very little since the morning she'd discovered Andre's treachery. Oh, there had been stabs now and again of shock and grief, but that was all. She felt self-congratulatory about that, thinking, I'm bearing it, I'm getting through, and going on. It gave her a kind of pride, a desolate sort of pleasure to think she was carrying a heavier weight than she'd dreamed it was possible to carry. She'd never realized the amount of strength she had.

Three weeks after arriving in San Francisco, she trudged home under shreds of fog one evening trying to make a choice: should she eat tonight, or save the money to pay her rent? Her financial situation had come down to that. She knew she'd become terribly thin—she was beginning to look swallowed in her clothes—and there was that queasiness, almost daily now. If she lost her health, that would be the end for her. She had to start taking better care of herself. But first she had to earn some money.

She turned at a flower stand and started down Fourth Street, then stopped before a brick building where a small shop sign read, KANE'S PHARMACY. It was one of the cheaper drug stores, yet a notice in the window—HELP WANTED—immediately snared her attention. A bell over the door announced her, but the only person present was arranging a display of hair dressings on top of a wooden showcase, and he didn't look up. She approached him, feeling very dubious, and stood waiting, looking about her as she did.

The place was small, over-stuffed, and barely lit. Shelves held a modest stock of fancy goods and myriad patent medicines. A side counter featured trusses, chest protectors, and several styles of supporters. At the rear stood the usual high, enclosed prescription counter with its grilled window. Nearer stood a display of Star's Balsam Wild Cherry Cough Syrup.

At last, knowing very well that she was hovering for his attention, the man turned: "Oh . . . may I help you?"

"Are you the proprietor?"

"George Kane, yes, ma'am." He had a square face, with features that seemed to have been chipped out of a block of hardwood with a dull chisel.

She gestured to the window. "You have a sign out for a helper. I would like to apply."

He frowned, looked her up and down, taking in her black gown—and her thinness, no doubt—then said, "Ever work in a drugstore before?"

"No, sir." A flicker of disappointment passed through her. She knew what came after that question, and to forestall it, said, "But I'm willing and able to learn."

To her surprise, he didn't shake his head. He said, "Well, the position doesn't really call for too much intelligence. My wife worked it until recently, but now she has my mother to care for."

In further conversation, Laura gathered that if she got the job she might one day make eleven dollars per week, the usual salary for a clerk. But that had to be worked up to. "If you want to come in for seven-fifty to begin with—well, all right, eight dollars—I might give you a chance, Mrs. Upton. Besides waiting on customers, the job includes dusting and tidying and stocking shelves—and sweeping out the store before we open at six-thirty—"

"Six-thirty? In the morning?" She didn't know how she would ever wake up so early.

She felt quite proud of herself when she climbed the stairs to her room. She had a job. She'd really done very nicely on her own.

But that night she woke in the dark and caught at her mattress, trying to still her shaking. Her heart thumped. Tears ran from her eyes into her hair. Suddenly, unexpectedly, all the emotional hardiness she'd so recently prided herself on seemed to bleed right out of her. Lying there alone, she felt all the wounds that hadn't healed, the wounds she'd denied, the wounds to her soul. She saw that she'd been maimed, maimed in a way no one else would ever see. And she would never forget.

Still daunted when the cold and colorless hour of 6:00 A.M. came, she went to her first day of work.

It was a long day. A long week. Her hours were from six in the morning until six in the evening, with a lunch period of one and a half hours. And as she'd suspected, Mr. Kane was a tyrant without a heart. Even so, her hours of work were better than her hours alone in her room. She grew to hate the solitude and the dark—and worse, the stillness, in which there were only certain echoes and no silencing them anymore. Andre seemed to fill her sordid little room. He found her alone—for having been hurt, she'd chosen to go alone, like an injured animal—and he tormented her.

Sunday came, her only day off, and she spent it grieving hopelessly. When Monday dawned, she was very sick. She arrived at the drugstore fifteen minutes late, white-faced and nauseated. Luckily Mr. Kane seemed for once to be in a halfway human mood, and only scolded her with, "Use your lunch hour to see a doctor, because if you can't get here on time, I'll have to replace you."

Dr. F. Kellogg's office and home was on the corner of Taylor and O'Farrell streets, in a narrow three-story building graced with spindly columns and jigsaw work. Laura was shown into the consultation room, and sat on a red plush sofa, behind which was a window where the day's rainstorm hammered like nails.

"Ah, here we are then, I'm Dr. Kellogg."

Laura was too startled to give her own name. For the doctor was a woman. A tall woman who held her shoulders like a soldier and dressed rather severely. Her outfit consisted of a mannish shirt, a bow tie, a masculine jacket, and a long, flared skirt of blue-gray tweed. She was perhaps thirty-five, and if not handsome, she had a certain incandescence—attributable to soft red hair and a face drenched

230

in freckles.

"Sorry to have kept you waiting. I had a house call, a little boy with the croup." Which accounted for the fact that she smelled faintly of eucalyptus leaves.

She didn't sit behind her desk, but took a small side chair near the sofa. "Mrs. Upton," she started briskly, "it's my experience that most people know exactly what's wrong with them, so why don't you give me your diagnosis and save us both a lot of time."

"Well . . . I think I just haven't been eating properly. Or sleeping well. Anyway, I've been feeling ill, almost every morning now."

"Hm-hmm, how long has this been going on?"

"I don't know. Two weeks maybe."

"How long have you been widowed?"

"A month or so."

"I see. And you haven't any idea what the problem is? Sick in the mornings? Have you discussed it with anyone? Your mother, sisters, women friends?"

Laura only gave her a solemn, sidelong glance. "I haven't—that is, I'm alone."

Dr. Kellogg stood. "Well, you need a thorough examination at any rate. I think you'd better come along with me."

Laura was a little shocked at the nature of the examination, and suffered a quick, horrible fear when she heard what the doctor concluded from it: "Mrs. Upton," Fredericka Kellogg said, smiling gently, "you're going to have a baby."

Laura said nothing from where she sat on the side on the examining table. She couldn't seem to react.

"Didn't you suspect?"

She shook her head.

"I see." After a moment she added, "You weren't happily married? Most women in your position would be overjoyed to know they were going to have a child by a husband lost so early in life."

"No, I wasn't happily married."

"I see. Would you care to talk about it?"

"No."

"You really have no one here in San Francisco?"

231

Andre . . . She envisioned it—finding him in some dark, rich background of tweed and smoke and oak-paneled rooms . . . a flash of husbandly emotion as he enfolded her terrified soul in the cape of his care . . .

The image wouldn't hold up. The words came huskily from her tightened throat: "No, no one who would care." She gazed at the doctor with the last of her shields smashed down. She was depleted, spent with torment, the nights without sleep, the tears of grief, the remorse and regret and pain that was endurable only because it had to be endured. She had no words for what she was thinking now: that she suspected Andre of knowing this might happen, that she suspected him of cruelty beyond her understanding.

"I see," the doctor said.

Laura doubted if she did. She looked down at herself, at her waist. The orderly, ordinary hopes she'd fallen back on—keeping her job, making a life for herself, forgetting somehow—were shattered about her.

"Well, from what you've told me, I think we can expect delivery next June." Dr. Kellogg still considered her. Her voice softened. "Are you terribly unhappy about it?"

"I-I don't know. I'm frightened." Indeed, her heart was beating like a small wing of fear. "I can't even seem to feed myself properly; and my room, my job—how will I take care of a baby and keep my job?"

"Perhaps you should think of adoption."

"Adoption? You mean . . . abandon my baby? No!" A sudden fierceness welled up in her, an obstinacy. "I wouldn't give my child away! I *will* take care of it—I just have to think how, that's all."

In a suddenly affectionate way Laura hadn't suspected was in her, Dr. Kellogg reached to put a hand on her shoulder. "I'm sure you will. And you'll love her—or him."

Laura spread her hands on her abdomen. She imagined she could already feel a new heartbeat there, one not entirely in accord with her own. A strange companionship shivered within her, the chimerical whisper of another pulse. She was going to have a baby. The thought had an insidious satisfaction.

She was going to have a baby, and she would protect it from all hurt, and offer it all her rejected love. And it would love her in return. As its father hadn't. Perhaps the victory was not entirely Andre's, after all.

She went back to work that afternoon, and went home to her room that night, and went to sleep feeling triumphant— only to awake within an hour racked with sobs, with salty, warm tears that tracked down her face and onto her pillow.

Twenty

During Laura's next visit to Dr. Kellogg, the doctor wasn't at all happy about her weight. "What are you eating?"

"I, uh, usually have the special at a restaurant near my rooming house."

"You're eating in a restaurant?"

"I don't have a kitchen . . . and I don't know how to cook."

Dr. Kellogg laughed. "That's one thing we have in common then. You're looking less haggard—but you really must gain a few pounds. A rat-cage room on Mission Street with nothing in the cupboard but soda crackers won't do to make a baby." She stood. "Put your coat back on. We're going out. My trap's just outside. There's someone I think you should meet."

She handled the trap and horse admirably. The brass buttons of her mannish jacket winked in the cold sunlight. Laura pulled her own coat tighter. The sea wind could cut with a razor's edge.

They halted on Eddy Street, before a small dwelling that was top-heavy with a high mansard roof. The lower windows held pots of Chinese primroses. Inside, Laura was introduced to a Mrs. Noah, a widow. "She and her daughter take in a boarder when they can find someone respectable."

"Oh, Mrs. Upton," said the plump, elfinlike woman who was pouring them cups of tea, "Holly will be so happy to have someone close to her own age. And a baby next spring!

How terrible it must be to have lost your husband so soon, but you'll be glad you have the child to remind you of him. Holly's been such a comfort to me."

"Holly is a year or two younger than you, I believe," Dr. Kellogg said. "She works at a fruit-canning factory—on Clay Street, isn't it, Mrs. Noah?" She set her porcelain cup and saucer back on the tea tray. "Perhaps Mrs. Upton could see the room."

It was a small and simple but perfectly clean room on the second floor. The bed was made neatly with a multicolored hand-stitched quilt. "What do you think?" Dr. Kellogg asked.

The fee was five times what Laura had been paying for her dingy place on Mission Street. But here hot nutritious meals would be included, and an atmosphere of propriety she needed for her child's sake. "I think it'll do fine."

"That settles it then." The doctor started down the stairs, drawing on her gloves. "I'll drop you off at work for now, before Mr. Kane fires you—though where he'd get someone else to work so hard for so little is beyond me. Then tonight we'll get your trunk. Mrs. Upton didn't know anyone when she came to town, Mrs. Noah, and had to take a room in a horrible place. She'll be grateful for your cooking, I can assure you. I think we can have both her and her things here before dinner. Is that convenient?"

When her trunk was stowed in her new room that night, she followed the doctor out to her trap. Darkness had settled over the streets. The fog was in. The edges of things— buildings, carriages, people—looked slightly smudged in the misty air. "Dr. Kellogg, I don't know how—"

"Now don't turn mushy on me, Laura—may I call you Laura? You've shown remarkable sense and courage so far."

The compliment was oblique, and yet Laura fancied she'd caught a glint of affection in the brusque words. The doctor already had one foot on the fender of her trap. "Wait," Laura said, placing her hand on the taller woman's arm. Droplets of the mist clung to the doctor's red hair and jeweled her pale brows and lashes. "You must let me thank you. You've done so much for me."

"Nonsense; I do the odd favor for people and they do the odd favor for me. It's a good way to live. Women making their way alone in the world must look out for one another." She pressed a professional hand to Laura's boned corset. "You're going to have to give up that contraption, you know." The distraction didn't work, so she paused, smiling tenderly at Laura's desperate need to voice her gratitude. "All right, you've thanked me—mostly by looking so relieved. And you're very welcome. This isn't the end of your problems, as I'm sure you realize, but you're safe for now."

She bent suddenly, unexpectedly, to kiss Laura on the cheek. She then stepped into the trap and seated herself, taking up her reins. "Now I expect you to start gaining some weight. Don't make me have to take up cooking for you! You'd be sorry, I promise." She drove off, leaving Laura with the warm knowledge that she wasn't totally alone in the world anymore.

Holly Noah turned out to be a spunky girl with a heart-shaped face and curly blond hair. She had a certain nimble impudence to her carriage and a likable pungency to her personality. Neither mother nor daughter were bookish or at all intellectual, but Holly was addicted to newspapers. That very first night she shook her evening paper open, like any man home from the office, and said, "I see Guiteau's lawyer isn't having much luck finding help with his assassination defense. Now I wonder why that is?"

Laura, sitting near the lace-curtained front windows on one of a pair of oval-backed chairs tufted in pale amethyst, didn't know if Holly's question was rhetorical or not, until the girl lowered the paper and looked directly at her. She said politely, "There must be a lot of reluctance to defend a man who has murdered a president."

"As long as a crook has money he never has to hunt far for a lawyer." She read a little further, then nodded her head in satisfaction. "Ah yes, here it is—Guiteau hasn't *got* any money. No money, no lawyers."

Mrs. Noah said, "Holly keeps abreast of all these things. She's so clever. Me, I find it hard to keep up with my reading for the temperance cause."

"Mama's a member of the National Christian Women's Temperance Union." Each seemed equally proud of the other.

Laura looked from one to the other with the tiniest pang of envy. If she could in any way become a part of the life of this tiny family, she wouldn't be discontent. She knew only too well that she could do much worse than the quiet, nonglaring love that warmed this home.

Richard Laird sat in his saddle in that invariable way of his, as if he lived there and couldn't imagine any good reason to venture down. Laura had seemed to admire the way he looked on a horse, and he'd made sure she saw him on one often when he'd been courting her. He was beginning to realize just how many little things he'd done to win her. He'd made sacrifices in order to make her his wife, when he'd never thought much about having a wife before. But there'd been something about her that he'd wanted. No one else, just her. Maybe that was why he'd gone so crazy to hear her say she'd fallen in love with Sheridan.

He sat looking eastward, in the direction she'd disappeared on their wedding night. Clouds closed off the mountain peaks; the air promised a storm.

There was still talk about them. It couldn't be otherwise. First he'd married her, then she'd disappeared, then she'd come back—but hadn't stayed long. How much else his neighbors knew, he wasn't sure—and didn't care—but he saw looks passed between his men, and he felt the silence they paid him, as though they saw something worse when they looked at him than what showed, and he found he did care about that. He still stopped and joked with them, but there were always whispers behind his back. He felt disapproval where before he'd been respected, admired. He imagined he heard the word coward, and another word, unmanly.

He was wearied of it past all bearing. Solitude had piled up on his shoulders. Even Page had closed up on him. The foreman spoke less now than he ever had—and he'd never been a blabbermouth. An anger burned in Page; Richard felt it. Anger and blame and outrage, all banked up like a night fire. Page would be gone come spring, the same way Harriet had taken off last month. The same way Laura had gone. He'd had a nice life, had things set up just the way he wanted them, with a nice future in store, and then that damned Sheridan had come back. When Richard thought about it, about how this was all because of that little Chinese bitch of Sheridan's—who hadn't even been that good and certainly not worth ruining his life over!—it made his blood boil.

Now a woman like Laura, a woman like that might be worth dying for, or killing for.

She'd gotten under his skin. He thought about her a lot more often than he liked, even though he was going to Aida's more often than ever.

There was a new girl at Aida's, Mildred, who complained in a soft, pained voice whenever she saw him come in the door, because every time he had her he left finger marks on her white sheeny rump. That's why he chose her—for that soft bruisable rump of hers. That and the way her tears flowed so plentifully. He liked the way she got so trembly and pleaded with him not to go so hard at her.

But as soon as he emerged from her he felt like he needed it again, sometimes worse than before. It wasn't working for him anymore, having Mildred, or even that Chinese girl who called herself May. None of Aida's girls satisfied him like they used to, and he figured that was Sheridan's fault, too.

Maybe he ought to be doing something about getting even. He knew Sheridan lived over San Francisco way. Probably had a house on Knob Hill. It shouldn't be too hard to find out. He could probably pay somebody to look into it for him.

Laura and San Francisco had had November, a somber stormy month, with rain and so much wind that it was difficult to walk to and from work. Then December and the holiday season arrived.

Once settled at the Noahs, she'd made the mistake of mentioning she had a stepmother in Massachusetts. Mrs. Noah urged her, in the kindest of terms, to send Alarice a Christmas greeting. Her landlady couldn't imagine a mother turning against her own daughter, not even a stepdaughter.

Eventually Laura did send a note wishing Alarice a pleasant Christmas. She wasn't surprised when she received no answer.

In the house on Eddy Street, the three women secreted gifts—small things, mostly made by hand and wrapped in inexpensive silver paper. Laura could afford to give only that which cost affection or talent. Mrs. Noah took the time to give her a few lessons in needlework, and Laura discovered she was quick and neat-fingered and that the creation of patterns in silk floss entertained her. So her gifts consisted of prettily embroidered handkerchiefs and collars. On Christmas Day, after a leisurely exchange of presents, the women went into the dining room, where they had a superb leg of lamb, and a pair of roasted stuffed ducks, followed by a handsome mince pie. Laura was as happy as she could be under the circumstances, grateful to be inside the glowing windows of this little house instead of, as could so easily have been the case, on the outside looking in.

Andre had been in San Francisco for two weeks, since selling his Texas ranch. He'd sold out on the spur of the moment. He'd been doing everything on the spur of the moment lately. He was drifting, purposeless for the first time in his life.

Tonight he'd finally been goaded by his managers to attack the pile of paperwork on his desk—three months' worth. It was late, but he couldn't sleep anyway, so he turned up the gaslights in his office and began with the unopened mail.

He sifted through the stack of envelopes, until he came across one with a familiar postmark. His heart thudded quickly, almost stopped, then started again as he ripped it open. There was a letter, but his eyes went right to the newspaper article folded in with it:

Sacramento, December 3, 1881. Mr. Richard Laird, of Laird Ranch, near Sloughouse, has been granted an annulment of his marriage to Miss Laura Upton, formerly of Abfalter Village, Massachusetts. Grounds for the annulment were based upon Miss Upton's disappearance from his home the evening of their wedding—with another man, Mr. Laird claims. After a two-week absence, she returned briefly, but declined to take up her marital duties. Miss Upton's present whereabouts are unknown.

With barely controlled anger, Andre slammed his fist down on the limp and smeary square of newspaper. He ran his hand over his eyes, took up the newsprint again:

. . . *declined to take up her marital duties* . . .

"Then why the hell did you leave me!"

Suddenly he realized why he'd been keeping his mind so carefully blank. That vision he'd had of her and Laird together—he hadn't dared think too hard about anything, lest that vision come back and break him.

. . . *present whereabouts are unknown* . . .

Where would she go?

He cursed her, long and hard. He was thinking now, at last, and feeling the threads that had been spinning out ever since she'd left him, threads that would always connect her to him, and that he knew he had to follow.

Laura! She was who-knew-where, getting into who-knew-what trouble, and by God, when he found her . . . when he found her . . .

January clamped winter skies over the city; the days shrank and lost their interest after New Year's. Several weeks went by in dull flat calm. The weather remained threatening but never made any real move. It wasn't until that cold month was nearly over that Laura met Yale Talbot.

"Good afternoon," said a male voice as soft as southern

summer nights.

She smiled the false smile she'd learned to put on for customers of the drugstore, and glanced up from the invoice that had come in with an order of Green's Corn Remedy—glanced up into the most piercing blue eyes she'd ever beheld.

"That there's about the thinnest smile I've ever seen—thin as March river ice."

A silence ensued; color rose in her cheeks. Mr. Kane called from behind his enclosed counter, "Mrs. Upton, are you attending to this gentleman?"

The stranger turned his attention to the pharmacist. "Sir, I'm afraid I've given the lady—er, Mrs. Upton—a bit of a surprise. She and I are old acquaintances," he drawled in an accent oozing dogwood and magnolia blossoms, "but I think I'm the last person on earth she expected to see crawl out of the south. Yale Talbot, at your service." He gestured debonairly with his homburg.

While he thus lied so adeptly to her employer, Laura had an instant to take him in more fully. He looked at ease in his tall, stiff collar and large, knotted, emerald-colored tie. His cuffs and shirt bosom were starched and ironed to a beautiful gloss. Over it he wore an impeccable high-buttoned, brown wool frock coat. His hands were square, uncallused, with finely turned knuckles. One finger sported a ring set with a golden-veined lapis lazuli. And his eyes, those startlingly attractive eyes, were an innocent, supernal blue.

The glint behind them went unnoticed by Mr. Kane, who muttered something about these not being social hours before he disappeared again into his private domain. Laura couldn't help a wry smile as the glib stranger turned back to her. That is, until he leaned over the counter and captured her right hand and located a warm kiss on her wrist, and then, quickly, another. A flustered feeling rushed all through her. She snatched her hand away. "You take liberties, sir," she said rigidly.

Lines of indulgent amusement deepened at the sides of his mouth. "A bold method is the best method, that's been my experience."

"And your experience has of course been very broad."

241

The minute she said it, she was sorry. It was terribly improper. Yet an intuition told her she was right. She turned her attention to a speck of lint caught in the ruching of her purple sleeve.

He leaned on the counter's edge, the picture of drowsy grace. "You blush right prettily, Mrs. Upton." His words only intensified the heat in her face. He laughed softly.

"Is there something I can help you with? I assume you came in here for a remedy."

"A remedy?" He glanced around. "Ah, yes." His yes was southern and slow, almost two syllables: *yeh-as.* "This here's a pharmacy." He shrugged, a casual gesture of broad shoulders. "Actually I'm standin' in need of a stiff tonic, you've got me so swimmy-headed, but I'll settle for a box of cough drops." He added in a confidential tone, "Truth is, I only came in because I saw you through the window: your hair shining against the white of your throat and those high-shadowed cheekbones . . ." Flattery seemed to fall from his lips as softly as petals fall from blown blossoms in warm moonlight.

"Horehound, licorice, or extract of lemon?"

"Licorice, by all means. Now I know that accent. You're a Yankee." His jawline went solemn as she handed him the box of cough drops with her left hand and he spotted her ring. "Are you really married?"

The question startled her. "I-I'm widowed." She hadn't the spirit for this kind of play. He made her feel nervous and anxious. And, unlike him, she didn't take pleasure in lying. Guiltily, she fingered the gilding of the cheap ring she'd purchased to document her claimed status.

"I see," he said, his voice once again deep and lazy as he laid down the coin for his purchase.

"I don't know what you see, but I do know I must get back to work."

"Do you mind if I just browse a while?"

She flushed again at his smile. "Feel free." She bent her head over her invoice once more.

He didn't remove himself from her counter, however, and after a disconcerting moment said, "Have you ever played

242

poker, Mrs. Upton?"

In spite of herself, she looked up at him again. Those eyes were truly stunning.

"There you are, holding your cards, waiting as the dealer turns over that last one. That instant is the essence of poker. It makes no difference, really, whether you win or lose. It's that instant of anticipation, of promise. That's what the game is played for, you know."

Abruptly, she caught a glimpse of Mr. Kane's face peeking through the grilled window again. "It's been so nice to see you, Mr.—" she searched her mind for the name he'd given, "Mr. Talbot. Perhaps we can talk again sometime when I'm not so busy." She looked at him meaningfully.

A look of laughing conspiracy slid into his blue eyes. "What a good idea. What time do you finish here?"

She glanced at the grill. She couldn't see Mr. Kane's face, yet she felt certain he was eavesdropping. She shook her head silently but emphatically at Mr. Talbot, saying aloud, "Quite late, I'm afraid."

As luck would have it, Mr. Kane chose just that moment to come down out of his pharmacy and bestow some of his questionable generosity. "You might as well go with him now, Mrs. Upton. I can see I'm not going to get any more work out of you today. You can make the time up by staying through your lunch hour tomorrow."

Laura glanced at the clock on the wall above her head. Only twenty minutes remained till closing—and for that she would have to work an extra hour and a half tomorrow.

"How kind of you, sir," Mr. Talbot said. "Mrs. Upton, I have transportation waiting, if you'll allow me to drive you home. It's such a nasty foggy day. I always hate to see a lady face the streets when it's so damp out. Do you have a hat and coat I can help you with?"

"I really can't—I haven't finished this invoice."

"Go," Mr. Kane said; "Come," Mr. Talbot urged. And in a very few minutes, the bell of the door tinkled behind her and the Southerner. "You're very sly," Laura said at once. She was pulling on her black kid gloves, which were rusty at the finger ends and needed to be restored yet again with black

243

ink and olive oil.

Mr. Talbot only grinned, put his hat rakishly on the back of his head, and took her arm. He did have a hired cab—evidently that much of what he'd said was true—for now a coachman urged a pair of clip-clopping white mares up the street from where they'd been tethered. Mr. Talbot looked at her with those eyes as blue as the Mediterranean Sea. "Good lawyers—and good poker players—have to learn to be sly."

"Somehow I think the trait came naturally to you, sir." She glanced down at her arm. "Please take your hand away. Surely you don't think I have any intention of getting into a carriage with you?"

He smiled down at her. "What? After I've gone to such trouble manipulatin' things to my advantage?"

"The poker game is over, I'm afraid, and you lose." She disentangled her arm and turned up the street, her trailing purple skirts sweeping the wet sidewalk behind her.

"Mrs. Upton!" He fell in beside her. "Now don't get cross-legged!" He stopped her with a hand on her arm again, this time gripping firmly enough to swing her toward him. "I do apologize if I've imposed myself on you. I plead temporary insanity. I saw you poised so pensively over your little invoice, your profile so perfect, and I said to myself, Yale, my boy, that's a right pretty woman. I simply had to meet you. I'm a brash man, I admit it," his smile had become merely a glance of teeth, "but I'm not completely without redeeming qualities. Tell me you'll forgive me."

She softened. He seemed sincere. And he was obviously a gentleman—of sorts. "Very well," she said tiredly, "your apology is accepted."

"Good—then you'll have dinner with me?"

"No! I couldn't possibly!"

There was that sly grin again. He had a way of bending his head when amused. "Sure you could. All you have to do is say yes. Now, don't just keep shaking your head—that's so monotonous—Mrs. Upton, don't you ever say yes?"

"Of course—"

"There, I knew I could get you to agree." He signaled his carriage again. "And I know just the place to take you; the

244

escalloped lobster is wonderful, not to mention the raspbery Bavarian cream." His hand went to the small of her back, urging her toward the vehicle at the curb.

"Mr. Talbot—really!"

"Shh—don't look now, but Mr. Kane is coming out."

She did look, sideways, pretending to adjust the brooch-fastened ends of her white lace collar, and just saw the chiseled-wood block shape of Mr. Kane's head as he stood locking the shop door for the night.

"I suppose, if you want to stalk off down the street without me you could explain to him tomorrow that we aren't really acquainted at all. But then he might wonder why you went along with me in there, wouldn't he? He might even feel you'd played him for a fool. As I understand it, employers take a dim view of that sort of thing. You might even lose your job. Why, if I were of a vulgar nature, I might remark that you're dependent upon my silence just now."

"You *are* vulgar, Mr. Talbot, a vulgar opportunist," she said through stiff lips.

"Indeed I am, Mrs. Upton—and fixin' to leave now." He held out his hand, grinning with enough charm to melt butter. "Better come along and stop acting so feisty."

He was lean, blond, and good-looking—too good-looking. She found herself viscerally attracted in spite of herself. And he seemed to know the instant her mind capitulated. "Smile," he whispered, "the old bulldog's watching us."

She forced an icy smile and, moving with reluctance, allowed her fingers to be caught in his warm grasp.

245

Twenty-One

According to Andre's informant, Laura had been at Gladwin's Boardinghouse during the first part of October, but had left with no forwarding address. If Mrs. Gladwin knew where she'd been bound for, Mrs. Gladwin wasn't telling. Andre decided to visit the lady himself.

"I'm sorry, I can't help you, Mr. Sheridan," she told him that evening in her parlor. It was going to be a dark night, with a gray valley mist muffling everything. The lamp on the table between them emitted a hissing brightness.

"But she was here," he said.

"She was here, yes."

"I can't believe you'd let her leave without knowing where she was headed for."

"She's a grown woman and not beholden to me."

"Where did she go, Mrs. Gladwin?" This was the woman who had told Laura about rabbits and husbands. There had to have been some friendship between them. He brought out his wallet and took out four fifty-dollar bills. "Just tell me what direction she went. North?" He separated one of the bills out and held it just over the little table.

Her eyes were caught by the money. They seemed to flower in her face. Fifty dollars was probably a third of a month's income to her. Slowly, she shook her head.

"Not north." He let the bill drop to the tabletop. "South?" He dangled another bill.

She shook her head again.

The second bill dropped. He dangled a third. "East?"

No. Laura had gone west. There was only one city of any size west of Sacramento. "San Francisco?" he said, a little disbelieving. But Mrs. Gladwin wasn't saying any more. She had a look on her face that told him she already wished she hadn't given in to his bribery. "Don't worry, Mrs. Gladwin, I don't intend her any harm."

"Who are you, Mr. Sheridan?" she asked suddenly.

"I'm a man who never forgets a promise."

Mr. Talbot followed Laura into the small restaurant, and held a chair for her at a corner table. He ordered for both of them. Laura hardly knew what she ate. Her companion chatted easily about his recent arrival in San Francisco, his new law practice, his rooms at the Palace Hotel, his hopes of being accepted into the University Club, his interest in boxing and baseball. Listening to his melodious drawl, Laura remained wary. "Why have you brought me here?" she said at last, putting down her fork.

He wore a teasing grin. "Why, because we have so much in common—both so alone in the world." When she didn't comment, he said, "I'm plumb tired of doing all the talkin'; tell me about yourself." After a long moment, he bent near and whispered, "You won't even tell me your first name?"

"I don't like to be coerced, Mr. Talbot."

"You won't forgive me for that? I've tried to explain I couldn't help myself. I find you challengin' and beautiful and a great mystery. I've never seen so little autobiography written on a face. Except for your eyes. Such knowin' eyes. Like two round, gray pebbles scoured by the surf along a rocky beach."

She gave a vacant laugh and struggled not to look away. The description was too apt. This man was too perceptive. She had to discourage him, here and now. Speaking with quick and throbbing urgency, she said, "My name is Laura and I'm not a widow; my husband is very much alive."

He considered her, and his grin slowly spread. She could have sworn there was a new ember of eagerness in his

247

expression. "Why, isn't that a coincidence? We have more in common than I thought. My wife is very much alive, too."

She was temporarily taken aback.

"Her name is Lois. And I have a son, little Brent. My beloved spouse stayed behind in Charleston. I left her in her daddy's drawin' room wearing a dotted white muslin gown with a blue sash and cute little black slippers with shiny bows; she was pouting like the spoiled child she is. The boy will probably grow up to be spoiled and childish, too, but since I'll seldom see him, it hardly matters to me. I got what I wanted from them, a partnership in the Griffin law firm, while Daddy Griffin got himself a grandson and heir. An even trade, I think.

"Now, I've bared my disreputable past; it's your turn, Mrs. Upton. A beautiful woman, not a widow but a wife, obviously reared as a lady, but working as a shopgirl. What a tale you must have to tell."

All of the many things she wanted to make clear to him tumbled together in her mind without form. "What do you want from me, Mr. Talbot?"

"Only your story . . . for now." He riveted his so-blue gaze on her.

"Very well. I ran away from my husband." She felt that in order to get rid of him, she must shock him thoroughly. "And in only a few months I will become the mother of another man's child." She folded her hands over her stomach, which was still so flat as to deny what she'd just said.

He raised his wineglass to his lips. His grip on the stem was tight. "A few months, you say?"

"Five, to be precise. Now, I would like to go home." She stood and began to make her way out of the restaurant.

On gaining the street, she was surprised to find him behind her. He reached for her arm. "Since I brought you out, Mrs. Upton, I'd be remiss not to see you home. We Southerners are sticklers for chivalry."

In his carriage, he was silent, then took her hand, willfully. "You said you live with friends. Do they know about your little indiscretions?"

"They, like Mr. Kane, believe I am a respectable widow carrying a posthumous child." She was now regretting her earlier candor. It didn't seem to have had the effect she'd hoped for. Meanwhile, it had made her vulnerable, as she realized by his new line of questioning. And he was the kind of man to take advantage. She appealed to the sense of chivalry he'd mentioned. "I have very little dignity left, Mr. Talbot; I would like to preserve what shreds I can. I would be grateful if you didn't change my friends' opinions of me."

"How grateful?" There was a pause; he added, "Now that was tacky, wasn't it? Have I told you I admire your nose, with that little chip out of the end of it? I'll call on you later in the week, when I'm better settled in my offices."

"Why?" Her heart was racing threadily. "What can come of it?"

He smiled. "Many things, Mrs. Upton, many things."

Andre had two detectives looking for Laura in San Francisco, but the city was large; they could pass her on the street without knowing it. She could be anywhere, behind any door, beyond the glass of any window, and the thought was driving him mad.

He wired her stepmother twice, but didn't receive a reply to either message. He began to believe a journey to Massachusetts was in order. The more he thought about it, the more obvious it seemed: She'd gone home to Abfalter Village, was back there now, telling her mama not to answer his queries. He could be there in seven days. His heart beat a little harder with hope. *And Laura, once I get my hands on you, you'll never get away from me again!*

The days continued gray, often with cold, drizzling rain. The realization that she had exposed her secret to a stranger did nothing for Laura's self-confidence. She feared Mr. Talbot might accost her again at the shop; she half-expected him to be waiting for her when she left work each day; but

249

each night she found herself alone along the dreary ten city blocks she walked home.

On Saturday evening she was reading the latest issue of *Century Magazine* in her room, when a knock came at her door. Mrs. Noah told her she had a caller. She knew who it was even before she entered the little parlor.

Yale gave her a grin. "Good evening, Mrs. Upton," he said, with a slight bow that was a model of politeness. "I hope I haven't chosen to call at a bad hour." (*Are,* he pronounced it.)

"Have you met . . ." She glanced behind her. "Mrs. Noah?"

"She said somethin' about gettin' some refreshments," he said placidly. Every time he spoke, Laura could all but smell jasmine blossoms. She had no doubt he'd already charmed Mrs. Noah into a dither with his Southern ways.

"May I sit down?"

"If you must," she said ungraciously. He took the sofa. She took one of the lavender chairs. Seeing him here, the sense of safety she'd managed to weave for herself felt suddenly like spun glass, fine, fragile. "Mr. Talbot, I truly believed that by telling you my circumstances you—"

"Ladybird," he said in a low voice, "the fact that we're both pretending to be widowed is perfect, don't you see?"

"No, I don't!" She stared at him for a moment, then rose and restlessly inspected the striped leaves of Mrs. Noah's cast iron plant. She knew she mustn't look too long into his eyes, for in them lay his charisma—and his danger.

"You're a little dumb and a little wise, aren't you, ladybird?"

"What does that mean?" she asked in exasperation. Being a lawyer, he had a way of using words; their shadings of intent were his métier, and their careful manipulation got him the results he wanted.

"I would love to explain, but I hear our tea coming." In a louder voice he said, "May I say that you're lovely this evening: you have just the coloring to wear black."

Mrs. Noah entered with a tray almost as big as she was. It was covered with a lace cloth and silver things that

250

glittered—things from the glass cabinet in the dining room, which Laura knew were only for special occasions.

"Here we are. Laura, why don't you pour, dear? I'm so glad Mr. Talbot found you. Laura hasn't made many new friends in San Francisco yet, Mr. Talbot. And an old friend is always so comforting."

Laura opened her mouth to mutter something, changed her mind, was silent. Mr. Talbot accepted a cup from her, ignoring her look. He seemed completely at ease—like a big cat dropped among a nest of small mice.

"Yes, it seemed like Fate herself had come to my rescue when I saw Laura in Mr. Kane's store. It's been so long since we've seen one another, you understand. I was just asking her to accompany me on a drive tomorrow. I'm interested in seeing the lay of the land around here."

"I'm sure you could find someone more informative, *Mr.* Talbot." His use of her first name hadn't escaped her.

"But Laura," Mrs. Noah said innocently, "you've been working so hard. Some fresh air would be wonderful for you."

"That settles it then," Mr. Talbot said. "You mustn't let your health slip, Laura. Not at a time like this."

Laura felt rather than saw the effect this had on Mrs. Noah—that he was a close enough friend to know, and mention, this intimate fact about her.

"I'll come around at one o'clock."

It was a good thing Mrs. Noah was smiling attentively at him, because Laura's face would surely have shocked her. For a moment she was sorely tempted to open Mrs. Noah's ears with a fact or two. But what if Mr. Talbot returned the favor? Where would she go if Mrs. Noah turned her out? So instead, she smiled a quick, nervous smile that twitched the muscles in her mouth without ever touching her eyes.

Mr. Talbot arrived the following day with a buggy pulled by a resigned-looking bay horse. He tipped his jaunty straw hat at Holly and Mrs. Noah, then apologized as he handed Laura up to the cracked black leather seat. "I couldn't rent

251

anything better on such short notice; I've got to find the time to buy a vehicle of my own."

To please Mrs. Noah, Laura had dressed carefully in a gray gown with a small lawn collar. The sleeves went straight to her wrists and had turned-back cuffs. Her hair was upswept, with a waterfall of curls down the nape.

She murmured, "Your father-in-law must be very generous to set you up in such style."

A slow grin climbed his cheeks. He settled a rug over their laps and took the reins and whip in his buff-colored gloves. "Daddy Griffin is above all a good businessman. He's earned a good return on all his investments in me: a husband for Lois—who won't actually take her away from him; and a grandson left for him to mold into his own likeness. He also wanted to open a branch of the firm on the West Coast—we deal with shipping mostly, you understand. He and I saw through one another from the start."

"I wonder if Lois saw through you?"

He regarded her from behind his gold lashes. "Lois will go on playing the virginal belle 'til she's old and wrinkled. She won't be a spinster, yet she won't have to be bothered with a real husband's attentions—which she found unpleasant, by the way. She, too, has what she wants. Not everyone is an innocent like you, Laura."

"What makes you think I'm an innocent?"

"You must be, to have ended up the way you are."

"I have my eyes wide-open now—my surf-scoured eyes."

"I'm glad. That makes it easier for me."

"You seem to think you're going to be a part of my life, Mr. Talbot."

"You may as well call me Yale, because I am a part of your life, and intend to become a bigger part." He held up a hand, "Now don't start protestin'. I don't want to start the day with a quarrel, even if you do manage to look more beautiful the madder you get."

The unsaid part of this lay huge, huger than anything that had come into her life since Andre. "You're totally outrageous."

"But you're learnin' to like me."

252

Was she? She liked the strength of his voice, his humor, the enticing sense of being with someone who was willing to speak the truth, even the unmentionable truth.

He turned back to the horse and gave all his attention to their drive. They left the city behind. She hadn't spoken for quite a while when he said, "Are you goin' to sulk all afternoon? Why don't you tell me about the father of your child?"

She felt suddenly stiff, as if he'd thrown cold water on her and it had frozen solid. "I don't want to talk about him, not ever."

"Surely you're not preservin' your memories. That's deadly, you know." He said this lightly, but there was a cutting edge to the lightness. "Are you still in love with him then?"

"Who said I ever was?"

"You're not the type to fool around on your husband just to pass the time of day. I suppose he seduced you. Does he know you're expectin'?"

"No."

"Would he care if he did?" He waited for an answer, and when she gave none, he said, "No again, I reckon."

That wounded. She made her face go blank. She wanted to cry, but instead stared straight ahead until all possibility of fears faded. Then she turned to look at his profile. He had his arms resting carelessly on his knees as he leaned forward, casual, at ease. What had possessed her to drive out with this man who held so little sacred—not marriage, certainly not fatherhood, not even love?

She felt unbearably weary suddenly. He was right, of course. She was preserving her memories of Andre. And it was deadly, for he surely did not preserve any memories of her, unless as a reminder of his triumph.

And yet it seemed to her that the worst thing of all would be for her great love to come to seem only an episode, a brief occurrence that had momentarily interrupted her life—that it should ever become so remote in her mind it might as well have happened to someone else.

Yale took a winding road to the top of the Twin Peaks,

where they could view both the growing city and the bay, that great wedge of water driven neatly into the state's heart. The air had a clean snap to it. A bird sang on the broken branch of a wind-bent tree. San Francisco itself bristled with the chimneys and peaked roofs of its narrow-shouldered buildings. Behind it, masted ships from all over the world lay anchored in the deep harbor water.

The wind teased a strand of Laura's hair against her cheek. Yale moved closer. The desire she saw in his eyes had a sobering effect. She said, "It's getting late. Shouldn't we go back?"

His smile mocked her. His arm went around her shoulders and his free hand, still gloved, brushed the errant strand of hair off her cheek.

When he kissed her, she felt no reciprocating passion, nothing but an odd ache for the strong-gentle, soothing-electric handling of Andre. And it was anger at that yearning, and at herself for feeling it, that made her let Yale kiss her a second time. And a third. Moist, fervent kisses on his part. His left arm pulled her to him tightly. His fingertips stroked her lower back. But it was no good. She found his technique overbearing and graceless, and she eventually eased away.

She sensed the sting her rejection gave him. He didn't relinquish his hold on her completely. Her head rested in the crook of his arm that lay along the back of the seat. "What do you want from me, Yale Talbot?"

His eyes shone, each with a jewel of light in its center. "I think you know."

That answer echoed through her as he took up the reins. Gray rags of fog followed them back to Mrs. Noah's. Laura said as he halted the buggy, "I don't want to see you again. I'm hardly a suitable candidate for seduction right now."

"What I have in mind would be good for you, ladybird."

"It wouldn't be good for me. You wouldn't. You would only encourage me to fall lower than I already have." She scrambled out of the buggy without waiting for his help, and hurried up the steps to the door.

Inside the parlor, Holly was sitting behind her Sunday

newspaper, reading to Mrs. Noah about a new invention called the telephone. Laura barely said hello to them before going up to her room. There she slumped on her bed, her head bowed. It was hardly a moment later that Mrs. Noah's knock came. "My dear, Mr. Talbot is downstairs and he insists he must see you."

"Please tell him—"

"Laura?" Yale's drawling voice carried up the stairwell. "If you don't come down, I'm goin' to have to come up there."

The tendons holding Mrs. Noah's mouth closed gave way. Laura's cheeks stung as if she'd been slapped. She said quickly, "We, er, we had a small difference of opinion. I'll go down and straighten it out."

She found him alone in the parlor; Holly had diplomatically disappeared. "You have a lot of nerve!"

"We hadn't finished our conversation."

"I thought we had quite finished."

"We hadn't even started."

She raised her eyebrows.

"If I'm going to settle in San Franciso, I will have to have a woman."

"You could have your wife."

"A woman," he said, "not a spoiled little girl."

"I'm sure there are women of the kind you're looking for, all of them willing to spend time with you."

His blue eyes shone. "My own woman. I don't like to share. I'm a bit fastidious about some things."

He would have a woman—as he would acquire a buggy. He wasn't a man who liked to rent; he preferred to own. She wasn't entirely unprepared for this, but now that it had been spoken aloud, distaste crept up in gooseflesh over her body. "What makes you think I would consider such a thing?" she said at last.

"Because you're in trouble."

"Yes—I'm going to have a baby!"

"What of it? I can afford nurses." He read her face. "Ah, I see, you're bothered by qualms—prenatal modesty. Don't be, because, as I told you, I'm not. And after all, you won't be with child forever. I'll view it as a temporary novelty."

255

She was shocked.

He took her hand and raised it to his lips. "I'm afraid, ladybird, you're already lost. Too lost to be proud." He gathered her and kissed her again, kissed her deeply. But she felt like a dead volcano.

"You don't respond," he said, for the first time showing he had the makings of anger in him. "You think your old lover hung the moon and the stars. But he's not around anymore, and I am." He kissed her yet again.

She stood still for it, but when he was finished, she said, "Get out."

His smile returned; it came like slow, sweet honey. "All right, I know you need time to think. But don't keep me waitin' for your answer too long, darlin'. My patience is not inexhaustible."

After dinner, Laura helped with the dishes, then joined Holly at the table for a game of Authors. Mrs. Noah came in briefly to say good-bye before going out for the Sunday evening meeting of her temperance society. As soon as she was gone, Holly said, "What have you got?"

"Two small pairs. Thackeray and George Eliot." Laura spread them out.

"Well, I've got a Hugo straight." Holly laid them down. "And that's the boss hand out." As she formed the cards into a deck, she spoke again: "I was in the dining room earlier. I couldn't help hearing your conversation with Mr. Talbot."

Laura didn't comment. She felt a weary, dumb anxiety. Was this the moment her life fell apart again? Holly's next statement hit her like a hammer: "If a man like that made me an offer like that, I'd jump at it."

Laura's lips fell slightly open. "You don't know what you're saying. He's not offering marriage, you know. He's offering nothing but . . . room and board . . . and that at an expensive price. It isn't a romantic proposal, Holly. Oh, to even be discussing it!"

Holly eyed her like a mother cat getting ready to swat its kitten. "He's got money, Laura, and he's going to make more. You'd have clothes, probably jewelry, and I heard him say something about a nurse for the baby."

"My baby doesn't need a nurse."

Holly laughed; her brows arched cynically for one so young. "Your baby's going to need a lot of things. Things you won't be able to provide, since you know as well as I do you're going to lose your job the minute Mr. Kane figures out you're expecting. And—I don't mean to sound unkind—but Mama and I can't afford to let you stay here for nothing. We'll help all we can, but—"

"I'm not asking for charity from anyone! I'm saving as much of my salary as—"

"How much have you got?"

"Twenty-six dollars."

Holly only looked at her. They both knew it was a pitiful sum. Before long she needed to buy infant sacques and receiving blankets and flannel for diapers. Then there were Dr. Kellogg's fees. She cast down her eyes. "You can't really know what it's been like for me, Holly. I don't ask for much. I'm trying, I'm trying desperately . . . and this," she gestured to the simple room, "or something like it, is all I ask."

"Then get it," Holly said sharply. "Make that your price: a home of your own. Do what he wants, and get what you want."

Laura's hands clenched in her lap. "How can I? It's not right!"

Conflicting emotions struggled in Holly's voice. "We all want what's right. I would like to have a decent job, maybe find a husband who wouldn't mind the fact that I have to help take care of my mother. But I've been working since I was fifteen. I haven't had time to get a real education, and without book-learning . . . and that cannery is no place to meet a man. Oh, Laura, maybe life was so lovely for you, growing up in Massachusetts, that now you're honestly ignorant of the realities, but not me. I don't think Mr. Talbot's offer sounds all that bad."

A house like this. Laura felt another sudden sledgehammer blow, this one of temptation. If she had a house, she could rent rooms, as Mrs. Noah did. As Mrs. Gladwin did. She could earn her way and rear her child and be at no man's mercy.

Alarm at what she was thinking rushed through her veins. "It's immoral! Have you stopped to wonder why he isn't offering marriage? It's because he lied to your mother. He's not a widower at all; he's got a wife and a son, both very much alive."

"I gathered as much." Holly seemed unshockable.

"I'm sorry I've given you the impression that I could live with another woman's husband just for the material benefits he would provide. I didn't realize I appeared ready to stoop so low."

Holly's young open face flushed with emotion, but her eyes rested on Laura in a manner startlingly mature. "You're alone in the world. You have to look out for yourself. You could get enough out of Mr. Talbot to make it worth your while. Be smart, Laura. Give him what he wants—and get all you can out of him in return."

Twenty=Two

Everyone could see now, no matter what Holly and
Mrs. Noah said; for as of this afternoon Dr. Kellogg had
forbidden Laura to wear her corset anymore, and she knew
her pregnancy was glaringly apparent. It was evening now.
The day had sunk soundlessly, a mere extraction of light
from the overcast city. But Laura was still upset about the
doctor's edict. "Look at me!" she complained to Holly, who
had followed her up to her room.

"You're going to have a baby," Holly said in a wooly-tired
voice. She sank down on the stool before Laura's dressing
table, obviously weary from her day's work. "Did you think
you wouldn't show at all? Even so, you don't look anywhere
near what most women do at five months."

Laura, however, felt huge. And she had other complaints:
her back often ached; and whenever she ate Mrs. Noah's
delicious apple pie she got indigestion. She could give up
apple pie, but her corset? "How am I going to keep my job
now? Without a corset, my dresses won't fasten!"

"Tell Mr. Kane you've been spoiling your clothes and
start wearing a big coverall apron."

Laura considered. "That's a good idea."

"Well, it will give you another month anyway."

Another month, then she was out of a job. She walked to
the window. A gentle muslin mist of rain clouded the view of
the street below. Staring vacantly, she felt a small sensation,
like a bubble bursting. This wasn't the first time the baby had

259

quickened, but she was still awed by it.

Remembering Holly, she turned. "Are you going to nag me again this evening?"

Holly seemed to rouse herself from a state of suspension between sleep and wakefulness. "I'm just trying to get you to listen to reason. You can't keep him waiting forever. It's already been a month."

Laura sat on the bed, hoping that if she didn't answer, Holly would go away. It didn't work.

"You're too smart not to take advantage of this, Laura. If I had your looks, you can bet I wouldn't be working in a factory."

"Holly, you have your own looks. You'll soon find some young man who loves you beyond anything, and you'll settle down happily-ever-after. And when your babies come, you'll stay home decently and not have to go out on the street where men make odd offers to women in my circumstances."

"Mr. Talbot could protect you from odd offers."

"Mr. Talbot is the *worst* when it comes to odd offers!"

"But if you accepted—"

"Holly, you can't know what he's asking! You've never . . . been with a man, and you just can't know!"

Holly moved to the bed, too, and took up a rose sachet bag Laura had tossed there earlier. "Oh, come on, a girl doesn't work alongside the kind of men I do without learning what's what. I probably even know a few things you don't."

"All right then, let me ask you: could you let just any man . . . ?" She decided she really couldn't ask.

Holly didn't flinch, however. "Make love to me? No, not just any man. If I didn't love him, he'd have to be awfully, awfully rich."

Laura was tempted to laugh. "You're impossible! If your mother ever heard you!"

Holly ignored her. "Not loving Mr. Talbot is an asset. You just haven't looked at this in a businesslike way."

"I should hope not!"

"Listen, as long as you've got your emotions capped off, you can demand your due."

Laura looked ceilingward. "It sounds so simple—but

look at me, Holly! I'm five months pregnant. I don't even know why he wants me—I'm round as a pumpkin."

"You're not. But I don't think he'd care if you were. I've heard some men like pregnant women. Gives them a special thrill or something."

"Holly—you're going too far."

"Tell him yes, Laura. You won't have another chance like this."

The house was surrounded by snowy, smooth-haunched hills. In the yard, elms arched and spread, leafless now, but tipped with a multitude of chestnut-brown buds. In another month or two they would burst with green, and the crowns of the trees would come alive with whistling, chickadees. But for now only snow lay piled in the forks of the heavy limbs.

Andre trudged up the poorly shoveled walk and knocked at the door. It opened into a dim hall where a staircase mounted into shadow. Alarice Upton led him into an unheated parlor furnished with dark, leather furniture. She folded back the draperies of one window, letting the icy white daylight seep in.

He walked to the piano. It was closed—and locked, he discovered. He tried to imagine Laura sitting in this cold room, trying to limber up her fingers with scales. He saw her vividly in his mind, playing Chopin, her eyes closed, her head tipped forward. He saw her hands, fragile-fingered, with delicate bones at the knuckles, her wrists arching gracefully, then falling, her tears . . .

Alarice cleared her throat pointedly. The piano strings in his mind vibrated into stillness. He turned.

Laura's stepmother was tall and spare, dressed in gray brocaded satin, with a thin gold chain descending from her neck. There was a queenly superiority in her carriage. She stood with an embroidered linen handkerchief in her joined hands, waiting for him to speak. "I'm looking for your daughter," he said.

Her voice was as barren and cold as the room, as the day, as the winter: "I have no daughter."

He sized her up. "Didn't you receive my telegrams?"

"I received them, yes. But I have no daughter."

"Mrs. Upton—"

"I have no daughter."

She stiffened him with disgust. Those cold, haughty eyes. "If you're Alarice Upton, then I happen to know you're Laura Upton's stepmother. And I'm not going to leave until you tell me what you know of her." He helped himself to a seat in a rigid leather chair.

She gave no indication that he'd angered her, except that her flat bosom seemed to puff. A silence ensued, broken only when she finally said, "Very well, what do you want to know, Mr. Sheridan?"

"Where is she?"

"California."

"Where in California?"

"San Francisco, I believe."

His heart leapt. "You've heard from her?"

"I received a letter just before Christmas."

"What did she write? Where's she living?"

Alarice responded with no more than a machinelike smile and an expression full of malevolence. "I threw the envelope in the fire as soon as I saw who it was from."

"Without reading it?"

"Without opening it."

Somehow he kept from clenching his fists. "But you did see who it was from—you read the return address."

Her eyes narrowed. "You'll leave if I tell you?"

He nodded.

"I don't remember the house number, of course, just the street name: Ed something, Edson, or Edward—"

"Eddy?"

"That sounds right. And that, sir, is all I know."

He rose.

At the door the malice that was brimming in her suddenly spilled over. "She was always a wicked girl, selfish, lazy, ungrateful. What's she done that you would go to such lengths to find her?"

He gave her a look he hoped was as icy as her own. "Why

262

would you care, Mrs. Upton? As I recall, you don't have a daughter."

Laura, in her new shoulder-to-knee apron, was shelving some merchandise. She finished the patent medicine almanacs and started on the chilblain remedy. The box of tins sat on the floor; the display shelf stood over her head. Stoop and reach. Her back complained fiercely, but the work had to be done.

The packing dust bothered her, too; she kept trying not to sneeze—and had her knuckle under her nose again when the door jingled. She felt someone there, studying the poufs and froufrous of the rear of her dress—but not until she had her sneeze under control for sure did she look over her shoulder.

Yale stood silently laughing. He came forward to salute the tips of her fingers with his bent head. Then his hands quickly spanned her waist. "Ah, that explains the apron. You've put on a pound or two. Oh, now, don't look at me that way, darlin'; I meant it as a compliment." Again he laughed, a soundless movement of his straight, broad shoulders.

"I've asked you not to come in here."

"I waited until I saw the old bulldog go home for his dinner." He took her into his arms. There was an eagerness about him. "I've just come from looking over a house, ladybird, a two-story brick place. It's small, but I think it'd be perfect for us. Come and take a look."

"I'm working."

"And I'm growin' impatient," he answered in a suddenly clipped tone. "You've been beatin' the devil around the stump for a month now; I'm afraid I'm going to have to ask you for a straight yes or no."

"Yale," she said, feeling harried, "even if I were to say yes, you couldn't expect me to . . . to live with you yet. The baby won't be born for nearly four months."

"That's nonsense; of course you'll live with me—and sleep with me." He slipped his hands under her arms, bracketing her breasts. "You don't have to be shy, darlin'." His thumbs grazed the bosom of the apron, unerringly finding her nipples. Before she could slap him away, the thumbs were gone. He gave her a grin that showed his china-white teeth. He could be as sinuous as a circling fish. "Come look at the house. I won't take it if you don't like it." He added in a cagey tone, "But there's a nursery—a nice sunny little room at the back, away from the noise of the street."

He had an infallible instinct for manipulation. She stared away, at the high naked windows on either side of the door. The sun's rays were streaking between the breaking clouds, making their marshmallow rims so bright they hurt her eyes. "Yale, I-I just don't think I can. Not now. If you would only give me more time—until after the baby comes—"

His face sobered. "You're beginning to annoy me, Laura, and I'm not a nice man when I'm annoyed. I want an answer and I want it now."

Her back ached so, and she was sleepy again, and all at once the luxury of being able to stay abed in the mornings and take a nap whenever she needed seemed to be more temptation than she could withstand. To be in a place she could call her own, to care for herself, and later for her child, to have a man who would come home to her at night—was it so much to ask?

She turned away from him, stared at the bottles and boxes and jars on the shelves. "Would you put the deed of this house in my name?"

"What?" he said, as if he didn't believe his hearing.

She tried to remember how Holly had advised her. "I—I must have some security. Something more than a wad of money in a sugar bowl. Would you buy the house in my name?"

"Yes," he said in his slow, southern way. He was smiling with a certain knowing as he turned her toward him. She could feel the current of victory running through him.

"And I would like to have an allowance, a regular one for myself, aside from household expenses."

His eyes narrowed. Losing her nerve suddenly, she said, "Oh, this sounds so mercenary!"

"I like it, Laura. I'm right surprised—but I like it. A

business deal. You'll give me certain things, and in return, I'll give you certain things. Much more honest than love, don't you think, where people pledge intangibles—their very hearts and souls? As if a woman could give away her heart or a man could take it."

It's possible! she wanted to cry. *Oh yes, it's possible!*

The lamplighters hastened along the streets with their ladders, opening glowing eyes in the gathering fog. Laura hurried up the steps to the house on Eddy Street. Inside was the warmth she'd never yet taken for granted. She found both Holly and Mrs. Noah in the kitchen, and announced, "I won't be dining in tonight. I'm going out with Mr. Talbot."

Mrs. Noah's eyes shone like a puppy's. Laura's blush became tormenting as she went on about "that wonderful man." Laura formed her usual pretext of a smile: that exercise of her facial muscles she'd learned since Andre had left her. "If you'll excuse me," she said at last, "I have to change."

She climbed the stairs to her room, pondering how and when she should tell Mrs. Noah that she was going to become that wonderful Mr. Talbot's—

Her mind veered away from the word she heard Richard's voice shouting at her. Funny how people always said time healed all. Time, she knew, didn't heal a thing.

She sat in her chemise by the hissing lamp at her dressing table. A knock came at the door and Holly burst in. "Laura, I'm so glad! Now don't look so scared. One man can't be much different from another."

You, Holly, know nothing of differences between men.

"You'd better let me help you dress. It's nearly eight o'clock already."

"I don't know what to wear. If I could wear a corset I'd have some choice, but as it is, my gowns are too snug."

Holly ignored her sulky mood. "You're not going to keep to mourning clothes anymore, are you?"

"I suppose it would look pretty hypocritical. But not that red, Holly! I already feel like a scarlet woman."

At last, they agreed on a rather plain dress of dark green. With a cape of creamy lace to cover the fact that the buttons wouldn't close at her waist, it would serve.

"Now stand very straight and keep the cape closed. Don't clench it—casually, yes. Really, I swear even I couldn't tell."

Laura drew the front of her hair sleekly up in a high knot, and with curling tongs formed ringlets at the back. She picked up a squeeze scent-spray that stood among her bottles. Rosewater wafted onto her throat. Finally she pinned on a hat, a velvet toque the startling green color of April grass. It was designed to perch just forward of the chignon gathered atop her head, and she hoped the color and effect would take people's eyes off her middle.

It must have worked, because Yale's eyes were blue sparks when she went down the stairs to meet him. "My," he drawled, "you look exceptionally fine tonight."

He himself was appallingly well dressed and handsome. She hesitated just beyond his reach, still dubious, then offered him her gloved hand. He swept her out of the house, while Mrs. Noah smiled after them in that puppyish manner, her small face radiant. Laura felt so guilty. How was she ever going to tell Mrs. Noah the truth?

The streets were quiet; there was a delicious sense all over the city of brushing-up and taking a quick meal before going out afresh for a Saturday evening. Yale drove his new buggy at a leisurely pace, turning up Sacramento Street. The blocks began to be lined with fantastic pagodalike structures, decorated in greens, reds, and yellows. It was like entering a garden of taboo.

"Little China" was steadily growing, despite bigotry and persecution. Laura had heard that gambling dens flourished here, and alley saloons, and dungeonlike basements that teemed with activity day and night. The idea of opium smoking and strange rites in smokey lairs both fascinated and revolted white Americans. The Chinese were even accused of importing prostitutes and keeping them in bondage.

None of this was evident along the crowded walks, however. Bits of carved ivory, richly lacquered game tables, tapestried screens, and choice selections of satsuma and cloisonné china glimmered in the darkened windows of the shops, while the Chinese populace moved along in their noiseless padded shoes. Here was a delicate lavender lining showing under a blue coat; there was a woman with sleek black hair rolled and held by a brilliant jade ornament; and across the way squatted an ancient-looking fortune-teller with drooping white moustaches.

Laura knew from Holly's incessant reading of the newspapers that many people wanted to abolish all further Oriental immigration. Both major political parties were anti-Chinese, and the daily press charged the "Moon-eyed Menace" with unfair labor competition. Orientals were also supposed to be drawing substantial sums of wealth out of the country and sending it back to China.

From what she saw, they were perhaps an unprogressive people, living in crowded, inferior, unsanitary dwellings. She couldn't believe, however, that they were "innately pagan, depraved, and vicious." She suspected it was more their lack of interest in assimilation that made them so inexcusable.

Yale stopped and helped her down. They strolled a short way to a building with elaborately carved balconies hung with yellow Chinese lamps. A number of Chinamen lounged about the street-level door. Laura felt uncomfortable. She'd never been in such a place. Then it occurred to her that this was the kind of place a man took his mistress. Other places, more conservative places, were reserved for wives.

He said, "This is the Golden Dragon. They serve a dish called *nok mai gai* that's supposed to be especially good." He preceded her up a flight of narrow stairs where a waiter greeted them with a shy smile. Pressing his palms and fingertips together to form a lotus blossom with his hands, he delicately dipped his chin to his fingertips. The gentle majesty of the salutation touched her. "What does it mean?" she murmured to Yale.

He shrugged. "Some sort of sign of respect, I imagine." He gestured her before him to an elaborately inlaid teakwood table. The dining room, though small, was humming. She

267

decided to abandon herself to a novel experience.

He ordered, and while they awaited their dinner she asked if they might step out onto the balcony. "You've already finagled a house and an allowance out of me today. I suppose I should consider myself lucky if all you ask for tonight is a view of Little China." He held her chair for her to rise.

The balcony was hung with those gorgeous lamps, bright paper bubbles that swayed in the breeze. And below—the moving throng, so amazingly quiet! "Don't they seem sad?" she asked.

"I haven't noticed. I was thinking of how much money they've made for Leland Stanford."

Something captured his interest. Laura followed his gaze to a beautiful girl in a violet coat threading her way through the somber crowd, a girl with high breasts and a head beautiful enough to have been made by a sculptor. Laura realized suddenly that Yale Talbot would never belong to just one woman. Nor even to two. She would have to be prepared to share him with occasional light-o'-loves if she expected to keep him at all. Thus came another glimpse into the foreign way of life she had agreed to embark upon.

The harsh jangle of an orchestra broke the murmur of the street scene, and the little balcony immediately filled with others eager to catch a glimpse of the parading musicians. Yale said, "I believe it's their New Year." As if to punctuate this, the sky erupted in an explosion of fireworks.

Andre was too angry to do more than glance up at the fireworks. He saw only something bright and flaming that left a great plume of smoke curving behind as he ducked into the Golden Dragon. He'd got back from Massachusetts two days ago, and had quickly placed men up and down Eddy Street. One of them had seen a woman fitting Laura's description a scant hour ago. Andre had reached the house where she was living just as she'd come out on the arm of a stranger.

It had stunned him. All during the past months, even when

268

he'd been determined not to think of her, in the depths of his mind she'd belonged to him. Yet here she was with someone else. Instead of going right up and making his presence known, he decided to follow them. The thought of her being so close made him feel dizzy. But who the hell was that dandy she was with, and what did he mean to her?

Laura was crowded uncomfortably. Yale offered his arm and shouldered a way for them through the gathering on the balcony. Their waiter placed steaming bowls of tea at their places as they reseated themselves. Sipping the fragrant greenish brew, Laura glanced discreetly at a table where a group of Chinamen were conversing in their curious singsong language while at the same time their hands, burnished to teak, dexterously handled thin chopsticks. One old man's nails were a good four inches long. In and out among the customers moved the waiters, balancing immense brown straw trays of food on their heads. Laura's senses swam in a riot of smells: hot soups, puffs of rice-flour dumplings, meat hissing in unseen woks . . .

An array of exotic dishes, each on its own lovely plate was placed between her and Yale: deep-fried spring rolls stuffed with shredded pork, stir-fried chicken, mushrooms, bamboo shoots, and bean sprouts, pork and shrimp dumplings. They both tried to use chopsticks with comic failure before Yale begged for some forks.

He talked of the friends he was making among the professionals of the city, of the men he hoped to entertain once he was established in a home. Men, he was careful to say, and Laura understood that though they might bring their own mistresses to meet her, she would never know their wives or daughters.

In spite of these realizations coming one after another about the life she had committed herself to, he was a charming escort. He could dazzle and impress with his education and his experiences. No matter how engaging his conversation, however, she wasn't able to relax and enjoy the evening. Something was wrong; for some reason she had a constant urge to look about her, as if she felt herself watched. She tried to put it down to self-consciousness, yet the feeling seemed more insistent than her appearance or her awkwardness amidst all these foreigners warranted.

When their table was cleared, a new pot of tea arrived, along with a selection of white rice cakes topped with shreds of cyrstalized coconut. "I'm glad you finally decided to be reasonable," Yale said. "In fact, why don't you come home with me tonight?"

She sipped her tea, and tried for a flirtatious tone. "You'll see so much of me, I wager there will soon be times when I'll have to remind you of your previous eagerness."

He accepted the dare. "I would like to see 'so much' of you," he said in his soft way. "To see all of you, in fact. And the sooner the better. I have been longin' to sleep wrapped around you like a tangled vine."

She took no comfort in this. He wanted to possess her as he would possess a good horse—a necessary amenity for a young man moving up in the world. Yet she had no reason not to suppose his sexual desire was real. She had felt it growing in intensity for some time, so that now it rang from his body to hers. She felt it in the way he merely stroked her hand lightly where it lay on the table. "Come home with me tonight, Laura," he repeated.

Twenty-Three

"Go with you to a public hotel?" Laura said cautiously. "I think not."

"You're an illogical, stubborn woman," Yale murmured. "Unfortunately it's part of your charm. Still, it's a good thing I'm not the vindictive sort. A man like that, when he had you at last, could make you very sorry." Smiling suddenly, he added, "No doubt we'll have quite a few entertainin' clashes of will."

Without warning, Richard's voice came through her memory again, bringing with it the words she'd been avoiding all evening: *You're nothing but a fancy little whore* . . .

Yale asked, "Are you all right? Laura? Darlin'?"

She shivered. "Yes, I—I'm fine. It's just been a long day for me."

"Of course; you're tired. You can quit that job come Monday mornin'." For a flicker of time his gaze held a sensitivity that caressed her sore soul. "We'll go now."

The bill paid, they passed back between the tables. Laura stopped to admire several brilliant red banners. A waiter told her they were for good luck and happiness. She touched one before starting down the stairs on watery legs. She was going to need all the luck she could get.

Outside they found a heavy mist had rolled in while they

271

had passed the evening away. The streetlamps were blurs, their rays dense-looking in the fog.

The fog was so thick, Andre almost lost them outside the restaurant. He had to follow them closely on the way back to Eddy Street. There the Southerner didn't let her get out of the buggy immediately. Andre had time to leave his horse at the end of the block and make his way through the shadows up the opposite side of the street. He stood hidden in a doorway where he could see them reasonably well. As the Southerner took Laura in his arms, Andre gritted his teeth. His fingers curled into fists when the bastard's hand slipped beneath that lace cape she was wearing.

To her credit, Laura drew back a little, but the Southerner was insistent. He laughed softly. Andre knew why: her nipples were probably hardening. He allowed himself no more than an instant of a remembrance, for the Southerner was saying, "You're my dessert, the sweetest part of the meal." And then he put his hand right under her skirt. "Let me; open your legs, darlin', just a little."

Christ, right here on the street? A dread came on Andre. *Laura, don't let him, don't.*

"Please, Yale, not here!" Andre knew that voice: she was struggling against tears.

Still the man—Yale—was feeling playful. He gave another soft laugh. "Oh come on, ladybird." He fumbled some more under her skirt, and Andre nearly growled aloud until she said, "I can't, not here, *please!*"

Andre wanted to smash his fists into something.

"You're awful shy, considerin'," Yale protested. Leaning over her, clumsily knocking her hat askew, he went back to fondling her breasts.

Was it wishful thinking, or was she trying hard not to push the guy away? Andre heard her make a small sound, which he interpreted as disgust—but the Southerner seemed to interpret it as encouragement, for he kept on. Andre stood there quaking with rage. He wasn't just trembling, he was

272

shuddering all over, like molten lava in a live volcano. He had to do something. He cleared his throat from within the shadows that were hiding him. That startled Yale. They both sat up and looked around. The Southerner seemed to remember they were on a public street—and Laura took the chance it gave her to say she wanted to go in now.

On the doorstep, Yale hovered over her some more, talking softly—yet with his hands on the sides of her breasts again, familiarly. Andre nearly roared when he saw her hands resting on his chest.

What the hell was going on? The Southerner was well dressed, Andre had to give him that. But it made him see red to see Laura's palms on the man's lapels. Yale's gaze seemed to linger on those tender flexions of her mouth that Andre knew so well. Yale made an exasperated sound and abruptly swept her against him, capturing her lips. The kiss was possessive, seasoned with impatience. And it seemed, when he released her, that reluctance corded his arms, so that it required effort and will for him to step back.

She remained on the doorstep until the buggy started away; and even then she lingered, her hands crossed over her stomach in a way Andre had never seen before.

He wanted her so badly, but the minute he made a step toward her, she took fright and hastily stepped inside. He hesitated, looking between her door and the retreating buggy. He chose to follow the buggy.

A peculiarly white-faced Yale assisted Laura into his buggy again the following day. He was as well dressed as ever, in a black suit and brownish yellow waistcoat. She even caught the scent of his cologne. It wasn't bay rum, but it was expensive and masculine and disturbing. He had a look of possession in his eyes as he touched her chin. "Are you always this beautiful of a mornin', or does bein' in the family way especially suit you?"

"I don't think it suits me," she said, tucking the lap rug well up over her thickened middle even though the day was

273

brilliantly sunny. "No one who looks like a winter squash is beautiful. But thank you for saying so," she added, remembering her manners.

As he snapped the reins, she noticed his pallor again. Every movement seemed to make him wince. "Are you ill?"

"I've felt better."

"We don't have to look at the house today. Perhaps you should go back to your hotel."

"After all the talkin' I had to do to get the owner to show it to you on a Sunday? Besides, fresh air will do me more good than anything. I'm afraid I did some extra celebratin' last night."

"You went out again after leaving me?"

He nodded his head—and winced yet again.

"I gather the second celebration was liquid in nature?"

"I tried to find a card game: I am constantly dumbfounded by how few people in California can play a decent hand of poker. There I was—no mistress, no card game—there was nothin' left but to get knee-walkin' drunk." He frowned. "I wonder how much I told to that fellow who was so generous with his bourbon? He was someone I've been wanting to meet, but . . . darlin', don't ever let me drink bourbon. Keep in a supply of blackberry brandy; that's more to my taste."

She remembered her own night, the waiting before sleep finally came, for it wasn't until she went to bed that the old despair descended. Night after night she embarked on the past, visited those refuges of happiness, evoked scattered memories, endearments, the brief sound of a nocturne; night after night she reconstructed her fall. Perhaps Yale could break the cords of those night journeys, teach her to live again. Teach her to live something better than this colorless, pieced-out existence, this life that was nothing—a life without Andre.

The brick house was all he'd said and more. That it was going to be hers didn't hearten her, however. Instead, she felt her conscience grow heavier. She asked not to be taken home right away. Yale was agreeable, and soon the buggy was following a westerly route through Golden Gate Park.

As they traveled, Yale talked about furnishings. "I like a

nice tapestry carpet—and I saw a parlor suite in raw silk the other day—"

"Can you afford all that?" Laura asked murmurously.

"Darlin', I can't afford *not* to put on a good show."

They came out of the park near some cliffs. Before them spread the grand vista of the Pacific. Gulls looped and circled past the cliff faces, and black swifts flashed by in fleet arcs. A curling wave, aquamarine and indigo, broke against a tide rock, its liquid ice shattering into blue-white crystals. Another breaker hit the cliffs broadside with terrific power. There was a wonderful sound of impact, a crash and splintering.

Yale turned them southward toward miles of clean, sandy beach. Winging birds cried overhead and spindrift blew in off the billowing sea. Laura felt exhilarated by the ocean, the blue-green surge and swell, the silver splash and slide-off.

At last Yale reined up among some inshore dunes and helped her down. He kissed her lightly, but she stepped away from him, murmuring, "We're not alone."

He turned in the direction of her gaze, his homburg tilted back at an inquiring angle. "Yes," he said, slower than ever, "and he seems to be watching us."

She stared at the tall figure on the splendid horse poised all alone on a bluff against the sky. He was perhaps a mile away, and she could distinguish little except that he was large and his horse was dark with a blowing black mane. She shuddered as the moment seemed for an instant distorted and dreamlike. It wasn't *him,* of course; it never actually was him.

Oddly, Yale said, "He looks familiar." But then the man turned his horse down the opposite side of the bluff, and Yale turned to take the rug from the buggy. "Probably don't know him from Adam's house cat, but he looked for a minute like that fellow I met last night, the one with the god-awful bourbon. If it is, and he comes by, I'll introduce you. He could do me a lot of good, businesswise, so be nice to him." He smiled weakly. "I hope he doesn't, though—come by, that is. I don't feel up to socializin' today. My head's about to explode."

She responded with only half her mind. "What you need is exercise—and to control your impulses better."

"What I *don't* need is to fight another War to Suppress Yankee Uppitiness." He threw the rug over the sand in a hollow between two dunes. "Sit, ladybird. I need a nap. But afterwards I've got a mind to claim my just reward for waitin' such a powerful long time for you."

She pretended she hadn't heard that. The spot he'd chosen was a bit too private. If he became insistent . . .

He loosened his high starched collar, sat down and leaned back, placing his head in her lap, stretching out his long legs and folding his hands on his chest. She didn't know what to do with her own hands. Perhaps she should massage his temples?

"Ahh, that's downright kind of you. Maybe there's hope for you after all, evil-tempered and blunt as you are. Kiss me, darlin'."

It was an order couched as a pleasant suggestion. She couldn't explain how it made her feel. She felt she couldn't bear it. Shame flooded her face. Yet within seconds she obeyed, so afraid of annoying him was she. This was what it was like to be owned.

He sighed contentedly, and after a while fell sound asleep. Now she had nothing to do but watch the gulls overhead. The hollow lay out of sight of the ocean. She eased from under Yale's head and climbed the dunes in search of the water.

On the upslope of the shore, the panorama of beach and sea and sky lay before her as if time and people were irrelevant. She gazed a long while at the undulating horizon. The role and roar of the surf drowned out all sound, except for the occasional sad, wild note of a gull.

She walked slowly along the packed sand above the thick ruffled foam, head down, looking for shells and tracking the triangular footprints of gulls, the daintier prints of sandpipers, and the tittled lines left by scrabbling crabs. The hands of the breeze pulled at her hair beneath her hat, and the fresh salt spray made even breathing a sensual delight.

The atmosphere was mesmerizing. Not until her shell-blue

skirts were wetted by a wave washing higher than any before it, did she realize the tide must be coming in. She looked back, and found most of her footprints had already been eased away by the sea. Yale would wake and wonder where she'd gone. She started back, stepping around a pile of floppy bladder kelp.

She tried to keep to the strip of the firm wet sand between the swash and the high tide line, but aggressive waves repeatedly chased her back to the softer sand, which was harder to walk in. Giving a belated thought to the chore of cleaning her skirts, she lifted them above her booted ankles.

She was in that attitude—skirts lifted, head down—when a man stood up from a crouch at the foot of a dune. She looked up from the sand, a polite smile on her face for Yale.

But it wasn't Yale that smile met.

Andre stood there in a trim suit of honey-brown and a matching flat-topped Stetson. Andre, with his strength in his face. Andre with his lips full and sensitive. A fleeting thought winged through her mind: this, this was the face she had hoped to stare into forever.

She felt the sand slipping from under her. She felt her heart pulsing in her throat, felt her blood leave her face. Her mouth moved to form his name, but no sound came out. She shook her head the tiniest bit, trying to deny what her eyes told her.

He stood like a cobra in a state of coiled attention. He scanned her summarily, allowing his gaze to float down to her cape-hidden waist in a way she didn't like. He was blocking the way to Yale, and there was certainly no place on the open beach to run to, yet she turned and tried to run anyway, her arms automatically wrapping her stomach. Her skirts whished around her ankles, and her gait was ungainly because of the shifting sand—and because of her pregnancy, which she felt acutely now. She wasn't even quite sure why she was running from him, when she so badly wanted to run to him, but that was what she did.

He was behind her in an instant, his strong arms wrapping over hers, both of them seeming to cradle the child in her womb. She struggled to keep going, and while his hold was gentle, it was unyielding. "Stop it, Laura." He tightened his arms just a fraction, moving one up under her breasts, pulling her back against his chest. She thrashed against him. "Stop—you're going to get hurt."

She realized she couldn't get away from him. She realized that he wasn't a ghost from out of her daydreams but real flesh and real blood, and she twisted to face him, to look up into his wrathful eyes with her own wrath.

He held her at arm's length now. Their eyes caught and held. The aqua sea-glare shimmered and shivered on his shaven cheeks. Her lungs locked; she couldn't breathe. Every muscle was frozen. Only her head moved, from side to side. *No.* Her fingers curled into a fist and smashed against his hard muscled chest. She punched at him again . . . and a third time, now hitting his boned shoulder, her blows ineffective except that he must surely feel the resentment and anger behind them. He let her continue to hammer at him for a while, then by degrees stepped closer, until there was no space between them, and her fists quit beating at him so uselessly and her face buried itself against his chest. Her fingers uncurled just long enough to find his coat, then they closed again, gripping the lapels, clasping him to her. And suddenly she was crying, silent, tearless, body-shaking sobs of anger and frustration and hopeless love.

"Laura, why?" His arms circled her. His cheek came to rest atop her head. His lips dropped onto her forehead.

"No!" she said again, abruptly pushing away from him. "Go away! Leave me alone!"

"As if I could," he said, cold again.

Her mouth twisted. "Why can't you? You do as you please. Do it quite well as I recall. Go on! Do you hear me?" She threw off the hands he tried to restrain her with, and started again for the sand dunes and Yale.

He caught her arm. "I'm not letting you walk out on me again, by God. Maybe you think you don't need me, but the baby will. And we're going to do what's right for it."

"I don't know what you're talking about." But she did. She knew exactly what he was talking about, and she also knew that look on his face, and his capacity for ruthlessness in its

278

presence. Desperate, she said, "The child is Richard's."

He glowered at her. "I'm afraid not."

"It *is!* You have nothing to do with it."

His eyes narrowed even more. "You really don't know, do you? I thought when your pretty boy up there—" he nodded toward the dunes, "claimed you were married, it was something you were telling him for propriety's sake."

Now she really didn't know what he was talking about, and she didn't care. "Let go of me!"

He gave her arm a brief, warning squeeze. She caught a glitter in his eyes, which made her quail. "Richard Laird was granted an annulment two months ago, Laura. It was in the Sacramento papers. You're not married to him anymore. It's as if you never were."

"I . . . Holly reads . . ." Holly read the San Francisco papers. "Annulment?"

"The grounds were—among other things—that you refused to let him consummate the marriage." He paused meaningfully. "That makes the baby mine."

Rather than continue to struggle against his hands, which was undignified and useless, she stood still. Could it be true? Yes, her reasoning mind told her, yes. Richard had wanted to be rid of her. She'd seen that light in his eyes as he raised his fists to her, that light that said he wished she'd never come into his life, that he wished her out of it now, that he wished her dead.

Her heart contracted. She felt faint. She felt cold, hollow. "What is it you want then?" she said in a cold, hollow voice.

"My child."

"You can't have it."

"Can't I, Laura?" he said slowly. That look, those dark eyes, that tone that had never boded well for her. "Can't I, sweetheart?"

A spark of caution flickered behind her eyelids. Her nostrils dilated slightly. "No, you can't." She stared at him, searching for some sign of relenting. "You can't, Andre." Her hard-won safety was crumbling again. "Yale!" She tried to pull herself from his hands again. "Yale!"

But there were, God help her, more shocks to come.

"He's gone."

That didn't register. "Yale!"

"Listen to me, Laura! Talbot is gone. I made him an offer he couldn't resist. And he's lucky he took it, lucky to be alive after what I saw between the two of you last night." He shook her a little. "Are you listening?"

She was too astounded to remember to nod. *Made him an offer . . . he took it . . .* She was in complete awe. In her mind she could all too well imagine the scene: Andre's money, Yale's desire for it, the two men dealing, the many smiles and gestures of male *bon homie*.

"He really left me?" She was on the verge of crying again, her face struggling against it.

He canted his head to one side. "You didn't think he loved you, did you?"

"No . . . no, I'll never make that mistake again." She swallowed. "Wh-what did you offer him?"

He started her over the sand dune. "What he wants more than he wants you: he's now one of my lawyers. He's ambitious; he knows getting me for a client is an open door to Stanford and Huntington and the like."

She stumbled, trying to keep up with his long, angry stride. He stopped, looked at her closely. "All right? You're not going to faint on me, are you?"

"Where are you taking me?"

"Back to town." He stepped closer, put his hands on her thickened waist, as if to steady her.

"Why? Why buy me from Yale? What do you want?" she whispered.

"Our child." His palms moved, as if discovering her new shape.

She tried to forget that and concentrate on his words. As the purport of them sifted in, she gradually stiffened. "No, Andre."

He started her walking again.

"No!" She stopped so abruptly he almost pulled her off her feet. Yet she stayed her ground. "If you think I'm going to let you drag me off again—let *go* of me!"

His hand didn't even loosen on her arm. "I'm going to

280

claim what's mine. The child—and you," he added dreadfully.

She was close to panic. "I'm not yours! I—I'm in love with Yale."

The look on his face made her shudder. "Then you have my sympathy."

"I don't need your sympathy." His face wavered in the film that rose before her eyes. "I despise you; I've never hated anyone the way I hate you."

"You'll love me again soon enough. You seem to love best whoever has you at the moment. And that's going to be me from now on. Now are you going to walk, or would you rather be carried?"

"Is this—Andre! is this another abduction?"

"With variations, and for the best of reasons." He pulled her along as he spoke. "I persuaded Talbot to take my horse and leave the buggy. Throwing you over a saddle didn't seem a good idea this time—considering your condition."

She thought the world must have gone mad. He was stealing her again, with nothing she could do about it. And Yale . . . Yale had sold her! She felt weak-kneed, clutched at his coat sleeve for support, feeling suddenly depleted and sick and shaken.

"Laura—are you all right?" he asked. She hardly noticed when he put his arm around her, lifted her, saying under his breath, "Good girl, you're doing fine. Keep your eyes open now, don't pass out."

The horse's ears were sharp with interest as he raised her into the buggy; then they were moving, he with his arm around her, supporting her, and the immediacy of being in such close quarters with him once more, after having come to believe that she would never see him again, made her feel sick and fluttery all over again.

She leaned sideways, away from his hold, and scanned all about to see if Yale was still in sight. He wasn't. Andre didn't stop her from looking, but he warned, "You're going to get that man shot yet." He spoke without even looking at her. "I will shoot him, too, don't doubt it, if that's what it takes to protect you from him."

"You're not my defender!" she said fiercely, but then, tentatively, she touched his sleeve. "Promise me you won't harm him."

"Touching," he said contemptuously. "But don't kid yourself that he feels the same way about you. Hell, he cares more about the straightness of the part in his hair than he does about you. I know his type."

Twenty-Four

"I know exactly how a man like Talbot goes courting," Andre sneered, "starting off with such careful attention to that pretty blond hair and sucking a licorice drop to make him oh-so fragrant. He's your classic Southern dandy, is Yale Talbot.

"Did he tell you he loved you? He's a damned liar if he did—but I wouldn't put it past him. He's got the instincts of a riverboat gambler—shuffles his cards so slick they hardly bend. A good trait in a lawyer, but not in a lover. You'd lose every time to him. He'd study you, and break you down, and make you his toy. As it is, he'll have a replacement for you in a week.

"*Damn* you, Laura! There's no more predictability in you than a swallow in a cyclone. What a damn fool thing! First Laird, then Talbot!" His voice was low with disgust. "Christ, you don't know the first thing about men, let alone what one expects from a mistress. Him and his southern drawl, pawing you last night—'Open your legs, darlin'. I could have killed him right then and there, and strangled you, too. And when he told me you were going to have a baby—*my* baby!" He'd worked up his anger to the point of being unable to express it coherently anymore. "Son-of-a-god-damn-son-of-a-bitch!"

He was leaning forward, his forearms on his spread knees, the reins clenched in his big fists. He tossed her a look as sour as swill. "Have you been to bed with him?"

"No!" she cried in absolute terror. Terror enough to

283

subdue for the moment all the other thoughts fanned out in her mind, such as that he had no say over what she did with her life, who she saw—or who she went to bed with. That none of this would have happened if it hadn't been for him. But the terror made her wise enough to keep quiet for now.

Instead, she stared ahead. What was he planning? She felt as if she were falling endlessly into an eerie place of *déjà vu*. She had to keep her wits, be tough as boiled eel, and somehow, somehow! see that he didn't get the last word this time. This time she had to make sure matters didn't pass her by before she could even see them coming. She was not going to let him make a fool of her again.

She met his eyes. With surprise, she read not anger, but only sadness and reproach now. "Laura, how could you?"

She assumed he meant her liaison with Yale. Anger she could deal with, but not this. She said hopelessly, "You couldn't understand." It was a weak excuse; she hadn't intended to make it. She would make no more.

When they exited Golden Gate Park, the angelus bell had already rung its pure, deliberate notes at the Mission Dolores. It was growing dark over the city's teeming wharves. The last birds were merely swift, sharp wings over Market Street. Laura sat up straighter when they neared Eddy Street, and looked at the golden squares of windows along its length, but Andre continued into the Little China section of town. He turned down a narrow alley, stopped, and jumped down. He came to her side and held up his arms to her. Not budging, she asked, "Where are we?"

"This is where Ling's uncle lives."

"Wonderful. But I don't care to meet Ling's uncle just now. Please take me home."

"Laura, you're not dense; you know what's happening."

"I want to go home."

His anger flashed once more: "What did I tell you? Did you think I didn't mean it?"

She knew that tone, and considering her baby's safety, decided not to give him cause to handle her roughly. Caught between struggle and submission, she put her hands on his upper arms, prepared to be helped down quickly.

Instead, he drew her into him, so that she lay against the length of him, the tips of her shoes above the ground. Powerful, his arms and legs felt powerful. And she knew she loved him with the same unremitting intensity she'd felt in the blue bedroom of his house outside Jackson. The carved cherry wood buttons of his coat pressed into her breasts and round stomach. He tipped his face up to her. She knew what he was doing—ruthlessly reminding her of the cords with which he had conquered and held her before. She had tried to rip them out of her thoughts, sledgehammer them with rationalizations, erase them with fatigue, but she saw now that they were still as strong as ever. All in an instant she remembered their lovemaking, how he had entered her . . . She felt a warm rush of pleasure.

He said, "You know, when I'm holding you, that you're right where you belong—don't you?" With those words echoing softly in her ears like the echo of the sea in a shell, he put her down.

His hand on her back, he knocked on what seemed a blank wall. A seam appeared in the darkness, broadened, a door opened and a thin bar of light fell on his face. A moment more of mysterious stillness, then the door was thrown wide and a Chinaman of indeterminate age, wearing thick spectacles and a queue hanging down the back of his long Prussian blue robe, bowed them inside.

The room smelled clean, with the faintest hint of a subtle incense. While Laura took it in, Andre and the Chinaman muttered a few brief words. Andre had a desperate look, and lifted his hat and smoothed a hand over his hair. The old Chinaman was full of servile smiles and bows, as if proud to even be noticed. He was all a-glimmer, gold teeth and gold spectacles, a volley in his laugh. His voice was a bit too exuberant, too happy, though, and Laura didn't anticipate the alarming caroom of his eyes behind the refracting magnification of those lenses: His eyes were the eyes of a man who had seen everything and was shocked by nothing.

He beckoned her through a narrow passage. She had no intention of following him, but Andre's hand at the small of her back again gently pushed her along. The passage led to a dark courtyard, walled in on all sides by neighboring buildings. Someone nearby was shooting off fireworks that burst into balls of burning glitter in the sky above. Laura looked up, then looked to find the old man stopped, indicating a steep flight of stairs leading down to a basement. She balked. "I'm not going down there; I want to go home!" Panic rose. Were they really going to imprison her in a dank cellar?

The old man continued to smile and bow—and make gestures with his hands that were like executioner's chops. Andre started down the narrow, unlit stairs, taking her wrist in his iron fingers so that she was forced to follow, the long train of her skirt trailing behind. "Andre, don't!"

He turned in grim silence.

"Please—please don't! I'll do whatever you say!" She was perfectly frantic.

He seemed to see her terror then, and though he frowned, he also relented. "It's all right, Laura. What do you think, that it's a dungeon? Just take a look inside."

Instead she swung around in a confusion of skirts to look behind her, hoping desperately for help from some quarter. The old man had already disappeared. When she looked back, Andre had unlocked and now threw open the door with his free hand, revealing a small room bathed in lamplight. He pulled her down the last steps.

She wasn't prepared for the wall hangings of silk in rainbow hues that shone and pulsed. Nor had she ever beheld such cupboards, of tulipwood and lacquer, with tiny clusters of drawers finely painted with pavilions and figures in gold. In a corner a brazier with a black and polished grate glowed with coals. Opposite was a bed-lounge strewn with brightly embroidered black silk cushions. Behind the door stood a table and two red lacquered chairs, and a rich chest gleaming with brass fittings. The room was saturated with color: royal blue, damson, green, red.

Andre stood watching her with the brim of his hat shading his heavy-lidded eyes. "This is lovely," she said to him, her voice breathless and pitched slightly high, "I'm so glad you brought me to see it. Now may I go home?"

He released her wrist. "Stop playing dumb." He was giving her an especially unpleasant and personal look.

She moved to a low, black lacquered table. On it stood a porcelain figurine, a woman who was slightly bowed with her hands clasped.

"Kuan Yin, goddess of mercy. You may need her."

"Because I can't look for any mercy from you?"

At first he didn't answer, but then he did, with such a resurrection of his wrath that she whirled to face him in surprise. "Who am I"—his voice built to a shout, *"Who am I, for God's sake, to show you mercy!"*

She trembled like a deer before a grizzly. He was immense, a violence at rest, broad shoulders, strong back, strong hands—a man capable of anything.

"This is no more than you deserve!" He was more angry than she had ever seen him, his face was white with it and his eyes glittered black. His hands came up, as if to close over her upper arms, and she braced herself. But instead of seizing her, he slung himself away, paced to the opposite end of the room, threw his hat down on the chest and clenched and unclenched his fists in an effort to control himself.

After a moment he turned and said, "I warn you, Laura, don't ever underestimate me again."

In command of himself once more, he came back to her. He drew her cape away. She didn't dare object. He put the lace to his nose briefly before he hung it over the carved back of a chair. "Everytime I steal you, you come to me smelling of French Milk of Roses."

"Why are you doing this?" she asked between teeth gritted against tears. She peered into his stark gaze that was still lined with something ominous.

"In four months we're going to have a baby."

"I'm going to have a baby."

"Don't forget how you conceived it."

The need to turn from him was overpowering, but he took her face into his hands. He spoke deliberately. "Remember

287

how it was, Laura, when we made love?" He brushed a thumb gently across her lips.

Her vision was glazed with unshed tears, yet the words fell from her lips slowly, like drops of acid: "I remember." Her feelings were much too strong for her to put them off, fear or no fear. "Oh, I remember. Especially how you used me and betrayed me. I remember, Andre, oh I remember exactly how it was." It was hard to breathe, as if someone she loved had just died, that keen a sorrow.

A muscle moved in his jaw. Why did that strike such a chord in her? But then his lips lifted in a silent snarl like a wolf's. "*I* betrayed *you?* You're the one who went back on your word; you're the one who makes promises you have no intention of keeping."

She was thrown off balance. "I don't!"

But his expression was closed now. He was refusing to listen to her. He moved away from her again, turned, took savage paces across the Oriental carpet. Then, as if he couldn't trust himself another moment in the same room with her, he grabbed his hat and, without a word, opened the door. He paused with his back to her. "I've got to meet Talbot at my mother's stable. No one will come if you make a fuss—these people have learned to mind their own business —so don't exhaust yourself trying anything foolish. You have the child to think about."

She gasped. That he could say that to her! "I've thought of nothing else for months! I've thought and thought about the child, Andre! The child you left me with!" she said to the closing door. Then came the sound of the key in the lock and his steps retreating up the stairs.

Her heart was beating so hard it hurt. She looked about her for some means of escape. The only window, located over the bed, was high, narrow, and barred. She stood on the red silk coverlet to look out, but saw only a narrow view of the alley, the buildings across the way, and a sliver of sky, now filled with rockets and red stars and golden rain. A faint, rasping, discordant sound burst from some nearby street. She recognized it as the Chinese orchestra she'd heard

288

last night when she was in this district with Yale. The music was punctuated by more bursting rockets and someone singing—a voice like an Irish tenor with adenoids.

She climbed off the bed, removed her hat, adjusted the fullness at the back of her skirt, and sank into one of the lacquered chairs at the table. She stared at the brazier, and the coals stared back, like eyes afire. Her will broke then, suddenly, like the snipping of a cord. She buried her face in her hands and wept. She was a captive in the very heart of oriental San Francisco, in a basement room that, despite its silken lining, was nothing but a cell. It took everything she had to keep her terror from spilling absurdly from each crack in her face.

An hour later, Andre eased the door open. The February air, drenched with ocean cold, pushed in with him. Laura was still sitting at the table, her head in her arms. She pretended sleep. The room had grown chill; she heard him replenishing the coals in the brazier. She raised her head, so that when he stood he found her watching him.

He had removed his brown coat and waistcoat, and stood in a white silk shirt. As he stared back at her, he slowly drew his hand across his lips, as if his mouth watered for her. It was a gesture totally at odds with the fury he'd directed at her earlier.

"I, uh, I'll ask Wong Yung to bring you something to eat," he said in a neutral tone that didn't match the gaunt passion in his face.

She kept looking at him; she felt afraid not to. "Don't bother, I'm not hungry." She made a desperate effort to appear calm, though she felt her nerves tight as drawn bowstrings.

"You should have something. He's got—"

"I'm not hungry."

"But you should eat."

"Can we introduce a new topic?" She rose. "Andre, this is so insane! You don't care a fig about me or the baby. Let me go!"

For a moment the air in the room seemed as cold as Alaska in December. He crossed to the bed-lounge and swept the horde of black silk cushions from it, then turned down the red coverlet and raw silk quilt. "Get some rest. You look tired; I noticed it last night."

"Last night?" She recalled now that he had mentioned seeing Yale "pawing" her in the buggy.

"I happened to be dining at the same restaurant as you and Talbot. I was right behind those red good-luck banners. I thought for sure you'd see me."

He'd *happened* to be dining there. An accident. He'd run across her by chance. And even then he'd been afraid she would see him. Well, what had she hoped for? That he'd looked for her? That he had felt some remorse over his betrayal and come to realize he cared?

"I'm not staying the night here, Andre. There are people who must be worried about me this very minute. And I have to go to work tomorrow, early."

"I sent Talbot to explain to your landlady that you're with me now. He's a charmer; he'll make it sound good. As for your working, that's all finished."

She stood. "I need that job! You have no right to make that decision!"

As her temper flared, he seemed to become more and more calm himself. "You have more important things to do with your hands than sell Tropic Fruit Laxative." He took a deep breath. "Come on, Laura; haven't you had enough for one day? Turn around and let me unfasten you."

She shrank back. "Don't touch me! I don't need your help, not for anything!"

"You're pushing me, Laura."

His voice was smooth as velvet, all but caressing—but she wasn't fooled. Underneath he was still furious. Carefully, she said, "I'm not going to stay here. I'm warning you, Andre, I'll fight you. If you're so worried about the baby, then *you* won't push *me*." For emphasis, she picked up a dark jade Buddha and held it like a weapon.

"You think that's going to stop me? Look, you know damn well I'm not going to let you go, so why don't you give in, and make it easy on both of us?"

"What sort of game are you playing? If what you say is true—that I'm not married to Richard anymore—then there's no reason for any of this. You can't get at him through me now. You never could. So why are you doing this? You don't really expect me to believe you feel any sense of duty to my baby, do you?"

"Put it down, Laura."

"You seduced me, you ruined Richard's marriage. Isn't that enough? When is it going to end?"

He took a step forward and said quietly, "If you don't put that thing down and get out of that dress and into bed right now, I'll give you a good idea how it *might* end."

She stood her ground, but when he took another step forward, she jumped back, out of reach of those powerful arms and hands.

"I think it would be easier to surrender, sweet. Easier on the baby, easier on me . . . easier on you."

She swallowed. "All right, but don't come any closer." Uncertain, she put the Buddha down. Just as uncertain, she put her hands to the fastenings at the back of her bodice.

He stood with his legs braced wide, his hands crossed over his chest, his strong-featured face scowling as she stubbornly struggled alone with the myriad tiny buttons and ties that had kept her dress draped properly, until she was down to her muslin chemise. Her body felt cool and vulnerable; she felt worse than naked. She self-consciously folded her hands over her convex tummy and cautiously stepped around him to sit on the side of the bed and remove her button boots, which were full of sand, and then her stockings. Finally she took down the bun on the crown of her head, and the ringlets that had cascaded down her nape, and let her hair fall over her shoulders. Would he notice that the pins and combs she'd removed were the ones he'd given her? Would he comment that her hair smelled of roses, too, for she always added a drop of scent to the rinse water when she washed it?

She met his gaze warily. Those heavy-lidded eyes, their gleam made her feel weak. Strength rose from his thighs and gathered in his shoulders; his whole body rang with it. It made her tremble to the sound of faraway chords. She'd fallen in love with that strength, that power to dominate. She had to turn her face away from it now. "I don't look quite the way I did last September, do I?" she said briskly.

"You're beautiful, more womanly and beautiful than—"

"*Please!* Don't do that—tell those kind of lies again. Don't humiliate me further, Andre, I'm begging you."

She sat taking in ragged breaths. He leaned to turn out the lamp above her head. In the sudden darkness the window flared with a white explosion, a rocket burst of color and cinder-fall. She looked up at him, and he seemed about to do something, but hesitated, then said, "Go to sleep, Lorelei." His voice was gentle.

Impulsively, she reached toward his face, inviting him down to sit beside her. Her fingertips touched his lips. She said softly, "Yale will teach me whatever I need to know to please him."

There was a long frozen moment before his smile came, crooked with contempt. "Talbot will never touch you again. There's no doubt he would've taught you a lot of things, though. He's lucky I found you when I did, because if you'd already gone to bed with him, I would've had to call him out." There was no sternness in his voice, and he had the strangest intent expression on his face. His hands went around her shoulders. Then, with a fluid movement, he laid her down on the feather pillow, his arms strong and firm about her. He whispered, "Sweet, forget Talbot; he's lost to you now. You're mine again." He kissed her with hunger.

And she let him kiss her, forgetting everything but his hands under her back, his mouth on hers. He lifted her legs onto the mattress and lay half over her. He held her as though he'd had part of his heart torn from him and it was barely restored. His voice was fierce, passionate: "Could Talbot make you tremble like this, make you want like this?"

Her heart thumped against his chest like something imprisoned and frantic.

"You're an artist, an angel, a dreamer, Laura, a dreamer who too often plays the fool."

A low moan escaped her and she arched away feebly.

"No . . . let me love you," he murmured, his mouth taking hers again. He was holding her hard, his hands confining her like manacles.

Her instincts overtook her reason completely, and she put her arms around him. His silk shirt was glossy and cool. She reached around his shoulders as far as she could, urging and stroking his back.

"So there are things you remember, then," he said, his tone satiny.

She remembered everything, and she knew that she had not been alive since he'd left her that night so long ago. Not really. She'd been dead, waiting for him to come and claim her. And now, in a moment, just this simply, she was set spinning into life again, spun by his careful hands and his tender mouth.

It was his big hand smoothing over her rounded stomach that caused her to stiffen, to regain her senses. The intimacy was like a whip of wind against her cheeks; it shattered her treacherous mood. She wrenched away, and felt dizzy from the complete fall from those heights the movement cost her. "Are you proud of yourself? Is that what this is all about— you made me pregnant and now you're feeling so proud? You want to know what I'm like now—after what you've done to me?"

He pressed his face into her hair as she began to cry. She hated to cry in front of him like this, but she didn't seem able to stop.

She felt him leave her, then felt him slip into bed beside her. She turned away, but that didn't stop him from molding her back and hips into the curve of his naked chest and groin. One of his long-boned, big-muscled calves slipped between her bare feet. She didn't struggle; she didn't want to struggle; she wanted to rest there in his arms endlessly. Let time stop. Let it stop now.

And she didn't forestall him when he fondled her stomach again, searchingly, seemingly awed by its solidness, by the thought of the child it carried. And when the baby moved——he lay stock-still, as if stunned, with his palm conforming to her flesh. He lay so long like that, making the acquaintance of the life within her, that she fell asleep.

Twenty-Five

The baby in Laura's womb quieted, and Andre's attention turned back to Laura herself. He turned her in his arms and began to open her cotton chemise without waking her: Light as a fern, his mouth brushed her lower lip while he unfastened the top button, and another, and another, until her breasts lay translucent in the dimness of the room. They had gathered fullness since he had last loved them; even so, beneath the delicacy of her shoulders, they seemed fragile. His lips traveled down her throat, her shoulder, to delicately nibble one nipple: he took it into his mouth and plied his tongue around it, just trifling and pleasuring himself.

As his hand strayed down beneath the nice roundness of her belly again, she stirred. He barely breathed. She'd be mad as hell if she woke up now. It was as if he held a wild creature in his arms, all but captivated, all but captured, all but possessed, one who wouldn't knowingly allow him to touch her. At any moment she might wake and see her danger—that she was being caressed and observed in her beauty by the enemy. She would scramble away and stare at him, stiff, cold-eyed, angry.

When it was evident that she was still sound asleep, he leaned up on his elbow. He eased the hem of her chemise up her legs. He bent to kiss her soft, pillow-downy thigh, high up, where she was fragrant of woman. She wasn't wearing underdrawers—probably because she couldn't button them around her waist. He smiled bemusedly. He'd never before considered the little problems like this a woman encountered when she carried a child.

In the dim red light put out by the brazier, his hand closed lightly about her knee. He was sorely tempted to lift it aside. It would thrill him to give his eyes a feast. But somehow that would be going too far, it would be too much of an invasion of her privacy.

Still, his mind wondered: What if he were to take her now, what if she woke to find him already within her? Would she surrender to the pleasure? Or would she struggle?

He groaned and lay back and covered them both. Not since he was a kid had he been so impatient, so pent-up, so ready to burst at the merest touch. He wanted her warmth and comfort, wanted to fill his hands with her, fill his mouth, fill his eyes. He lay carefully away from her, and willed his mind to think of horses, of the salmon fishing business, of possible names for the baby.

But underneath everything was his anticipation. How soon could he openly explore all the subtle and mysterious changes in her body, by touch as well as by sight and smell? How soon could he reach for her for succor in the night?

A light tap at the door awakened Laura. She watched Andre answer it. Wong Yung smiled and bowed, his gold-rimmed spectacles and gold tooth glittering, as he handed in a breakfast tray. As Andre shut the door, Laura sat up—and found that her chemise was twisted up around her waist. She vaguely recalled coming to the edge of sleep several times in the night and feeling Andre's hand tucked between her bare thighs with easy familiarity.

In the few seconds it took him to place the tray on the table she'd discovered that she was unbuttoned as well. She quickly began to right herself. He saw that she was awake then, and saw what she was doing. His grin was infuriatingly sheepish. "Did you enjoy yourself?" she asked bitingly.

Before he could answer, her hand moved to her stomach.

296

"Kicking again is he?" He came to sit beside her and nudge his hand under hers. "Here?" The baby treacherously elbowed exactly where his palm lay. He laughed. "That's either a symphony conductor or a mule you've got in there."

She brushed him away. "He?"

"Or she. Which do you want?"

"I don't know. A girl, I guess; I don't know much about little boys."

"I know a lot about little boys, so we have the situation covered in either case. Convenient how that works out, isn't it?"

She saw how easy it would be to fall in with this, to share the burden. And the pleasure. But she'd trusted him once before, to her loss, and the experience had left her wounded. She must be careful this time, oh so very careful. "May I get up?"

He allowed her to get into her clothes. She said, twisting her hair into a temporary rope over her shoulder and stretching her arms back to reach the upper buttons of her eggshell-blue dress, "How long must I stay here?"

"Why? Don't you like this place?" He glanced about blithely. "And I was so sure you would, what with Talbot's plans for you. This room was furnished for a whore."

That hurt. She clenched her teeth before taking a helpless sort of retaliation. "Your Mr. Wong must certainly be an honorable old man. Quite a family, your late wife's: a hateful old servant for a father, a procuring uncle, and for a husband—"

"That's enough, Laura. I'm going to try very hard to be patient and fair with you today."

"Oh, are you? How kind."

She grudgingly accepted the pocket comb he offered, and styled her hair into a severe and sleek chignon. He held a chair for her and she sat down to a breakfast of steamed shrimp dumplings. His hands moved from the back of the chair to her shoulders, and he bent and spoke softly in her ear: "Funny you're still using Grandmother Sheridan's combs—when you hate me so much."

He sat across from her, smiling to himself. "As for Wong Yung, he left China under conditions only slightly different from slavery. When the Central Pacific Railroad was being built, a man by the name of Mark Hopkins supervised the founding of companies to import and use Chinese labor. They were responsible for the immigation of around nine thousand Chinese in the early sixties.

"Crocker's Pets, the railroad workers were called. Named for Judge Crocker, who is so admired in Sacramento these days for benefiting the city with his art collection. Laborers were bound to the companies by contracts, and were purposely kept poor and malnourished. In no way were they free, but pretty much owned by the speculators, who paid them a few pennies an hour.

"This room was furnished for a girl brought over against her will for one of our leading San Francisco millionaires. I won't mention any names, because my mother still entertains his family at odd times. Wong Yung was her keeper, yes, but he only did what he was forced to do.

"Now, as for how long you'll stay here, that depends on how hidebound you are with this show of antagonism."

"*Show* of antagonism?" She swallowed down her retort. She wanted to be set free as soon as possible. "What is it you want, Andre?"

"I've told you."

"Well, tell me again."

He began to eat.

"Tell me, damn you!"

He affected a frown. "I was hoping you'd forgotten that bad habit." He ignored her exasperation. "I want to be a father to my child—for starters. I've always had a hankering to be a father. The paternal instinct and all."

"The only reproductive instinct you have . . ." She stared at the bowlful of solid-headed marigolds Wong Yung had handed in with the tray.

"You were saying, Laura? I'm afraid I missed the end of that sentence," he said with grave, outrageous politeness.

"Please, just tell me what you really want."

"I just told you—to be a father to my baby. At the same time, I'm going to save your honor—what's left of it. I'm going to make an honest woman of you, Laura: I'm going to marry you."

She nearly spilled the bowl of tea she'd brought to her lips. She put it down cautiously. Her fingertip followed the circle of its rim. "And how do you intend to accomplish that," she looked up at him, "without my cooperation?"

His teasing mood disappeared. "You'll cooperate. You're not so dumb you'd pass up a respectable 'Mrs.' in front of your name, in favor of a life of backstreet restaurants and degrading fondling. A man doesn't ask his *wife* to spread her legs in a buggy on a public street, I can tell you that!" He paused, took a deep breath, and went on more calmly. "You ran away from home to find yourself a husband and have some babies, as I recall. I've given you the one—a bit beforehand, I admit; now there's only the other, and your wishes are fulfilled."

"You don't want to marry me. You never did. I can only assume you're feeling some sense of duty to the baby, but you don't have to. I'm perfectly able to take care of it."

"By becoming Talbot's doxie? By letting my child grow up illegitimate?"

"No one has to think the baby is illegitimate. I've established myself as a widow; I'm having a posthumous child."

"A widow about to become a common whore!"

"If I'm a whore it's because you made me one!"

He immediately became calm. "I suppose that's fair enough. But I made love to you with the express intention of marrying you as soon as possible."

"How can you say that? How can you sit there and—"

He held up his hand. "All right, I understand that you were under a strain. You didn't understand annulments, you felt you were married to Laird—and I guess you were, legally. I'll give you that much. For the time being, we'll forget about the fact that you didn't come to me when you left Laird, not even when you found out you were pregnant.

299

And we won't even go into the affair with Talbot—Christ, you're easy, Laura! Seems anyone can have you!"

He was confusing her. She had to keep to the point. "I won't marry you."

"The child has a right to my name and my inheritance."

"You can't make me marry you. Presumably there would have to be a clergyman present, and at least two witnesses. I don't see how you can force me under those circumstances. Someone would be bound to notice you twisting my arm."

His chair tipped as he rose. "Don't be too sure! As they say around here, you haven't got a Chinaman's chance, because if I can't make you see reason, if you haven't got enough sense to accept an honorable proposal—if you're going to be the one kind of fool I can't even find an ounce of pity for, the kind who won't help herself—then what happens won't be my fault! And as for mercy," he moved to the low table that held the statuette of the goddess and gave it a vicious kick, shattering the porcelain on the floor, "I don't figure you've got any coming."

She was wise enough not to respond. Instead she watched him gather his coat and hat and slam out the door. She sat quietly for a moment, then went to the door and tried the knob. "Andre?" she called tentatively; then louder, "Andre!" She rattled the lock. "Don't you leave me here alone again!"

All that day Laura paced the floor, reliving everything that had happened between her and Andre, hour by hour, as a geologist devotedly pulverizes a rock. When he didn't return that evening, and she couldn't get anything but more bows out of Wong Yung, she went to bed in exhaustion.

In the morning, he was back. He was sitting beside the bed when she woke, dressed in a white, stiff-fronted evening shirt, its high collar open. A cambric bow tie lay at the foot of the bed atop a black tuxedo jacket. Evidently he'd been to some formal affair last night, while she'd been imprisoned here.

He was silent; his gaze went over her face slowly. She had

the feeling he was even less in grasp of his emotions than he had been yesterday or the day before. A man in mid-hesitation, not knowing which way he should pivot.

"For Christ sakes, stop looking at me as if I were some sort of ogre. It's only been six months since you went to bed with me—and enjoyed it pretty thoroughly, as I recall."

She felt her face tighten. "You took advantage of me."

He thought about this for a time. "I did. But you loved me in spite of it—for a little while, at least."

He rubbed his face as if to wipe a dream from it. "I could use a shot of bourbon," he said sullenly, leaning forward with his elbows on his knees. "But I suppose all we're going to get out of Wong Yung is more green tea." He took a lock of her long hair that had fallen over the edge of the pillow, and idly stroked the silky skein back and forth between his index and middle fingers.

"You're playing the fool now, Andre. None of this makes any sense. I know you don't care about me, and I can't believe you really feel a sense of duty toward my baby—"

"Sense of duty?" An unkind smile appeared on his face. "Is that what you think this is all about?" He shook his head, and his smile changed his face to something more pleasant. "I've missed your simplistic viewpoints, Laura."

He slowly brought his elbows off his knees, straightened his shoulders muscle by muscle, sighed deeply, then rose from the chair to walk about, finally stopping before a piece of embroidery on an electric blue background, studying it as though he were thinking of stealing it. She took the opportunity to begin to dress. He turned to watch her put on her stockings, his face quiet, speculative. Then he moved quickly, taking her wrist and pulling her up to him.

Oh! it was so unexpected! A long, delicious kiss, fervent, eager, familiar. Their tongues met and intertwined, smooth as syrup; his palms pressed softly against the sides of her breasts as his thighs pushed her back to the wall. He continued fondling her breasts, finding and squeezing the nubs beneath the thin muslin of her chemise, and kissing her neck. And she allowed it, amazed at how little sin she felt at letting him handle her so intimately.

He put his forearms on the wall on either side of her head to brace himself, bending his knees to put his mouth on the same level as hers. His lips were warm and sweet, their pressure ravishingly gentle. Hers opened again in languorous acceptance. She hardly realized when she arched the peaks of her breasts to him, trying to flatten them against the broad hardness of his chest.

Eventually he lifted his head away, and she saw a smug smile rest a moment on his mouth. His body leaned into her. She was a little ill at ease, but not so much as she might have thought. She knew he could feel the swell of her belly, but evidently her new shape didn't repulse him. Not if she were to judge by his own unembarrassed tumescence.

His mouth came over hers a third time, and clung to her lips a moment more. When he raised his head again, his eyes were onyx-bright. He smiled—a slow tantalizing curve of his lips—but didn't move or speak. Realizing that her left wrist had somehow come up to lie against his shoulder, she lifted it. Still he stayed, hovered, an overwhelming, intensely masculine presence. "Sweet Laura," he said with a ragged chuckle, "you are easy, so easy I don't see how you're going to hold out on marrying me."

Wong Yung's knock came at the door. Andre flexed the muscles of his powerful arms and pushed off the wall. "Just a minute!" he called. He found her dress and efficiently threw it over her head and buttoned her into it—letting fly an unconscious profanity when he found that several of the waist buttons wouldn't meet.

She squirmed, self-conscious again. "Where's my cape?" As she found it, he unlocked the door to accept their breakfast. They seated themselves at the table.

He reached across the table and fingered her chin. "Sorry about this beard; looks like I scratched you some."

She didn't meet his eyes, but stared at his white single-breasted waistcoat. "Where were you yesterday?"

"Making arrangements. I meant to get back by dinner time, but at the last minute I remembered I had to go to a

302

reception. Since it was in my honor, I couldn't think of a way out of it, short of saying, 'Sorry, but I have a woman locked in a cellar in Little China and can't get away just now.' Of all the times to have a birthday party! I came in about one o'clock, but you were already asleep."

Their breakfast only consisted of bread, still warm and soft at the heart, and fruit, and yes, green Chinese tea. It satisfied Laura, however.

As soon as she'd eaten her fill, he suggested they go up into the courtyard. "You need some daylight." He unlocked the door and preceded her up the narrow steps.

He was taking no real risks in letting her out of her silken cage. The court had no exit except through Wong Yung's rooms. Andre heaved himself up onto a low, wide, brick wall, the remnant of some older building destroyed by one of the city's famous fires, while she paced, her bedraggled blue skirts sweeping the pavement. The surrounding buildings blocked all the ocean breeze and for once the sun poured down so bright her shadow was stark as ink at her feet.

"You said you spent yesterday making arrangements?"

He lounged on the half-wall, balanced, his ankles crossed, his broad shoulders braced. "For the wedding," he said at last. "It's set for this evening."

With an effort at scorn, she said, "I thought I made myself clear: I'm not going to marry you."

"Mulier est hominous confusio: Woman is the confusion of man. Funny that I should remember that particular remnant of Latin out of all my old lessons, isn't it?" His next statement was devoid of all sarcasm. "If you won't cooperate, I'll take you to Jackson."

She stared at him, tried to fathom what he meant. "I won't go."

Hie eyes flicked over her face. "I'll have a closed carriage here tonight. I arranged for that, too, just in case. We'll take the southern road around the bay. I'll keep you there till the baby's born. After that you can do whatever you want. Talbot might even still be interested. But you're not going to

303

bring my child up in that sort of situation. I'll see that junior is decently raised."

Her blood pounded in her temples. She could hardly hear him for the noise of it. Her face tipped up to where a lone gull wheeled quietly above, flying in a silent, circular pattern. It wheeled and wheeled. The summery sun in the courtyard dimmed. A sickening darkness began to smother her, to press down on her. Her legs felt watery. They had no strength. Something in her soul had broken open and all her strength was spilling out. She groped for something to support her. Her hand went out, found nothing. She was sinking, falling.

Hands caught her an instant before she hit the hard pavement. She vaguely felt herself being lifted and carried, being placed on the bed-lounge in the basement room. The cool black cushions felt so good, the cool silk coverlet. Her eyes struggled to focus. The question was there, just waiting to be asked: "You're going to take my baby away from me, Andre?"

"God knows I don't want to! He'll need you. You have to marry me, Laura! It's the only way, can't you see? I can't have my son or daughter brought up behind the stairs."

"You would take my baby." She said it as if it were something she needed to memorize. Once again he would take her dreams and disappear with them.

His face became blankly controlled. "Laura, you *will* marry me! It doesn't have to be this evening. I'll give you more time to think about it. You can think about it in Jackson. I'll give you years—you know I have tremendous patience. If need be I'll seduce you all over again! Laura? God *damn* you!"

He stood straight and glared down at her. When next he spoke his voice was soft, every word laced with sour control. "That's just about enough! You'll marry me, by God, you *will!* And today's as good as any other day, so just make up your mind to it!"

She had no reserves to throw out passion in return. She

304

hadn't even the strength to cry.

For a brief hour just after noon, the sun found its way through the high narrow window and fell in barred squares across Laura's hands folded on the table. The key turned in the lock of the door; Andre stepped in. "Well," he said without prelude, "have you made up your mind?"

Her nerves were stretched as tight as corset strings. "What choice do I have? You're going to take my baby away from me if I don't do exactly what you want."

"You have a choice. Even marrying me you have a choice—to go into it willingly."

"How can I? You don't love me. I married a man who didn't love me once. I don't want to do it again." She stared at her hands engulfed by his larger ones, remembering a night of pain and fear that she had never spoken of to anyone—and would certainly never speak of to Andre. "For some perverse reason you've decided you're going to force me to marry you, and if I won't," she nearly broke down saying it, and only just managed to keep her voice in control, "you're going to take my baby."

He took the chair opposite her so that he could lean toward her over the table. He separated her hands, studied the cheap gold band on her finger, brought her knuckles to his lips and kissed them. "You wouldn't be marrying a man who doesn't love you this time. It's my misfortune to have to admit that I do. I tried not to, but it just wouldn't wash. So I'm not going to deny it; I love you, despite everything you've done. Maybe that makes me a fool—"

She seemed to turn to granite all through. "Oh, don't!" She pulled both hands away violently. "You can't do that to me again!" Suddenly she was furious. "You *liar!* And what do you mean, in spite of everything I've done?"

He unhitched himself from the table. "You call *me* liar— when it was you who said you loved me and then ran out on me the first chance you got?"

"*I* ran out on *you?*"

"That seemed to be the gist of the situation when I got back to Jackson and found you gone."

"When you . . . you got . . . *back?*" The last word was a mere whisper. She considered the weight of it before she asked: "What do you mean?"

He turned his chair sideways and sat down again. "Come on, Laura. I came back exactly when I said I would. It was plain as day in my letter."

Twenty-Six

"What letter?" Laura said.

Andre gave her an exasperated look. "The letter I left propped against a bowl of apples in the dining room. The letter you read just before you helped yourself to the cash in my desk to buy yourself a ticket back to your beloved Richard."

"Soo bought me the ticket. There was no letter! Soo—" Their eyes caught. The truth dawned. "Soo," she said.

"He thought if he sent you back to Laird, I'd go after you."

"Andre," she whispered, "Andre." She knew her face must be terrible to look at, yet she couldn't help it. So much pain, and all for nothing. "He told me you only left one word for me: Revenge. I was so hurt, and so confused, and he kept telling me I had to go back to Richard—and Richard was my husband—I just did what he said."

"What a hellish six months we've put in. At least I have, scouring the western hemisphere for you. You had your paramour to cuddle up to."

"You looked for me?" she said in a flutey, rather high voice, ignoring his slur.

He stared at her, then shook his head. "At first I damned you to hell—and I figured Laird would see to that. But you'd chosen him over me, and I figured you deserved each other. But then I found out about the annulment." He leaned forward on his elbows again. "Think, think of all you know about me, Laura. What did I do next?"

"But you said you only happened to see me in there."

He explained more fully, about selling his ranch in Texas, about coaxing that tiny bit of information out of Bessie Gladwin, about walking the streets in fruitless search, about traveling all the way to Massachusetts to badger Alarice. "That was enlightening; now I understand why you deny yourself the pleasure music was meant to give you." And finally he explained how he had found her: "I followed Talbot after he took you home, and got him drunk, and when he told me you were expecting—" He shook his head slowly. "That didn't make me happy, Laura. You've known all along that my mother and I have a house here, yet you didn't even try to contact me."

"I couldn't."

"Proud? But not too proud to consider an offer like Talbot's. You certainly have a leaning toward venturing among the lions. You must like dangerous men."

"I thought you'd deserted me."

"You should have known better."

"How could I?"

"I told you I loved you."

"And I told you the same!"

"And then you hurried back to Laird."

The silence in the opulent room grew uncomfortable. How could he blame her for the way she'd felt that morning, finding him gone?

"Well, that's all in the past now, isn't it? The business of the moment is my proposal: Are you going to marry me or not?"

"I—I need to think."

"By all means, think, sweet. But don't take too long. The wedding's at seven o'clock sharp."

She ran her hands back through her tangled hair. "I seem to be without a comb again."

He smiled, ever so slightly, as if at shadowed memories, and handed her his pocket comb. "Did Talbot ever lend you his comb? His shirts? He's a pretty fellow—and easier to get along with than me, isn't he?"

"Quite frankly, yes."

"And so ready to make love to you right on the street."

"Really, Andre."

"Don't deny it. I saw him trying to get his hands up your skirt. Has he ever touched you there?"

With an effort, she burst into soft laughter, as though this were a wonderful tribute to her ability to attract men. "I think I'll let you figure that one out for yourself."

"Don't try to be clever, Laura." He stood and swung away. When he turned back to her his voice was as silken. "You were going to go to bed with him—despite the fact you're carrying my child. Didn't that bother you at all?"

His cruelty went right into her. Her voice was bright-edged. "What right do you have to question anything I've done? How do you dare?" She rose slowly, with great dignity. "I don't owe you any explanations! And to think I loved you once!"

He crossed the room and caught her wrists. "Love?" He looked at her for an eternity more, then said, blandly vicious, "You loved me? The way you loved Laird? The way you loved Talbot? I don't think you know what love is."

Did he want her to argue the matter with him, to convince him? Couldn't he see for himself that her heart was full of unfailing love, for him and no one else, love she didn't think he deserved anymore?

His look still stung. He eyed her anatomy as if he were minutely choosing his bone. "Are you going to marry me?"

The hardest thing wasn't agreeing. The hardest thing was saying she agreed. Both fear and want constricted her throat. If only she could hide. But his gaze pursued her, his hands held her, hands which she couldn't—and didn't want to—escape.

His strong grip on her wrists brought her closer. "Come here." His command was tinged with gruff emotion. He drew her slowly toward him, until finally she stood toe to toe with him, mute, looking hungrily into his eyes.

Why couldn't it be like it used to be? Why did he have to be so rancorous? For a man who claimed to love her, he seemed awfully close to hating. She couldn't bear it. Tears gathered. She lowered her head. If she looked at him anymore, she would cry. Her mouth was trembling already. If she blinked, the tears would spill.

"Damn!" His hands released her wrists to smooth her hair back, to brush a stray tendril from her forehead; then he tilted her head and held her chin so she couldn't move. He forced her to look him full in the face. "Just say yes."

She couldn't see him for the tears standing in her eyes, but she heard it, the love in his voice, the love he'd been keeping back for days now. It was reluctant and bitter, but it was true. All promptings quieted within her. Her body eased, and she stood absolutely still, in his power again and glad to be. "Yes," she said.

He drew her into his embrace, and nudged her lips with a blandishment so weightless it might have been little more than a shadow cast by his bent head. Then his mouth pressed down. As her lips parted, a small sound welled up from deep within her. Her eyes closed; the tears fell and made two tracks down her cheeks. His kiss went deeper. With a groan, he lifted her and sat on the edge of the bed-lounge with her on his lap. "Don't cry, sweet. It's for the best. You know it is."

"You h-hate me . . . b-because of Yale."

"I don't. How could I hate you when I don't know how to live without you? It's only that I'm not sure of you anymore." He turned his face from her. "I counted on you to be there when I got back, to understand that I would act on my promise, that I was only gone to make it right for us. But you weren't, you didn't."

"But that's not fair. You could have simply wakened me, told me you were going. Oh, if only you had, Andre!"

He smiled sadly. "I considered it, but I was afraid if you kissed me, or moved in my arms, I wouldn't have the willpower to leave, and I felt I had to get Laird out of our lives as soon as possible."

"Soo was so mean, so cold, and when he told me you were gone—*gone*, Andre!" She was crying again. "I thought I would die."

"You should have known I could never be so heartless."

"How could I have known? Did you know the same about

me when he told you I'd left?"

"I know I would have gone after you right away, if I'd thought you'd run anywhere but back to Laird. While you—you didn't even come to me when you found out about the baby, and you knew where you could find me. And then Talbot. I don't hate you for that, but I'm afraid I'm going to be leery about letting you out in the world. I'm afraid you'd give yourself to the first scoundrel who came along and flattered you in the right way. And there are scoundrels in this world, believe me, men who are even worse than I am. Even worse than Talbot."

"Andre!" she said. She took his face between her hands. "I swear I love you. Only you. You must believe that."

His head came down. Everything took on a dream-sprinkled quality as he enfolded her with his big body and outlined her lips with his tongue. She felt a rush of anticipation. She imagined a great light radiating from them. Life stretched ahead like a gleaming filament.

But then he murmured, "You did love me, a little. I believe that. Enough to give yourself to me. And if I'd had more time with you, I could have taught you to love me completely. But you have to admit, you give yourself too easily, to whomever has your attention at the moment." He paused; it seemed he was thinking hard about this. "I guess I'll just have to keep a close watch on you, won't I? At least until you learn who you belong to."

He didn't believe her. She was disappointed, but tired of quarreling, and so kept her silence and simply drank him in. She'd made her decision: she was going to love him, and cling to him, no matter what he believed of her, until he believed the truth. She felt the strange terror and exhilaration of a woman walking willingly into flames.

He wiped away the dampness on her face with his thumb, then studied her. "Do you have any idea how good you look to me, even with your eyes swollen and your nose red? Tonight, ah, tonight, my sweeting, I'm going to make such love to you." His finger stilled her lips before she could protest. "I'll go easy."

Her breath caught on another sob. It wasn't fear of pain—

311

he had never taken her except by caresses—but a very real fear of rejection. She said, "I'm big and round and funny-looking." She looked away, confused and embarrassed.

He placed his big hand on her stomach, and got an odd little smile on his face. "It's you I want, and I don't care what shape you happen to take on temporarily." He laughed softly. "Besides, the important parts of you are still soft and beautiful. I know—I looked at some of them."

"Oh!" Heat flooded her face. She buried her forehead against his chest.

But he wanted her lips, and lifted her face to his. "Tell me you want me to make love to you."

Against his mouth she breathed, "I . . . yes—I mean if—if you want to, then I want you to." She pressed even closer to him, slipping into the webbed and radiant dream he'd always been able to spin about her.

"You should have turned to me," he whispered back in a disapproving, regretful voice, "not Talbot."

He held her a while longer, then said, "I'm awfully tempted to take you here and now, so you'd better stop provoking me like this and get up. It must be two o'clock already. That leaves us just five hours. I hope you don't have any strong objections to a civil ceremony."

She looked down at her figure as he helped her to stand. "Who will be there?"

He could still smile a little. "No one who doesn't already know you're a little this side of blushing virginity—except," he added thoughtfully, "my mother."

"You haven't told your mother?" Her hands came up to her tear-stained face, her unbound hair. Her eyes went to her bedraggled dress that she'd worn now for three days. "I have to go home, change, bathe. What will she think of me? She'll think— Oh, Andre! She'll think I'm loose."

"The only place you're going is with me. And she'll think you're perfect." He grimaced. "It's me she's going to tear to shreds." He breathed a soft imprecation.

Laura immediately pictured a harridan. "I can't meet her in these clothes—and I can't be married in them! You have to let me go home first."

312

"I've already arranged for your things to be packed and delivered. The Noahs are coming to the wedding, by the way. That little Holly is quite a piece of baggage. She gave me a pretty good raking over this morning, while her mother tittered like a dove in the background."

"What did you tell them? How did you explain?"

"I told them something close to the truth—that we fell in love shortly after your marriage and that the baby is mine. I didn't think you would want them to know you'd lied to them, so they still think you're widowed. You were torn with guilt when your husband died, because you'd been unfaithful to him—once, just once—and you wouldn't consider marrying me then. You ran away from me. But now you see you must become my wife, for the child's sake."

"Andre! Such an elaborate story!"

"'Oh what a tangled web we weave,' et cetera."

"Did Holly believe you?"

"She allowed herself to be convinced when I showed her this." He brought a small box out of his pocket, flipped it open to show her a ring with an ice-clear stone. "Give me your hand."

She started to, then quickly wrenched off the gold band she'd been wearing. He took it from her. "Where'd you get that? It's not the one Laird gave you; even he wasn't that cheap."

"I bought it at a pawn shop."

He shook his head and tossed it into the brazier, then slid the glittering diamond onto her finger.

Laura hadn't been to Nob Hill before. She gawked at the views of the bay, the elaborate homes that reflected money earned from the trinity of wealth that had built San Francisco: gold, railroads, and shipping. From within a carriage that obviously was not rented, Andre pointed out Mark Hopkins's mansion and Leland Stanford's, which stood just behind and slightly down the hill.

"My father's railroad shares bought him membership in the club that rules most of the state's business, but I sold them when they came to me. Mother and I are still included in their social set, though. These are the people your boyfriend Talbot wanted to mix with so badly, the Central Pacific crowd. He'll prove himself useful to them, no doubt. And he'll love Stanford's quiet little poker parties—and his other virile entertainments—at the Palace Hotel. Stanford has a penchant for harlots."

The carriage turned into an elegantly arcaded street. It let them out before a grand establishment built in the eighteenth-century style. Laura found herself facing a magnificent pair of boldly sculpted limestone lions sitting on their haunches, guarding the doors of the mansion. She stared like an ignorant rustic.

Andre placed her hand in the crook of his arm. "A bit much, isn't it?" He seemed to square his shoulders. "Shall we go in?"

He ushered her up the wide stone steps into a large hall that ran the length of the second floor. He didn't glance at any of the several visiting cards lying on a silver tray on a sidetable finished with delicate floral marquetry. He kept her hand firmly and showed her through a pair of huge sliding doors into the first room on the left, a drawing room— actually two large drawing rooms opening one into the other.

Both were empty. They had an air of opulence, done as they were in gold and white, with gas lamps in the form of brass mermaids on the walls. Mirrors, silvered and gilded, caught the light from the windows. Beautiful craftsmanship had gone into the frescoed ceilings and parquet hardwood floors, even the moldings over the doorways.

Andre said, "Mother must be up in her sitting room." He rubbed his hands together.

Laura tried to think back, but she couldn't remember that she'd ever seen him nervous before. Mrs. Sheridan must be an awful harpy. He said, "I guess I'd better go on up and get this over with."

She raised her chin, "Perhaps I should go—if you're afraid that is. Or is it that you're ashamed of me?"

He squared his shoulders as he turned. "Don't move out of

314

this room. Sit—there."

She sat in the tapestried armchair he indicated, while he went out. Ten minutes passed . . . twenty . . . thirty; they seemed like thirty hours. But finally a small, fair-haired woman entered the room with a rustle of dark lilac satin. In her fine, rich dress, with her head meticulously coiffed, her nails buffed and shaped into neat ovals, she was the picture of an aristocrat. Laura stood politely. The woman paused midway across the room, as if surprised by her youth, or her size, or her condition—or by all three. She sent a slicing glance back at Andre coming in behind her. *I'll deal further with you later,* that glance said. Then she came straight on and took both Laura's gloved hands in her own. Her aging but lively green eyes suffused with pity.

"My dear Miss Upton, I am Elexa Sheridan." She spoke with a surprisingly soft and husky French accent. She seemed shaken, yet in control. "The tale I have just heard—" She said on a clenched breath, *"Fantastique!* It has left me reeling. Please, please sit down, *ma fille."* Keeping Laura's hands, she led her to a gold plush sofa. "I have had to apologize for many of my son's misdeeds—oh yes—but this—" she shot her eyes toward Andre again. "This is beyond belief! I must ask myself if I did something terribly wrong to have reared such a monster."

"Mother," Andre interjected irritably. He was squatted near the fireplace with the poker on his knees. The low-burning logs threw an almost tragic light onto his face.

His tone didn't seem to intimidate Mrs. Sheridan in the least. She glowed with a theatrical fire. "Oh, you flinch at the word monster, do you? I imagine Miss Upton has called you that, if not aloud, then in her mind, and with far more cause than I have. I suddenly understand so many things, *oui:* why you have been so mysterious and reluctant to talk to me these past months; why you have lingered here in San Francisco when you never have before. Your conscience must have been very heavy, Andre."

He peevishly raked at the ashes beneath the grate.

"Very heavy indeed," she went on regardless. "I have never been so horrified, so disgusted, so sickened." She turned back to Laura, her bearing regal, yet her face frozen, becoming paler and paler as she spoke. "Did he hurt you? What a question—of course he did. Abducted! I cannot even imagine . . . and then . . . Well, we won't speak of that here." She threw another shriveling glance at her son. "But he has told me." Tears of shame shimmered in her eyes. "How could he? Knowing you had nothing to do with poor Ling! How could he do that?"

There was silence in all the house. Laura could hear the fire burning with a soft rustle, like a slight wind in a great tree. She began to realize that Andre had told Elexa, or at least given his mother the impression, that he'd taken her by force. The pain this woman must be feeling to think the son she had labored over and loved had done something so despicable! And Andre's pain, to have his mother believe him so low!

"Mrs. Sheridan," she said gently, "I don't know what he told you . . . it's true that he has been mean on occasion, but he never . . . he was never brutal. That is," she floundered, "there was no force used, not ultimately. He did take certain liberties . . . but I assure you, I'm as much to blame for my present situation as he is. Please, you mustn't think—"

"She was completely innocent, Mother," Andre ground out, standing. He reseated the poker in its stand with a clang of metal. "Laird hadn't touched her yet. She hadn't even had the facts of life made plain to her. She's never had a mother of her own, at least none to speak of. The closest approach is the snow-coldest bitch I've ever had the unhappy experience of meeting."

His glance for Laura was admiring, yet he went on: "Her only fault is that she has a naive and malleable heart. Naive enough to marry Richard Laird without knowing what sort of man he is, and malleable enough to be easily seduced by just about any man who shows her the least bit of kindness— even dangerous men. It was like I told you upstairs: I took her from Laird, and when he didn't have the guts to come get her from me, I decided to keep her for myself. She tried to keep to her marriage promises to Laird, tried very hard—"

"But you raped her!"

316

"No!" Laura said.

Elexa patted her hand, but kept her eyes on her son.

"Seduced . . . let's use the word seduced." He leaned back, settled his huge frame comfortably against the white marble mantel. He gazed out in the direction of the windows as if he had nothing more to do but look out through the day or through the distance. "It was fairly easy, really, considering she had no idea how one thing can lead to another, how a man can break a woman down, lead her into wanting what she should be damned leery of, and coax her into letting him go just a little further each time."

"Andre, please," Laura murmured, her face heating up.

"No more idea than a child," he went on regardless. "And speaking of children, since her carnal education was left to me, I naturally concentrated on the pleasanter aspects. I believe I left out the details about the relationship between consorting and conceiving. She didn't have the foggiest notion I could be so graceless as to make her pregnant. So you can't blame her for anything; you don't blame the kitten who gets too close to the flames when its tail catches fire. The blame lies solely with me—because, of course, I knew exactly what I was doing. The minute I laid eyes on her I felt a terrible pulling in every vein. I wanted her and I was bound to have her—and whatever it took to capture her irreversibly was all right with me."

Elexa regarded him coolly before turning her attention back to Laura. "I will tell you what I think. I am a woman, small like yourself, and I know what it is to be bullied by a large man, a man twice your size. My husband was like Andre, a great lout of a man. But you—" She gestured to a small statue on a nearby table. Obviously by a master, it was the image of a nubile girl shyly trying to hide her complete nakedness. "You, *ma fille,* were like *La Timide,* were you not? Intimidated and frightened? He was taken by you, he wanted you, and, afraid for your very life, you twisted your heart to accommodate him. Am I close to the truth?"

"Exactly," Andre answered for Laura. With a smile nailed onto his face, he added, "I even had her convinced she was in love with me. Of course, as soon as I was gone for a few hours, she realized her mistake. When Soo offered her a ticket to get back home, she jumped at the chance."

"Of course you did, *ma fille.*" Elexa patted Laura's wringing hands. "And I suspect you do not know if you want to marry my son now, he has been so crude and so cruel. "But," she added gently, "I think you must. You do not have to be afraid. I will see that he does not—"

"Don't make any promises you can't keep, Mother."

"Andre Sheridan, you are not going to threaten and abuse this poor girl in *my* house! I am going to have the servants prepare the rooms next to mine for her." She turned back to Laura. "You will be safe there."

Twenty-Seven

Andre's face was thunderous, though his voice was quiet. Too quiet, Laura thought. "As my wife, Laura will naturally be sharing my rooms."

Elexa stood and faced him. "I will not have it, Andre! Not here!"

"Then I'll take her somewhere else." His tone was mild, yet utterly menacing.

It occurred to Laura that they were arguing over her as if she were unable to think for herself. But she had thought, and had made her decision. She loved Andre, wanted him, wanted a life with him. "Pardon me," she said, standing, "but I think I have a voice in this matter. Thank you for trying to protect me, Mrs. Sheridan, but as I said—and you must believe it—Andre has never been willfully cruel to me, not . . . that way. Quite the opposite; he . . . he was always tender." She felt her face flooding with yet more color. It was so awful to have to speak aloud of the private thudding of their passion. "It's one of the few ways I'm not afraid of him."

Now she looked at him. "Where I do need protection is against his distressing habit of keeping me either bound and gagged or under lock and key—his insufferable habit of keeping me his prisoner! He *would* take me somewhere else, Mrs. Sheridan. You may think you could stop him, but I'm not at all convinced. And the fact is, I would much rather share a room with him than be locked up in one by him!"

"How fierce you are," Andre said mockingly, "but that's the first smart decision you've made." His eyes sparkled with the same lights that beckon from the ends of space. "Well, maybe not the first—giving me your maidenhead wasn't bad—but one of the few."

"Andre!" Elexa said, shocked.

"Enough, Mother." He was looking at Laura, slowly and thoroughly. And Laura was aware of a tension growing in her. He crossed the room to place his hands possessively on her shoulders. "I've played at being remorseful all I'm going to, when the truth is, I'm not really sorry for anything I've done—except to let this woman out of my sight long enough for her to run wild. Laura, if you'll take my arm, I'll show you upstairs to our room. Mother, will you order her a bath? The ceremony is at seven, remember."

They swept out, leaving Elexa speechless.

The impressive curving staircase he led her up was wide, carpeted with an opulent scarlet runner. It had heavy oak bannisters and bracketed gaslights. The landing had an enormous oval window bearing a cut design, with a sprawling fern on a table below it. Then more stairs, gracefully rising to the third floor. Here were more chandeliers and wall lights, a walnut hall table with a centerpiece of fresh sweet peas, a Chinese Chippendale mirror, other tables with porcelains. The interiors were all eighteenth century, keeping with the style of the house. Laura counted five doors toward the front, and two more in the rear. Seven bedrooms! To her it was a castle, nothing less, a cultured mosaic in which every element had its proper position.

"Andre," she murmured, "you aren't going to dress in the same room as me, are you?"

"Didn't I just hear you declare you were looking forward to sharing a room with me?"

"That's not exactly what I said."

"But it's what I said, and now that I've won that war, it would be a poor show not to oblige myself of the spoils."

"But it's bad luck for the groom to see the bride beforehand."

He took two more steps, then burst out laughing. "Laura, you say the damnedest things! Bad luck? We've already had our bad luck. But all right, if it's important to you, I suppose I can find a spare room to dress in. It would make Mother feel less scandalized—since we aren't married yet!" Again he laughed.

However, neither his mother's nor Laura's sensibilities stoped him from entering the foyer of his suite with her and closing the door and leaning back against it. She twirled to face him anxiously. His left hand on her arm drew her near; his right hand reached to circle her throat, his thumb grazing the hollow at its base. His parted lips touched hers, playing so tenderly and erotically that she was reluctant to be let go. When she was, she sighed.

"Such a melodic sigh," he murmured, "such a leaning pitch. Remind me to resolve it in to a chord later. But for now . . . there's something I've been wanting to do forever."

He kissed her throat as he turned her like a waltzer and pinned her against the door. They kissed for a long time as he lifted her skirts and went in search of her wetness.

"Andre, you mustn't!" But it was too late. With her hems bunched at her waist, she sighed as he found her. Moaning, she rolled her head. Her knees began to give way. He held her harder against the wall with his weight. She moved against his fingers, urging him to reach inside.

He teased. "How wet you are . . . you're very wet. Because of me?" He stroked again with slippery silken fingers. Her head was thrown to the side, her neck arched. Quakes ran up and down her spine. He gazed at her with soft and open eyes, while she closed hers and bided in that quiet, hollow anteroom of joy until she saw flames lapping in behind her closed lids. She quivered, then shattered around his pleasuring fingers. The stars came loose from the sky and rained down like Chinese fireworks.

"Ah, Laura, sweet Laura." He lifted her and carried her into the bedroom, and placed her on the big, waist-high, mahogany bed. Slowly she recovered from his caresses; she returned, clinging to him, breathing in heavy gasps. "You look a little shaken, love. Maybe you'd better rest for a

321

few minutes."

Amazed at what he'd done, and how she'd responded, she could give him no more than a silent wide-eyed nod. He straightened slowly and gazed down at her as though she held him bewitched. His face creased into a slow grin. "I'll get my things out of the dressing room. Your bath will be coming. And probably a maid to help you. I'll see you later." His voice was silken.

In the foyer he let his laughter break free.

Laura had to drag herself from the drifting, hazy cloud of sensual wonder in which he left her. The diminished sounds of the day were givng way to those of the evening, and she had things to do. She sat up, feeling scandalous now. Oh! She slid to the edge of the high bed. There were steps, but they'd been kicked out of Andre's way. She had to slip to the floor without them.

She briefly explored her whereabouts. Knowing how Andre cherished his privacy, she wasn't surprised by his rooms. First, there was the entrance foyer where he had kissed and pleasured her. Beyond ice-blue velvet portieres was the bedroom proper, dominated by the tall bed of masculine proportions. To the right and left of the foyer were two glass-paned doorways, one leading to a study, obviously his refuge, where he could both work and relax. The other led to a dressing room tastefully decorated with screen-printed wallpaper and tasseled draperies. Within was a bathing space floored in slate; it had its own small fireplace.

She only had time to satisfy her curiosity with a quick peek into these rooms, for within minutes her trunk arrived. Two male Chinese servants put it in the dressing room. As soon as they were gone, she chose a simple plum-colored dress that buttoned up the front and had neat tucking and delicate English embroidery on the shoulders, a high, lace-trimmed collar and wrist cuffs. A Chinese maid arrived to take this to be sponged and pressed.

More servants brought hot water, and Laura bathed and did her hair in a style that gave her what she hoped was a regal appearance. Before she considered herself completely dressed, she found a shawl of the palest beige lace, the tint of engraved stationery. This she closed over her breasts with a brooch, so that the ends covered her inconvenient waist. Even with leaving four buttons unfastened, the baby had grown to the point that bending over in the gown without forethought was out of the question.

The Chinese maid came in again, breathless in her rush to deliver a huge nosegay that had just arrived, made of mixed flowers and lace and trailing pastel ribbons. There was a delicate diadem of the same for Laura's hair. Once this was pinned in place, she swished quietly into the hall.

Andre was waiting for her, leaning against the wall, playing idly with a penknife out of his waistcoat pocket. He was dressed in a gray frock coat with matching trousers and a gray silk bow tie. She inhaled the scent of fragrant bay rum as she took his proffered arm.

He explained, as they descended the stairs, that his witness was going to be an old friend of his, Captain Parry Glenn. "He's Stingy's owner—remember Stingy? It wasn't easy finding someone at such short notice, but Parry's in port just now. Oh, and the Noahs suggested you might like your doctor to stand up with you. A woman doctor, Laura? Is she any good?"

"Oh yes, Dr. Kellogg's been such a good friend to me. Andre," she added, making him look down at her, "thank you."

"For getting you a witness?"

"For being so thoughtful. It was you who ordered the flowers, wasn't it?"

"Actually, that's the one thing I forgot. It must have been Mother. I told you she'd take to you."

In the drawing room, the gas jets behind the brass mermaids were lit, so that the marble statuettes and gold sofas and Austrian blinds bloomed with mellow light. In this splendid setting the bridal pair came to a stop before a judge with a precise black moustache trimmed as if to military specifications. Andre introduced Justice Broadbent.

The ceremony wasn't elaborate. There were no violins, no singing of "Oh Promise Me." Justice Broadbent cleared his throat and began: "We are gathered to join this couple in marriage. Who witnesses this union?" And Captain Glenn, who looked a sailor through and through, and Dr. Frederica Kellogg promptly came forward to take their places.

Andre's responses were strong and clear, while Laura's were barely audible, even to herself. ". . . till death do us part," she said in a reedy, tremulous voice. She'd said that once before and it hadn't held true; would it this time? Or would it again lead to bruised eyes and broken bones? She felt light-headed, visions of Richard springing into her mind. She was weak with emotion and fright when Andre took her trembling hand to remove the large diamond from her finger, slip on a matching gold band, then replace the diamond. And then he was tilting her chin up. She raised tear-filled eyes. In the angular lines of his jaw she saw a muscle move. His mouth came down tenderly, then he kissed her once more, this time hard, abrupt.

His embrace was soon interrupted by the congratulations of Captain Glenn and the bustled women.

Elexa, dressed in yellow grained silk, had wept softly all through the ceremony. Her hair was in an elaborate high chignon, clasped by jeweled combs. Her yellow gown had a close-fitting, low-cut bodice, and a skirt tight before and full behind with gathered flounces and train. She and Laura kissed delicately. Then she clung to Andre. Laura didn't doubt he'd always been a worrisome offspring.

Holly beamed brightly from beneath a special occasion hat of navy blue decorated with bright plumes. Her eyes sparkled with reflections of the flaring gaslights. "You've certainly fallen on your feet," she said in a voice only Laura could hear. "From Mr. Kane's to this palace. And that man! So handsome—so rich! And willing to *marry* you!"

Mrs. Noah was next in line, dressed in her best somber indigo with elbow-length sleeves that had lace ruffles. She offered her best wishes so sincerely that Laura felt guilty for not having been more truthful with her.

Now Captain Glenn was taking advantage of the traditions to take the bride in a bearish, brotherly embrace. He was a physically impressive man, tall and well propor-

324

tioned, good-looking, and gracious. He had a mustache and side whiskers, and a fresh, frosty flash, like sea light, in his eyes. "Too bad"; he teased in a rather husky, but quick, no-nonsense voice, "as I was standing there, I was really kind of hoping you might tell him no at the last minute." He dropped his face to touch his lips to hers. "Best wishes, little Laura. Got your work cut out for you, marrying my friend the timber wolf."

He moved on to clasp Andre's shoulder and shake his hand. Laura overheard enough of their exchange to realize the hug the man had taken from her had told him things Andre apparently hadn't: "Pretty little thing, and going to make you a father soon, I see. Be interested to hear why you waited so long to marry her. Got a good excuse, I hope."

Justice Broadbent was apparently moved by weddings. He massaged his eyelids vigorously before he bowed and touched his black mustache to her hand in a courtly manner.

At last there was Dr. Kellogg, dressed in what for her was a feminine gown of simple brown trimmed with cinnamon ruffles and bows. "I wondered why you missed your appointment yesterday."

"I'm sorry, I-I forgot." She couldn't say she'd been locked in a tart's boudoir. "I'm awfully glad you came."

"Oh yes, I came, especially after the tale passed on to me by the Noahs. I hope Mr. Sheridan is not chronically weak in his morals. To seduce a young woman right after her marriage . . . I remember you once told me you hadn't been happily married. I assume he took advantage of that. Well, at least he's doing the right thing by you now."

Laura blushed. Andre rescued her by bringing her and the doctor fluted glasses of champagne. A cup of tea was found for Mrs. Noah, who, as a member of the temperance movement, had signed the pledge. Then came the toasts.

Whereas Andre had clashed frequently with Laura, and irritated and exasperated her with his insolent manner, she saw now that when he chose he could sweep people along with his charm and bravado. During a private moment he dropped a kiss onto the tip of her nose, and let his tongue quickly swipe along its hint of a cleft. "Mmm, I always wanted to marry a woman with a dented nose."

The play of amber light descending on him from the gaslights, his dark eyes (merry for once), his grin, all enchanted her. She felt herself more open to him, more profoundly willing to be dominated by him than she had ever considered possible. She smiled, suddenly and desperately happy, and reached up to flatten his strong nose with a fingertip. "Watch out, dented noses may be catchy with too close an association."

He grabbed her wrist playfully. "Back off, woman, I have to offer more champagne to our guests before I can concentrate on you alone."

That drew her thoughts to the big machogany bed upstairs. She shivered, watching him refill Holly's glass. That was when the butler, an Englishman, spoke discreetly in her ear. "A caller asking to speak to you, madam. I've shown him into the library."

"Thank you," she said. "Er, could you show me where the library is?"

She entered the gas-lit room across the hall with a soft swish of skirts. A fire was burning in a fireplace of gold-veined black marble. Above it was a mirror with Shakespeare's profile carved into the frame. The back half of the room was divided into bays—vertical banks of shelves that stretched high overhead and could be reached only by ladder. These were arranged with leather-bound volumes titled in gold, some apparently so valuable they needed to be enclosed behind glass doors.

As she rounded the first of these bays in search of her caller, she found herself suddenly face to face with Yale Talbot. She started back. He sent her a slow contemplative look that began with the flowered diadem atop her head, and ended with her hands, which she held together over her shawl, her new rings uppermost.

A little smile played about his mouth. "It seems I've come at an inopportune moment, darlin'."

She felt him following her every movement as she returned to the heath. "What do you want?" Her thoughts were: What if Andre finds him here? What will he do? What will he think? "What do you want, Yale?" she said again.

"Just checkin' on you, ladybird."

"Why? Weren't you paid enough for selling me?"

"I wouldn't say I sold you; he's a persuasive man, your new husband. Still, I was worried about you. I got to thinkin' maybe there was a dead cat on the line. But I see it was unnecessary." He took her hand, smiling faintly at the big diamond. "So he's the old boyfriend, the father of the babe and all? Do you still love him?"

She sent him a look that was at once incensed and bitter. "You told him I was in love with you!"

His brows arched provocatively. "And he believed me? My, I must be a better liar than I thought. Or maybe he just wants to believe it. Maybe he's hopin' you won't cling too closely, darlin'." He was still in possession of her hand, running his thumb inattentively over the facets of her diamond. "Maybe, after all, you'll be as free as I am to pursue your inclinations."

Her lips parted at the suggestion lying beneath his words, and she snatched her hand away. "Despite what others may think, I try to be faithful to my word. I have just given it to Andre, and I plan to keep it."

He laughed, evidently amused by her prim answer. "You gave your word to your first husband, though, and that didn't keep you from sleepin' with Sheridan."

He laughed again when she found herself speechless. "I think I'll just leave you with that thought, darlin'." He bent to graze her brow with his lips. She turned her head away quickly.

It was at that moment that the door opened. Yale straightened. Laura didn't need to turn to know who stood there; she felt Andre's eyes on her back.

"I thought you understood the terms of our deal, Talbot," came his voice from behind her.

Too quiet, too quiet, that voice.

"I did—and do. I simply had to make sure you weren't trickin' the girl."

"I gave you my word about her."

"Your word? People are fond of givin' their word. I'm

afraid we lawyers require harder evidence."

"And are you satisfied now that you've seen it?"

"I'm right satisfied, yes."

"Then you'll be leaving."

Yale bowed ever so slightly and made for the door. "Goodnight, Laura." She didn't answer.

"Talbot," Andre stopped him, "stay away from her. The least I could do is ruin you professionally. The very least."

Yale left without speaking again. Laura felt relieved to know she wouldn't have to see him any more, for he surely realized that Andre could, and would, do exactly what he threatened.

"Laura."

She turned to look at her husband. He stood just inside the room, his hand still on the door. He remained motionless as she crossed to him, then held out his hand for hers. She gave him what he wanted.

He didn't berate her for Yale's intrusion, yet his grip was so tight her rings cut into her fingers. He drew her back into the drawing room celebration. She found herself smiling twice as much as before. Elexa saved her face from cracking by calling, "Come, children, our supper is waiting."

The older Mrs. Sheridan led them out of the double drawing rooms, all the while tossing comments in French into the conversation like bits of confetti. The party followed her with a great silken rustle into a dining room that was nothing less than a pleasure to behold. Laura felt she had left San Francisco for somewhere in the Far East. The wainscoting was inlaid with ebony; a pair of blue and white vases were definitely antique Chinese; and the table was laden with an impressive collection of Chinese floral porcelain. To complete the picture, they were served by a Chinese steward who kept bowing himself in half.

Laura heard Mrs. Noah say, "You're a very lucky man to have Laura, Mr. Sheridan."

He smiled a little and said, "Many people agree with you. Nearly every man she meets, in fact. It's not her fault, I suppose. Moths, and all sorts of unsightly creatures hover about a lit candle. Can the candle stop it?"

"Why, I suppose not."

"No. But I'm the one who has her now, and I intend to keep her out of the others' reach. Will you have some curried rabbit, ma'am?"

At the other end of the table, Dr. Kellogg and Captain Glenn had somehow stumbled into controversy:

"I challenge you to give me one good reason for keeping women from voting—a good reason, I say, which excludes the real reason: that you couldn't exploit us anymore the way you do now."

"Exploit you, Doctor? I doubt any man could exploit you without your cooperation." Captain Glenn laughed. "Though it might be entertaining to try."

They both seemed to notice at the same time that everyone else at the table had fallen silent. Captain Glenn looked around, then back at Dr. Kellogg with teasing eyes. "I apologize. A pleasant dinner table's not the place to display such an obsessive interest in, uh, politics."

She nodded her head in a regally forgiving fashion, and he laughed again.

The dessert course, strawberry ice, was hardly finished when Dr. Kellogg used her rose-scented fingerbowl and stood, saying, "I'm sorry to be such a social boor, but I must visit a patient yet this evening."

Laura felt terribly proud of her friend as she stood ready to take her leave, a perfectly wonderful woman who had made an important place for herself in the world.

All three men rose politely, but only Captain Glenn said, "I'll see you home."

"That's quite all right. I have my own trap."

"I'll just ride along with you then," he insisted.

"But, as I said, I have a patient to visit on my way."

"Should be interesting."

"A case of corns?"

"Always been interested in corns. Sometimes my sailors get 'em and I never know what to recommend."

"But, Captain," she put a little more meaning in her voice, "if you ride along with me, then you'll have no way to get home."

"I'll tie my horse to the back of your trap," he said smoothly, making it all sound a simple matter.

At this point Andre took Laura's hand and pulled her up with him. "Since it looks as if Parry and the good doctor will surely work this out eventually, shall we say goodnight to our other guests, Laura?"

"Going up so early?" Elexa said.

"I think so, Mother. Laura tires easily these days."

"Goodnight, Mrs. Sheridan." Laura smiled at her mother-in-law nervously. "Captain Glenn, Holly, Mrs. Noah, thank you all for coming. And Dr. Kellogg, it meant so much to me to have you here." She nodded and murmured a thank you to Justice Broadbent as Andre turned her toward the door.

Twenty-Eight

On the stairs, Laura and Andre could hear Dr. Kellogg and Captain Glenn debating still as they gathered their wraps in the hall below. Andre said, with a flicker of a grin, "That'll end in thunder, or my name's not Sheridan."

"Dr. Kellogg is very independent, I'm afraid."

"And Parry's used to being the king of his ship. Wouldn't it be interesting to ride along with them tonight?"

His grin was gone, however, when he bolted the door of his rooms. The bed had been turned down by someone, the airy down pillows plumped, and fresh roses stood in a vase nearby. Andre shrugged out of his jacket, throwing it into one of the pair of easy chairs that bracketed the Italian marble fireplace. He tugged at his tie. "Would you like another glass of champagne? I could order some."

"Thank you, no."

He unbuttoned his shirt, pulling it out of the waistband of his trousers, watching her at the same time. "It might relax you."

"I'm quite relaxed."

Deliberately, he removed his gold stud cufflinks, then stripped off his shirt entirely and cast it onto the chair. His hair gleamed with dark iridescence in the firelight; his body was supple with athletic grace, the browned skin slipped over his mature muscles like water over smooth stones. "Funny, you don't look relaxed," he said. "Are you afraid of me after all, sweetness—despite that brave little speech you

331

gave Mother?"

"I—I'm not afraid of you, no." But in these final moments she was filled with doubts as to his mood just now, and his purpose, and his methods of gaining it.

"Then why don't you stop strangling that poor bouquet and come here?" He stood waiting beside the hearth where the flames of a small fire trembled.

She hesitated, then took a step forward. Suddenly she said, "Andre, I wouldn't have gone to the library if I'd known who was there."

He reached out to take her bouquet, then to unfasten the brooch that held her shawl closed. He began to unfasten the draped outer skirt of her plum-colored dress, his big fingers sure and quick at the ties. Nonchalantly, he laid the puffy skirt over his own discarded jacket and shirt. He started on her bodice next, and soon was spreading the neck, pushing it back over her shoulders, stripping her arms of the close-fitting sleeves, easing the skirt over her hips. She stepped out of it.

Now he took the hem of her chemise in his purposeful hands and lifted it upward. At the last moment she stopped him from uncovering her completely. He tilted his head to one side, stood just looking at her, waiting, until slowly she let her arms go up so that he could pull the garment over her head.

He knelt to release her shoe buttons with a hook. She placed a balancing hand on his shoulder as he pulled off first one and then the other. He rolled her white stockings down and slipped them off her feet. As he stood again, she covered her breasts with her forearms.

His eyelids seemed heavy. "Put your arms down, Laura."

"Do you believe me?"

"I don't know."

"Ask the butler."

"And make it plain to the servants that I can't quite trust my wife?" He didn't seem angry; he seemed terribly reasonable. "It was bad enough to have everyone see how reluctant you were to marry me."

"Reluctant!"

"Oh, you tried to hide it, but you were shaking as if you had a fever, and trying so hard not to cry." His tone was still neutral. "Put your arms down. Show me your breasts."

When she couldn't seem to do it, he took her wrists, gently, and placed them at her sides. He stepped back, as if to better see her. Totally naked, she stood trembling. The flames of the fire glowed behind the dark stillness of his jetty eyes; in them she saw herself reflected, the heat from the hearth casting a warm and golden glow onto the lines of her shoulders. His gaze, as it fastened on her breasts, was a bit terrifying. She couldn't keep them from quivering; she would have to quit breathing. She knew they were smoother and fuller than before and, standing there so blatantly naked, it seemed as if she were offering them to him, as if they were crying to be caressed and kissed.

His right hand came up. With aching quiet, his knuckles grazed her jaw, traced a line down her throat. His fingers spread to sweep down over one breast and then come up under it. He lifted it, as if to test its new weight. "Like a ripe peach, almost bursting with nectar." He grazed its tip with the end of his thumb, and obediently it stiffened.

The exploring hand continued downward to her abdomen. His left hand came up, so that both palms smoothed over the taut skin of her rounded belly. He skimmed his palms over and over that warm solid curve, discovering the changes their unborn child was causing. She recognized his right to do this, yet she couldn't help whispering, "You're making me self-conscious."

He stepped closer, his hands slid around her. Her lower body was pulled into his groin. The fabric of his trousers caressed her thighs and triggered another involuntary tremor. Holding her there with one hand spread at the back of her waist, he used the other to remove the flowered diadem in her hair. She bent her neck, first this way, then that, to allow him to find the several pins and combs her heavy hair had required to be tamed into its upswept style. He seemed in no hurry, but finally her hair tumbled onto her shoulders and fell down her back.

He lifted her then, carried her to the bed, and laid her

down while he sat beside her, putting his hand casually between her legs. She felt anxious and uncertain, like a sacrificial maiden. His fingers moved idly. She felt the promise in them like faint music arching over an immense distance, low and sweet.

"So, Laura, we are man and wife. I'll do everything I can to make you happy. But in return . . . I've waited a long time to have my captured Lorelei back in my arms. Do you have any idea how much I've wanted to punish you and love you and hear you cry out? And here you are."

"Andre, don't talk anymore." She lifted her face for his mouth, thinking a kiss would reassure her. He granted her wish, kissed her with the same authority he'd used when claiming her as his wife a few hours ago; but his lips didn't linger, for he straightened and went to the nearer chair, there to sit and pull off his dress shoes and socks. She didn't dare look him in the face, but saw him stand again, saw his hands at the waistband of his gray trousers. Off they came, and his white underdrawers. He turned to lay them aside, displaying his buttocks, tough and round and muscular. When he turned toward her again, flames shot through her core at the sight of him. Her eyes riveted to that place between his legs, and she felt startled anew.

He lay beside her and placed his lips on her partly open mouth. His kiss was warm and certain, and she was run through with so rare a sensation that her own lips stayed in their kissed attitude even after he lifted his head. "More?" he drawled softly. "Like Oliver Twist and the porridge?" For the first time she saw a flash of a smile. He stretched beside her and kissed her as she wished. And when he stopped, she whispered, "'Please sir, I want some more.'"

Another ghost of a smile; but then it seemed he did mean to punish her a little, for this time he seized her by the nape and drove his tongue between her lips. For a long while he probed, discovering the very back of her mouth. His free hand meanwhile was moving over her thighs. In spite of herself she experienced a tingling everywhere he touched her, as if his hand had some magical power.

He began to concentrate, to contemplate, slowly, her

breasts. His fingers went from one to the other, turned each hopeful tip this way and that, and tested the delicate circles of skin around them, until her breath became uneven, and she knew there was moisture between her legs again. The sensations became torturing, and she balked, bringing up her hands to stop him.

He captured her wrists easily and pressed them to the pillow on either side of her head. "You promised me three things: to love, honor, and obey me. I'll settle for one at a time; obey will do for starters."

It suddenly seemed he was monstrously stronger than she, a strong *strong* man. To struggle against him was unthinkable. Besides, he was her husband now. He had every right to examine her body, to use it for his pleasure. "I'm sorry," she murmured. She tried to regain her calm, but it eluded her. She couldn't look at him, she closed her eyes. He had every right, every right.

"Open your eyes," he ordered quietly. He held her gaze as surely as he held her wrists. "I love you, Laura; I think you're beautiful. I want to see all of you and touch all of you and taste all of you. I won't hurt you, that's my promise. All I ask is that you don't resist me. Can you lie still for it?"

She nodded her head, slowly.

His hands left her wrists, but when she started to lower them, he said, "Leave them there, sweetness. Don't move them from the pillow. I think that will make it easier for you."

And so she didn't, even when he parted her thighs.

"You said you weren't afraid of me," he reminded her. And he lifted her knees and spread her legs—until she felt graceless. She thought she could not bear it as he knelt between her spread feet. A half-frightened, half-thrilling response ran through her as she glanced into his face briefly. But she was made too nervous by his shadowy and searching eyes that were lowered to those other parts of her.

Smoothing the fine skin of her upper thighs, he murmured, "You're as fragile as bone china, but warm and soft, this white skin . . . like something skimmed off fresh milk." Her hands clenched into small fists and she stared at the ceiling above her as his careful fingers opened her. His head lowered.

She pushed her head back into the pillow at the first contact of his tongue, tried to set herself to bear it as she'd promised. His tongue moved in slow voluptuous circles, sampling, touching. Gradually it began to feel more right and comfortable than she could have ever dared hope. Nearly note perfect. Though she had her eyes closed again, mentally she saw his hands holding her thighs while he buried his face in her. Presently all her attention was centered down there, on herself and his mouth.

She became alive to a rising within her body. Her pelvis lifted, her nipples hardened into pebbles, and involuntary gasps escaped her. She wondered how he could carry her into this weightless, gilded yearning place after so much had happened to her because of him. Knowing that he believed her to be inconstant. She didn't understand, but he *had* carried her here; her body was on fire.

Wildly she began to peak. Flower after golden flower blossomed inside her, a huge wedding bouquet opened and closed and opened once more. Her thighs clasped his head. "Enough!" she cried, even while she continued to rise to his tongue. "Andre, oh, I can't stand it!"

Yet he demanded she stand it, for his lips and tongue prolonged what he had begun while she thrashed and spasmed.

When he finally desisted, when her shuddering finally ceased, he came toward her on his knees. She saw his arousal again and knew she wanted that part of him now.

Gradually he inserted himself into her. There was no effort, no jarring. He cushioned her in his arms so that his strength absorbed his inward nudges. He felt big, however, and when he was well in, he simply filled her.

His strong muscles flexed in the low gaslight and the half-light of the fire. When he lifted her hips off the bed in order to invade her better, his biceps seemed to explode under his skin. His shoulders and chest gleamed and moved with muscles.

"Am I hurting you?" he murmured. But he was taking her

even as he spoke, as if unable to resist the need, thrusting into her gently at first, then more willfully as she seemed able to endure it. "You must tell me if—if—"

"No—no, don't stop."

At last he left off talking to insert himself in rapid strokes that took her fast, farther, out into radiance. She felt his body grow hard, hard. He leaned forward suddenly. His chest grazed her belly. He moaned softly into her breasts. With her breath held, she remained absolutely still. And her reward was to feel him quiver, to feel him filling her with his hot succulent liquid.

"Oh, Andre, I love you so much."

He released her slowly, and withdrew himself and fell onto the pillow beside her, breathing deeply. Her hands still rested where he had told her to keep them. He pulled the nearest to his face and took the tip of each finger into his mouth, one at a time. He tugged her body into the curve of his own, took her face between his hands, and kissed her fully on the mouth, drawing on her tongue.

His upper leg curled around her thighs. His mouth went to her temple. For a time their bodies floated together, married indeed. Then she felt his jaw move; his voice was gruff. "Tell me again."

She knew what he wanted to hear. "I love you," she said, obedient.

"Tell me you're mine."

"I love you; I'm yours."

"Whether you love me yet or not, you're mine."

"Yes, I'm yours."

The baby moved. He felt it and inhaled sharply. He spread his fingers over her stomach, in invitation, but when nothing more happened, his hand once more sought the intimate world between her thighs.

It was past midnight. Richard Laird was fixing a broken fence in a far pasture by the light of a lantern. He looked leaner than ever, lean and unhealthy, like a steer that had wintered in deep snow.

Beginning on Christmas Day, he'd got himself drunk on brandy and stayed that way for two weeks. He'd had women, lots of them—pretty nice lookers, too. But then Aida banished him for leaving tooth marks on the Chinese girl.

For the next couple of weeks he mostly drank beer, and the women he found in the various saloons around Sacramento were a little shabbier than what he was used to.

For the first two weeks of February, he started on straight wine and sluts in their shacks outside town. The difference, in his mind, between a whore and a slut was not what you could make them do, but whether they did it meekly, or with an arousing reluctance. It took a little more clearheadedness than he sometimes possessed, what with the wine and all, to think of something even a broken-willed slut would object to. Nothing was less fun than a woman who was too degraded to even care how she was used. But he'd exerted himself, believing this would get Laura out of his system at last. Then maybe her name wouldn't keep coming into his head at odd times, as clear as if someone had whispered it in his ear. Whatever secret cavity or recess of his brain she occupied, he wanted it shoveled out.

Just yesterday he'd let Zacariah collect him from the shack of the fat squaw he'd stayed the night with. He came home to find Page had quit ten days ago. The ranch was already going to hell.

But the minute he entered the door of the ranch house he'd thought of Laura again. He saw her gray eyes that reflected shadow and light in equal measure, and he knew his weeks of cure hadn't worked at all.

Page would be out here helping him with this damned fence right now, and Laura would be waiting for him at home, if it hadn't been for that bastard who'd fouled her and everything else in his life.

He put his pliers back in his pocket, the fence patched good enough. There was only one way he could get back his self-respect. Only one way. He was going to have to kill Andre Sheridan.

*   *   *

338

It was late morning. The bedroom ceiling was high and light, the carpeted floor cast with lances of sun. Andre, impatient, woke Laura with a kiss. She opened her eyes slowly. "Good morning," he murmured, shifting to hold her closer in the quilted bed. Her blank expression amused him. She was the deepest sleeper! "Remember me?"

"What are you doing still in bed?" she asked. "I thought you were an incurable before-dawn waker."

"I am. I've even had a bath already. And when I came back to bed the little one was awake, too." His hand slid to her stomach. "You're the only one who's been sleeping."

He'd already ordered a tray for her. And while she ate her cereal and eggs, he had the bath filled for her in the slate-floored dressing room. When the servants were finally gone, he pulled her naked and protesting from bed, intent on washing her himself.

At first the still, clear bathwater made each submerged movement of his hands visible. Then he reached for a bar of rose-scented soap. He smoothed and smoothed creamy lather over her breasts, murmuring, "Do you know what pretty breasts you have? They're so white, with a sort of shine, like watered silk."

He was only holding her breasts loosely, but she sat there, naked for him, kept by nothing but his eyes—yet he thought she still seemed a little afraid. Had he been too rough last night? He reached up and began to stroke her cheek. It was his way of gentling her, of saying, "Easy, easy now."

An hour or so later she lay beside him in the sun-soaked bed, in the cradle of his arms. She was spent. He loved the ease of their bodies relaxing so intimately, her belly brushing his, his thigh grazing her thigh. His mind drifted, he floated anchorless on a calm ocean, out of sight of land.

She drowsed—it seemed she had a lot of sleep to catch up on—though she was aware enough to separate her legs when his hand stroked up her thighs. He felt more satisfaction at that small act of compliance than she could ever know. She was losing her shyness, learning to anticipate the pleasure he could give her, learning to enjoy giving him pleasure in return.

He held her in his palm without pressing for a deeper intimacy just now. He was erect and wanted her again, but—for once he wished his father were alive. Who else could he speak to, man to man, about the loving of an expectant wife? There were things he needed to know.

"Shouldn't we get up?" she said murmurously. "Aren't we expected downstairs?"

He sighed, commanding his hand to slide up to the relative safety of her breast. "Not today. I'm keeping you all to myself today."

They did arise eventually, but he wouldn't allow her to put up her hair, let alone get dressed. When she pointed out that he had his trousers on and that she was chilly, he relented enough to envelop her in his dressing gown, which robed her to the floor. She trailed around all the clear bright afternoon with his voluminous dark jade satin sleeves folded back three times on her slender wrists. She looked as awkward as an adolescent, but he murmured, nuzzling her throat, "I love to see you wearing my clothes—an acquired taste, I think."

He held her on his lap in the study, and fed her candied flowers and fruit, and apologized for their wedding—"You probably wanted a stiff white church"—and for the meagerness of their honeymoon, and, in a light bantering voice, promised her a grand wedding trip after the child was born.

"I don't need a trip," she said in a slightly dazed tone. (He was doing his best to keep her dazed by fondling her, offhand and casually, yet almost continuously.)

"Don't be uppish," he scolded. "You're going to let me give you everything from now on. You'll have a wedding trip, and that's that." He selected a strawberry, all a-sparkle with sugar, and held it over her lips, so that she had to lift her chin to bite into it. She managed to take a playful nip of his finger, as well. "I figure pregnancy makes you hungrier, but I didn't expect viciousness."

"Mmm, well, maybe you should be careful." She batted her eyelashes. Evidently she didn't realize how close she was to being ravished again. She didn't realize, he supposed, that he was rationing himself to the pleasures between her legs in consideration of her condition.

"Rich man that you are, Mr. Sheridan, will you ever let me get dressed in something I can wear outside these rooms?" She held up her arm so that the sleeve of his robe drooped. "Clothes that aren't made for someone the size of a whale?"

"A whale?" His brows arched. He offered the remainder of fruit.

"No more, I'll be sick."

He set the plate aside. "Right now I like you as you are, my own private, nearly naked, newly wedded wife. And when I do let you get dressed, it won't be in those things that don't even fit you anymore. You need to have some clothes made. I could get tired of that trick with the shawl. Was that Talbot's idea—to hide your condition while he squired you around?"

She smiled stiffly, demurely folding her hands back on her rounded stomach. He placed his hand there, too. "Is it moving?"

After a moment he said, "I seem to remember from out of the jumble of last autumn that you needed clothes then, too. You especially wanted a corset. Is that why you ran back to Laird—because you couldn't wait?"

Thus, playing on the keyboard of her memory, even while fondling and caressing her, he also gently persecuted her, for the intense yearning he had for her was something for which his soul thirsted, despite disappointment and vexation.

He loved her thoroughly, even if she wasn't mature enough to be capable of experiencing anything but a cloudy and doubtful presentiment of love in return. He had the rest of their lives to teach her: first obedience, then honor, and finally love. He was a patient man.

The sun set in streaks of deep pink, rich amethyst, and golden yellow; then the fog rolled in. Andre tended the fire in the study—and Laura sensed a heat of quite a different kind within the room. An ever stronger thread of anticipation glided beneath their idle talk.

A knock came at the outer door. He answered it, and Laura overheard the English butler say, "A boy brought this,

341

sir. He said it was important, or I wouldn't have disturbed you."

The door closed, there came the sound of an envelope torn open, then Andre murmured a sibilant curse.

When he came back into the study, his eyes had gone cold as arctic ice. He held a folded piece of paper in his hand. "I have to go out for a while." He waved the paper without showing it to her. "Some unfinished business. Shouldn't take too long. Can you be faithful to me if I leave you alone for an hour? Can I trust you not to fall into bed with one of the servants?"

She ignored his jibes and leaned forward in her chair, so that his dark satin robe rustled about her. "What is it?"

"Just business. Nothing to get your eyes so wide over."

"But it must be close to eight o'clock. Can't it wait until tomorrow?"

"I'm afraid not. Now don't look like that. What's this little snapped purse doing where your mouth should be? Come on, kiss me nicely—you know you want to."

She fidgeted under this strained bit of teasing, until he went to dress. After a while, she followed him into the dressing room, holding up the hem of his robe so she wouldn't trip on it. He was already pulling on his high top boots. "Can I help you with anything?" she said.

"No." He seemed to make an effort to grin. "I'm beyond help now. You should have offered a few minutes earlier; I would have let you button me into my trousers."

She wanted to ask where he was going what it was all about, why she had this nagging feeling of foreboding. But he'd put such a constant slight on her loyalty to him, she was afraid he wouldn't believe her concern.

He shrugged into a jacket of rough charcoal tweed that made him look lazily distinguished. She trailed behind him into the foyer, wanting so much to say: *I love you; with all my heart and soul, I love you. Andre, you must believe me!* Instead, she tentatively slid her hand up his forearm, saying only, "I wish you didn't have to go."

He kissed her. His arm banded her thickened waist and caught her close, holding her until she felt weak and more

342

frightened than ever, for she sensed an awful desperation in him. He slipped his free hand into the satin robe and cupped a breast. A rush of heat flooded her throat and cheeks. "Ah, sweet, when you respond to me like that . . ." Hastily he freed the belt of the robe, so that the front of her was naked to him in the gaslight. He bent down to circle a nipple with his lips. "There's cider wine in this one, and . . . mmm, champagne over here." He sucked as if to drink from her, and it was as though he tugged on a long nerve, which extended through her breast and body, all the way down to the core of her. "Andre, don't go. Stay with me."

Her words seemed to have a negative effect, for abruptly he let her go and went out the door.

Twenty=Nine

Laura's heart seemed to fold up like a flower at dusk as the door closed on Andre. She managed to tuck her breasts away, though they didn't seem so easy to ignore now. She felt a little angry with him, a little as though he'd deliberately tormented her.

Even absent, he threaded his way all through her thoughts. She went back into the study, then wandered into the bedroom. Though she had a book—a copy of Robert Lewis Stevenson's newest, *Treasure Island*—she didn't turn the gaslights up. The fire in the fireplace was the only light in the room.

Sitting in one of the easy chairs, an unexpected shiver ran through her. She couldn't account for her apprehension—except that he had all but refused to tell her where he was going. It had something to do with that message, of course, which he'd taken with him.

She spread her left hand over the forgotten book's marbled cover and studied the rings he'd placed on her finger. They were heavy, these symbols of the oaths by which he held her. But what a relief to know they would weigh upon her hand forever! How reassuring was this man who laid her upon a bed of rock, who knew how to take what he loved ruthlessly.

Oh, if only he would return! Where was he? Why did she have this terrible feeling of dread?

She heard music, a faraway melody. She went to the

window and held the velvet draperies aside. Someone along the street must be entertaining. She couldn't see much, however, for fog completely blanketed the city. It seemed especially thick tonight; it reminded her of the mists in her worst nightmares.

Andre halted his horse under a streetlamp and took the handwritten mesage out of his pocket:

It's not over, Sheridan. Meet me at the Pacific Mail Steamship Company docks. R. L.

He crumpled the note and tossed it to the ground. It was one of those damnably foggy nights. The pier stretching out into the bay seemed empty. He sat his horse looking at it for several minutes—and was shocked when it dawned on him that he didn't really want this confrontation, at least not right now, not tonight. All he really wanted tonight was to return to Laura and spend hours with her gentle arms wrapped around his neck, her knees parted around his thighs. He wanted to tell her things that would make her blush—he loved the way she blushed. He would pull her into his arms the minute he got home, and kiss her behind the ear, and open her robe again and whisper, "I want to feel those pretty breasts of yours some more." Something that simple could make her glow pink. He nearly chuckled aloud to think of it.

And then nearly moaned at the thought of lowering his face between her thighs. She would be wet for him there—but tender, because he hadn't restrained his hands today the way he'd meant to, the way he should have. He would just lick her a little, carefully, with delicate touches of his tongue, hungry for the smell and taste of her. And maybe, to soothe and balm her, his tongue would roam inside . . .

His mouth watered and waves of heat swept through his lower body. There seemed to be nothing but distilled essence of sex flowing in his veins these days. It made him prone to slide off into daydreams like this, prone to a jumpy

345

awareness of his strong needs. The love he felt for her was a constant pain made more aching by the need to temper his passions. Consequently, it took all his willpower to think of Ling now, to remember how he'd loved her and what she'd suffered.

And she had suffered. He forced himself to remember the bruises she hadn't let him touch, the toothmarks on her breasts—that bastard had bit her!

Dutiful, the old hatred surfaced. He began to sweat, despite the chill of the damp night. Hatred almost trickled out of his pores.

He dismounted and crossed the Embarcadero on foot. The wooden pier echoed under his first steps. He recognized a coarse smell. Someone had just recently blown out a stinking, whale oil lantern here. He stopped, every hair on his body at attention.

"Down here, Sheridan," came a hollow call from the very end of the structure. Water lapped at the underpilings. Along the side of the pier were occasional stacks of crates, shadowy in the fog.

"Is that you, Laird? Why don't you come out where I can see you? Or are you as much a coward as you ever were?"

His only answer was a dry sound of laughter. He took a few more steps, reaching for his pistol. He went forward with it in his hand ,scanning the darkness intently. He started past the first stack of crates, lug boxes of raisins—

—and felt the blow to his back immediately. He'd never been knifed before, yet he knew beyond a doubt that he'd been knifed now. The blade plunged into him, jarred on a bone, then went on swiftly, like a bullet, but with a viciousness unlike any blunt-headed bullet, unlike anything he'd ever felt, a sensation that had no pain in it at first, yet made him go weak with its sliding, slicing penetration, deep into his flesh.

"Understand you got married yesterday, Sheridan," muttered the wielder of the knife. He knew that voice; it pierced his eardrums like another steel blade. "How was the wedding night? Bet a hen couldn't snuggle into a nest any better than you snuggled into hers. Think of this as just a

346

little wedding present, from one bridegroom to another."

The blade was withdrawn, bringing with it a rush of warm blood. Andre arched his back with the senation of its reverse slide, then collapsed.

"You get him?" came the voice from the end of the pier.

"Yeah!" Laird was running toward his friend, who presumably had a boat.

Andre lifted his pistol belatedly. But the fog was so damn thick—or was it just that he couldn't see? Laird's boot steps halted, there was a sound of oars. Finally there was only a stealthy, cold silence.

The pain in Andre's back was like a white-hot stitch. A thought filled his consciousness: the feel of Laura arousing to a nub beneath his fingers . . .

Laura had been dozing in the chair when she woke with a little cry out of an unhappy dream. She opened her eyes with something like shock to the unfamiliar bedroom. What had wakened her? Was it only that she'd suddenly felt the hours Andre had been gone? Or had she heard the fall of a log in the fireplace? Or had there been a noise at the door? She hesitated, listened, then rose and moved through the portieres, hesitated again, then threw back her loose hair, and turned the elaborate cast bronze doorknob.

Andre was there, lounging peculiarly against the door frame, his forehead turned and pressed into the wood. His tweed jacket hung open, exposing his turquoise waistcoat. He seemed a little pale, yet his smile was friendly enough, if a bit nonsensical.

"Have you been drinking?" she asked.

With what seemed like an effort, he stood and swung his arm over her shoulders. It came down on her like a dead weight, so heavy she staggered. Somehow she maneuvered him through the portieres, but then he stopped her, pulled her around in front of him and dropped his face, his mouth meeting hers.

He didn't taste like alcohol. Her tongue was all mingled with his and love whispered to her so softly she could hear

347

nothing else for the moment. Then he began leaning more and more heavily on her, until it wasn't a lean anymore, it was a fall. She threw her arms around him, but he continued to bow over, near to fainting. Her spine nearly snapped with the pressure. They both crashed to their knees on the carpet, then he slumped onto his side.

"Andre?" There was silence where his voice should have answered her. "Andre!" she cried, shaking him. That was when she felt the dark wet stain soaking the back of his tweed coat.

She strained to drag his coat, waistcoat, and shirt off his upper shoulder, revealing a deep puncture steadily oozing. She stared with horrified enthrallment at the bloody mess. "Oh my God—a doctor, you need a doctor!" She struggled to her feet.

"Laura," he called softly, trying to reach for her.

"Don't move," she pleaded, going to her knees again.

His eyes focused on her face. They were the man's soul, those eyes, and for a brief moment she knew how very much he must love her. He took hold of her bare knee. "Are you all right?"

"I'm fine, I'm fine," she said, trying to control the inclination of her voice to become a falsetto.

"Don't leave the house . . . until . . . I can go with you. Promise me."

She thought this was no time for his mistrust of her. But with him looking at her as though he were storing up for the next thousand years she said, "Yes, all right, I promise!" Then she watched him lose consciousness.

She raced to the door, flung it open, and shouted up and down the hall. "Help! Someone! Please help me!" She raced back to Andre, unsure if her calls had even been heard. But Elexa appeared in the foyer, hurriedly tying a peach-colored dressing gown around her waist. "What is it, *cherie?*" she said, her voice crisp with its accent.

Laura was crying; her hands were red with blood. "We need Dr. Kellogg! I can't stop it, we've got to stop it! He can't die, he *can't!*"

Elexa came forward another step into the bedroom, and

then in a surge of peach satin, fell to her knees, and embraced her son. *"André—mon cher!"*

"Please send someone for Dr. Kellogg!"

What Elexa thought she didn't say as she wordlessly left to give orders to her staff. In only moments she was back with a compress made of a clean folded towel. "We will combine our strength." She placed her hand over Laura's. "Together now."

It seemed hours later that Dr. Kellogg finally arrived. Andre was lifted onto the bed by several of the male servants, and undressed. Laura refused to leave the room when she was told to. Though she didn't have a strong stomach, she assisted the doctor in cleaning and sewing his wound. She willed Andre not to leave her again with silent desperation, sending pleas from her heart to find his, wherever it might be.

At last the doctor placed a clean pad over the injury and bound it. Laura wiped at her lips. "Who would do this?"

The doctor said sensibly, "Probably a thief." She gripped Laura's arm sympathetically. Then, businesslike again, she washed and dried her hands, and tied on her Rubens hat, which she'd discarded hurriedly upon coming in. "The blade pricked an artery. It could have been worse. A little deeper and . . . well, he's lucky to have so much deflecting muscle and bone. And blood—the man does seem to have plenty of blood, doesn't he?" A small intent smile trailed the corners of her mouth. "He'll pull through, Laura. He strikes me as a man who wants badly to live just now."

"He was conscious for a moment," Laura told Dr. Kellogg in the morning. Andre's breathing had been uneven sometimes during the night, as if the rise and fall of his chest pained him. Propping him with pillows had helped, but there had been drawn-out, nightmarish moments when his chest stopped moving at all. Laura, with Elexa, had sat for long hours witnessing his struggles, her own lungs aching with the desire to breathe for him. Dr. Kellogg was informed of all this, but not that he'd tried to rise twice, reaching instinctively for his hip where he wore his gun when he wasn't within the walls of his home.

After examining him, the doctor said, "Yes, he's doing fine—or as well as can be expected. The wound itself wasn't that bad; it's mostly his loss of blood that's laid him flat. He's building that back even now. He'll amaze you with his rapid recovery."

"Laura?"

"I'm here, Andre!" she answered quickly. He was lying on his stomach, and she leaned by him to help him onto his side and support his head while Dr. Kellogg gave him a spoonful of tonic. He made an awful face.

"Bitter, Mr. Sheridan?"

"Not as sweet as some of the things I've tasted lately." He coughed, and winced at the pain it caused him. "What was it, gentian root?"

"Gentian root, as you know well enough, is for horses. But now that you mention it, a horse tonic might prove best for someone of your physique. Seeing that you're well enough to joke, I think you're well enough for us to get something nourishing down you. Mrs. Sheridan," she turned to Elexa, "could we have some beef tea?"

Laura supported Andre's head again when the steamy bowl arrived. He said, between sips, "You look tired, sweet. You should crawl in here with me and get some rest."

Embarrassed, she spoke briskly: "I'll rest when you've taken this broth." She nodded to Elexa, who carried another spoonful of it to his mouth.

"That's enough for now," Dr. Kellogg said. "Let him rest."

He didn't sleep immediately, however, but asked to speak to Laura alone. "Just want to tell you about the attack, sweet. Don't want to be bothered with police questions, so you're not to report it."

"But who was it? Who would stab you?"

"City's full of thieves."

Elexa seemed to accept this, when Laura relayed it to her, and Laura was too anxious about his health to question him further.

He slept again, and didn't waken until evening, when it

was dusky once more on Nob Hill. The two women again fed him, and again he mentioned that Laura looked tired.

"He's right, child," Elexa said. "Go lie down. Choose any room."

"I'll just have a nap right here," she said, taking the easy chair by his bed once more.

Dr. Kellogg seemed pleased with the healing of his wound when she returned in the late evening. She beckoned Laura into the foyer and touched her cheek with a cool, professional palm. "Did you sleep at all today?"

"I napped a bit."

"In that chair? You've got another life to think of, remember."

When Laura went back into the bedroom, Elexa asked, "What did she say?"

"Only that Andre was doing better."

They sat on opposite sides of the bed for another hour or so. Though Andre slept, he held Laura's hand, and she couldn't bring herself to be separated from contact with his warm skin. She knew everyone was right; she needed to lie down. Her back ached terribly. She had strained it in trying to break his fall the night before, and the pain seemed a part of her now.

When he moved restlessly in his sleep, and his hand fell away, she stretched. She would have excused herself then, but Elexa sat dozing in her chair, and Laura thought one of them ought to remain alert in case he needed something.

She bent to touch her lips to his forehead. His eyes opened suddenly, and she wasn't at all surprised to find herself falling into them, drifting weightlessly down . . .

Andre tried to catch her. The effort cost him, and he wasn't quick enough anyway. He had never loved her so *sorely* as when he saw her lying there on the floor and himself too weak to help her. "Mother," he said in a croaky voice, "Mother . . . you'd better get that butler of yours. Laura needs to be picked up off the carpet over here."

"I warned you," Dr. Kellogg scolded.

"I'm sorry," Laura said from the bed of one of the mansion's many spare rooms. She vaguely recalled being carried here—recalled the fresh-starched scent of the butler's shirt more than anything else. "I told them I didn't need you."

"Oh, didn't you? Now listen to me, young lady, I don't want you on your feet again until I say so."

"But Andre—"

"Your Andre doesn't need to watch you tumbling to the floor beside his bed. He's in there now growling at everybody for not taking better care of you. You've only managed to make it harder for us to take care of him."

Laura averted her eyes.

"You need rest and quiet, Laura. Have one of that army of maids I see scurrying around here help you undress and get into this bed properly."

"Are you saying I could lose the baby?"

"I don't see any sign of that." She seemed to hesitate, then spoke plainly, as was her habit. "Which reminds me, I think I should have a talk with your new husband. I have a feeling we won't keep him convalescing for very long, and he must understand that he has to handle you with care."

"He isn't . . . that is . . ."

"He loves you, I can see that. But sometimes men in love get carried away; they get . . . exuberant, shall we say?"

The morning weather looked miserably raw outside Laura's windows. She learned that Andre had been restless with a fever during the night. Dr. Kellogg visited them both in the afternoon and assured Laura that the fever hadn't been unexpected—that it had passed without incident and not returned. Indeed, he was recuperating nicely now. Still, Laura couldn't quite believe these secondhand reports. It was frustrating to be kept abed when she felt perfectly fit. She would have gotten up, but Dr. Kellogg had gained Elexa's complicity to keep her where she was. And Elexa, like her son, was proving to be a difficult person to circumvent.

Night came again; the house quieted. Laura fell asleep

early on, but woke within an hour. She lay alone in the big guest bed, wide-awake, staring at the ceiling of the strange room, listening to the cold, rainy wind at the windows. Everyone said she must rest for the baby's sake, but how could she when she was fretting herself to tatters?

Suddenly she threw back the green chintz quilt, and in nothing but her white nightdress and with her hair unbound, tiptoed out into the hall.

In Andre's rooms the only light came from the fire on the hearth, which was dying to red-gray embers. She paused under the portieres to let her eyes adjust. His voice startled her: "Come here, Lorelei."

"I—I didn't mean to wake you, I just wanted to see if you were all right."

He tried to sit up, made it to one elbow, and held out a hand. "Come here."

She moved around the bed, but stayed just beyond that hand which waited, palm up.

"Closer," he said, "I can't reach you."

She finally laid her thin hand in his big one. In his touch was welcome, without a trace of the unyielding hardness or anger he'd sometimes displayed since finding her. He drew her to the side of the bed. "You're not supposed to be up."

"They're silly to fuss."

He smiled. "They'd better fuss, or I'll know the reason why. Were you so afraid you didn't feel you could even rest? There are several emotions I like to arouse in you, but fear isn't one of them."

"What a shame, when you're so good at it."

His eyes gleamed. "Are you afraid now?"

She shook her head.

"Well then . . ." He held the blankets open to her. "Come on, get in before your toes freeze."

She said, letting her lashes hide her eyes, "Very well." She found the steps and snuggled in beside him.

He threaded his hand through the hair at her temple; she saw something wicked shape his face. "Your Dr. Kellogg had a talk with me this evening. Something to the effect that I'd better temper my stallion instincts for a few months. I almost blushed."

"But she told me it would be all right as long as—" And she did blush, for she'd revealed herself and now he was grinning.

"Temper my instincts, she said; not corral the horse altogether. I'm to be mindful of your condition. I assured her I am mindful, very mindful, of everything about you."

Lying on his good side, he pressed her head onto his arm. She relaxed as his warm, slightly rough hand smoothed over her belly. "Where did you get this god-awful flannel nightdress?" he murmured.

"I've had it. Mama bought it, I suppose."

"Remind me to buy you one or two French negligees when we go shopping for your new clothes. One should be enough, for times when you're ill. Otherwise I'd rather have you naked . . . naked as the day . . ." he spoke softly, with meditative pauses, "naked as the moon."

"I thought you liked flannel. You own so many flannel shirts." They were talking nonsense, the kind of midnight talk married people everywhere must make. Golden talk in drowsy voices. Using up bits of heartstring too short for daylight conversations.

"Well, if this were one of my shirts, I might like it better. But then it wouldn't be so long and I could get to your legs." He moved to make himself more comfortable, coincidentally pulling up her gown and tangling his knees between her bare thighs. "Umm, that's better. That's nice. Ten minutes ago I was in here damning the bastard who laid me up—but all of a sudden it's not so bad—being stuck in bed that is. I wonder what made the difference?"

"This flannel nightdress."

"You think so?"

"I'm sure of it. Shall I leave it here to comfort you when I go?"

"I'm tempted to say yes, just to see your bare bottom bounce out of here without it, but you're not going anywhere, so I'll have to decline."

"I have to go sooner or later. You're not well. You need room to thrash around and get comfortable."

"I'm very comfortable—and very tempted to thrash around."

"Dr. Kellogg wouldn't like that."

"Dr. Kellogg can just—"

"She's very kind really, and very skilled."

"Yes, she changed my bandages today with all the skill of a practiced torturer. Why is it that I get the feeling she doesn't approve of me?"

They listened for a while to the violent blasts of rain at the windows, and the rages of the wind, then she said, "How old are you, Andre?"

He raised his head a bit to look at her.

"I'm just curious. You said you had a birthday party last week."

"Oh, yes, that. Friends of the family—Parry's parents, as a matter of fact. They found out I was in town and nothing would do but a big flowery banquet. It's nice that you're expecting, so we can have an excuse to get out of that sort of invitation for a while."

"You don't like parties?"

"Not the oversized and over-lavish kind. Do you like parties?"

"I haven't been to many. Only my weddings . . ." She could have bitten her tongue off. This peaceful moment was hardly the time to remind him she'd married another man before him, the man who was his worst enemy.

Thirty

Andre said quietly, "From what I saw, you didn't seem to enjoy either of your weddings much, Laura." There was a silence before he went on. "Anyway, to go back to what we were talking about, I doubt you would like San Francisco-style entertainments. They're posh and vulgar and I think they would just fret you. Wouldn't you prefer a quiet corner with a piano where you could make music?"

She sighed. She hadn't thought of making music for a long time. Had she missed it? Yes, she knew she had, though she didn't like to admit it.

She wanted to change the subject, and remembered that he hadn't answered her original question. "Are you thirty? Thirty-one?"

"Only twenty-nine," he said petulantly. "*Just* twenty-nine. *Barely* twenty-nine. A long way from thirty."

She giggled, suddenly lighthearted. "Twenty-nine is very old, though, isn't it? So close to middle-age."

"Huh! Just remember that I was celebrating while you were locked in a cellar in Little China. There's a lesson there, woman."

Piqued, she said, "No doubt you sat next to some eligible miss—you in your fancy tuxedo and she in . . . what? Some luscious gown of silk and satin?"

"It was blue, and she was blond—and pretty, as I recall. And she fairly hung upon my every word."

"Andre!"

He chuckled. "You asked. I was quite eligible myself at the time. A bachelor—a *young* bachelor—good-looking—*very* good-looking—with a little money to spare. Any woman in her right mind would set her sights on me. You're lucky to have me, you know."

She settled deeper into his arms. "You're dreadful."

"I know and an unclean beast and a fatuous cad—remember all those names you called me?" He nuzzled her forehead with his lips. "My horse's ears were shocked. He'd never heard such unladylike cursing."

"Your horse should have been shocked the first night, when you were so mean to me."

"Was I mean? I tried to make you as comfortable as I could. Mostly what I remember about that is having you in my arms, bound and so helpless, your soft mouth a little swollen from the gag. I wanted to kiss you, kiss away that fright and find out if your lips really did taste like ripe plums . . ." His head lowered.

"Andre," she breathed a long moment later.

He sighed hugely. "That debutant in blue—"

"What debutant?"

"The one who sat next to me the other night—your attention darts around like a bird, love; you have a mind like a swallow. I've been talking all along about the girl in blue, trying to tell you she wouldn't even tempt me if I'd had her over my saddlebow in her underwear. In fact, she struck me as being someone who would strip to her underwear in a minute had I cared enough to ask. While you came to me such an unwilling temptress, and a thousand times more potent because of it. And I doubt if she could match you, carnal as she was and delicate as you are, in sexual passion. You've always been easy, my easy easy Laura, my swallow who caught up my heart and trailed it after her like streamers."

"You're terrible."

"Yes, and lecherous, too, for I want you, dear captured wife. I've longed this whole day to make this soft body of yours writhe."

"Really terrible."

"But not terrible to you, so stop fidgeting and twitching; I'm in no condition to wrestle you tonight."

"Then move your hand."

"What hand? Oh, this one? But it's comfortable—I'm comfortable."

"Andre, you're in no condition to make love to me—"

"I'm just holding you. I like to. I like the way you fit in my palm. You really think I'm capable of almost any depravity, don't you?"

"I know exactly what you're capable o-of . . ." Her scolding was ruined by a yawn she couldn't suppress. She knew she must seem as ferocious as an egg.

He chuckled dryly, and said with false meekness, "Yes, ma'am. Now you'd better get to sleep."

"I have to go back to my own bed."

"You are in your own bed." He tightened his hold on her, indicating he had no intention of letting her go.

"But—"

"*Hush.*" He gave her a little squeeze. "You're going to upset me and I'm a sick man; I need to be humored. Besides, as my wife, it's your duty to hover about my bed of pain. Now kiss me goodnight . . . ummm. Once more . . . come on, Laura, give me a real kiss."

"Move your hand and I will."

"Move it—like this?"

"Ohh . . . Andre, don't tease."

"Kiss me then. Mmm, that's better, much better."

The wind was still blowing in furious gusts when Laura awakened. She stretched like a cat unwinding from a nap, and finally propped herself on her elbows, her hair trailing the pillows behind her. Andre, up and dressed, had on trousers, and a loose, untucked shirt. He smiled at her over the top of his newspaper. Flickering rainlight played on his face and danced on the wall behind him. He sat in one of the easy chairs with his long legs thrust out, one black-booted ankle atop the other.

Before she could even ask him what time it was, a knock

came at the outer door. He gestured her to stay put while he went to see who it was.

She heard Elexa questioning him, a worried note in her husky voice. Laura flung her hair back, to better hear his reassuring responses: "She's with me . . . yes, but at least this way I don't have to go sneaking around the halls at night to check on her . . . I'm feeling much better, a little sore . . . I promise I won't go further today than this foyer . . . yes, I will, Mother. And I think you could use some extra rest yourself. Let the servants worry about fetching and carrying for us today."

When Dr. Kellogg arrived after lunch, she found Andre lounging in his chair again, while Laura lay luxuriously in the big bed. Her hair was brushed and braided, and her face felt shiny from soap and water. "Well, Mr. Sheridan," the doctor said, "I see you take better care of your wife than you do of yourself. I recall saying you might get up today, but this wasn't exactly what I meant."

"Andre, you told me—"

"Now you see how you're upsetting Laura, Doctor?"

Dr. Kellogg remained unsmiling. "Let's look at you."

He took off his shirt and sat on the arm of the chair for her to examine his wound. He was so bronzed and sleek, so hard and insolent and unapproachable, Laura wondered how any woman could touch him as coolly as Dr. Kellogg did, without a single sign of the feelings simply looking at him engendered in Laura.

Evidently the doctor found his wound much improved, for she said, "All right, Mr. Sheridan, I concede the point this time. When a patient is as feisty as you, it's usually time to let him up anyway." She turned to the bed. "And how about you? Has the baby been moving?"

Laura avoided Andre's laughing eyes. "A little."

Dr. Kellogg cocked her brow. The corners of her mouth twitched as she said, "Was your sleep disturbed last night, Mr. Sheridan? By tiny knees and elbows perhaps? Seems a big enough bed. Maybe if you were to allow your wife more room in it, you both might rest better."

Laura's face felt hot. The doctor bent to brush her hand

over her forehead. "I suppose you want me to let you up, too? You wouldn't want to get too soft with all this luxury." She gestured at the well-appointed room. "Quite a change from your circumstances when we first met, hmm?"

"And what circumstances were those?" Andre asked.

"You don't know, Mr. Sheridan?"

Laura, who had never forgotten, who would never forget the confusion and hurt of those days, nevertheless said, "Doctor—"

"If I knew, I wouldn't have to ask, would I?"

"Andre—"

"Well, I think you should know: Laura came to me quite ill. She'd hardly been eating at all for weeks. I don't think she had the money to eat and pay her rent, too. She was living in a perfectly awful place, and was making do on a single meal a day at a greasy restaurant. She was about to lose her job because she was feeling sick every morning, and hadn't the least idea what her symptoms meant."

Andre got to his feet.

"Shocking, isn't it?" Dr. Kellogg seemed quite satisfied with his reaction. "I'm not surprised she hasn't told you. Just as, at the time, she didn't tell me the father of her child was alive and right here in the city. I asked her if there was anyone who would help her. She told me, 'No one who would care.' Now that doesn't go along with your claim of begging her to marry you, does it, Mr. Sheridan? I doubt if she'll ever tell me the real story, though. There are a good many things she keeps to herself—things that the persons responsible should feel embarrassed about."

After the doctor had gone, Andre stood staring at Laura, his eyes awful. Laura said, "I don't know why she told you that. She exaggerated, of course."

He'd put his shirt back on and now rolled up the sleeves, watching her all the while. "Which part did she exaggerate, love?"

"Well, I certainly wasn't starving. I didn't eat much because I didn't have an appetite."

"And you didn't have an appetite because you were sick. And you were sick because you were pregnant—or was that exaggerated, too?" His voice, though not loud, sounded hard and faceted.

"It wasn't as bad as it sounds."

"Stop looking at me with those great eyes begging for your life. You know damned well I'm not going to hurt you. It would be flattering, this famous fear of me, except that it's so inconvenient. I just want some answers: You came to San Francisco without any money?"

"I had a little. But I had trouble getting a job, and got rather short before Mr. Kane took me on. That's why I worried when I felt sick each morning and started being late for work."

She dared to search his face, which she felt she knew as well as she knew her own, but found it shut. "I didn't know that getting sick meant I was pregnant. If I'd known . . ."

"What?"

"I—I don't know," she whispered.

"I thought you were going to lie and claim you would have come here. But you were sick, desperate, afraid—and still you didn't come."

"I thought you'd left me! I thought . . ." She felt so angry suddenly, and hurt, and offended, and—she couldn't find the right name for it! Tears set up in her eyes. The moment they began there, he took a step toward her, cursing under his breath. That gave her the power to hold them back. "I thought you wouldn't care," she said with what she hoped was a touch of dignity.

He swore again, still softly. "You damned me out of hand, without even giving me a chance. And now I have to take the blame for your suffering—when the truth is I did beg you to marry me! I did everything I could to break you without cowing you—a mercy I should never have shown."

"I was going by what evidence I had—your absence and Soo's word!"

After a dead silence, he said, "Go on: you learned you were pregnant, and moved to a better house."

"Dr. Kellogg introduced me to Mrs. Noah."

"And Yale Talbot? Did she introduce you to him, too?"

"No. Yale found me."

"And found you very willing, too, didn't he, after you'd apprenticed at love with me? After you'd let me teach you just enough to know how to give yourself. He must have wondered at his luck in finding a virtue as soft as apple butter." His voice held an edge she'd heard before, which promised sure retaliation.

He turned restlessly and knelt to mend the fire, though it hardly needed it. The flames crackled and sputtered. But he turned back to her with a glacial light in his gaze. "I could sympathize with this tale of horrors and hunger except that none of it was necessary. If you'd come here when you were down on your luck—at the very least when you found out you were pregnant—"

"And humiliate myself? You weren't even here at the time. If it hadn't come from your own mouth, would your mother have believed me—that I'd been bound and stolen and seduced by her beloved son? I doubt it! You're blaming me, Andre, when the truth is none of this would have happened if you hadn't been so determined to steal Richard's wife in the first place!"

"He stole mine!"

"I know that!" she said in frustration. "That's not the point!"

That startled him out of his wide-legged stance. He let his lids half-conceal his eyes. "How do you know—unless you confronted him? What happened when you went back to him?" He took a step toward her.

"I—I confronted him, like you said. And I found out you were right about him on several points: that he didn't want me back, for instance. He only wanted me . . . h-he only wanted me . . . gone. So I left as quickly as I could."

She saw him trying to figure it out in his mind. She swung her legs out of the bed and searched for the steps with her bare feet.

"How long did you stay with him before moving back to Mrs. Gladwin's?"

"Not long. Two days."

"Did he—God damn it! Did he—"

"No! And that's the last I'm going to say about it!"

"Oh, is it?"

"Some things are none of your business, Andre! I'm a separate and individual human being, you know. You may never believe I love you, but this I swear: I have never been intimate with another man. I'm yours—yours and no other's."

As she tried to pass by him without looking into his face again, he stopped her with an accusing hand. She softened like a kitten, as if to preclude triggering some taut spring in his arms.

Andre—this is Andre, not Richard. He would never strike me.

"Why don't you go ahead and cry?"

"Because I don't want to!"

"You do! You're on your way to the dressing room now to cry by yourself."

"I'll never cry over you again!" As false a pronouncement as was ever made, for she was all but crying already. She felt a strange helplessness as she stood looking up at him. She wanted him to take her in his arms. She didn't understand why she craved that when he was being so cruel, but she did.

"Can't you bring your suffering to me even now, Laura? You ran back to Laird because he was your husband—well, I'm your husband now. Run to me."

She stood trembling, helpless, with shameful tears rolling down her cheeks . . . and then her hands were about him and very pore of her body released like a floodgate. He anchored her against his large chest with his correspondingly large hands. Despite her disproportion, they seemed to fit together so snug that not an inch of space remained between them.

"Laura, Laura, you should have come to me then. Sick and scared—you must have been so scared. God, half of me wants to shake you and the other half wants to cry with you! Shhh," he whispered, "it's all right. You're with me now, and safe. You'll always be safe with me." He had a hand behind her head; she kept her face turned into his shirt, her hands hugged his sides. He rubbed his chin over the top of her head lightly.

363

When she'd cried herself out, and dared to peek up at him, his mouth opened over hers, hard, yes, but savoring. Pleasure filled her immediately, like an ardent mist. She tried to keep her silence, but it was impossible; she moaned without reservation. All her anger was gone. He made her feel soft with desire, and weak—totally his possession. She let her hands wander beneath the tails of his shirt, onto his naked back, then her fingers moved to undo the buttons of his trousers. His hands dropped to her hips. He held her against him, pressed her round stomach into his pelvis. "We shouldn't."

She swallowed, hard. "I'm sorry, your wound . . ."

"It's not me I'm worried about." With his hands on her shoulders, he pushed her gently back against the bed.

"Oh." She blinked. "But I'm fine."

"Are you sure?" He lifted her to sit on the edge of the high mattress, and unbottoned the neck of her nightdress. He pushed it off her shoulders, bent, and his mouth enclosed the puffy peak of one breast, then the other, again and again, till both throbbed with exquisite sensation and she was warm and all yielding womanliness.

He pulled away. "I really don't think we should. I need to talk to Dr. Kellogg again . . ."

She whispered entreatingly, "Couldn't you at least kiss me?" At the same time she spread open his loosened trousers and unfastened his underdrawers. She was somewhat daunted by such obvious virility as she found there, yet the sight of him, stiff and delicately curved, aroused her. She took him in hand, and stroked him, marveling at his suede smoothness.

He kissed her, as she'd asked, and then bent so his mouth could again open on a nipple. His erotic suckling caused a peculiar tightening low in her stomach. He moved to nibble the pointed crown of the other breast—

—then ripped his mouth away and closed his hand over the hands she had on him. "Laura, are you seducing me?"

"I think so."

"You think so, Lorelei?" His slight smile was rueful as he wedged her legs apart. "Lie back." He lifted her nightdress,

364

so that it covered nothing but her stomach now, and took her knees over his forearms. He pushed her legs up and back, and positioned himself and slid into her inch by inch.

And with fluid, stunning grace the music rose. The firm power of his body was a voluptuous delight, making her shiver with each impact. She closed her eyes and moaned each time he entered her. He seemed to go deep, deep.

He increased the cadence of his thrusts. They became swifter, stronger, his smooth-sliding entries went ever deeper. She felt his trousers along the backs of her buttocks. He whispered, "Laura . . . Laura . . ." He slid his hips toward her one last time, pressed in. And just the feel of him, hard, warm, alive, so surely present at the center of her, sent swift fountains of joy through her. She shuddered. At the same time she felt him swell and throb and flow.

"My Lorelei," he murmured when he could speak again. "I can't live without you anymore. There was a time when I knew exactly what I had to do with my life, and why. But you make me forget. Everything seems to stop with you; I can't see any further. You seduce me—and I can't resist."

Despite the fact that the weather was still wretchedly stormy the following day, Elexa came into Andre's study fresh from a jaunt outdoors. Her full-length coat of sable, with matching hat, sparkled with raindrops as she placed a dressmaker's box in Laura's arms. Inside was a gown made of shimmering satin.

"I've never seen anything like it," she said later, as she modeled it. The simple underdress, the color of wine, hung loose from her shoulders. Over it went a heavier, rose-colored satin coat, rather like the tunics of the women of Chinatown. There were bands of the darker wine material at the neckline and around the shoulders. The coat hung below her hips, concealing her round stomach attractively.

"I am not surprised," Elexa said with expansive Gallic affection, "since Andre sketched the rough idea for it himself and asked me to have my dressmaker sew one up."

Andre, surveying Laura with an air of proprietorship,

said, "If you like it, we'll have more made."

She stared at him incredulously. Not only handsome, big, and vital, not only a man to have the heart out of her with a smile or a phrase—but one who would take time to design maternity gowns for her comfort.

Seeing her look, he smiled. "Going around half-unbuttoned for months at a time would definitely lower my self-esteem. Do you think this design will do?"

"Oh yes. If I could have one or two more, maybe in more practical daytime fabrics." She wouldn't need much in the way of evening clothes, since now she could properly "disappear from public view."

"You'll have as many as you want, but at least—what, Mother? Half a dozen?"

Elexa gave a mellow, easy laugh, that was either very artless or very comprehending. "Half a dozen for evening, *cheri*. She will want to dress for dinner even if she cannot go out just now. And another half dozen at least for day wear."

Thus Laura got a glimmer of what marriage to a rich man meant in terms of style of living.

There were other glimmers delivered that day: a gold case holding calling cards engraved with "Mrs. Andre Sheridan" in flowing script; a bottle of French Milk of Roses *parfum* in a cut crystal bottle; a dozen pairs of handmade French kid gloves in assorted colors; sets of jet and horn hair ornaments; and finally, a flat, black velvet box containing a choker of diamonds.

Conscious of the weight of the jewels around her throat, Laura tried to thank Andre again as they sat down to dinner at the long polished table in the formal dining room. The lovely profusion of Elexa's china and crystal gleamed before them. A bowl of early camellias sat between two candelabra; the candles' flaring light picked out gilt details in the glassed cabinets.

"You've thanked me, sweet, and you're welcome," he said with mocking courtesy. "And I haven't forgotten, I still owe you those corsets. I just didn't think they'd be very comfortable right now—and I admit I'm glad."

The bowing steward served their meal. It seemed a

daunting task, but she found her way through the stemware and silver utensils at her place without fumbling—water goblets, wine glasses, forks for one thing, forks for another, soup and dessert and coffee spoons, salmon knives, meat knives . . .

"The General trains her soldiers to set a properly appointed table," Andre commented wryly.

The wind continued to shake the house as they ate, like breakings of the sea. Rain dashed at the tall windows behind their silk draperies. During the several courses, Andre showed his conversational abilities. His wit made the best possible sauce to the delicious dinner. As soon as he leaned back in his chair, stretching his long legs beneath the table, the butler made his crisp and well-groomed appearance.

"Brandy, sir?"

"I'll have coffee with Mrs. Sheridan in the music room."

Thirty-One

Andre escorted Laura into the room next to the library,
where paintings lined the walls and a grand piano dominated
a draperied alcove. She had occasionally heard faint music
through the house these past few days. Someone, Elexa, she
guessed, had played a lot of Liszt. The music, though
capably executed, had had certain weaknesses Laura's
fingers had involuntarily tensed to correct.

She sat with Andre on a small red plush sofa. She poured
the coffee and passed him the platter of fresh fruits and
Monterey Jack cheese, asking politely, "Where did you say
your mother went this evening?"

"A party, as usual."

"Oh." Her eyes wandered to the piano, on which a shaded
lamp threw a circle of light over the music rack. "A Nob Hill
party?"

He grinned, not answering her, but saying, "I don't
suppose you'd play for me? Go on; you're more interested in
that piano right now than Mother's social life."

She crossed the red Turkish carpet and seated herself on
the bench with mixed feelings. The piano was a square
rosewood Steinway with heavy, turned legs and a glasslike
finish. Like a Haydn symphony, it was all balanced shape, all
clarity, all elegance of construction.

Ready on the rack was Tchaikovsky's melancholy "None
But the Lonely Heart." She bowed over the keys still. Her
hands trembled a little, then . . .

The piece was meant to open with a sense of pathos, almost a sob—but there was nothing! Her rendition was terrible! She all but cringed.

She decided to try some of the pieces with which she was more familiar. Unfortunately, even Chopin seemed to be more full of annoying dissonances and eccentricities than he should have been. She tried to forget everything except the intricate arrangement of the melody, looked for the emotion, but what she ground out left her cold. She stopped abruptly in the middle and bowed her head over the keys in shame—and despair.

Andre came behind her and placed his hands on her shoulders. "What is it?"

She shook her head dumbly, mortified. "I can't . . . I seem to have lost something . . . everything."

"It sounded good to me. At least—I'm amazed at how someone as small as you can get so much sound from a piano."

"So much *sound!*"

"I'm sorry; I didn't mean it that way. But it was a compliment really: You're going to have a baby and—"

"You don't have to find excuses for me."

"You're too hard on yourself. You haven't been near a piano for months. Believe me, Laura, you play much better, even without practice, than any amateur I've ever heard."

"I'm no amateur!" she said in a voice rich with disdain. "I'm an—" She realized what she had been about to say, modified it, and finished in a whisper, "I was trained to be an artist."

Trained. Yes, that was the word for it. Like a monkey trained to perform for the hurdy-gurdy man, she'd been trained to satisfy Alarice Upton's unquenchable ambitions. But she'd escaped those ambitions—or had she? If so, then why was she feeling so panicked to find her skills dying now? That old dream of artistry (whoever had originated it) was well on its way toward being lost—as she'd meant it to be lost, when she ran away from Abfalter Village a year ago! So why feel its going so strongly at this late date? Why feel so utterly empty to realize it might truly be something left behind, to become irreclaimable as she grew older, irredeemable with the passage of the years?

She hugged herself. The baby turned fretfully within her, as if commisserating. Suddenly she felt resentful of it, and of Andre. She rose away from him. "I think I'll go up."

"Laura," he reached for her hands and pried at her clenched fingers, "the only proper attitude is patience."

She pulled away. "You don't have to come up with me. I know it's early." Quickly she added, "Goodnight."

He wasn't long in following her. She was just slipping her nightdress over her head when she heard the foyer door open and close; his footsteps went into the bedroom. Though they were muffled by the deep pile of the Turkish carpet, she knew his quiet walk. She took her hair down and began to brush it.

After a few moments, he opened the glass-paned door of the dressing room. He stood leaning there with his necktie loose and his coat slung from one finger behind his right shoulder. His left arm was braced across the doorway as if to bar her escape. "Do you want to talk about it?"

"About what?"

"Your music, Laura. You've always been a little silly about it. I can't imagine anyone with a talent like yours even considering letting it wither."

"I'm a married woman now, and soon to be a mother. Where am I supposed to find the time to traipse around the world giving concerts anyway?"

"Don't blame it on me or the baby. You'll have servants to run your home and nurses to see to the tedious details of raising a child. You're going to have to decide what you want, Laura. If you give up on yourself, it's your decision, not anyone else's."

He was so self-assured, so smug, so certain of everything he did. He couldn't understand uncertainty in others. To him it was a simple matter of making up her mind—as if making up one's mind was ever all that simple!

She said, "Your mother will be home soon. Why don't you go down and spend some time with her? She would appreciate it, and surely you're getting tired of my company."

"I don't want to spend an hour chatting with Mother

370

about San Francisco society. I want to go to bed with you."

He eased her back from the mirrored chest where she was still brushing her hair in a self-punishing way. A hand on the small of her back, he ushered her into the bedroom. He'd turned down the bed earlier, and as she used the bedsteps, he went about the room turning out the gaslights. Each made a gentle sound, like a snuffed candle.

It was dark then. No light came through the window, for the fog clouded any view of moon or stars. The fire in the fireplace had gone out while they were downstairs. In the big bed he took her in his arms, tenderly, yet firmly. He reached for the buttons at the yoke of her nightdress.

"Don't. I want to wear it; I feel chilly."

He left off his unbuttoning and took her hand and kissed the palm and each finger, slowly, attentively. But when he lowered his head, meaning to capture her mouth, she turned her face into the warm indentation beneath his collarbone. His warm hand slid into the open bosom of her gown. "Don't, Andre." She pushed lightly away from his wide chest.

With a faint smile of indulgence, he said, "I thought you were cold. I'm just trying to warm you." His lips pressed against her temple, his breath brushed her ear.

"Don't try to make love to me tonight," she said petulantly. "It won't be any good."

He laughed softly. "Are you sure? You've never disappointed me yet." He nudged her onto her side and moved behind her. The musky smell of him filled her senses. Her breasts swelled and their caps grew hard in his fingers. His lips caressed her nape, then moved to her ear. "You never have, Laura."

The matter of her music was still foremost on her mind, and her fury at herself was melting toward tears. She tried to scoot away from him. "I don't want to, not tonight!"

"Well, surely you won't begrudge me just one kiss. Turn over and let me button you—and give you a little goodnight kiss." He leaned forward over her shoulder, but she buried her face in the pillow.

"That afraid, hmmm?"

"Afraid of what?" She turned onto her back defiantly.

Propped on an elbow, looking down on her, his fingers traced across her cheekbones, over her mouth, to that little throbbing place in the cupped hollow at the base of her throat. "This," he said, "gives away all your secrets."

"I don't have any secrets."

"Oh, I think you do. For instance," he said with a fearfully casual focus, "what took place between you and Laird when you went back to him."

She lay quiet; a caution had come on her. "Well, you have secrets, too," she parried. "Like how you got yourself stabbed. If it was a thief, why was your wallet still in your coat pocket? And there was that mysterious message that took you out that night. You always change the subject when someone brings any of that up."

He said consideringly, "You really want to know? I'll tell you then—it was Laird."

She gasped.

"He and a friend—Zacariah, I imagine. They ambushed me down at the docks."

Her mind roared with white noise. "Why, *why?*" She remembered Richard's fists, and his eyes—eyes like thin sharp blades turning in the darkness.

"He said it was a wedding present. Evidently he's having me watched now, the way I've watched him for the last five years. Which suits me fine, because it means sooner or later I'll get him to meet me in the open."

The hand that had been idly shaping her breast spread with a different purpose. "Laura? God, your heart's gone berserk. Look, I'm sorry I told you, but I wanted you to understand why you can't go anywhere by yourself just now. Not that he'd hurt you, but there's always the chance he might try to use you to get at me. It won't be for long. I've got him squirming now; he's at the point where he's just about got to vent his spleen."

She lay rigid beside him. Richard knew where she lived! He had tried to murder Andre! And Andre was still intent on his revenge. My God, my God! The madness was boiling to a terrifying peak. Her every instinct cried, *Run!* For a long moment she battled for self-possession. Andre's hand, during their conversation, had rested on her breast. She reached for it instinctively. "Andre! Love me!"

"I don't think so now, sweet. You're too upset."

Willfully, she lifted her head, offering her mouth to his. She felt the warmth of his sigh as he leaned down and took her lips, but softly, gently, with measured desire. "Laura, you don't have to. I was just teasing earlier."

"Make me want to, Andre—you know how. Kiss me hard!"

He put a hand on her neck, under her loose hair, and pulled her face close. His tongue met hers and played within her mouth, until he lifted his head again and said, "Let's leave it for tomorrow, love."

Impetuously, she took his hand and placed it at the fork of her legs. Obliging, his fingers slid into her silky fleece. She opened herself to him, and he couldn't seem to resist beginning an affectionate search of her close moistness. She knew exactly when he grew excited. One hand remained beneath her head, bracing her for his kisses, while the other continued to prepare her, until she was loose and more than wanting.

He got between her knees, priming her again with his fingers before attempting entry. He seemed to sense just when she was about to climax. He moved above her, careful to hold himself off her, and thrust in. She arched up to cling to his muscled neck. Her small cries almost immediately became a long shuddering sigh. The piercing fulfillment cascaded within her. He moved gently until the ripples receded.

"Better now?" he whispered.

She lay sated on the pillow, covered with downy peace. The only pain was in her soul, an ache, a memory of havoc. "Yes; but what about you?"

"Are you sure?" he said doubtfully. "I don't mind holding off this time."

She answered by undulating into him. He took the cue. At first he was slow and gentle, but as his desire gained momentum, he grew less capable of moderation, and finally gathered his own satisfaction with compelling insistence.

He fell spent beside her afterwards; they lay together in pleasant, placid repletion. Into her languor he murmured, "How about if I ask your Dr. Kellogg if you could travel as far as Jackson? Would you like to get away from the city, at least until after the baby is born?"

She felt his hand move over her breasts again, shaping one and then the other for his mouth. Going to Jackson would mean she wouldn't have Dr. Kellogg to help her when her time came, but . . . She thought of Richard, who knew where she was now. She remembered the look in his eyes that said he wanted her dead, remembered uncovering the terrible wound to Andre's back. "Yes, I would like that." Jackson. Out of the dark into the sunlight.

"We'll go, then." His hand came to rest on her stomach. "We'll take junior here back to the bed where he began—maybe show him how it was accomplished, hmmm?"

"As I recall, I had to coax you a bit then, too."

She felt rather than saw his face crease into a silent smile. "Oh woman, you just haven't caught on to me, yet. I find that if I pretend a little reluctance now and then, I get the pleasure of hearing you beg for it."

"You don't!"

He chuckled. "Worked tonight, didn't it? I loved the way you pushed my hand right down into you."

"You're not that calculating!"

"There you go, suspecting me of being kind again. That was always your mistake, love. It's given me an edge time and time again."

"Andre . . ."

He chuckled evilly.

The fog settled over San Francisco right after lunch. The lonely ringing of a bell buoy drifted to Nob Hill from the bay. Laura was taking the daily afternoon nap Dr. Kellogg prescribed. She lay on the bed in her morning robe, too restless to really sleep, however. Last evening's attempt at making music had left her with an anxious yearning. Andre was out making arrangements for their trip, and Elexa was making calls; Laura was alone except for the servants. In all, there was no one to know if she cheated on her nap time.

She dressed and crept down to the music room, where she surprised a maid on her knees gently sweeping the fine red Turkish carpet with a soft brush. "Please, don't mind me," Laura murmured, pretending a casual air. Yet the dark-haired Chinese girl quickly gathered her things and bowed out of the room. After only a moment, the space she'd vacated was filled with a quiet pavane.

The dark Steinway was very, very finely crafted. Its sounding board quivered like a living thing, even if the player of its keys was unpracticed. An hour passed, or maybe two. Laura's stiff fingers got looser; the results she coaxed out of the piano became clearer, braver; she felt close to knitting the old knot—then turned with a sudden and visceral instinct to find she wasn't alone anymore.

Elexa sat in one of two Russian chairs that flanked the sofa. She wore a walking suit of navy plaid velvet, a hat of blue straw, brimmed and garlanded, and had carnelian bobs in her ears. "Oh!" Laura said, "I didn't know anyone was home."

"I have not been here long." Laura saw in her green eyes something of the teasing she glimpsed in Andre's darker gaze sometimes. "And I will not tell on you. You should take your naps, chéri—but I am glad you did not today; I would not have missed this for anything.

"I had no idea," she went on. "Of course, Andre mentioned something about . . . but you play brilliantly! Listening to you, one can almost believe you *are* the music. Now I know how my son came to forget his great grief at last, how he came to fall in love with you."

Laura looked down at the rings on her hand. She said, "I'm afraid you're just being kind."

She felt Elexa studying her. "About your playing, or about Andre's love?"

"Both. I'm quite out of practice—and he loves me, but not enough to forget Ling. He still plans to avenge her."

Elexa sighed. "Men can be such fools." After a moment

she said, "Did you know I was a performer? I came to America to sing and do Molière in the mining camps. Hangtown, Angel's Camp, Fiddletown . . . 'Mademoiselle Elexa Brogunièr!' I dined with Mark Twain once." She chuckled. "He called me a hoyden."

Laura left the piano to sit as straight as a duenna in the other of the Russian chairs. Elexa was encouraged to continue: "If you think Andre can be stubborn, you should have known his father. There was a man wrought of iron. He was so big and could look so mean! But I was enthralled. His embrace was firm, conquering. Men had pursued me before, but no one successfully until I met that persistent and penniless Californian. He had no social status, yet importance fairly radiated from him. It was unthinkable that he would not make his way in the world."

She sighed at her memories. "He wooed me—actually followed me from camp to camp! The determination of such a strong-willed man is not easy to evade. Though I tried to deny it, there was that about him which made me love him from the first; it was . . ." she shrugged, *"je ne sais quois*—I know not what.

"But he was a wolf disguised as a big puppy, and I did not realize until it was too late that the soft paws with which he fed me sweetmeats hid sheathed claws."

A waft of delicious perfume drifted to Laura as Elexa rearranged the skirts of her elegant gown. "He won me, but our vows were hardly consecrated when the first clash took place. I was young and obstinate and termperamental—and held the novel notion that matrimony was intended to be conducted on equal terms. Drew—ah! such a beautiful man! those dark, penetrating looks he gave me! He held without apology the conventional view that the male of the species is the unquestioned master. My outlook was incomprehensible to him. He often laughed at me, said I was 'full of sass and vinegar'—a term I still find utterly disgusting. And in the midst of this turmoil Andre was born."

She opened her handbag to take out a fine, lace-edged handkerchief, which she began to draw between her hands idly. "Andre is like Drew, so like Drew—more than he will ever admit. And both of them like the wolf, with the skill of the solitary predator. Men like them bring a bit of the wild into our paved and artificial world—but at a cost, *non?*"

Seeming to gaze at one of the landscape paintings on the wall behind Laura, she added, "Andre was always careful and thoughtful. Even as a young child he seemed reflective about life. He was an adult early, almost self-sufficient from birth. He took his decisions seriously, considering situations before acting. Such care and persistence demands tremendous patience."

"Yes, he's patient," Laura murmured, "and persistent."

"Like the wolf, *non?* But like the wolf he can be made to heel. Your beloved husband is both independent and needful at the same time. It is his mystery, is it not?"

Laura nodded ruefully.

"I was shocked at first to learn of his treatment of you, but not really surprised once it was all revealed."

After a moment, Laura asked, "What was Ling like?"

"Ah, that one. She was pretty and small and—to be plain—much like you, *mon coeur.* She had the dark hair and the small garnet mouth—and just the kind of fragility that brings out all the tender and gentle feelings a hardened man like Andre keeps hidden inside himself. She was quiet and unobtrusive, a true lady such as only the Orientals seem able to breed—though there is something of it in you, too. It emerges as a quiet poise—like the convent novice, *oui?*— which seems always to challenge a virile man. A homely nun he will accept, but a beautiful one is an insult to his masculinity."

"Your husband didn't like Ling."

Elexa's eyebrows arched delicately. "He did not even know her. He and Andre were ever at odds. One moment they seemed to understand each other on some entirely male level, and the next they were like strangers. Drew, always domineering, used his money to make it hard for Andre to break away. I always thought my son's love for Ling was at least partly a convenient excuse. Drew forbade their marriage and that, in the end, gave Andre a reason not to have to live another minute under the same roof with his father. And—I tell you this in confidence—I have many times wondered if in some corner of his mind, Andre realizes this pretext poor Ling served, and if perhaps there is a taint of guilt in his desperation to avenge her death."

This would give Laura much to think about in the days to come, but for now she wanted to learn all she could, while Elexa was in such a communicative mood. "Did you like Ling?"

The older woman smiled. "Yes, I did. But I could not accept her for my daughter. She was different—mysterious and alien. You, now, are something else. We have much in common, you and I. We both love music. And we will both love your child—my first grandchild. And we both love Andre with all our hearts, do we not?"

"Yes," Laura admitted, "we do." She added carefully, "Your husband—did he approve of your career?"

Her gaze became shadow-green and faraway. "I had no career after I married Drew."

Laura nodded, unsurprised. "Andre once offered to take me to Germany to study. Of course, it was impossible—I was married to Richard at the time. And I didn't want to go anyway. You see, I didn't want a career. My stepmother made it seem so unpleasant. Now, with the baby coming . . ."

Elexa studied her. "No, you could not go with the baby coming. But after . . . what will you want to do after, *cherie?*"

"Well, I'll be busy taking care of it then, and of Andre."

"Has Andre told you he expects this from you?"

"Well, no, he . . . I think he still wants me to go."

"And what do you want?"

"I don't know anymore. I'm afraid to have my life overtaken and overwhelmed again, to lose control."

"But who will take control? You are not a child anymore, but a woman full-grown."

Laura picked up a little of the material of her skirt and twisted it. "Were you terribly unhappy being just a wife and mother?"

Elexa took time to form an answer. "No, I was not. Despite all I say about Drew, I loved him unspeakably.

378

And—the truth, *chérie*—I was not a great talent. Oh, at the time I thought I was, but I can see now that it was no large loss to the world that I resigned from the stage to take shelter in the iron curve of my husband's arms. But you—you have *un talent prononcé,* the gift, the great capacity inherent in you. People spend their whole lives seeking such a thing. Andre, I believe, acknowledges that this is within you. If he encourages you to unleash it into the world, to develop it and enlarge it and offer it to others, then, *chérie,* my poor dear, I think you must."

Thirty-Two

In March of 1882, Laura and Andre arrived in the Mother
Lode. Laura's sense of homecoming was sharp and sweet.
The high china-blue sky. The silence, the vast silence after so
much city tumult. While the earliest small flowers spread
themselves like gold dust on the hills, and the redbud
sprayed into bloom, she spent her mornings practicing—
Mozart, Beethoven, Chopin, and Shubert—and spent her
afternoons sewing baby things. Both skills were improving,
as they must, considering how she tackled each with
clenched teeth, with such dreadful uncertainty of which
should become her life's work.

Andre spent his mornings doing general chores. With
a claw hammer and a mouth full of nails, he repaired the
neglected "necessary," he thoroughly cleaned out the wild
animals nested in the washhouse beyond the kitchen, he
sanded and varnished all the rusted iron in the icehouse, and
replaced some wood that had splintered in the stables. In the
somnolence of the early afternoons, he sat in his office
across the hall from the parlor, doing paperwork concerning
his various business enterprises.

On the twentieth of the month, though it was not yet
dawn, Laura rose to look out the window at the solemn
shadowy cedars that outlined the sideyard. She'd been
uncomfortable all night. Unfortunately she'd eaten a portion
of crab apple tart last evening. Even as she stood there, her
womb suddenly contracted. It was a bit frightening, but not

really painful, and when it stopped, she decided not to mention it to Andre.

Their relationship had become as patterned as their activities over the past weeks. He didn't seem to feel the need to keep a tight hold on her here. He still voiced skepticism of there being any strength to her love for him, but at least his eyes had let up on her a little. Though they hadn't mentioned it aloud, they'd called a truce. She felt that they were at last joined in a rhythm, making music together, their own music, necessarily quiet so they could both live with it, a music without darkness, enabling their better feelings for one another to arise naturally.

Almost every evening he said to her, "Play for me," as her father had before him. And she played, idly and softly, heart-healing melodies. He wisely refrained from speaking to her about why she practiced so many hours each day. She had the feeling he knew about the tug-of-war going on within her, and she was grateful to him for letting her keep the struggle personal.

In all, it was a good time for them, a good place to be, and theirs was a good music to make. She felt it as a simple sound at her heart, played *sordine,* and was invisibly sustained by it.

She half-wished they might stay here forever, and make these gentle, unhurried foothills their home—except for the one mar in the otherwise perfect peace: the presence of Soo.

She'd been surprised to find him still working for Andre when they arrived. Supper that first night had been about as lively as a death hymn. As soon as she and Andre were alone, though she was afraid of treading into that darker side of his nature, she was also recklessly sure that she must, and so she brought up the subject of dismissing Soo immediately: "He hid your letter from me, Andre! He urged me to go home to Richard where—" *Careful!* "Don't you see how he wants to hurt us?"

Andre's face remained deceptively emotionless in the lamp shine of the blue bedroom. "He didn't mean to hurt us so much, as just remind me of my promise."

"Just what exactly did you promise him?"

"To make Laird pay for what he did."

"And haven't you done that?"

"Ling's dead, Laura. What do you want me to do, just scrape the memory of her off my shoe, the way Laird scrapes steer manure off his boots?"

She looked into his eyes, looked most desperately into them. "Richard's death isn't going to bring Ling back."

"My God, the man *raped* her! She was no bigger than you and he left her . . . broken." The word came out deep and husky.

"It was an ordeal for her, I'm sure, and I'm sorry she felt the dishonor so strongly," her heart felt cold and clouded, "but other people have lived through ordeals, and they don't necessarily commit suicide, or need to see the person who hurt them killed—let alone want to watch someone they love give his life over to this kind of vengeance. I don't really think Ling would be made any happier by what you've done, or plan to do."

"What would you know about it, Laura?" he said frigidly.

And, of course, she couldn't answer, couldn't tell him that she knew nearly everything about it, so much that in comparison he knew very little.

"If only the bastard would come out in the open and fight me!"

"I wouldn't fight you myself! There's nothing to be gained by this feud—on either side! *Give it up, Andre!*"

Thus she urged, knowing it was perhaps impossible for a man like him to ever give up anything, let alone a woman he'd loved enough to take to wife against all the stern dictates of his family and his culture and his race. Such a woman was surely graven too deeply on his heart for the memories ever to be effaced—or replaced. Yet Laura foolishly hoped that with time . . . no, she didn't have any hopes of the sort. It was merely wishful thinking. Oh, she just wanted it to be over! She wanted it to be over so badly.

A faint cool light was seeping into the room as she left the window and slipped back into bed. She curled into Andre's side, until he rolled toward her, his eyes still closed. She nestled even closer into his wide chest. Wakened out of the warmth of his dreaming, he smiled a little and took her in his arms. Feeling a bit desperate, she pressed closer yet, wishing she could burrow right into him, past the perception that he, the father of her child, guarded silences she could never penetrate, thoughts she could never know, and longings for a dead woman against which all her living charms failed.

Oh, don't think of Ling anymore, don't listen to that voice I can't hear, don't remember whatever it was she gave you that I can't seem to give you.

She sighed a troubled sigh.

Andre, wakened by her restless nestling, smiled a warmer smile. "What is it, sweeting?"

"Hold me."

"I am." Nevertheless, he wrapped her right up and squeezed. Their legs entwined. He grew harder. And with touching and kissing and suckling, he began to love her. So often their sleep drifted into loving and back to sleeping. She never failed to revel in coming gradually awake to the lean masculinity of his limbs around her, or his hand between her legs working her. A very gentle hand it was, full of melodies. He caressed her there now, until her hips rose and fell, until she felt the ultimate pleasure and shuddered with release from his handmade delight.

Then she was lost in the loving, floating sea of his entry. Stabs of pleasure took her further into their private world. He laved her in the flood of his release; she felt his swift spasms and hot fluid satiating her body, and she loved him so. She drifted back to sleep while he yet occupied her.

As usual, she slept in later than he did. When she descended to the dining room, Soo looked up from clearing away the dishes of Andre's earlier meal.

She couldn't fault Soo's work. He excelled in cookery, he ran the house faultlessly, the recently waxed floor of the dining room gleamed. But each day she disliked more the way he looked at her, the slyness and malevolence hidden just behind the bland expression on his face.

Still regretting that apple tart, she paused only long enough to pour a glass of milk from the stone jug on the buffet. She drank it standing up, staring at the wild flowers she'd arranged in an amber-glazed vase yesterday.

But then she turned suddenly, and said, "Soo, can't you let it go? Can't you let go of the past—of Andre—please?"

She got no answer from him, not even a sign that he'd heard her, other than a glimpse of joyous malice in his eyes.

Depressed, she started down the hall to begin her daily practice. Andre, whistling "Oh! Susanna," came in the front door. His bright, teasing gaze greeted her. "'Morning, lazybones. Finally getting up, huh? I've been to town and back already—oh, here's a letter for you."

"For me?"

He whipped it behind his back. "Not till I get a kiss."

"Well," she looked up at him, "bend down for heaven's sake! Not all of us were born giants, you know."

He deigned to lower his head a few inches, but she still had to go up on tiptoe to reach him, and since she failed to compensate for her enlarged front, she fell into him. He laughingly steadied her in his arms, saying, "If you'd only fallen for me that way in the first place."

"I did fall for you that way in the first place—and just look at what kind of trouble you got me into." She looked down at her bulging middle with a mock frown.

He chuckled, and gathered her nearer and took her mouth quickly and voluptuously. "Mmm, you taste like milk."

"My letter?" she reminded him.

"Mmm . . . I like milk, warm milk . . ."

"Can I have my letter now?"

"You're rather read a letter than kiss me?" He shook his head in disbelief. "Women are incalculable."

She snatched the envelope from him. "It's from Holly!" She tore open the flap and extracted a note scrawled on azure paper as she followed him into his office. She perched on a side chair to read, and gradually her smile faded. "Oh, Andre, we can't . . ." Her voice trailed off as she looked up to where he was seated at his enormous rolltop desk.

He swiveled in his chair. "What's the baggage up to?"

"It's . . ." She hesitated, considering how he might react. "It's about Yale."

He seemed to go prickly and unreasonable at the mere

mention of the name. "What? Passing messages to your old lover by way of your bold little friend?"

She ignored that. "He still works for you, doesn't he?"

He poked his pen into its inkwell and leaned back in his squeaky chair. "I've thrown him enough work to introduce him to Stanford and Sharon. That was our agreement."

"Then you have some influence over him?"

His mouth twisted. "That seems debatable."

He had her under a disadvantage with his pride. She gained her feet, as best she could, and handed him Holly's letter. "Can you stop him from doing this?"

Holly's laborious hand had resolved many of the words into an oversized scrawl, but the gist of what she'd written was that Yale had asked her to take the place Laura had never occupied—in his bed. She wrote ecstatically about what an opportunity it was for her—

> . . . to get out of that factory! Yale promises to introduce me to the richest men in town. We'll go to parties at the Palace Hotel. He says he can't buy me a home just yet, as he was going to for you, but I can have a little allowance. Oh, I'm going to have so many clothes, and be such a well-dressed, smooth-spoken lady!

Andre said, "What does she mean—this part about him buying you a house?"

Laura folded her hands over the expanse of her stomach. "Those were my terms. A house and a personal allowance. But Holly . . . oh, it's so foolish! She's not under the pressure I was. She could very well meet someone, fall in love, and—"

"Terms?" Andre repeated, and went on slowly, "Terms, Laura? You asked Talbot for a house? I don't recall you ever asking me for a god damned thing!"

She was taken aback. "It was for the baby—some security when he tired of me," she said, wishing they could keep the conversation to Holly.

He stared fixedly at the letter. "You knew he'd tire of you, and yet you loved him anyway?"

385

She saw then what he was working out in his mind. She didn't answer—until his eyes veered up and leveled at her. Eyes much too keen for comfort. She said, "I never loved Yale Talbot. I wasn't even sure I could go through with it, though I knew if I didn't I would be forced to rely on charity when the baby came. But when he kissed me, when he put his hands on me . . . I felt sick," she whispered. Then went on, feigning a quite alien cynicism now. "But I suppose I would have steeled myself. After all, a house, a little money to put by—what more could I want? What more could I possibly expect—pregnant, alone? I'd learned hunger by then, and I wanted better for my child."

With a smile that chilled her, he said, "He told me you were in love with him."

"And you believed him."

"You said so yourself."

"Because I was frightened of you, that you would blame him and—you said you would shoot him. And because . . . because you were so arrogant and contemptuous and I didn't want you to know that I still loved you so pitifully. You'd made up your mind about me, that I was inconstant, and—" suddenly she was angry, "—and when have you ever changed your mind once you've made it up, Andre? Who knows what set purposes Mr. Andre Sheridan has half as well as I do? Who knows better just how steady his memory is? I learned the hard way what you have to teach. I've looked into your soul when it's at its strangest and most shocking."

A silence ensued. He handed her back the letter. "I'll wire Talbot," he said in a clipped voice. "I need someone to go to Los Angeles for me right away. Meanwhile, your little friend might be persuaded to get herself some schooling, since she hates that factory so much. There's a teachers' college in Chico, in the northern part of the valley. That should be far enough away from San Francisco to keep her out of Talbot's reach. I'll have one of my other lawyers handle getting her up there, while she's still a virgin."

"Thank you," Laura whispered, embarrassed now by her emotional outburst.

"You wouldn't thank me if you knew what I feel like doing

386

right now." He looked up at her with a searching glance that pried into her heart and probed her wounds. He said in a soft voice, "I could thrash the sauce out of you." Then added, softer yet, "So proud, so God damned proud, you wouldn't even explain yourself." But, belying his harsh words, he looked at her with a kind of calm marveling.

Her heart leapt. He understood, at last!

"I've been accusing you of being in love with love."

"I've never loved anyone but you. I tried to tell you, but you refused to listen." She felt the color rise to her face, and turned her shoulder to him. Her lips trembled. "I've tried to show you."

"Yes, I guess you have. Yes, I guess you've told me pretty often."

She knew there was a bright flush upon her face. "As you've told me."

Though nothing more was said, it was with them. How it had arrived she wasn't sure, but it had. It was there in the room: Love, like sunlight shafting into a dark place, glittering bronze and gold, moving slowly as in some dream, picking out, of all the people on earth, the two of them.

Laura, wearing her favorite blue maternity dress, moved restlessly in a wicker rocking chair in the corner of the porch. Even here, where the great black oak cast its shade, it was unseasonably warm. She'd stopped sewing and was using her embroidery hoop as a fan to relieve the sunset heat.

She'd come to love this porch, especially since Andre had told her how as a boy he'd played under the wisteria at the other end, brandishing a whittled sword as he'd swashbuckled across the seas of his imagination.

Laura rocked back a bit in the creaky chair. It was still hard for her to believe they were finally able to give and take the full measure of love they each felt for the other. She'd been happy about having his baby before, but she hadn't felt so keenly that they were making this child *together* as she did now.

Nothing was ever perfect, of course. There was a deep fear

387

in the back of her mind, that even at so late a date as this, something would come to obstruct their well-being. She did her best to be cheerful and unconcerned, yet . . .

She tilted the rocking chair further back. She'd overdone it today. She'd practiced this morning, as usual, and early this afternoon she'd devoted her time to sewing the fine seams of a long baby dress and putting the hems in several squares of bird's-eye cloth for diapers. Then she'd come outside. Impulsively, she'd decided to weed the flowerbeds down the sideyard. She'd gotten nearly halfway along before Andre, in a blue-checked shirt, had come around the house and stood looming over her, demanding what-the-hell she thought she was going? He looked her up and down with vexation, making her feel more clumsily pregnant than ever, until her eyes dropped in shame. "Woman, you're going to be my undoing!" And with a none too gentle hand steadying her back, he propelled her to the kitchen pump to wash the grime from her hands.

And then this evening she'd made the mistake of eating a bowl of the well-sugared cherries for dessert. Evidently cherries were as off-limits to her as apples.

Her hand moved over her taut stomach. Well, only another month to go.

Andre was upstairs putting the finishing touches to his paint job of the wainscoting in the bedroom that was to be the babe's nursery. He'd hung red and white striped paper yesterday. She could hear him whistling occasionally from inside the open doors and windows. She would like to be up there where he was, but the combined odors of fresh wallpaper glue and paint were too much for her.

In the open spaces between the scattered oaks across the road, the Mother Lode's only remaining hoard of gold— California's sunny orange poppies—were flourishing with bright prodigality. A progression of wildflowers had embroidered the green of the awakening slopes: buttercups, yellow violets, and baby blue-eyes, then fiddleneck, lupin, and clover. But none were as eye-catching as these tangy orange poppies. From among them came the sounds of mating doves, open and lonesome as flutes and oboes; and when a meadowlark sang from above its nest, the notes fell like flakes of fire.

In such peace, the appearance of a single rider making the bend of the road was jarring. Laura had been having more of those disturbing contractions, and all she needed now was to have to entertain a caller. As the horseman drew nearer, the tall slimness of his figure gave her an especially uncomfortable twinge.

She stood, in order to see better, and accidentally dropped her thimble. By the time it stopped rolling and she retrieved it and stood again, the rider was much closer. She peered his way, shading her eyes against the winking arrows of sun coming through the great tree.

The man sat his horse as though he were sitting upon the world itself. She recognized that head-up, life-has-never-stopped-me-yet way of riding. And she couldn't move; she stood where she was, fixed. She saw him, and she saw . . . everything that was about to happen.

He reined in, slid from his cow pony, and tethered it to the hitching post outside the wrought iron fence. There was an unholy light in his golden eyes. "Hello, Laura," he said, swinging the gate open with the toe of his boot, setting his spurs to ringing on the paved walk.

Her voice was hardly a whisper: "What do you want?" Her pulse beat hard; her hands were locked together over her stomach. She was reminded of those ghastly dreams in which she struggled with all her might to escape some fearful peril, but remained stuck powerlessly in the same place.

"Is that any way to greet an old husband?" He grinned fiercely—a smile that did nothing to warm his topaz eyes.

She could only stare at him, while the sunset forgot to breathe and nothing moved. He didn't look well; he was terribly thin. The lines of weather about his mouth were deeper than she remembered. Apparently he'd ridden long hours to get here: his hat was darkened with sweat and there was a streak down his face where he'd rubbed the back of his hand. Nevertheless, she felt no pity for him. "Go away. Please, Richard, go away."

"I come a long way to see you, Laura." He was advancing

up the walk a step at a time, his golden eyes sweeping the lower and then the upper windows of the house. When they came back to her, he snarled, "You got under my skin, honey."

She gripped a post to steady herself. The front door opened, and Andre stepped past her to stand at the top of the steps. "Go inside, Laura." He was buckling his gun belt, tying the string around his thigh, settling the holster.

"Sheridan!" Richard tilted his hat to the back of his head. His eyes glowed like melted gold. "We meet again."

Andre spoke to Laura: "Get inside before you're hurt."

"Yeah, we wouldn't want Laura to get hurt." His eyes slid to her again, and glinted wickedly. "Looks like she's carrying a full litter there. I wonder if it's really yours, Sheridan. You never can tell with stray cats like her. If I hadn't kicked her out when I did, she'd have tried to pass it off on me, that's for sure."

Laura's breathing slowed. She was nauseated; she was afraid she was going to be sick. Here were all her nightmares, her most terrible nightmares, being enacted before her eyes.

Andre's apparent detachment seemed to increase Richard's gall. When Andre failed to move, Richard went on: "I'm surprised you didn't lose it, Laura." His eyes flicked back to Andre. "Did she tell you about our little fist fight? No? She likes to keep secrets, our Laura does. She wouldn't tell me a thing about you. I had to pry it out of her."

"What's he talking about?" Andre muttered, giving her a sideways look.

Laura's voice throbbed as she took a step forward. "Don't do this, Richard."

"She told me what I wanted to know in the end—enough of it anyway. I heard I left plenty of bruises, honey. Heard you were unconscious for three days, and couldn't lift your head off Bessie Gladwin's pillows for another week. Concussion and three cracked ribs—have I got that right? Was it three, or four? It really is a wonder you kept that kid."

He looked at her with eyes that were only a step away from violence even now. They swiveled back to Andre, who seemed paralyzed by what he'd just heard.

"Ever hit a woman, Sheridan? There's fun to be had in it. You don't want to hit 'em quite so hard they go out too fast. Just little punches, you know what I mean? Laura took quite a few. Now your little Chinee gal, she didn't fight. She just lay there like a dead thing."

Andre's right hand clenched and unclenched near his holster. It was the only part of his body that wasn't stiff.

"You're a real persistent bastard, Sheridan. Waited all those years. Was Laura any better than your slant-eyed girl? Now that I think about it, that one was so tame she all but sang encouragement when the load was going in her."

Andre half-turned to Laura again. "Go in the house! Inside—*now!*"

But she couldn't move. And she wouldn't have, anyway, because the only reason he wanted her to, was so that he could draw his gun on Richard, and not have to worry about her taking a stray bullet.

Richard was taunting him again. "Tell me, when it came to having your pigtail after I had her, could you do it? Could you bring yourself to touch her? Didn't you just want to kill her yourself? I sure wanted to kill Laura. Would have, too, if—"

Andre's voice was a roar as he lunged and landed a slogging blow to Richard's jaw, a blow that would have killed a lesser man. He had the immediate advantage, and he swung again, with his whole shoulder behind his fist, knocking Richard down and then falling on him as if he wanted to pulverize him.

Madness. The air was filled with the honey of wild flowers and vintage grief and the dry scent of madness.

They rolled; Richard was on top. He planted a left on Andre's jaw. But when he followed up with a right, Andre blocked it with his left arm, and sent his own right fist crashing into Richard's face a third time.

Andre was on top again. His big hands went around Richard's throat, intent on strangling him. He was flushed and panting—while Richard grew white and desperate. His scrabbling hands left Andre's wrists and found a brick, one of the many loose ones in the old walkway. He rooted it up

391

and brought it down with savage force on Andre's head, stunning him for an instant.

Richard scrambled to his knees, but Andre, though swaying, somehow made it to his feet. Richard raised his arms while Andre smashed blow after blow into him with both hands. At last Richard grabbed him around the legs, tackling him. Andre was trying to get up when Richard found the brick and hit him again, in the forehead this time.

As the blow took effect, Andre slumped slowly, and then much faster; he fell face down on the grass.

Thirty-Three

Richard staggered to his feet while Andre lifted himself onto his hands and knees. Richard took a step backward, swayed . . . and in his face, plain for Laura to see, was that intent to kill. He fumbled for his revolver.

In those few seconds left to her, Laura felt a great yearning terror. She thought, *No, don't. Don't take him from me.*

Everything happened so fast she hardly realized she had backed inside the front door. Without taking her eyes off Richard, she reached toward the gun rack. Her hand found the shotgun. It felt miraculously light, a wand.

Andre shook off his daze just in time to look down the muzzle of Richard's pistol barrel. He dove to the side the instant it went off. Richard turned with him, turned with grim creases around his thin, pressed mouth, swiveled the barrel of his gun to find his target again. The sight made Laura seethe with sick fury. She did what she had to do.

A tremendous explosion came from the shotgun; it shoveled back into her shoulder and sent her stumbling sideways against the house. Echoes and vibrations resounded through her gravid body, roared and reverberated against the hillsides. When she righted herself, and blinked Richard clear, she saw he was a mass of blood. Slowly he twisted to look at her, his eyes wide. Without her being able to say exactly when, those round tawny eyes were suddenly open on nothing. His face drained of all color; his gun slipped from his grasp, fell with a clatter to the brick walk; he leaned leftward in a sudden disengagement of life.

What lay on the grass then, a last breath bubbling out of its throat, was no longer a man. Richard Laird had left that closed, uninhabited face. Laura's eyes filmed with tears. She felt the last of her innocence slipping away. Henceforth parts of her would be old, as old as time.

Andre lumbered to his feet. His back braced momentarily against the fence. He stepped away, weaved for a moment, then knelt on one knee over Richard's body. "He's dead." His voice held a touch of disbelief. He lifted his head like a war horse about to breathe fire, and looked at Laura standing above him on the porch with the shotgun still in her hands. "I thought I told you to get inside!"

"He would have killed you," she said dully. She lowered the gun that was trailing a gray-blue streamer of smoke. The acrid smell caught sharply at the back of her throat. She moved, on knees that shook beneath their enveloping skirts, to the nearest post for support.

Andre pitched to his feet. "But . . . but I wanted . . . damn it, Laura, *I* wanted to kill him! It was my *right* to kill him!"

"I'm so sorry, my love." The words, though only a flutter of sound in this atmosphere gone suddenly quiet, somehow contained a loud and bitter defiance.

An agony of frustration and confusion distorted his face. He swung from foot to foot, as if he didn't know which way to turn anymore with the object of his hatred gone. His eyes came to rest on her again, where she hung unmoving by the post. "He beat you." He seemed near to tears. "God damn, the bastard beat you! And you didn't tell me!"

He stood before her now, a great tree swaying in the wind. A thin thread of blood trickled from his forehead down the side of his nose; otherwise his face was perfectly white. He took another tilting step toward her. Unafraid, she said, "We'd better take him into town." She slowly sat on the top step, carefully laid the shotgun to one side.

She looked at Richard again, stared at the white shirt dappled with bright blood, like bright flecks of red paint. Here was a man she'd once thought to share her life with, a man so tense with life he fairly hummed. "He didn't know he was a bad man," she said, apropros of nothing perhaps. "Can you imagine—he didn't even know it?"

He'd hurt her, but he could never hurt her again, for she'd killed him.

And what she felt about that was a crystal cold thing.

Andre swung away and went to the barn.

Soo came out of the house. He never looked at Laura, but went down the steps and stood staring at Richard's body until Andre returned and threw a blanket over it. He hoisted it over his shoulder and carried it to the wagon he'd brought to the front gate. His face was expressionless now. Something of his heart seemed to have died with his nemesis; at least he had that appearance.

He tied the dead man's cow pony behind the wagon. The horse backed with a shrill whinny pitching up her head, but she couldn't elude the hard grip that held her. Laura watched the animal's ears swivel to follow Andre's progress back toward the porch.

He picked up the shotgun. A gleam of the setting sun shone redly in his face. "I don't know what's going to happen in town," his voice was calm on the surface, but beneath it was an iron anger, "but listen to me: no matter what anyone says, you never touched this gun. Never. I killed him. Do you hear?"

"Andre—"

The harshness broke from behind that thin and brittle veneer. *"Do you want to have that baby in San Quentin!"*

She shook her head.

"It was self-defense. I'll get off on self-defense. He came here—jealous of you—and tried to kill me. We fought, he drew on me, and I killed him. That's the story, Laura. They'll ask you—can you remember? It's near enough the truth anyway."

Yes, it was near enough the truth. Richard had certainly been determined to kill someone today, at least as determined as Andre.

She wanted him to hold her. Her longing was so great she had to clench her fingers and close her eyes when he turned his back on her and went to the wagon and climbed up to the driver's bench. The wheels started to turn with a jerk. Down the road he went, leaving only the blood-smeared grass as evidence that there had been any tragedy enacted here today.

She watched the wagon getting farther away. Thoughts skimmed the surface of her mind like dragonflies. A hollowness grew inside her, an empty space that she tried to fill by taking a deep breath. Her shoulder ached from the recoil of the shotgun. That hollowness seemed to move, to become intention, and then—*pain! Pain sharp as splintered glass!* It contracted her abdomen and took her in-held breath away. She wrapped her arms about her middle and hung onto herself, until gradually, gradually, it slackened.

She straightened. So this was the pain of birth, this is how it comes, and then fades, and yet lies waiting, like a flickering light, over a woman's splintered body.

The wagon neared the bend, the horses moved in an easy rhythm, a sleepy kind of cadence; soon they would be out of view. "Andre?" she called in a small voice. Then louder, "Andre!" She started down the walk.

She made it as far as the middle of the road, had her hands raised and was about to call him once more when a gush of warm fluid spilled down the insides of her legs, and with it the pain came again, swirling, building, breaking her.

"It'll pass," she whispered through clenched teeth, her arms wrapped as she bent double. "It'll pass."

When it did, the wagon was gone. She staggered back to the gate with infinite care, seeing the garden walk lengthened, back, back, back—how far away the house seemed! Could she make it that far?

She moved cautiously, made it to the porch, looked through the open door into the warm interior of the hall.

Soo was standing there, just inside the door, watching her. "Soo! Go after him, please. Tell him to come back. I—I need him."

The old man didn't move.

Her eyes attentively and entreatingly settled upon him, she picked up her damp skirts and mounted the porch steps and slowly, cautiously crossed the threshold into the house. "Soo? Did you hear me?"

He only looked at her, his slanted eyes burning like hot coals, his hatred blatant. "Had good man for daughter to marry. Good Chinese man. She be alive now, have babies herself. I have descendants to honor me, to take care of me in old age, to worship me as ancestor."

"I'm sorry—but she's dead. And now Richard is dead." Another pain was tightening like a fist within her. "It's finish—uhn!" She went rigid, as if suspended on an everlasting edge.

"Yes, finished." He looked at her pitilessly, then turned. "I go home now."

She loosened and took a deep breath as the spasm passed. "Soo!" But she knew he wasn't going to help her. He'd wanted revenge as much as Andre, had goaded Andre to it all these years, silently, using his presence as a constant reminder. But he hadn't just hated Richard—he'd hated Andre, as well. And he had no intention of helping Andre's wife and child survive. She understood all this in a flash, and realized the hopelessness of pleading with him.

"But it's too soon," she said to the now-empty hall. The baby couldn't really be coming. That was logical, wasn't it? The baby couldn't be coming, because it was too soon. And because she had no one to help her.

Another contraction ascended, engulfed her, wrenching a whimper out of her—the helplessness of it! Oh God, the baby *was* coming, and she couldn't do anything to stop it!

When this contraction receded, she blessed the relief. She moved down the hall, her long blue untidy skirt rustling. She made it to the dining table, only to be bent double by a new pang that brought a wet choking cry out of her.

Would another come? She waited to see.

It did.

"Upstairs. I'll wash up . . . and lie down . . . and Andre will be back soon."

But what if he wasn't? What if they put him in jail for killing Richard?

The pain came squeezing again when she was only halfway up the stairs. And again when she reached the upper hall. In the bedroom, she could do no more than pull the blankets

397

from the bed and roll onto the cool white sheet as yet more tendrils reached through her abdomen and threaded around her back and *squeezed* . . .

The setting sun shone full through the window. She wished she'd closed the draperies before she'd lain down. There was no one to do it for her now. Soo was gone already. She knew it; she felt it. The house was strangely silent. He must have left everything, perhaps only taking whatever money he'd saved toward this day.

She was wrenched again. She dug her heels into the mattress, realizing she still had her shoes on. She was having a baby with her shoes on!

The last gleam of the sun slanted through the open window into her eyes. Her face twisted as a new contraction came on, grew, gripped her in its monstrous fingers, and only gradually let her go. Then the light was gone and she lay alone in the folding dusk.

It was deep dark when Andre returned. It had taken time to find the reigning lawman in Jackson, to explain things. He'd half-feared he would be jailed, but his history in the area, his standing, and the unlikelihood that he would or could disappear if let go, all spoke for him, as well as the fact—which he kept stressing—that he had a pregnant wife at home, frightened by what had happened, and with no one but a servant to look after her. The lawman insisted he see the local doctor before leaving, hence he was arriving home with a white bandage haloing his headache.

"Soo!" he called into the vacancy of the house. There were no lights burning, no signs of life—and it sent prickles down the back of his neck, for he had come home to this place once before when it had been deserted of all he loved. With a reeling of his mind he suddenly remembered that time all too well: that dull gray pain about his heart, that frenzy of desire for a woman who was gone.

Please, Laura, be here.

He remembered how he'd left her earlier today. She'd sat on the step wearing that blue dress. He recalled what he'd said to her, how he'd treated her. And how she was unamazed, how she looked at him, her eyes, her face so wan she might have been graven of ivory . . . of stone, of diamond. He remembered all this so well.

In the dark of the dining room, he stood with his Stetson in one hand, the other going to his battered head. He heard a sound cut the silence, a sound such as he'd never heard before. A thin wail, held-back, like an animal in some agony. It came from a room above. Suddenly afraid, he took the stairs three at a time.

He found her in the bedroom. She clutched his shirt. Her voice was childishly small. "Help me."

"Laura, my God, I'll send Soo for—"

"Soo left," she panted. A heated flood of feeling seemed to spring up and spill from her eyes. "He left me all alone."

"I'll go then."

"Don't leave me . . . *An-dre!*" Another wail that scraped his very bones. It seemed to be torn from her, from somewhere deep inside, as if something unseen had gripped her by surprise and was killing her.

"Laura! . . . Laura!" he said helplessly, his hands fluttering over her without knowing where best to land.

When the contraction was finished with her, she panted, "Don't leave me. I think something's wrong; it won't be born." Her face was still marked by her tears; her wet lashes stood in starry tips. Her fear showed. It stirred the pity in him.

Oh, Laura! My sweet, tranquil, noble love—what's happening to you?

He felt her despair during these past hours of exquisite pain, he felt her suffering as plainly as if it were his own body wrenched and wracked. "No, I won't leave, shh, no, no, I won't leave you. Pulling a baby is probably a lot easier than untangling a leggy calf from inside a heifer, and God knows, I've done that often enough." He took her wrists, pulled her fingers from his shirt. "Let's get your clothes off, sweet. You can't have a baby with your shoes on."

He lit the lamps and undressed her and helped her into a plain white nightdress. A contraction came in the middle of this. She clutched his hands until the murderous clamps loosened, slid off, leaving her breathless, weeping with the violence of it. "Yes," he said, "it's coming a little crooked. Just a little. I think it'll straighten out." He reached calmly to finish fastening the tiny buttons of her bodice. He took down her hair and sponged her face with cool water and meanwhile gave her his hands to grip with each contraction that came.

They came again and again, wringing her body, and her sweating face gleamed like alabaster in the dimness of the gaslights. When the child didn't seem to turn, he decided he must do something. He opened his hands over her belly, and the muscles of his arms bunched cautiously as he pressed in a sideways direction.

She cried out. He quickly stopped what he was doing. The sweat stood on her face, and he wiped at it with his hand. "I'm sorry, sweet, I'm sorry. I thought I might be able to turn it."

Her hand lifted to his face; her fingertips outlined his mouth, then rested beside his chin. It was a gesture eloquent beyond words, a gesture of suffering and forlorn love. His free hand lay open on her stomach, and he felt the next spasm seize her—and something else—a sudden dislocation, a movement, as if something had been released.

"It's coming!" Every fiber of her suddenly strained.

The infant had turned. "Push, love!"

"Out," she cried between clenched teeth, "out . . . out . . ."

He whispered encouragement: "Yes, yes, sweetheart, you're doing fine."

She held her breath for as long as she could, gulped air and held it again. He was thinking she couldn't sustain this tension much longer. She choked back a cry. The infant descended, moved into his hands. Such a poor, wet, tiny, blue-faced thing.

Laura fell back in exhaustion. He checked her first, tended to her, then quickly looked back to the infant. It looked nothing like the pink and chubby babies he'd seen before. It wasn't breathing, for one thing. Acting on instinct, he tilted it to let the waters drain from its minute mouth. The little creature sneezed, filled its lungs, and yelped its first, life-making cry. A thin cry, like a reed in the wind, yet it filled the silence of the room.

"A girl." He stared down at the tiny life, awkward in his sudden amazement, in his sudden feeling of joy—a joy so pungent it burned. "A girl, Laura."

The blade of his jackknife flashed. He reached into a drawer and slashed a strip off one of his best white shirts. Only the best would do. Even before he was done tying and severing the cord, Laura breathed, "Let me see her."

The child sputtered and choked and then cried again as he lifted her and placed her in Laura's shaking, waiting, mother's arms. His own hands were trembling.

"So small! Oh, my poor little baby, you're so small." She looked up from the puffy, crimson face, her eyes alight with something indestructible, a flicker of indestructible love. She exchanged something with him, something very glad. He put his outstretched palm on her shoulder. Without warning, two tears slid down his cheeks. And with a laughing groan his mouth came down on her lips that were soft and sweet with exhaustion.

He straightened, backhanded his face quickly, and looking down at the pair from his considerable height, said, "What shall we name her?"

"Her name is Jean. Jean Ann Sheridan. For my mother." Then she added, her fatigue apparent, "She needs to be washed and swaddled, Papa."

Papa!

He moved again. Downstairs to get warm water, to the nursery for soft blankets and diapers and a tiny saque. He was tentative and clumsy, and took longer than a woman probably would have, but eventually Laura was settled in a clean gown on clean sheets, and he stood holding his washed and swaddled child. He stared at her for what seemed an eternity, looking into her eyes that were unfocused and watching her fists wave slowly and aimlessly. He felt a little alien from her—after all, she wasn't the boy he'd expected from the strength of her pre-natal kicks—and at the same time he was possessed by an insistence—an insistence in which there was nothing like gentleness, in which there was more savagery and fury than anything like gentleness—that she must survive, and that nothing bad should ever *ever* befall her. Not Jean. Not his daughter Jean.

Laura felt very slim and fashionable in her white summer dress of wrought Indian muslin edged with real Hamburg lace. The ringlets of her hair were caught up by white ribbons in the latest top-heavy fashion, leaving her neck exposed.

Frederica Kellogg also looked stylish in a lilac chambray dress. Her hair shone reddish gold as the drowsy afternoon sun struck it in the silent porch air. She'd arrived yesterday, and now was enjoying some refreshments with Laura—samples of the new cook's ginger cookies, served with a pitcher of chilled root beer.

Jean slept here in the afternoons, here in this place that had been the scene of hope and downfall, burgeoning love and sudden demise. Laura had spent many hours here herself in the past weeks, regaining her strength, breathing the sweet foothill air as a tonic, watching spring's green give way to the brasses of summer.

"She's such a pretty thing," Dr. Kellogg said of the baby on her lap, who was dressed in a pink satin gown with white lace and silk ribbons, who to Laura was the essence of everything good. "But so tiny! You and she are both very lucky just to be here."

Laura shuddered. That night was still too close; she didn't want to talk about it, or even to think of it. To change the subject, she said, "Have you heard from Holly?"

"Mrs. Noah has. Holly's encouraging her to move to Chico. Evidently Holly loves it there."

Laura smiled faintly. "Does she still have time to read the newspapers?"

"Oh yes, her letters are full of Guiteau's trial."

"He'll be hanged," Laura said dully.

"I should hope so, after all Mr. Garfield suffered."

Laura said quietly, "I wonder how Andre's hearing is going." She looked to the road, but the folding hills trapped

402

her vision. There was a haze of light on the day. "I feel so guilty—being excused from testifying, I mean."

"They have your statement—and you have your health to think of. You're still pale as bone china." Dr. Kellogg jiggled Jean on her knee, and the child's mouth went round with wonder and surprise. The doctor chuckled.

Laura clicked her tongue. "I'm fine." She'd had a brief bout of fever after Jean's birth, and ever since had been cosseted and indulged and largely treated like a lovely but particularly brittle piece of pottery—while Andre went back and forth to hearings and meetings concerning the man she had killed.

Dr. Kellogg, innocent of the facts, scolded, "Now don't break out in stubbornness."

Laura smiled back, a smile that felt hollow. "It's been two months since Jean was born. Two months of having this hearing hanging over our heads. It's been so hard on Andre. I know it has."

She knew, but not because he'd told her. He was still sleeping in one of the spare rooms. The local doctor had scared him away from her after Jean's birth, and he had never returned. It seemed he'd set a shell about her, one that said, Don't touch! Worse, he seldom looked directly at her anymore, and when he did, it was a look that kept things from her, a look she'd never seen before and couldn't understand. Perhaps, like her, he couldn't reconcile his feelings.

She knew how her own eyes had taken up peering into the heat-hazed distances. How she woke in the night crying, longing for him, wanting him as the stars marched in mute procession through the darkest hours, yet when finally she saw him a physical sensation of cold seemed to diffuse from the center of her outward. She'd lived through so much unhappiness because of him, and in the end had been forced to kill to save his life—only to have him turn on her in a rage for it. But then he'd delivered her child and undoubtedly saved her and Jean's lives. And he'd taken on the blame for Richard's death in order to spare her. Perhaps he felt the same jumble of confused love and anger when he looked at her, as she did when she looked at him. Perhaps that was why he seldom spoke to her of anything more than the mundane.

The sun coming through the black oak cast dapples of shade and light on the lap of her white dress where her hands were clasped tightly. "If he's not acquitted," she said, "I don't know what I'll do." He'd spoken to her of this much at least, saying that even if the opinion of the judge was manslaughter, he would probably get only a light sentence, a few months or a year in prison—"And I'll know you're home with Jean and that will make it right. You're not to come forward with any last-minute confessions, do you hear?"

But could she carry it that far? Could she let him answer for an act she had committed? How could she live with that? She asked herself that question through the sleepless hours of every night. And in the dawns there were never any answers. Yet, like him, she kept her determined silence. They were both in pain, yet didn't dare turn to one another, neither for advice nor for comfort.

Instead they both turned to Jean. They both held very dear this treasure given to them. For the time being a mere child was their only link against the night, against the shadows, against all the ills of the world.

"That bout of fever is nothing to pass off lightly, Laura," Dr. Kellogg scolded. "Your Andre has been very wise to protect you as much as possible from this business."

Laura realized how self-centered she must sound to an outsider who didn't know all the story. "I'm sorry to complain." She unclasped her fingers and flexed her weary hands. She'd been at the piano all morning, trying to keep her sanity in the only way she could while she waited. She gave the doctor another small, meaningless smile, then lifted her glass of root beer and studied it, as if it were a fluted glass of chablis. "I'm so glad Andre persuaded you and Captain Glenn to visit us."

She knew why he'd done it, of course. So that if he didn't come home today, she wouldn't be alone.

"I'm glad he invited us—me." Was that a blush on the doctor's cheek? "I don't know about Captain Glenn, but I needed a vacation." The two had arrived just yesterday, and today the captain had gone to the hearing with Andre.

"I wish we would hear something," Laura mused.

"All in good time." The doctor seemed to think it was best to talk of pleasanter things. "Andre surprises me, I must say. I've never seen a man sit and hold a baby like he does, with never even a frown when the little dear predictably soaks through the trousers of his suit."

"Yes, he loves Jean, there's no doubt about that." *But does he love me anymore?* She sipped her root beer, looking off into the distance, into the veil of the heat haze.

Thirty-Four

Dr. Kellogg went for a walk, and except for the baby and the new servant in the kitchen, Laura was alone in the house. She'd just finished nursing Jean in the upstairs nursery, and now diapered her daughter with slow care, marveling over the tiny, chinalike ears and the thatch of ebon hair that curled over the perfectly shaped head. The child looked so like her father.

Andre. Suddenly Laura felt a tingling in all her uncovered nerve endings. Her fear and need and longing swept over her, and a pair of quick tears dripped into Jean's crib. With a rush of tenderness, she picked up the infant and held her achingly close, pressing her own face into the sweet, curved, tiny neck, inhaling the fragrance of the little body.

"Laura?"

She spun, startled at Andre's voice coming from down the hall. So softly had he climbed the stairs, she hadn't heard him. That was his way now, that quiet step. She called, "In here," and put the baby down in order to swipe at her tears.

He came in. His face—his presence in fact—told her what she wanted to hear even before he spoke: "Acquitted. Self-defense. It's over, Laura."

"Over," she breathed. One word, so much meaning. She felt like a bee tasting a whole summer in one goldenrod.

He made no move toward her, and she made none toward him. The reticence which had grown between them hung heavy. Insects outside the screened windows made a close curtain of sound around the house, yet the silence inside was complete.

He stepped closer to the crib. Jean cooed upon seeing him. He lifted her, and got a flicker of a smile for it.

"Laura . . ." he said, holding their child against his heart so that her small head nodded beneath his jaw. He was full of strength, yet held his burden so gently he couldn't have bruised a rose petal.

He didn't finish whatever he'd meant to say. To fill the awkward silence, Laura said, "She's growing so."

"Yes. She's growing." Pain grazed his face, a patient sort of pain, long-suffered. It was like a wound, that look. It was the look she couldn't understand.

Suddenly he said, "Why did he come here? Why did he finally dare? You said yourself he didn't have anything to gain by it."

She answered without hesitation: "His fear of you broke what little there was of him. And his need for me, such as it was."

"And you had to kill him—because of me, you had to kill a man." He faltered, then whispered, suddenly stricken, "Forgive me."

In an instant, she felt the ice frozen about her heart burn away.

"Stolen . . . beaten . . . driven to the brink of harlotry . . . even forced to kill a man . . . and afterward, blamed instead of thanked. You have every reason to hate me. You must mourn the minute you first set eyes on me."

This was a painful thing to hear—a man testifying against himself. She reached into the crib to plump the baby's lace-trimmed pillow. "None of that matters any—"

"It matters!" His words intersected hers like a knife. "Laura!" then calmer, "Laura. Can you . . . do you think you can ever forgive me for all the pain I've brought you?"

"What pain?" There was a knot in her throat. He was so close—she felt dizzy with the nearness of him, all out of breath. She saw that he didn't know what to do. Andre, who always knew exactly what to do—but it was clear he wasn't sure now.

He took an uncertain step toward her, then drew back. "I've been afraid . . ." He started again, "I suppose there's been too much that happened, for you to ever love me again." He placed his fingers gently behind Jean's dark head and tipped her so as to look down at her little face. "Well, I already have more than I deserve. Far more. That you survived, and Jean. That's all I feel I can ask for."

Was he trying to tell her that that was all he wanted? Was he trying to say that the passion he'd felt for her was gone now, replaced by gratitude, by guilt, by duty? That hurt her almost more than anything else. The pain, which she'd just denied so blithely, was in fact deep everywhere. Yet she said, "You still don't understand; I've always loved you. I never stopped. I love you now, and I always will."

The baby fussed. Laura laid her hand on his arm. "Let me put her down." He yielded the child; Laura laid her in the crib. Her fingertip gently traced the delicate curves and creases of the round button mouth. Jean lay on her tummy, holding herself up on her arms, her knees bent, her feet waving.

Andre said, "You've changed, Laura."

"Yes." She wasn't an innocent anymore. Never again. Yet she'd begun to mature in a way she thought was right. It wasn't something to speak of, but once there had been things she'd desired, foolish things—a protector, a hiding place, a clearly forseeable future. But having been reduced to mere survival, she now had a crystal vision of what was most important to her. The things she cherished now were Andre's arms, Jean's smile, her music. She knew she would gladly trade all else—all the fairy pledges that life was so full of— for just these three.

"I love you, too—but you know that," he said gruffly.

She looked at Jean's face, and up at his, and suddenly she began to weep. Standing there with her arms empty, she wept, "Oh Andre, I hoped you did, I hoped you did!"

Several reactions passed over his face, then he smiled sadly. "But you weren't sure? Since the night Jean came, I've been so head over heels in love with you . . . I thought before that I loved you as much as a man could love, but this . . .

408

this has paralyzed me. I've never felt anything like it before. It's made me uncertain, because I was sure you must hate me. I'm changed too, Laura; I've learned that there's a kind of love that doesn't speak up, for dread of offending, for dread of being rejected and losing all hope."

"I thought you didn't care. I thought, because I'd robbed you of your revenge . . . and I felt so guilty, letting you take the blame for what I did."

"It was my blame to take. Mine—all of it! And I was glad that at least I could spare you that much—because I've spared you so little otherwise."

"Oh, Andre! In my mind I've returned and returned to where all our lives came together and made their bend, and, God forgive me, I can't truly say I'm sorry for that night when you stole me. And if I can't be sorry for that, then what *can* I regret?"

He didn't answer for a moment, then said, rather abruptly, with a touch of his old iron, "You know, Laura, I'm just about out of willpower. If you want the gospel truth, I want to make love to you so bad it hurts!"

She stared up at him, her tears stopped by shock. "Oh!"

He grinned a bit sheepishly, but more of his old self was returning. "Come here, sweeting." He pulled her to him slowly. His eyes were all pupils as his mouth came down. Her lips opened to him and her hands slid up his chest, around his neck, while his arms went about her waist. "Laura." He held her very tight. "We'll find one another again. We will— won't we?"

His next kiss was all sparkles and joyous whorls of tongue. The scent of him was fresh and manly and utterly intoxicating. He lifted his head an inch. "Is it all right? I mean, are you well enough?"

She groaned, "Yes!" and felt a pang, low in her abdomen, in anticipation of the reach of his body inside her own.

He swept her up, swept up the rustly skirts of her white gown and held her to his chest. She let him, trusted him, clung to his neck as he carried her down the hall to their room and swung the door shut with his foot. As soon as she was on her feet, he turned his attention to the small fastenings down the front of her bodice. And she was caught by an incredible and startling rise of wantonness as his hard dark fingers covered the milk-fullness of her breasts.

Her corset was disposed of, and her chemise and underdrawers, and he removed the ribbons and pins from her hair, releasing it to fall about her shoulders. He let the hairpins clatter from his hand onto the bureau—but used the white ribbons to playfully tether her waist. "I'm going to have my will with you, Mrs. Sheridan. If you struggle, I'll have to bind you with these satin cords."

"Then I suppose I may as well surrender from the start."

"Smart girl." He wrapped the ends of the ribbons around his palm, reining her in. "Remember our first time in here?"

"No."

"No!" He spanned her waist and tossed her onto the hobnail bedspread.

She lay as she fell, arms and legs akimbo, her hair strewn across the pillows. The bed blazed with the afternoon sun coming through the windows, and she lay naked in this glory of light. He'd taken her virginity and delivered her child here—had given her Jean's life twice in this room. Oh, she remembered, yes, very well. Still, she said lazily, "Refresh my memory."

Looking at her, it seemed his mouth was dry. He seemed to roll his tongue around inside before he said, huskily, "Don't move." And with the summer sun cascading through the windows behind him, he yanked off his boots.

When he came to her, she shivered a little at the look on his face—and coincidentally recalled that they had houseguests. She tried to rise from the pillow. "Andre, Dr. Kellogg might be back—and what about Captain Glenn?"

"We saw the doctor from the road and Parry decided to find out where she was heading. He had a certain glint in his eyes . . . and I think they'll be a while getting back." He had a glint in his own eye and tipped her chin up for a kiss.

"Are you sure?"

He chuckled deep in his throat, to cover, she suspected, emotions too deep to be conveyed any other way. "If I were you, Lorelei, I'd be worried about my own fate just now.

Surrender or else."

She softened and smiled and opened her arms to him.

But he didn't go into them. Instead, his own smile faded. He said, "When will Jean be old enough to travel? Do you think we can leave before December?"

"Leave?"

"For Germany. Mother is writing letters to Guizot, Liszt, and some others she used to know. You can interview them, and they you . . ."

"Andre—"

He stopped her with a finger over her lips. His callused hand found hers and grasped it, ever so gently, and turned the wrist up. "There's power here," he said, tracing the faint lines of her palm with his forefinger. "Not many men have the power this hand has. It could bring an entire world to heel if only you would use it."

She stared at him, speechless; then looked at her own hand as if quite suddenly she saw her heart beating in it.

He twined his fingers between hers, and smiled and asked his question again, in a way that was seduction itself: "Will you go to Germany, Laura? Will you be all that you can be? Will you let me take you, and travel with you, and see how the years pass?"

She felt tears gathering again. Total happiness was more overwhelming than she'd ever imagined.

He fell onto his back and pulled her over him, smoothing his hands gently over her shoulders. "There's no reason for crying now, sweet." He sleeked back her hair and took her in his arms and held her with great tenderness. "Lorelei, don't. You know I never could stand to see you cry."

She laid her cheek against his chest. She heard his strong heart beating, the heart he had given to her.

"To think I could have gone on for years living like . . . like a wolf, but for you," he murmured. She looked up to find him staring out the windows, staring with the far lost eyes of a man too hard to cry for himself. He held her within the strength of his arms, and gradually his eyes lowered to her again, and darkened, and filled with promises. "Will you give yourself to me, Laura?"

411

"I'm yours."

His desire was in his eyes, wide as his chest was wide. He rolled her beneath him, pillowing her head with one arm, his right hand spread over her throat, smoothing it while he slowly fitted his mouth to hers and ravished her parted lips. He seemed hungry, and didn't lift his head until she'd begun to tremble. He lay half over her with his hand on her breast. She relished the feeling of his enormous body, the strength and power of him. She gave him her mouth again with a soft sigh. In that moment she would have given him anything he wanted.

What he wanted his fingers found and made round luscious circles, while he paused to lightly kiss each of her breasts.

The bed creaked a little as he moved fully over her and opened her and went into her all at once. He was hard, hard as flint, striking sparks and light, striking summer lightning, striking July rockets and explosions and bright flickers in a dark sky. She placed her fingertips in the hard small place where his back and buttocks met and urged him on. She nipped his shoulders with her teeth. She called out in that high, helpless voice he so seemed to love. At the same time his rich moan went directly through her. They pulsed, pulsed . . .

And in the quiet tender protection of one another's arms, they were without nightmares, without memories, lovers bound whole and new.

The Coda . . .

March, 1884. The concert stage was shadowy but for a shaft of gaslight illuminating a piano and bench. The hall beyond buzzed as members of the audience found their seats. Pearls and swan-white shoulders glimmered as the women strolled down the aisles in tied-back skirts, while their escorts occasionally removed their top hats to make lazy, courtly bows.

When the lights went down, the audience quieted, then applauded politely as a young woman came onstage. They watched her cross the boards with skepticism: An American? an unknown? and so beautiful, too? Unlikely! Yet there were a few who immediately felt the presence of a honed concentration, a poised and balanced intent. Gradually the whispers died away and the hall stood as silent as a cathedral. A magic seemed to fall; the very air was full of it—a tingling, a feeling of . . . *perchance . . .*

She wore black satin, with a long square train trimmed in silver cording. Her hair was piled in glossy twists atop her head, with ringlets falling onto one bare shoulder. Her face was somber as she took her place, her black satin skirts puffed behind and spread beside her. The audience now waited with pent expectancy, until, with utter calm, she bent her head to the keyboard. Her hands, her long shapely fingers, discovered the desired keys.

The music rose softly. She didn't use her body to perform, as so many pianists did, but remained reserved, rapt. And the faces watching her grew rapt as well, while she folded trills and *arpeggios* into sheer poetry.

The smell of scent in the hall, the flicker of white shirt fronts and creamy, bejeweled throats in the vast dim house, were forgotten. All were drowned in a voluptuous sonata. The woman's cheeks paled and paled as her focus drained them, but her hands . . . her hands were alive, they blazed with souls of their own.

An hour passed. She played Liszt's lingering "Liebestraume," sustaining every note for its full value, letting the measures ring; and then, while the harp of the piano still resounded, she rose. The lights went up; she blinked as if waking from a dream. Her shoulders and throat were glazed by her exertions. The shadows cast upon her face by the gaslights emphasized the purity of her skin and soft silver of her eyes. In all, she was a haunting beauty.

The glittering assembly sat eerily silent for long seconds as she stood facing the soft colors of their gowns and the shimmers of their furs. A few voices murmured, the spell unraveled . . . and then, all at once, the place erupted—with applause, with shouts of "Brava! Brava!" and again while the applause became deafening, "Brava! Brava! Brava!" She had come finally into the world to which she belonged, the world which had for a time frightened her, and now would honor her. She lowered into a curtsey under its wash of approval.

Her pale eyes, which shone like moons beneath water, scanned the sea of faces until they found a tall, jet-eyed, startlingly handsome man. He had with him—unusual in this setting—a child.

He wasn't applauding, but he was smiling, *carezzando*—caressingly—and now, only now, did she smile in return. A beautiful smile, as if her very heart opened and set free a song.

They smiled at one another, this man and woman; and they seemed to speak across the space of the concert hall, with their smiles, with their eyes, with their hearts. And for those who are able to hear such things, there was music.

<u>FREE</u> Preview Each Month and $ave

Zebra has made arrangements for you to preview 4 brand new HEARTFIRE novels each month...FREE for 10 days. You'll get them as soon as they are published. If you are not delighted with any of them, just return them with no questions asked. But if you decide these are everything we said they are, you'll pay just $3.25 each— a total of $13.00 (a $15.00 value). **That's a $2.00 saving each month off the regular price.** Plus there is NO shipping or handling charge. These are delivered right to your door absolutely free! There is no obligation and there is no minimum number of books to buy.

TO GET YOUR FIRST MONTH'S PREVIEW... Mail the Coupon Below!